Praise

Loved. This. Book. It reads ~~~~~~~~~~~~~~~~~~~~~~~~~~~
Morisot painting, wishing sh~~~~~~~~~~~~~~~~ you —and then quietly,
privately, she does. And not just about her daring brush strokes or her use
of quiet color, but also the secrets, the stories and the struggles hidden in
each canvas. Yes, you will be fascinated to read about Morisot's scandalous
love triangle with the Manet brothers, but at its heart, this book is about
a woman's greatest passion: her art.

- **Margie White,** Founder of the blog The American Girls Art Club in Paris

This is an exquisitely imagined and written novel about the artist Berthe
Morisot, her determined but, also, instinctive approach to art and life and
love. This novel is a beautiful, seductive linguistic dance, subtly expressive
like Morisot's art.

- **D. M. Denton,** author of *Without the Veil Between,* *Anne Brontë: A Fine and Subtle Spirit*

Today a woman of Berthe Morisot's talent and vision would be celebrated
and admired, but in 19th century Paris she was considered odd and
brazen. Weaving a pioneering Impressionist's life story with meditations
on art and its purpose, *La Luministe* is an inspiring tale of a woman who
would not back down until she claimed her rightful place at the table.

- **P. K Adams,** author of *The Greenest Branch* and *The Column of Burning Spices*

The colors and swirl of 19th century Paris come to life in this touching
novel about learning to truly see—in art and in love. Berthe Morisot lived
an impressive life, and Paula Butterfield has written a novel worthy of her.

- **Carrie Callaghan,** author of *A Light of Her Own*

With *La Luministe* Paula Butterfield delivers a touching and compelling
chronicle of female artist Berthe Morisot and the nineteenth century
Impressionist world she helped to birth. From unpaved streets of Paris
to Baccarat-crystal lined parlors, we are treated to a vivid dramatization
of the beginnings of modern Paris. Surviving the Franco-Prussian war,
the Siege of Paris, and a dogged love for Manet, Berthe Morisot masters
light and becomes the first Impressionist whose work hangs in a public
museum. From Ms. Butterfield's artful pen, we are handed one more
narrative to illuminate women's history.

- **Donna DiGiuseppe,** author of *Lady in Ermine: The Story of a Woman Who Painted the Renaissance*

La Luministe

Berthe Morisot: Painter of Light

A novel by

Paula Butterfield

Regal House Publishing

Published by
Regal House Publishing, LLC
Raleigh, NC 27612
All rights reserved

ISBN -13 (paperback): 9781947548022
ISBN -13 (epub): 9781947548039
Library of Congress Control Number: 2018911296

Interior, cover image and design © by Lafayette & Greene
lafayetteandgreene.com
"Jeune fille au bal" by Berthe Marie Pauline Morisot, Musée Marmottan, Paris -
Public Doman Royalty Free/CCO

Regal House Publishing, LLC
https://regalhousepublishing.com

Printed in the United States of America

For my grandmother, who knew how to make anything a
little more beautiful.

"I wondered if all creatures were drawn to what was dangerous or if we merely wanted light at any cost and were willing to burn for our desires."

- Alice Hoffman
The Marriage of Opposites

PART ONE

La Luministe

The Painter of Light

Chapter One

Paris

September 1858

"Barbarian!"

"Madman!"

The mutterings from two men hunched behind their easels had broken the silence in the Great Gallery and hung in the air for an instant before echoing up the walls to the soaring, arched, glass skylights of the Louvre. My sister and I had been immersed in our work, copying the paintings of the Renaissance Masters, before their outburst, which was followed by the approaching *tap-tap-tap* of a silver-tipped cane on the parquet floor. I'd looked up to see the most revered and reviled artist in Paris swagger the length of the gallery.

"Edma!" I hissed to my sister, "It's Édouard Manet." She slipped me a look out of the corner of her eye and gave the slightest of nods in acknowledgement.

I recognized Manet from our friend Fantin's portrait of him, but he was more handsome in person, with a long, narrow nose and wavy, dark blonde hair and whiskers. With his proud carriage, he needed only a red sash and a white ruff around his neck to resemble the Dutch Captain of the Guard in Rembrandt's *Night Watch*. He was tall—even taller in his glossy black silk top hat—dressed in well-cut clothes with fine leather gloves and boots and carrying a wooden paint case tucked under his arm. The haunting sea chantey he whistled contrasted with his elegance—and sent shivers up my arms.

"*Comment ça va, mon ami?*" Manet greeted Fantin, not ten feet away from us, with a vulpine grin, ignoring the malicious murmurs of those around him. Manet and Fantin bantered and joked for a bit, their deep laughter resounding up to the skylights. I had never known anyone to make the earnest Fantin laugh. And then the men turned

2

toward Edma and me, the shift sudden enough for the men to catch me staring. Although he appeared to be no more than ten years older than I, Manet smiled at me as one smiles at a precocious child. True, on his side of that decade divide was a life of independence, even decadence, while on my side I still lived the life of a sheltered *jeune fille*. But I was *not* a young girl; I was almost a woman.

My sister, Edma, and I were eighteen and seventeen years old, and we were determined to become Great Artists. Our older sister, Yves, had once shared our ambition, but she'd succumbed to marriage, a fate I planned to evade. On that fresh, breezy morning in September of 1858, when the Louvre, like the rest of Paris, re-opened after closing for the month of August, Edma and I were eager to resume the copying routine we had begun in the spring, mastering the techniques that would enable us to reach our own artistic eminence.

"Think how glorious it will be to be celebrated, independent artists," I had whispered to Edma that morning as we left our home in Passy on the western edge of Paris, dressed in bonnets and short capes, toting palettes and paints. We traversed two worlds twice-weekly when we left our village of tile-roofed white houses and marched down the Trocadero Hill—rows of trees had replaced the windmills on the rue de Moulins—to catch a horse-drawn tram. Leaving behind open spaces and wide skies as the tram rattled on its tracks, we followed the curve of the Seine past bridges, barges docked at the *quais*, and solitary fishermen angling for a perch or a pike to take home for dinner.

"Think of how marriageable my accomplished daughters will be," came our mother's voice from behind as we stepped off the tram into the bustle of the Place de la Concorde. Maman escorted us between the golden-tipped Egyptian obelisk and the sea-themed fountain where naiads held fish spouting water into the large, lower stone basin. The upper basin was supported by figures personifying the arts, but we never lingered long enough for me to determine which writhing nude represented painting. I didn't want Maman to suspect my interest in the naked male form. So, eyes straight ahead, I marched on past *les palais* surrounding the square and rounded the corner on to the rue di Castiglione, where a gilded statue of Jeanne d'Arc sparkled in the morning sun.

We continued past the shops under the arcade along the long rue de Rivoli. First, Gagliani's Bookstore, that narrow shop with dark depths lined floor-to-ceiling in mahogany shelves and filled with tables piled high with still more books. Then we were enveloped in the intoxicating scent from the *Chocolat Mexicain Masson*—chocolate infused with cinnamon and cayenne—the only advantage to France's rule of Mexico that I could see.

I remembered when, as a child, we would only traverse this street by carriage, for fear of stepping in the sewage that had run down every road in Paris until a few years ago. Edma and I had made a game of scattering sofa cushions on our drawing room floor and jumping from one to the next, pretending that missing a cushion would land us in the sludge of a city street. Now the rue de Rivoli was wide, airy, and clean enough for fashionable people to cross. In fact, at that moment, a fastidiously attired *flâneur* strolled down the middle of the street. I observed his gray plaid trousers and double-breasted black frock coat with just enough cravat protruding above the top button to require a stick-pin. He was the height of fashion, although his umbrella and dainty shoes struck me as less than manly.

The *flâneur* stopped to contemplate a pretty flower vendor, a girl my age or perhaps younger. There were no match sellers to be found here in the elegant center of the city, and it was too early in the autumn for the roasted chestnut vendor, so this girl with her arms around a basket of posies and *boutonnières* had the broad boulevard to herself. The cuffs of her fresh white blouse were frayed, but her copper hair caught the shimmering sunshine, and in the Jardin de Tuileries the leaves of the plane trees behind her flickered in the breeze from green to gold like daubs of paint, creating an appealing portrait.

"A flower, monsieur?" she asked, her deferent tone edged with defiance.

He selected a flower and was sneaking a look down the flower girl's bodice as he positioned the gardenia—Maman had cautioned us that this was the most seductive of scents—on his lapel when we passed him. "Hold your breath, girls," came Maman's voice, as if my conscience were speaking aloud.

The privilege afforded by position and education elevated a *flâneur* above a mere *voyeur* and made his opinions matter. What such an idle man observed as he strolled the city became fodder for café conversations, or perhaps even a perceptive essay in *Le Monde*. I wondered if this gentleman's keen insight also allowed him to discern the flower girl's uneasiness—she must have felt vulnerable, yet she needed to sell her wares. The nurse who aimed a disapproving glance at the *flâneur* as she pushed a baby carriage to the Tuileries did not have the same authority as my Maman, who walked close behind us to discourage advances.

Just past the Tuileries, we crossed the street to the arched side entrance to the Palais de Louvre. After signing the artists' roster at the museum, "Berthe Morisot" and "Edma Morisot," we turned left and passed through the pre-Classical Greek gallery, stepping with care in our leather-soled boots up the slippery marble stairs to the statue of the Winged Victory, then through endless, echoing rooms to the hush of the Great Gallery. Young men from the Academy were already positioned in front of the paintings they'd chosen to copy, industriously applying themselves, but we found two available easels in front of the Italian paintings. Edma and I prepared for our copying session as our mother, a discrete but watchful chaperone, found a chair behind a pillar close by. We slipped on our smocks, set up our small canvases, squeezed colors onto our paint-stained palettes, and set to work copying Titian's *Woman with a Mirror*.

That fine autumn morning, we had no way of knowing that this was the momentous day when we would meet the most renowned artist in Paris, Édouard Manet.

Henri Fantin-Latour had arrived soon after we did that morning, brandishing a print in the air. He was a young man a few years older than we were, whom we had met months before. Monsieur Guichard, our painting instructor, had introduced us on the first day we'd copied.

"Mesdemoiselles Morisot, behold my latest find," Fantin said. "A print by Utamaro. Now *this* is realism. A fresh view of everyday life with all unnecessary details stripped away." The Japanese artist had used the fewest lines possible to depict a woman brushing her long hair and had made no attempt to indicate the volume of the model. A black rectangle represented her hair and a white oval, her face. The only color accenting the print was the red of her lips. How strange that the spare woodblock print felt familiar, as if my most private hours in my boudoir were revealed by an artist half a world away.

Fantin and I stood behind Edma, who contined working. I examined the print, but Fantin couldn't take his eyes off my beautiful sister, although, as usual, he didn't speak to her directly.

"This is why we have disavowed l'École des Beaux Arts!" Fantin told the light tendrils trailing down the back of Edma's long neck. "The state school rewards clichéd allegorical paintings and overlooks real life." He waved the Utamaro print at the ornate gilt-framed paintings that surrounded us, immense works peopled with Greek deities and swarming warriors who looked polished rather than painted. Some young men like Fantin were choosing to leave the school—the one Edma and I would have given anything to attend—to find new and original ways to paint.

"What does such nonsense have to do with life today?" Fantin railed. Edma glanced up from her painting. "If that is how you feel, Monsieur Fantin," she asked in the measured tone she used to ensure that she offended no one, "why do you come to copy the Old Masters?"

He blushed and looked away from Edma's hooded blue eyes, timid again after his outburst. "I must make a living. But on my own, I am exploring more immediate effects, as Manet does. Now there is a man who paints simply, as the eye sees."

Édouard Manet had become the idol of the younger artists when he had abandoned Academic style in favor of the hard edges of the great Spanish artists. Although propriety prohibited young women from viewing any of Manet's paintings, I longed to see them.

The intriguing Édouard Manet was gaining fame by breaking the rules for technique and subject matter, while I only got in trouble when I did the same. Edma was a far more meticulous copier than I was. I sometimes left out details like facial features if I felt like colors and shapes were the more compelling parts of the composition.

"Edma, did you know that Fantin has painted a portrait of the great Manet, surrounded by his acolytes?" I asked for Fantin to hear. I so envied his many freedoms that it was a cruel pleasure to tease him and watch him blush.

Fantin hung his head and mumbled. "My homage to the great draftsman."

"Edma?" I repeated. She sighed and leaned closer to her canvas because I was interrupting her concentration, so I stifled my question. How was it that my sister's painting smock was spotless, while mine resembled a painting itself? And how did her coiffure remain perfect, while my dark curls tumbled down my neck no matter how many pins and ribbons I wove into them? Edma was only a year older than I, but I felt that I would never catch up to her.

I tried to focus on the work before me, as Edma did, but after Manet had arrived and positioned himself next to Fantin, I'd found myself observing him instead as he set to copying Tintoretto's self-portrait. Like Fantin, he too attacked his canvas, but with elegance. His long nose ended in flared nostrils that seemed to signal his intensity. If I hadn't know who he was, would I have suspected that this refined gentleman was the renegade who was taking on the art world with his own two hands? I tried to imagine having that kind of confidence. In truth, my *Woman with a Mirror* didn't look too bad. What if I got rid of the half-tones and gave the figures harder edges, as Manet was said to do? I outlined my *Woman* in black, and she became a cartoon. *Oof!*

Old Monsieur Guichard hobbled into the Great Gallery at that moment to gauge our progress, his shabby shoes squeaking a warning. He turned his pockmarked face so close to my work that I was suffocated by his sour breath when he asked, "How is *Woman with a Mirror* coming along?"

"Another woman trapped indoors!" I complained. "And notice, monsieur, a man-servant holding her mirror. Absurd! No man is allowed in the cloistered world of the toilette."

"That is beside the point. You are here to study the skin tones. Titian has made her flesh positively luminous…"

"But the rest of the painting is all murky shadows." When Maman or my sisters were at their toilette, everything seemed full of light. It reflected off the mirrors, the lacquered cosmetic cases, the glittering silver hairbrushes, the crystal bud vases. And it was as soft as their billowing white lace peignoirs, their powder puffs, the rustle of silk, and our whispered gossip. I could conjure up the scent of lavender water even in that cold, marble gallery.

"Surely you are not criticizing one of the Masters," he grumbled. It was not the first time that I had exasperated Monsieur Guichard. He wanted us to study a painting for hours upon hours without forming any opinion about it, yet another in a growing list of prohibitions that I found difficult to obey.

"I think I would like to try painting something different," I retorted, still thinking of my sisters. "Is that a crime?"

"It *is* a crime, of a sort." It appeared to be costing our teacher great effort to keep his voice low in the hushed gallery, but he couldn't help but throw his hands in the air and demand, "Who are you to think you can improve on Titian?"

Put that way, I sounded proud and vain. But I was an expert in one area, so I shrugged my shoulders and pronounced, "I am a girl who knows more about the private lives of women than any master could."

Monsieur Guichard snorted and turned to Maman. "Madame Morisot, may I have a word with you?" He pulled a chair close to Maman's behind the pillar and lowered his voice, but he was near enough that I could still hear him.

"I've been meaning to talk with you, madame, to warn you…"

Maman folded her newspaper and held it to one side so that no ink would stain the skirt of her aubergine-striped taffeta day gown. "Warn me of what?"

"With characters such as your daughters possess, my teaching will make them painters, not minor amateur talents."

Guichard thought that we were good enough to become professional artists! My pride was tempered by my fear that his warning might lead to Maman putting an end to our painting lessons.

But she only laughed in the manner that charmed men.

"Do you understand what I'm saying?" Guichard sputtered. "In your world, it would be a revolution. I would even say a catastrophe."

"Surely you exaggerate. There are no geniuses in my family, nor my husband's. Painting gives my girls pleasure. They will be the most cultivated of wives and mothers—certainly not a catastrophic outcome, monsieur." She snapped her newspaper open again. Guichard understood that he was excused, and he shuffled out of the gallery, shaking his head.

One moment Fantin was tilted toward his painting, his upturned nose almost touching his canvas and his lank hair hanging over the collar of his ill-fitting suit, but the instant that Monsieur Guichard left the gallery, Fantin stepped forward to introduce Manet to our mother. At thirty-eight, Cornélie Morisot was still a slender, fashionable beauty, with Edma's light hair and seductive eyes, capable of fascinating the stodgiest politician—or the most disreputable *roué*.

I listened to Manet's deep voice. I couldn't make out his words, but they were followed by Maman's melodic, lilting laughter. "It will be my great pleasure to make your mother's acquaintance," she said. The Manet name was well known in Paris. Édouard Manet's father was a magistrate and a judge, and his mother was the god-daughter of the crown prince of Sweden.

I thought of what Maman would want me to do and willed myself
not to turn to witness this polite but profound social transaction.
What luck that we were friends with Fantin, who could provide a
formal introduction to the most promising artist in Paris! I didn't
know to what event this meeting might lead, but I intended to be the
belle of that particular ball.

Absorbed in my fantasy of winning Manet's attention, I failed to
notice that Fantin had crept up behind me. "Mesdesmoiselles," he
said in his most proper diction. "Allow me to introduce Monsieur
Édouard Manet." I swung around on my stool, discerning the faint
scent of lilacs amid the odor of oil paints around us.

"How delightful it is to meet lady painters." Manet's voice had a
sailor's husky intonation. "One does not encounter them in art
school." His eyes swept over me and came to rest on—I didn't follow
his glance to see where it would land. From the vantage point on my
stool, facing his chest and square shoulders, I focused on his beard
that was brushed into two tidy points. Manet's lascivious look left me
understanding how disconcerting that *flâneur*'s gaze must have felt
for the little flower seller.

"As long as we are not permitted to attend l'École des Beaux Arts,
this is our school," came a low-voiced retort. I was astonished to
realize that I had spoken my thoughts aloud.

Manet clucked his tongue and smiled in approval. "You have a sharp
wit for someone so soft-spoken. I have no doubt that you will learn
quickly from the Old Masters—and Mistresses."

I dared to look up at Manet from under my dark eyebrows, with what
Maman called my *fierce expression*. "Mistresses? Certainly you will not
find any women's paintings on these walls." I could see that Edma
was horrified. I did not dare to look for Maman's reaction. Why
was I saying these things? Had I lost my mind, speaking with such
discourtesy to a superior artist? I must have also lost control of my
body, because with an awkward jerk back to my painting, I dropped
my bamboo maulstick. I wished my bandeau weren't holding back

my chaotic curls; I would have liked to hide behind my hair at that moment.

Monsieur Manet swooped down to recover the stick and to present it to me with a flourish. "Not yet," he said, his thin lips spreading into a mocking smile. "Perhaps yours will be the first."

Later, we retraced our steps down the rue de Rivoli, the afternoon sun setting the sandstone arcade ablaze in myriad hues of yellow and pink. All that had seemed plain to me only that morning now felt as jumbled the colors surrounding me. Was my life's ambition to become a consummate Academic painter or to please a husband by keeping house and making myself beautiful, like my sister Yves? Or was I a renegade like Manet? I resolved to do everything in my power to avoid the domestic life in store for me for as long as I possibly could.

Then, one day, when I was a Great Artist, I would make paintings of modern women making themselves beautiful. A woman's world as it *really* was—more Utamaro than Titian. More intimate than heroic. That was a subject about which I knew more than even Édouard Manet.

Chapter Two

*O*ur last conversation with Monsieur Guichard had left no room for compromise.

"I only want to experiment with brighter colors," I'd told him. "The world itself is bright and I want to capture it."

"That's impossible. You cannot make paints any brighter."

"But we can! The Masters were limited to earthy ochres and umbers, but we now have the new metallic paints—manganese blue and cadmium red." Scientists in recent decades had isolated these elements and artists had lost no time in adopting the radiant colors for their own applications.

"To achieve light bright enough to match those colors, you would need to paint out of doors." That idea had obviously displeased him. None of the Masters he revered would have dreamed of such a thing. I hadn't understood his reservations. "It's not as if we have to grind and mix our paints and carry them in pigs' bladders any longer. What is to keep us from simply packing our tubes of paint and collapsible easels and taking the train to the countryside for the day?"

"I should turn you over to Camille Corot for instruction," he'd grumbled. I could only shrug. I had seen Corot's atmospheric landscapes, and they fascinated me. He was creating naturalistic yet dreamy outdoor scenes rather than Classical heroic landscapes. I'd smiled to myself. Corot was a friend of Papa's, and it would have only required a word to persuade the artist to take us on as pupils. Still, because I wanted to be chosen on my own merit, I preferred to wait for Corot to invite us himself.

☙

Since Edma and I had broken away from Guichard, we'd continued to study and paint on our own.

By the turn of the new decade, we were spending part of each summer on painting expeditions. Maman may have been running out of ideas as to what to do with unmarried daughters approaching their mid-twenties. Once, she took us to visit Toulouse, our grandmère's birthplace. There, she put us in the hands of a capable guide, and we trekked the Pyrénées on mules. We could look up and admire the peaks of Trois Seigneurs Massif, or look down through the trees at the immense walls of a Romanesque church tucked deep in a valley. The most exciting sight was the ruin of the Cathar castle at Roquefixade, bleached white stones on a rocky outcropping overlooking the churning Mediterranean Sea.

I tried to save up memories to share with my sainted sister, Yves, who had left her own family in the south of France and traveled to Paris to take care of Papa and our younger brother, Tiburce, in our absence. But in the end, there were too many impressions to impart—the fragrance of pine trees and wildflowers, the eagle that swooped overhead one morning—so I kept my memories to myself. Wherever we traveled, we entered paintings in the local Friends of Art Society competitions. After a few regional victories, Edma and I summoned the courage to submit work to the 1863 Paris Salon, and we each had two paintings accepted. Maman and Papa were jubilant. They worked the story of our success into conversation with every neighbor in Passy, and with anyone else who would listen, from the milk deliveryman to the *modiste* who sold us hats. As for Edma and I, we were thrilled. We felt sure that the Salon's acceptance of our paintings marked the first time that two sisters were represented in the exhibition. Now we were genuine, Salon-sanctioned artists, ready to conquer the art world.

The critics would write about us.

We would begin to receive commissions for paintings.

Our careers would begin in earnest.

The Morisot sisters' style was compared to Corot's. When he heard this, Camille Corot finally offered to instruct us in painting outdoors that summer, and we were happy to accept his invitation. We joined him in Barbizon, on the edge of the Forest of Fontainebleau, only thirty miles but a world away from the scintillating city of Paris.

"Nature gives herself only to her true lovers," Corot said. He sat on a folding stool at his easel outside, under his landscapist's umbrella, with Edma and me looking over his shoulder as he executed a painting. I shifted from foot to foot, wanting to paint, not watch. But as our teacher laid in a silvery stream beneath billowing trees that dwarfed the figures below them, with pale skies that covered the largest part of the canvas, I was beguiled.

"Even a small landscape, you see, can convey an openness that cannot be achieved in the studio," he said. I did see. Gazing up at endless blue sky dotted by scuttering clouds, I felt myself falling in love with nature.

Corot's silvery-white palette matched his own long mane of hair. He added a scrim of shining specks to his pastoral paintings. How did he convey the outdoors without color?

"Your sky—it's almost transparent," I observed. "How do you achieve that?"

"You must use a pale palette to paint the atmosphere," he explained. Learning how to paint the air became my new goal. One morning, I packed my knapsack, grabbed my walking stick, and slipped away from the ivy-covered, half-timber shops and inns of Barbizon unchaperoned—willing to endure the disapproving lecture that was sure to follow for a few hours of freedom. I counted on Edma making some excuse for my absence while I explored the forest, seeking out the precise vantage point from which to paint. This changed with the light, so that I was on the move most of the time. Corot had told me, "Never forget the first impression that moves you." How to catch one's first impression when it continually changed? It was glorious to try.

I decided upon a grove of birch trees where the dappled light on a thatched-roofed cottage called out to be captured. The challenge would be to capture the areas of morning light and slanting shade. I set up my easel and stool on a slight rise in an open field and squinted up at the sky.

Sunlit specks of pollen drifted around me. The sun itself I had presumed to be yellow but it turned white as I studied at it. The clouds appeared to be white, but had whispers of gray, yellow, even the blue of the sky. I remembered lying on the bench in our garden as a small child and the shock of discovering the actual colors of the clouds above me.

I rubbed my eyes and began to sketch in my composition, trying to see with that child's fresh eyes. Soon I was absorbed, undisturbed until a farmer and his family in a horse-drawn cart stopped on the narrow lane nearby. I was a strange sight, a woman alone, painting outdoors. The children pointed and giggled. Their mother tried to quiet them, and the farmer called out, "Are you lost, mademoiselle?"

"*Non,* I am right where I want to be," I assured him.

He cocked his head and waited a moment to convince himself of my safety before he called to his horse to move along.

By summer's end, I had mastered Corot's techniques for conveying the effects of light. He paid Edma the compliment of asking to exchange paintings with her, but he didn't ask for any of my work. He may have sensed my growing impatience with nostalgic poetic effects, which I associated with the out-of-date Romantic style. *Tant pis.* I was no longer interested in being considered "the student of" anybody.

I'd mastered composition and color, light and atmosphere. It was time to develop my own style, even if I wasn't yet sure what that was. I promised myself that I'd know by next year's Salon.

After Edma and I returned to Paris, I lined up all of my paintings from Barbizon against the wall in my studio. Most of them resembled Corot's work. I took up one small canvas of a hazy grotto, then another. Both of them could go and not be missed. I worked my way down the row of paintings, discarding one after another as too much like my teacher's.

Only *Thatched Cottage* was unlike any of Corot's silvery studies. It was a small pastoral scene of a green grove with a white cottage glimpsed through a stand of bare tree trunks in the foreground. A pattern of yellow blobs indicated the heads of the smudged grasses. It was the only painting from the entire line-up that contained the germ of something that was unique, mine alone.

I was still enthralled with the idea of painting the atmosphere. But, back in Paris, scenes of modern life also seized my imagination, most of which featured Manet, the man who personified Paris as the center of the art world. I pictured him against the backdrop of Haussmann's new boulevards and buildings, striding into the opéra in top hat and tails, or at a café concert with a singer perched on his knee. Perhaps by painting his world, I could make it mine. A century of revolutions had laid the groundwork for artistic upheaval, and now an abundance of new art movements called into question the relevance of the Salon. Every artist would need to decide whether to continue to paint antique themes or to depict modern Paris in a new style.

I cast my vote for modernity. As soon as I'd made my decision, I felt compelled to empty my studio. I needed to be surrounded by bare walls awaiting future paintings. One by one, I carried each of my Barbizon paintings out into the courtyard until only *Thatched Cottage* remained in the studio. I took the can of turpentine we used to clean our brushes and poured it over my stacked canvases. The fluid blotched the pallid trees, clouds, and streams. I paused for an instant, anticipating doubt, which did not arrive. I would not compromise.

With one touch of a match, I burned the rest of my summer's work.

Chapter Three

*W*hen the social season resumed, Maman invited Alfred Stevens, whom all the fashionable ladies were hiring to paint their portraits, and his strikingly beautiful wife, Marie, to dinner. At the last minute, Édouard Manet also joined us. Maman and Manet's mother had become fast friends. We saw the Manets at their regular Thursday gatherings, and they had an open invitation to our Tuesday evenings. Now Monsieur Manet slid into the chair between my restless adolescent brother, Tiburce, and me at the dining table just as the soup bowls were cleared.

Papa greeted him. "It's good to see you again, Monsieur Manet." Despite the fact that our dining table was round, Papa gave the impression of sitting at its head, a contented host.

"Bonsoir, Monsieur Morisot, Madame Morisot."

I leaned back as our maid stepped between Manet and me to serve the entrée. Manet leaned back, too. "Bonsoir, Mademoiselle Berthe," he said, behind her.

"Welcome, Monsieur Manet. I hope you like *boeuf au carrottes.*"

"I'm sure I will enjoy it. But I'll enjoy the delightful company even more."

Our maid stepped away, and I directed my attention to my dinner plate. Being deemed delightful flustered me. And now I felt pressure to think of something fascinating to say.

"We lost the great Delacroix over the summer. Do you think Romanticism is dead, monsieur?" I asked.

Manet laughed. He sounded more surprised than amused. "As an art movement, oui. As a way of life, never." Papa and Monsieur Stevens commenced a conversation about the results of the recent legislative election, which allowed me to turn back to my carrots.

It was a warm, late summer evening, so after dessert, Edma invited the Stevenses to our studio in the courtyard to show them our paintings. As we rose from the table, I hoped that Manet would choose to join us, but Tiburce, a loquacious fifteen-year-old hoping to impress our suave visitor, held him captive with a rambling story about a clever strategy that had led to his victory at a card game with his friends. While we were crossing the courtyard, though, I heard a chair scrape the floor and footsteps that hurried to catch up with us. By the time we reached the studio, Manet was close enough for me to feel his breath on the nape of my neck. I shivered and stepped into the studio.

"Papa studied architecture in his youth," Edma was saying. "He designed this studio for us."

The light of the gas lamp revealed a clutter of canvases, portfolios, a green gauze butterfly net, a parakeet cage, and straw hats. I brushed aside the litter of models' accessories to better show one of Edma's Barbizon paintings, which stood on the easel near the door.

"Expertly realized," was Alfred Stevens's polite comment. And the work *was* an example of successful technique, if not of inspiration. The complex composition included every element of a country scene. A sailboat glided down a meandering river bordered by blowsy trees. Tiny figures stood at the river's edge and a village stood on a hill in the distance.

Stevens leaned closer to the canvas and observed, "There is a story in this scene…"

"Oui, laundresses *and* a fisherman," interrupted Manet. "So many stories—you have neglected nothing." Did I detect sarcasm in his voice? I turned back to see his expression, a look he returned with an arched eyebrow that confirmed my suspicion. I had seen this side of him before and been amused by his mischief. During our growing acquaintance, Édouard Manet always outwardly appeared to be a gentleman, but he would flash his sly smile at Edma and me when no one was looking. His disparaging comments about other guests made us laugh at inappropriate times, such as the evening when, stroking his blonde beard into points with a flat thumb as he ogled a lady's plunging neckline, he murmured, "It appears that she's bringing them out for air." He said things that I wished I could say. But I did not see the humor in belittling my sister in front of me.

Edma was of too gentle a nature to notice that she was being teased. "Merci, monsieur," she responded.

Madame Stevens asked, "Which of these works is yours, Berthe?"

"I have a few recent pieces on the back wall." They would think me a madwoman if I described the fiery death of my earlier work. Instead, I steered the group to a recent watercolor of Edma sitting on a bench in the Bois de Boulogne.

"I see, a study for an oil painting," said Stevens. Of course the transparent washes of color would look unfinished to him, nothing more than preparation for a true work of art.

"Possibly." I had liked how the first wavering brushstrokes of green behind Edma had made the trees look as if they were moving in a breeze, so I had left them like that. But I was still unsure how to convey what I was striving for and unready to express my muddled ideas to a prominent artist like Stevens.

"I think it is quite marvelous to find two such talented sisters working together," gushed Madame Stevens.

"There is no doubt that one day soon you both will receive honors from the Academy," Alfred Stevens added. I wondered if that was likely. We hadn't received any commissions or sales resulting from our paintings being shown at the Salon in the spring. Those rewards, we had learned over the last few months, were reserved for the artists who had studios in the Academy, where they could court interested patrons who visited to see their work.

After we'd accepted the requisite flattering remarks, Edma led the Stevenses back into the house. But Manet lingered. He stroked his beard, riveted, it seemed, by my *Thatched Cottage*. I was surprised by how much I wanted to touch that silky beard and to have those fingers stroking *my* chin. But his ungentlemanly remark about Edma kept me from forgetting his reputation as a libertine.

I waited by the door, unsure of whether I should risk the impropriety of being alone with a man in order to take advantage of this chance to have the great Édouard Manet appraise my work. I was trying to muster the moral fiber to leave when Manet spoke.

"The house is almost hidden in the trees," he said.

"I wanted it to be enclosed by the trees, as if embraced by them."

Embraced? Why did I not say *surrounded?* We had all worn short-sleeved dresses for dinner, a decision I now regretted because my exposed skin so cried for the pressure of an embrace that I had said the word aloud. It was confusing to crave the touch of a man I had decided I should dislike.

Still, despite Manet's rude remark and my dangerous attraction to a notorious ladies' man, I was determined to hear his artistic assessment. Could he discern my effort to depict the atmosphere? I came back across the room to point out the pale background. "Do you think I should have shown more sky?" I asked him.

"That depends. What is the story you were trying to tell?"

His question was condescending. I knew from his own work that Manet disdained melodramatic scenes. Was he trying to belittle me, as he had Edma? "Do you expect me to paint a woman swooning over a letter from her beloved?" I whispered, to hide my irritation. "Or at her window, watching her lover depart, like Monsieur Stevens's paintings?" In my opinion, the subject matter and the lavish details of the luxurious dresses in Stevens's work—the highlighted sheen on silk, the voluminous drapery pooled on the ground—were better suited for fashion plates in *La Revue de la Mode.* "His work is beautiful, but without soul."

Manet kept his eyes on my *Thatched Cottage,* waiting for me to finish. "There is no story." My diatribe had drained me, and I cast about for the words to explain my objective. "I only wanted to paint the air."

He turned to me with a look of surprise. "How on earth does one do that?"

Again I became aware of my bare arms prickling as I remembered the sensation of the air on my skin when I painted in the Forest of Fontainebleu. I realized that it wasn't only that I wanted to paint how things looked. I also wanted to convey the sensation of being *en plein air.* "One feels it first, I suppose."

Manet said nothing. I looked up to gauge his response. But he was not looking at the painting at all. He was studying me, instead. I felt my face grow hot as his eyes glided down my nose, my lips, my upturned chin. "I knew when we met that in one year or perhaps two, you would be exquisite," he murmured. "And I was right."

I was dumbstruck. So he was attracted to me, perhaps even as much as I was to him.

His eyes gleamed in the gaslight as he moved toward me. Whatever happened next would be wrong, so I stepped back.

He matched my step like the most deft of dancers, while at the same time reaching out to take my hand. I tried to pull away but found that I could not move—nor did I want to. My features still inflamed, I closed my eyes, awaiting my first kiss. But it did not come. I peeked through my dark lashes just in time to see Manet, at the last second, bend to kiss my hand.

Had he seen my pursed lips, ready to be kissed? If so, he must have been shocked to understand that while he was able to control his impulse, I was no better than one of the *grisettes* who lurked around the artists' cafés.

"Shall we rejoin the others, mademoiselle?" Manet asked. He looked away from me, but I could see that his face was as flushed as mine. Determined not to reveal my own confusion, I dimmed the gaslight by the door, turned on my heel, and led the way back to the house. As I stepped into the light from the glass-paned drawing room doors, I saw that my left hand was cupped protectively over the hand that Manet had kissed, trying to trap the burning sensation that lingered there.

Chapter Four

As girls, Edma and I had seen Rosa Bonheur's great *Plowing in the Nivernais,* and we were quick to start a secret club, the Bonheur Society. Our older sister, Yves, had chosen needlework over painting, so we had not invited her to join us. Inspired by the artist who had earned the Legion of Honor medal for her body of work—presented by the Empress Eugénie herself—we had vowed that we, too, would devote our lives to art. I never tired of trying to figure out how Bonheur had captured the sun on her canvas. In *Plowing in the Nivernais,* yellow light was coming from the left, so it was the edge of the day, but was it dawn or dusk? Were the straining cows beginning their travails or trudging home? I hoped one day to catch sunlight on canvas as well as did Rosa Bonheur.

One afternoon during the week after my encounter with Manet, both members of the Bonheur Society were at work in our studio. I was laying in the background for a still life of fruit and flowers that I'd set up under a window while Edma painted me. I caught a glimpse of her canvas and saw a mirror image of myself, my long, dark hair pulled back from my face, the profile of my straight nose and my turned-up chin. Depending on my disposition, my features could look either finely-formed or sharp and angular. Today it appeared that Edma had shown me in a good mood.

A pattering of rain drummed the window over my still life. "It looks like autumn is here," I observed. "I shall miss the summer."

Edma brought up the episode that had occurred one day during the summer when Corot left us under the tutelage of his assistant, Monsieur Oudinet. "Do you remember the incident of the Rocher de l'Elephant...?" I stopped her with a black look before she could recount the story of my foolish behavior.

That day, under the spell of the ancient oaks of the Forest of Fontainebleau, I had transformed into a druid. Intoxicated by the freedom of the forest, I had detoured from the Allée aux Vaches to run across the fields.

"Mademoiselle!" Oudinet had called.

I hoped Oudinet noticed how nimble I was scampering up those strange, primordial boulders.

"Be careful!" He came running after me. I stumbled and Oudinet was forced to catch me. He was young and athletic, with prodigious muscles. I suppose I thought him handsome, in the rugged, bearded fashion of the Barbizon artist. This attraction seemed preposterous once I became familiar with the elegant refinement of Édouard Manet. Nonetheless, in that moment Oudinet's face was only inches away, with eyebrows like two *accents circonflexe*. His extraordinary, long fingers gripped my shoulders, but I pretended to lose my balance again so that I fell against him. The feeling of his massive arms around me was thrilling. The pressure of his body against mine elicited the most surprising sensation. Something in Oudinet's eyes shifted; he knew that I was aroused.

I was twenty-two years old. That was the first and only time I had been embraced by a man.

While I considered how to brush the play of light on the apples in my still life, Edma told me about an item she had read in our maid's copy of the gossipy newspaper, *Le Petit Journal*, concerning our current favorite subject, Édouard Manet, and his last Salon submission, *Luncheon on the Grass*. The subject was a party in the country, with two men dressed in cravats, collars, and caps, and two women who were nude. Edma and I recognized that Manet had reworked a theme painted by Titian, which hung in the Louvre, but the Renaissance master had depicted Classical figures, not a contemporary scene of debauchery. The idea of being naked around not one, but *two* fully

23

dressed men, in the open air, was frightening. I would often slip into Edma's bed to giggle about what we'd read that day concerning Édouard Manet. But when I thought about his latest painting alone in my bed at night, I became aware of my own naked body under my nightgown, my breasts loose and an almost painful feeling in my *bas ventre.*

I was still visualizing this painting, which we had not been allowed to see, when Edma brought up Manet's latest lover—the Spanish dancer, Lola de Valance.

"Do you suppose that she dances for him when they are alone?" Edma wondered. I imagined a nude, exotic beauty undulating for Manet's pleasure. This vision did nothing to diminish the sensations of the shameful, voluptuous sort that I felt more and more often when Édouard Manet was mentioned.

"With your dark eyes, you could pass for a Spanish dancer," she said, examining her portrait of me.

I twirled my skirt. "I have a fan. Shall we see if I can gain his attention at our next Tuesday evening?"

In the midst of our giggles, we heard a tap at the door and Maman swept in, exhilarated by her afternoon of social calls.

"Back from your calls so soon, Maman?" asked Edma, always the one of us best able to compose herself.

"Oh, I didn't call on the Boursiers," said Maman, unpinning the tiny hat from the front of her elaborate chignon and sliding out of her braid-trimmed half-coat as she perched on the pouf in the middle of the room. "I've heard such surprising news that I came home early to tell you."

She must have been in a rush to share her news as she hadn't even paused to hand her hat and coat over to the maid when she came in the door. This was sure to be some gossip about one of the bachelors in the city, her chief concern as the mother of two daughters approaching the far side of marriageable age.

"What is it?" asked Edma.

"I was having tea with Madame Manet…" Maman paused, attempting to create suspense.

"What is your news, Maman?" Edma asked again.

"Oh, yes. It's about one of Madame Manet's sons." With that, she claimed my full attention.

"Which one?" Edma asked what I was afraid to. Édouard had a brother, Eugène, also a painter, a reserved man whom we seldom saw. Maybe he had taken a docile young woman for his wife.

"She said that Édouard left for Holland unexpectedly," Maman paused for us to take in the full importance of her information before finishing triumphantly, "and he was married there."

Married! Edma saw that I was stunned; she herself must have been embarrassed that Maman would discover our silly infatuations. But for once Maman wasn't reading my every expression, too caught up was she in the excitement about her news and her plans for us. My head whirled, and my hands went numb as I clutched them tight. I could only trust that my face did not reveal the effect her announcement had upon me.

"The pool of potential suitors is diminishing by the day. Those Manet boys are mad. Still, I wouldn't be unhappy if one of you girls decided to marry in haste." Her eyes twinkled. "If it were the right man, of course." She picked up her hat and hat-pins as she left the studio. "And speaking of that, don't forget that Papa has invited some interesting young men from his ministry to dine with us tonight. Come in soon to dress, girls," she called over her shoulder from the courtyard.

The instant she closed the door, I sank down on the pouf, wringing my hands. Edma sat beside me and covered my hands with her own. "That's it then," she said. "Our obsession with Édouard Manet is over." She would simply move on to reading about someone else in the gossip columns.

"*Certainment*, of course it is over," I agreed, although I couldn't remember ever disagreeing with anything more. I had not shared with Edma what had occurred between Manet and me in our studio the week before, ashamed by how eager I'd been to think he wanted to kiss me. I didn't yet fully understand what I expected from Manet, so for the first time, I wanted to keep my feelings to myself. Still, Edma perceived that while her *béguin* for Manet was as casual as those she felt for the latest tenor at the opéra or a handsome young man at a ball, my feelings had grown into more than an infatuation. "Oh, poor Berthe," she whispered.

The shock of this man-about-town settling down distilled into the thought of no longer being able to see Manet, unencumbered by a wife, on Tuesday or Thursday evenings, something I hadn't realized I had come to count on.

Despite our frequent whispered conversations about this man and his many affairs with women of the demi-monde, I realized in that moment how Manet was more to me than a subject for gossip. More, even, than my artistic idol. There was no one else like him. He stood for both an example of what could be and of what I might become. But now he would never consider me, as an artist or a woman. What had I expected? I noticed now that in the portrait Edma was painting of me, my eyes were shadowed and dark, and the corners of my mouth turned down.

Would I still be able to follow in Manet's footsteps, now that he was married? I wasn't brave enough to break away from the Academy's restrictive rules *and* my parents' plans for me without watching to see how Édouard Manet managed to circumvent society's proscriptions. "But married?" I asked. "To whom?"

16 September 1863

Mademoiselle Berthe,
After last night, I feel compelled to explain my circumstances to you, or at least put my thoughts together. I must write to you, although I will not post this letter.
No one *ever* expected me to marry, least of all me. And I'd had no intention of ever having children.

But when my father died last year, leaving me nine thousand francs and a share in the family estate in Gennevilliers, I was able to do the honorable thing and marry the placid Dutch woman with whom I had been living for three years. Suzanne is neither brilliant nor a beauty, but she is calm, an excellent cook, and possesses a comforting, cushiony body.

Not even my closest friends knew that I had been living with someone. When I visited my friend Baudelaire to tell him the news of my upcoming marriage, his sardonic response about my wife was that she sounded as if she were beautiful, very kind, and a very great artist. So many treasures in a single female. Isn't that quite monstrous?

Suzanne has an eleven-year-old son. The law allowed me to adopt him, but that did not make him legitimate because his father—a man I had known very well—was married when Suzanne conceived. I thought I could help her out of a difficult situation while gaining a wife who would tend to my needs without interfering with my life. She insisted in maintaining the fiction that the boy was her brother and that his name was Léon Leenhoff.

Our arrangement works well enough. I paint in my studio, I socialize at my mother's Thursday evenings, I continue to attend concerts and balls, frequent the cafés, carry on with the demi-mondaines, and seldom return to the apartment where my wife waits for me.

Since I have provided her with a respectable marriage and adopted her son, Suzanne realizes that she is in no position to complain about the fact that I keep my life separate from hers. Given Suzanne's phlegmatic nature, we could go on like this for years.

Except...

Someone is beginning to creep at the edges of my consciousness, like the idea for a new painting before it is fully formed. My family had been friendly with yours for several years before I noticed last night that, just as I had predicted, the youngest Morisot daughter had transformed from a pretty, spirited girl into a sultry, sensual woman. Yet you are more than merely alluring.

You are curious and questioning and fervent about your painting.

In your eyes, I recognize my own nervous intensity. You never stop scanning your surroundings, a habit that makes you appear removed from those around you. Some would say distant.

But I see you, Berthe, and I suspect that quite the opposite is the case. Your demeanor and dress are flawless, but I believe that your breathy voice hints at a wild turbulence within, like the wisp of smoke that appears above a volcano before it erupts.

Of late, I've noticed you watching me during evenings at my mother's apartment or at the Morisot home. I flatter myself that many women take note of me, but unlike my other conquests, you, a young, sheltered woman, seem to see past my polished appearance, searching for the authentic Édouard. Up to this point, I've used wit to defuse the attraction between us.

But after last night, I understand that we teeter on the edge of a cliff over which it would be all too easy to fall. I can see that avoiding you altogether may soon be the only solution. Or is it? Many men keep mistresses. But a woman of your refined breeding would never agree to that. And I'm not sure that I would ever want such a woman to learn all of my secrets.

How is it right that I find you now that I am trapped in a marriage that is no marriage by anyone's definition? The comforting, contented woman I married now seems to me no more than a bland, bovine creature.

Berthe, it is an aching irony to discover you now. I may have committed myself to someone else, but I am

Yours,
Édouard

Chapter Five

*M*aman's girlhood training as a vocalist led to her lifelong love of the opéra. When she'd read in the newspapers that Giuseppe Verdi's new opéra, *Don Carlos*, would début on 11 March, she lost no time in ordering new gowns for her daughters and herself. This performance was the first of the season that we would be attending, so we required gowns in this year's fashion. Edma and I both chose the new low-cut, off-the-shoulder style with tiny puff sleeves. Edma's was a pale blue satin with rosettes at the neckline, while I preferred the simplicity of an unadorned white gown. We couldn't wait to be seen in our finery. The rue le Peletier was jammed with carriages when we arrived for the opening, but after an interminable wait, we pulled up in front of the Théâtre Impérial de l'Opéra and joined the crowd moving toward the arched entrance at the corner of the building.

When Papa, Edme Tiburce Morisot of the Ministry of Finance, strutted through the foyer of the theatre on the night of the première, he was a distinguished man of fifty. But he was as smiling and pink-cheeked as a much younger man as he displayed his Ministry ribbon and mayoral medals on his chest and his *trés belle* wife on his arm. "I am surrounded by beautiful women," he boasted as he guided us into the grand salle, as if we were about to be received by royalty. Indeed, the gilded columns stretching up to the painted, domed ceiling rivaled the pictures I'd seen of the opulent Palace of Versailles. Almost-blinding light bounced off every surface, emanating from an immense central chandelier and dozens of smaller surrounding chandeliers overhead, as well as from the glowing gaslight sconces on each column.

Inside the auditorium, the pulsating drone from the orchestra pit as musicians tuned their violins and cellos set my blood humming. By the time we took our seats in the loge, my body was almost vibrating with excitement. Edma and I sat next to each other, and Maman and Papa anchored us on either side. No gentlemen could approach us without first running the parental gauntlet, but that didn't keep us from observing the well-dressed gentlemen around us. We handed mother-of-pearl opéra glasses back and forth as the seats filled. From our position in the loge, we could look up into the four levels of box seats encircling us and make up stories about the audience members there.

"They are remembering their first time at the opéra," Edma said, pointing her fan toward an overdressed older woman and her white-haired escort.

I spotted a wide-eyed ingénue accompanied by a nervous young man who couldn't stop patting his handkerchief pocket. "He is planning to propose to her tonight," I predicted. Would she look back on this as the most magical night of her life, or might she feel trapped, as I would? Like Rosa Bonheur, I eschewed marriage for my art. Easily done, since I'd yet to receive a proposal. Or was my resistance to marriage based on the fact that I could not marry the one man who seemed meant for me?

My eyes moved to the box above my soon-to-be-betrothed couple when a group of men crowded into a side box on the upper balcony. Instead of taking their seats, they leaned against the railing like a row of black crows on a clothesline. They conversed with great animation, breaking into boisterous laughter and slapping one another's backs. It was evident that these gentlemen had been enjoying champagne, if not something stronger, while watching the corps de ballet in the rehearsal hall stretch in preparation for their performance.

"They've just come from the *foyer de danse*," I told Edma. Men courted the young "ballet rats" with money and jewelry in exchange for their favors. I leaned forward to observe the occupants of the box above us from a better angle.

"Mon Dieu!" Edma gasped snatching the opéra glasses from my hand.

"Sit back," she hissed. "When you lean forward, they can see right down the front of your gown."

I blushed and sat back in my plush seat, careful to appear nonchalant, until I was certain that all anyone looking down on me could see was the arrangement of flowers and combs on my head. I fidgeted with my fan and made a show of studying my program. Then, ever so gradually, I tilted my face upward until I was leaning back in my seat and looking straight up. By now, the gentlemen in the box had settled into their seats and sat scanning the audience below. One man was a head taller than the rest of them—Édouard Manet. Light glinted off his beard, turning it to spun gold. He must have been watching me, because the instant I caught sight of him, he doffed his top hat and nodded.

From where I sat, his smile appeared to be a lascivious leer. I looked down at my lap and saw that the light on my white gown made me a bright beacon. Of course my acrobatic twists and turns had called attention to my search for him. I was engulfed in fiery mortification. Manet had avoided me since the incident in my studio, not attending my family's Tuesday evenings, nor his mother's on Thursdays. Did he imagine that I had been pining for him during these last six months? By some great mercy, at that moment the lights began to dim.

The overture began. When the baritone playing Don Carlos broke into his first aria, Maman was in ecstasy, transported to her private musical world where she no doubt pictured herself on the stage.

As the story unfolded, it struck me as the height of hypocrisy that my parents saw fit to protect my innocent eyes from improper paintings, but found nothing wrong with exposing me to the story of a father and son vying for the same woman.

I always looked forward to the ballet traditionally danced during an opéra's second act. For *Don Carlos,* it was *La Ballet de la Reine,* featuring the tormented queen who pined for her stepson. The prima ballerina evoked the tragedy of the story in every longing gesture. My own hands mimicked her movements. To be able to express one's emotions with one's body seemed a marvelous thing, so much easier than trying to convey a static scene with strokes of paint. If I were on that stage, experiencing the freedom of leaps and pirouettes, what feelings would I reveal? I wasn't certain, but I had an idea that they would have to do with Monsieur Manet.

"Maman," I breathed.

She understood that I was moved. "I wish you could have seen Marie Tagliani in *La Sylphide*," she whispered back. "There was true grace." How often had Maman told us about the ballerina she had idolized in her youth? *La Tagliani's* angelic, ethereal style and fair coloring remained her standard of beauty to this day. I always chose to dress in white or black, partly because with my dark looks, colorful, embellished gowns would have made me look like a gypsy.

When the queen collapsed in anguish at the end of the act, the audience's applause was long and loud. As the soprano took her bows and collected the bouquets of roses landing at her feet, I took the opportunity to peek up again at Édouard Manet. He alone did not applaud the performance. In fact, if I was reading his expression correctly in the dim light, his face was as grim as if he himself were a part of the heart-wrenching story being played out on the stage. Lifting the opéra glasses to my eyes confirmed that his jaw was locked and that he stared into space with a furious expression. I confess that I spent the third act of the opéra trying to guess what had so upset him about *Don Carlos*. And I pondered once again why Manet was so often seen with his companions, rather than with his wife.

The house lights came up, startling me out of my speculation. We rose from our seats and Papa led us to the foyer, where Maman, Edma, and I waited at the foot of the grand staircase while he went to fetch us champagne. We watched the audience descend from the balcony and box seats, light from the chandeliers glinting from the women's jewels in accord with their effervescent chatter.

Then, familiar booming laughter as Manet and his companions filled the width of the staircase. Manet spotted us from the stairs and he spoke to the man whose red sash over his naval uniform set him apart from the rest. They broke away from their other friends and hurried to join the Morisot ladies.

"Bonsoir, Madame Morisot. May I introduce my old friend, Lieutenant Pontillon?" The officer bowed to each of us. "We met on a training voyage to Rio de Janeiro, and he's gone on to a career in the Navy while I've been conquering the art world." This claim was quite an exaggeration of the facts, as many members of the art world considered Manet's work more offensive than triumphant, but Manet was so charming that no one thought to question him.

Only after Pontillion was engaged in conversation with Edma did Manet shift his focus to me. "You look lovely this evening, Mademoiselle Berthe," he said, in that deep voice that always sounded like an invitation I must decline. "Are you enjoying the performance?"

"Oui, very much. But it looked as though you were not." No one would have described that statement as subtle, but I was always aware that my conversations with Manet could be timed in minutes, if not seconds, so I did not waste any of them on nuance. Still, I regretted my lack of tact when Manet's face fell.

"The story reminded me of…" he began. His expression did not change, but I detected pain in his eyes. "I was thinking of something else," he said. What I would have given to know just what *something* could cause such a reaction.

"Madame Manet could not join you this evening?"

He chuckled to himself. "No, she prefers to remain at home with Léon."

"I suppose that opposites attract. Anyone who reads the society columns knows that you are loathe to spend an evening at home."

"*C'est vrai.* Suzanne and I have an arrangement which allows me to carry on with my life as I did before marrying." Indeed, *le Petit Journal* reported on all of the women with whom Manet "carried on."

"So she stays at home with Léon?" I persisted.

Manet took longer than necessary to respond. He trained his eyes on me as he sought his answer to my question, in the end deciding on a discreet "Oui, Mademoiselle Berthe. That is correct."

His wife sounded like little more than a glorified housekeeper. I didn't understand such an arrangement.

Papa returned just when it seemed that Manet might have been about to take me into his confidence. A waiter with a tray of champagne flutes followed and handed us each a glass.

Manet turned to speak to Edma as I reflected on his hidden depths. I suspected there was a sensitive side to this rogue, and I would have liked to explore it if there had been an opportunity. As I sipped my champagne, Manet watched me over Edma's shoulder. I tucked my chin and looked back at him from under my eyebrows. Did he remember that night in my studio? Did he wish he had kissed me then?

Did he still think I was exquisite?

Chapter Six

Passy

Spring 1868

We enjoyed the quiet of the country in our house on the rue Franklin in Passy, within walking distance of the forested Bois de Boulogne, yet there was quite enough going on to entertain even my society-loving Maman. There were dinners, concerts, and occasional balls. Gioachino Rossini and his wife hosted dazzling affairs. But our social lives entered another sphere altogether at Maman's regular Tuesday evenings *chez* Morisot, as the campaign to marry off the Morisot girls commenced in earnest.

Maman would be a shrewd negotiator for any marital alliance, partly because she was an astute judge of character and partly because, if she judged one's character to be acceptable, she was a born hostess who knew how to put anyone at ease. While she was the picture of propriety, she was also considered rather original, as comfortable surrounded by artists who were generally outside our social circle as she was with the high government officials who worked with Papa in the Ministry of Finance.

One spring evening, Maman invited the congenial group from Barbizon, with whom we had reunited on the Normandy coast the summer before, to join our friends and neighbors for one of her Tuesday evenings. All of them adored Cornélie Morisot so much that they were willing to make the hour-long carriage ride here to the outskirts of Paris. Maman was a contented woman who had fallen in love with Papa at sixteen and was still happily married. Maybe that was what kept her so beautiful.

Camille Corot arrived first, and Edma ran to hug him in the foyer. With nostalgic affection, we now called him *Papa Corot*.

"Thank you for venturing into the western frontier to visit with us,"

Maman said in greeting as she joined us in the entry.

"I remember when rue de Moulins led to a summer retreat where aristocrats came to take the waters," Corot said as he shrugged his overcoat onto the new maid, a pretty little sixteen-year-old girl named Pasie whom Maman had brought back from a trip to Toulouse. Tiburce insisted on calling her "Mademoiselle Pasie de Passy."

"Ah, and surely you recall the days when Benjamin Franklin lived here as an ambassador and installed a lightning rod on his house at the top of the hill," teased Maman.

After shaking out his shock of white hair and adjusting his vest, Corot stared longingly at the blazing fire across the drawing room. The journey must have been arduous for a man approaching seventy. Maman responded by taking his arm and guiding him to a spot near the hearth.

I loved our drawing room and had often painted in it before I had my own studio. Across from the entrance was the fireplace where Maman seated Corot. To the left were tall front windows with a view of our village of white houses on a hill; double glass doors to the right led to the garden. Gilded moldings were Maman's only concession to the frippery of the Second Empire. Her own simple taste ran to striped *moiré* wallpaper and polished, parquet floors. Overstuffed sofas sat side by side with treasured pieces handed down from Papa's father. My favorite was the cabriolet-legged table in the center of the room, topped by a bouquet of flowers from the south of France, delivered to the florist by train this morning and to our home only hours later.

The Rossinis arrived next. "What a lovely gown," Madame Rossini commented to me as Pasie took her heavy velvet cloak, struggling under the voluminous garment.

My new Worth gown was of white Lyon silk, with a fitted bodice and a wide sash that drew up at the back to drape over my crinoline. It was in the new oval shape so that I did not bump into everyone like a huge shrub. I would have loved to talk about it, but not to a courtesan, and according to our dressmaker, Madame Rossini was rumored to have a past as a kept woman who may have given her husband *la verole*—syphilis. Indeed, Monsieur Rossini did make his way through the front hall with a stiff gait, which even a young woman as sheltered as myself knew to be a symptom of the disease. I kept my eyes down and smiled like the polite, well-bred daughter I was.

Once we were seated in the drawing room and Pasie had served apéritifs, Maman started the conversation by recalling an incident that had occurred while we were all together last summer in Normandy, when some of us went on an outing down the hill from Beuzeval to La Mer, a village on the seashore.

"Do you remember?" she asked Monsieur Corot. "It involved you and some local fishermen." I folded my hands in my lap and resigned myself to another evening of ennui.

Reprieve—Lieutenant Pontillion arrived. I would have judged him to be quite dashing in his gold-buttoned uniform and fringed epaulets, the anchor insignia on his sleeves broadcasting his rank, if he weren't yet another potential suitor for my hand or Edma's. But every bourgeois gentleman under the age of fifty in possession of property and income qualified for the role.

I still had no wish to marry, but if I ever had to, I would prefer to be matched with another artist who shared my ambition. I was quite fond of a young man whose friends called him "the tall Bazille," who had given up his medical studies to pursue painting. I'd been disappointed to learn that Frédéric Bazille had a fiancée waiting for him in Montpellier.

I was lost in the confusion of thoughts about marriage when the Duchess of Colonna entered with a gliding grace, lighting up the drawing room. With her retroussé nose, ash-blonde hair, and pink-and-white complexion, she would have had only to add a hooped skirt to fit perfectly in the court of Louis XIV. She was absolute perfection.

Only a few years older than I, the duchess had been widowed after a brief marriage to the Compte Castiglione-Colonna. But she had no shortage of companions; her name had been linked with the great

Romantic artist Delacroix when he was alive.

On top of her romantic background, the Widow Colonna was a promising sculptor. I'd met her when she rented a lighthouse in Normandy last summer, close to where my family was staying, where she created vibrant bronzes of Classical figures. She and I had quickly developed a sympathetic rapport. I think I reminded her of the young woman she'd been, growing up in Switzerland, before she became a titled artistocrat. She said she found it refreshing to relax by the sea after spending time with the court at the Palais de Fontainebleau. Although she was so successful that she'd been asked to sculpt a bust for the Empress Eugénie, she was still interested in hearing about my studies with Corot and how I was trying to use light in a new way to create a style of my own. She told me the story of how she had devoted herself to art after being inspired by the sculptures that brought her solace during the months she spent in a convent in Rome, grieving her husband's death. Her given name was Adèle d'Affry, but she exhibited her work as "Marcello," thinking to avoid the taint of a woman artist's reputation by hiding behind a man's name. I just called her "the duchess."

I jumped up to claim her for myself.

As we moved to chairs near the garden doors, I noticed that Lieutenant Pontillion had seated himself next to Edma on the blue velvet settee under the front windows. I already regretted that Édouard Manet had introduced us to the lieutenant at the opéra. Edma was not available to shield me from bachelors while she was entertaining an officer. Pontillion could not help but be charmed by Edma's gown of the same aquamarine blue as her eyes, with its new square collar—so wide that it was almost off the shoulder—which showed her collarbones to good advantage.

"Corot, have you heard the latest about Napoleon's fiasco in Mexico with Maximillian?" Papa asked.

"I'm more interested in his latest courtesan, that little circus rider who lives here in Passy," said Maman. Her cheeks were already pink from the *pastis* that Pasie continued to circulate, which might have explained her choice of conversation topic, but she maintained her exquisite posture in her favorite First Empire, ebony, spindle-backed chair. "I would have given anything to be there the day that Empress Eugénie stormed her apartment to end the affair."

Knowing laughter followed.

Papa Corot, nestled in the armchair near the fire, changed the subject. "We can't ignore the biggest news—the Salon."

At this conversational turn to the annual art exhibition judged by members of l'École des Beaux Arts, I felt indignation bubbling up. "When the Salon refuses so many hundreds of submissions that the state is forced to hold a second exhibition for the artists who have been rejected, something is terribly wrong!"

"Isn't it reasonable that the Salon can only accept as many paintings as fit on the walls of the exhibition?" Maman asked.

"The jury was more concerned with rejecting anything that broke with Academic subject matter or style than it was with the number of paintings to include. There are always more walls," I snapped.

Maman didn't look at me, but I could feel her disappointment at my outburst. An outspoken daughter could be even more difficult to marry off than one who insisted on pursuing a career as an artist. I promised myself that I would earn back her approval.

The duchess agreed with me, I knew, but she was far too refined to appear angry. "Come, let's get to the most important work in the exhibition," she said, "Manet's *Olympia*. He's painted a classical nude, but she is clearly a contemporary courtesan." I noticed the Rossinis exchanging a glance and remembered that Madame Rossini's first name was Olympia. "Is he paying homage to Titian," continued the duchess, "or mocking him?"

Corot sat back and lit his pipe. "I believe Manet is incapable of mastering scale and perspective."

"If he wants to be accepted by the Salon, he has a funny way of going about it!" Maman said. "He must prove that he's mastered art fundamentals to win the approbation of the Academy."

"And why should anyone want to be associated with that archive of the old-fashioned?" I exclaimed. Maman gave me the look that said *Don't flash your dark eyes like that!* I clasped my hands, struggling to compose myself. I wanted so much to please my mother, but it grew more and more difficult as her focus narrowed. The woman who used to be amused by my idiosyncrasies now saw them as impediments to her goal of finding me a husband.

"Ah, change is coming, mademoiselle," Papa Corot assured me. "Didn't anyone else notice how many more landscapes were accepted this year?"

That development was encouraging. As we had learned in our studies, in the inviolable hierarchy of l'École des Beaux Arts, history paintings were at the top of the list and landscapes were near the bottom. I was happy to hear that perhaps the old order was breaking down.

"Isn't it interesting," I interjected, careful this time to modulate my voice, "that Manet is referring to a painting by a Renaissance master in a scene of modern life?" I was thinking of an essay I'd read by Baudelaire in *Figaro*, who wrote:

> He will be a painter, a real painter who will know how to seize on the epic quality of modern life, to make us see and understand how grand and poetic we are in our neckties and our polished boots.

…and our bustles and silks, too, I thought. Oui, I wanted to be a real painter, a painter of modern life.

"Everything is *modern life* these days." Papa complained. "This is what comes of letting our girls converse with the young artists, Cornélie." I shrugged with impatience, and the duchess laid her hand on my shoulder.

"Those fellows have no brains; they're weathercocks who play games with our girls,"

Maman agreed.

The room was still filled with lights, conversation, and gaiety. But I felt detached, as if I did not understand anyone, least of all my own parents. And it was clear that they did not comprehend me, nor my ambition. It was sad to feel so alone amid family and friends in my own drawing room. I longed for an opportunity to have one of my intimate, candid conversations with the duchess.

My elegant mother glided to the piano and took her position to sing, calling over her shoulder, "Berthe, will you please accompany me?"

I played the piano quite well, thanks to many years of lessons. Rossini had said as much. What's more, he had selected our piano for us and signed it. But I was weary of displaying my accomplishments to prove my worth.

"Shouldn't we wait until after dinner, Maman?" I asked, stalling for time.

"I wish you to play now, *ma chère.*"

I shook my head—a small, desperate gesture—disappointing her once again. Without a pause, Maman turned to our guest of honor, saying, "I would be honored if you would accompany me, Monsieur Rossini." said Maman.

Madame Rossini aimed a smug smile at the duchess, the only aristocrat in the room. As a former courtesan, she might have been shunned by ladies in polite society, but she would not be denied the status accorded her as the wife of a celebrated composer.

When Maman began to sing in her fine soprano, I took the duchess by the elbow. "Let me show you the studio Papa had built for Edma and me," I whispered.

"By all means!" the duchess replied. We slipped behind the potted palms and outside through the glass doors to the courtyard.

The scent of lilies just beginning to bloom in the garden was replaced by the acrid smell of turpentine once inside the studio. "The light must pour in through those high windows in the morning," she observed, turning her long neck one way and another. I could see that the duchess approved. "This is what will make you an artist. You see, your papa does believe in you."

The duchess was referring to one of our conversations during which I'd described feeling Papa's pride in escorting his daughters to our first drawing lessons dissipate when he learned that I hadn't been following my teacher's instructions to the letter. Those first lessons were a misery. The tedious cross-hatching—straight lines for flat surfaces and curved lines for rounded ones. I couldn't help that my attention wandered and I ended up sketching Edma instead of the plaster busts we were expected to copy. Papa believed that I was stubborn, but did he believe in *me*? If the worldly-wise duchess said so, it might be true.

I remembered how excited I'd been when Papa invited Edma and me into his study to show us his new prints by Paul Gavarni, whose witty, satirical caricatures were in all the magazines, including the fashion plates. We had thought this invitation meant that Papa respected our talent, that he would be speaking to us as an art collector to artists. The first lithograph Papa hung was from the series *Les Femmes Artistes*. A woman in a loose painting jacket leaned against a mantel, above which hung her painting. I stood a little straighter at the thought that this was how Papa saw me.

But that changed when he hung a second print next to the woman artist, this one called *La Lorette*, a kept woman of the type scorned by society. "Take note, *mes filles*, that only inches separate the artist and the prostitute," Papa had pronounced. "If you are to be artists, you must protect your reputations above all."

"He believes in keeping me occupied," I replied to the duchess.

During my rumination, she had spotted my little painting of the thatched cottage on the wall of my studio. "I remember this house near Barbizon."

Standing before the painting, the memory of Manet's warm lips and soft moustache brushing my hand returned, unbidden. I suppressed those thoughts and explained to the duchess, "For me, this was the painting that captured the impression of being surrounded by light and air." I was thrilled that she had noticed my favorite work.

"My dear girl, let me take you to the Salon to see Manet's newest painting." My heart jumped. Had she read my thoughts?

"Does this mean that you think that I have promise?"

"*Certainment!* I'd love to expose you to a wider world."

Then I remembered. While Edma and I had attended the Salon in years past, Maman and Papa had instructed us not to this year, in order to avoid the moral corrosion that would surely result from seeing Manet's *Olympia.* We'd both had paintings accepted that I would have liked to have seen hanging in the exhibition. "My parents would never permit me to go," I said.

The duchess gave me a conspirator's smile. "All they need know is that you will be spending an afternoon with the Duchess Adèle d'Affrey, Countess of Colonna, and they will be content."

We left the studio, pausing under blossoming chestnut trees to survey the distant lights on the Left Bank of Paris. I envisioned entering that glittering world, taking my place among the sophisticated artists who were less concerned with Édouard Manet's shocking subject matter than with his revolutionary ideas about art. I imagined talking with Manet as an equal—and also as the kind of alluring woman who could captivate him.

I longed to see his newest painting at the Salon, but I had never dreamed of lying to my parents. How could I start now? Spring's promise of new possibilities seemed to suggest that there might be a way. The light-filled drawing room showed the way back to the house.

We paused at the doors, unwilling to give up our time together in the soft evening air. More guests had arrived. I could see Puvis de Chavannes, deep in discussion with Corot. He was a staid, older aristocrat we'd met at the Stevens' whom Maman must have invited to be the duchess's dinner partner.

I noticed that Eugène Manet was also in the drawing room. At a glance, he passed for his brother Édouard, with light hair and beard and aristocratic nose, albeit without his brother's height or insouciant air. I was disappointed that Eugène's brother, that provocateur of challenging conversation and teasing smiles, that breaker of rules both social and artistic, was missing. Not that I had expected him. We seldom saw him anymore. Perhaps he was too ashamed of his behavior with me to show his face here, although I had put the incident in the studio behind me. I was flattered to have drawn his attention for a while, but I told myself that I was nothing more than another of the attractive young mesdemoiselles whom Manet met by the dozens.

Struck by the fact that of all of our guests, only Eugène was gracious enough to talk to Tiburce, I went to greet him, with the indulgent duchess trailing behind. "I see that you did not bring your brother," I commented. "He must be immersed in familial bliss."

"Nothing else could keep him away from such a pleasant gathering, I am sure," Eugène said, his diffident eyes averted. Although I didn't see him much in society, I knew that Eugène had done his military service and studied law. Now he was a man of leisure, a status to which my brother aspired. Eugène gave an awkward, abbreviated bow as Tiburce pulled him away, no doubt to discuss how to attain that status.

The duchess chuckled at my exchange with Eugène. She knew that Édouard Manet's bride had returned from a visit to her family in Holland years before with an infant "brother" who was, in truth, her son. Did she know, too, that the boy was said to be Manet's son and the impetus for Manet's marriage?

"It is obvious to anyone with eyes that the boy is not Manet's child," she said, as if reading my mind once again.

"Yet the new Madame Manet seems to have gained complete acceptance in our circle of acquaintances. I don't understand how she can get away with such bohemian behavior."

"My dear, some events are so outrageous that society maintains an unspoken agreement not to mention them." I added illegitimate children to the list of unmentionable topics that already included prostitution and syphilis.

"I certainly can't comprehend why Édouard Manet would marry such a woman."

"It is a great mystery," the duchess agreed.

Five years after Manet's marriage, I still could not accept the finality of this event. I had yet to meet the wife with whom he was never seen, but I felt certain that he would recognize his mistake one day and find a pretext for having the union dissolved. He was an intelligent man, one used to having his way. I was prepared to wait.

The instant Maman noticed that we had re-entered the drawing room, she fell upon me. "Berthe, I want you to meet someone. Allow him to escort you to dinner."

"Oui, Maman, but please, not yet!" I wanted to hold on to my attentions from the duchess for a moment longer, not to feign interest in yet another eligible young man. That the dinner entrée was to be Tourandos Rossini, named after the composer—filet mignon fried in butter, topped with foie gras and a Madeira demi-glace sauce—made the situation even worse. My throat closed in circumstances when I felt powerless, as I did in this marriage market masquerading as a dinner party.

Once, when I was still in the nursery, my English governess, Louisa, was so determined to make me eat enough to become as stout as she was that I began stuffing food down my throat until I vomited. Only then did she let me be. Ever since then, I'd never had much appetite. The odor of the rich fare seeping in from the dining room choked me. Just thinking of it made me sick.

Still, I remembered my pledge not to disappoint Maman another time, so I allowed her to take my hand and guide me through people, potted plants, and overstuffed furniture. I saw that Edma was still sitting with Lieutenant Pontillion, who wore the enraptured expression of a mortal man before a goddess. "Maman, should I rescue her?" I asked.

She shook her head, saying, "She is perfectly happy where she is," and we continued to where Papa was deep in conversation with Jules Ferry, a tall, mutton-chopped young lawyer my father had noted for his driving political ambition. I reached behind to make sure that the duchess, smiling in amusement as she watched my little drama, stayed near me. She handed me a glass of Dubonnet from Pasie's heavy silver tray. Poor little Pasie was pink-cheeked and disheveled from struggling with it all evening. Considering the nauseating dinner and tedious conversation that lay ahead of me, I would have gladly traded burdens with her.

"The expense has almost drained the treasury," Papa was saying when we reached him. "The demolition of so many ancient neighborhoods has cost a fortune."

"But the project is almost complete. Haussmann's redesign of Paris will be worth it in the end. The wide, airy streets will prevent disease," the young man insisted.

Maman tapped my father's shoulder. He put his hand over hers to keep her with him a moment longer. "Berthe has not met our guest," she whispered. Papa brightened when he saw me. "Ah, Monsieur Ferry, please allow me to introduce my daughter. She is a talented artist." Ferry straightened up from where he had been leaning against the mantel, reluctant to leave his discussion with Papa, but too polite not to display some interest in a young lady of the house.

"It is a pleasure, Mademoiselle Morisot." His manner was absent, and his posture, when he bowed to kiss my hand, was awkward. It was obvious that he was no more interested in me than I was in him. In the normal course of things, Edma would have made sure that she and her escort were seated next to me at dinner, but tonight she was too preoccupied to think of her sister. I would have to endure dinner with Monsieur Ferry unassisted. I managed a gracious smile, but turned to the duchess with a dark look, seething with frustration. Marriage was the farthest thing from my mind. Besides, I had assessed every man in the room, and not one of them was the equal of Édouard Manet in talent or distinction nor worthy of the woman I intended to become.

"Think of the Salon!" the duchess whispered.

I nodded, and for the rest of the evening, I thought of nothing else.

Chapter Seven

Passy

Spring 1868

The scrape of a chair being pulled to my bedside woke me the next morning.

"Bonjour, Bértât," trilled Maman. She used the diminutive form of my name as she had when I was a child, but I wasn't fooled by her cheerful air—she was up early to receive an apology for my behavior at her Tuesday evening. Best to get it over with, then.

"I'm sorry that I disappointed you last night, Maman," I began as she pulled back the curtains with vigor, opening them to allow searing light from the window to blind me.

"You embarrassed me in front of our guests," she said without turning around.

"I don't know what came over me. I felt as if I were suffocating in a cloud of stale ideas—the worship of the Academy and the mockery of Manet. But I should have played the piano when you asked me to."

She came and sat down next to my bed. "I can't say I wasn't warned. I should have listened to Monsieur Guichard. How could I have guessed that those first drawing lessons would only whet your appetite? But you were only girls then and I assumed art would be a passing interest. By the time you were painting half of every day, I should have seen that things were beyond my control."

In the years since the summer we'd studied with Corot, I'd been trying to develop my own style. I remembered how my white dress had glowed under the chandelier at the opéra and wanted to reproduce that play of light, so I enlisted my friends to model for me. When Rosalie Reisener came to call, I painted her perched on an armchair under the chandelier in the dining room, still wearing her long coat and hat. The result was a decent likeness, but there was not enough light in the painting, only murky grays and sepias.

Despite my dedicated efforts, I hadn't yet succeeded in incorporating the luminous atmosphere I so much wished to paint. My progress had stalled, which left me wondering whether or not I could find my way on my own.

"But non," Maman went on. "I was an enlightened mother." I was considering her unpredictable swings between enlightenment and convention when Edma tapped on the door and slipped into my room.

"I've asked Edma to join us," Maman said as Edma took a seat on the tufted stool by my vanity. "It's time we three had a serious talk about marriage."

"That's *all* we talk about these days!"

"It didn't look as though you appreciated the effort I made to assemble a group of marriageable men last night—a politician, a military officer. It's no small task to marry off three daughters!"

"I know, I know. *Une fille, ce n'est rien, deux, c'est assez, trois c'est trop.*" I was the living embodiment of the old expression, *One daughter is nothing, two is enough, three is too many.* "I am the one daughter too many, the disappointment."

"Yves managed to find a husband by the time she was twenty."

"Oui, Yves is perfect." Did Maman imagine that I would settle for a one-armed, one-eyed war veteran, as Yves had?

"But you two are nearing thirty years old—I've been more than generous in the amount of time I've allowed you to pursue your interests. I assumed that fate would take its course, and that one of the young men you've met would catch your attention."

Edma nodded. Why on earth was she agreeing with Maman?

"Why must I marry at all? I would be happy to continue living here and painting in our studio. You've always said that being an accomplished artist could only make us more marriageable."

Maman sighed. "Generally, a young woman acquires her accomplishments during the years between her schooling and marriage. Collecting pretty watercolors in an album is quite a different thing from showing your work in public exhibitions, which is putting yourself forward more than is proper in the strictest sense. And what gentleman wants to come home to a wife with paint up to her elbows? The more that art becomes a profession rather than an accomplishment, the less likely you are to attract a husband, should you ever change your mind about marrying."

She paused, choosing her words with care. "You have my charm, to be sure, but as your charms pale, you will have many fewer admirers than you now have."

"You don't want to be seen as a bluestocking," Edma said. "No man wants one of those."

"And let's say you never marry," Maman continued. "What do you think you'll do when Papa and I are gone?"

"I don't like to think about that."

"We will leave you the income from my family, but if the worst happens? Revolutions occur with alarming regularity. What will you do?"

"I assume that by then I will be a successful artist."

"And if not, then what? Become a ladies' art instructor? Your painting would be restricted to what you taught your students."

That image silenced me.

"I don't want to let you expect too much, then be disappointed." Maman sighed again before she went on. "The real science of life is to adjust to things rather than wanting them to adjust to you."

Edma nodded as if she understood, but I sat straight up. "How much more adjusting can I be expected to do? I cannot attend art school. And there is no one in Paris I wish to marry," I lied. There was no point in bringing up an impossible candidate.

"It is better to be married having made compromises than to remain independent. But you are so headstrong, who but an artist would have you? And I have introduced you to all of the marriageable artists in our circle until the only eligible men remaining are Puvis de Chavannes, whom I'd find very appealing if he weren't so pretentious, or Eugène Manet, who won't look me in the eye and is said to be three-quarters crazy."

"My point, *exactement*!"

"I would prefer someone else," she conceded, "even if he were less intelligent and from a less congenial background."

I threw off my duvet and jumped out of bed in exasperation. "Unintelligent and uncongenial! Is that truly the kind of husband that you wish for me, Maman?"

There was that look again—*You must control your fierce expression.* Maman tried to remain calm as she explained, "The man I wish for you is one who is of our social class, with the means to support you—and a family.

"Someone reliable and kind," added Edma, stroking my hairbrush against her palm.

"And so I must compromise my life's dream in order to find someone who will deign to give me his name?" I paced the room as if it were a prison cell.

Now Maman's could no longer hide her irritation. "Who is to say what might have happened if I had insisted on pursuing my passion for music?" She stood and threw open her arms, the picture of a soprano on a stage, as she had her say. "Would I have sacrificed the possibility of husband and family for the adulation of a cheering crowd at the opéra? Being fêted in every European capitol and enjoying international acclaim?" The flush in her cheeks disclosed her excitement; her return to erect posture and disciplined composure as she walked to the door revealed her regret.

With a performer's perfect timing, she had the last word as she walked out of the room. "Bien, that line of thinking gets one nowhere."

Chapter Eight

Paris

Spring 1868

*H*ere we are, *Salle M*," the duchess announced. The walls of this gallery, like all of the others in the Palais de l'Industrie, were covered with paintings hung side-by-side, floor to ceiling, illuminated by light filtered through the white muslin-covered skylights. There were landscapes and seascapes next to history paintings illustrating everything from Bible stories and Greek mythology to the morally uplifting depictions of Napoleonic battles painted by Ernest Meissonier, the undisputed master of the Salon for ten years past.

"We must have seen a dozen nudes in Salles A through L, all with demure gazes, all surrounded by swarms of pudgy cupids."

"Indeed, with so many Venuses and Aphrodites, one would think that we were living in ancient times, not in the world's most modern city," the duchess said as she led me through the gallery.

"Neither passive women nor mighty warriors hold any interest for me."

"Just as well," the duchess said with a serene smile, "since neither is an acceptable subject for a female artist."

"How could I paint an epic historical scene without models or a large studio in the Academy, in any case?"

Women were expected to stay within our natural realm—still lifes and portraits. Neither genre was likely to earn the Prix de Rome, which provided its winner with five years of study in Italy, yet another benefit bestowed by l'École des Beaux-Arts upon its members that no woman could enjoy. It was difficult not to become bitter.

The duchess led me through the swarming crowds with supreme confidence. Heads turned in quick succession as my striking friend swept through the room. This attention was so common for her that she didn't appear to notice.

But my heart was racing. It was terribly flattering that the duchess wanted to spend time with me. And we were equals in one regard: I too had submitted work to the Salon and been accepted for three years running.

"There is my entry, four rows up, next to Edma's *Pot of Flowers*. I can hardly see either of them."

"You haven't yet earned the right to be hung at eye level," the duchess pointed out.

"Next year, that is where my submission will hang," I promised her.

"Did you paint that?" asked a viewer standing next to me, pointing to my *Study by the Water's Edge*. "Not at all bad!"

"Merci, monsieur." My *Study* was a copy of a work by Corot from a few years before, a woman lying on the grassy bank of a stream. But where Corot's woman was the typical nude accompanied by a cherub, mine was clothed and lost in thought. When I had painted her, I was interested in the effect of her white garment against her skin. I'd added a red band in her hair as an accent.

"Indeed, a delicate feeling for light and color." I turned around to see if the duchess had heard the compliment. I would have loved to have had her approval, too. She was an artist and a feminine woman, both roles to which I aspired.

But she said nothing except, "Stay close to me." I struggled to do so as we lurched through the crowd, which grew thicker as we made our way to the other end of Salle M, where Édouard Manet's scandalous *Olympia* had been hung.

When we drew closer, though, it seemed that something was wrong. A low roar broke up into more distinct sounds as we approached, until we were swallowed up by crazed laughter. Two bewildered guards were attempting to funnel viewers through the gallery in some kind of order. Ladies' crinolines crushed us, and we had to take care not to trip over gentlemen's canes. The warmth and odors of too many bodies pressed against us. For an instant, I felt faint.

"What is happening?" I asked the duchess.

She had to raise her voice to answer, something she was unaccustomed to doing. "I'm not certain—there is a crowd blocking Manet's painting."

In front of me, a gentleman tall enough to see the painting from where we stood shouted, "Her skin is yellowish-green, like putrefied meat!" He waved his umbrella in a reckless manner that endangered the painting.

"She is syphilitic, without a doubt," roared his companion. The two "gentlemen" having this conversation next to me found Olympia disgusting, but I found *them* to be repulsive. They wore heavy gold watch-chains over their waistcoats, *boutonnières* on their lapels, and an absurd amount of jewelry—rings, gaudy cufflinks, and tie-pins. To choose not to buy one of Manet's paintings was one thing— few people did—but how did these vulgar men believe that they had the right to discuss the great Manet in such a way? I had never encountered such crude creatures parading themselves as gentlemen. The duchess sensed my revulsion. "Don't pay any attention to those *nouveau riches*, my dear," she whispered. "They are unsophisticated coal merchants."

The man with the umbrella must have heard her, as he gave us a contemptuous glare, emphasized by a glinting monocle, and stepped closer to his companion to ensure that we would be unable to view the painting. Without a pause, the duchess moved forward and, placing a dainty elbow between the two of them, issued a smiling but emphatic "*Excusez-moi.*" Decency forced the men to part, leaving behind a trail of pungent eau de cologne.

Then, through the opening, I saw *Olympia*. She looked right back at me with an insolent stare. Contrary to her classical name, the orchid in her hair and her expensive jewelry made it clear that Olympia was a courtesan and that the bouquet her African maid brought was from a patron. She wasn't a nude; she was naked.

The infamous model Victorine Meurant who had posed as the courtesan must have been Manet's lover. What other outcome could she expect, standing naked in front of a man who was not her husband? That would be a hundred times more stimulating than being in the arms of Oudinet. I allowed myself to imagine unbuttoning my bodice and sliding it off my shoulder as Édouard Manet watched, until I felt faint again.

To turn my thoughts away from the idea of being the lover of the great Manet, I forced myself to study his painting technique. That, too, was shocking. At least I could understand how the public would not know what to make of the flatness of Olympia's body. Anyone could tell that Manet was mimicking Titian's *Venus of Urbino*, but why didn't he use Titian's rounded forms? Where were the shadows? The half-tones? The Renaissance master had portrayed an alluring woman, but Manet had painted a hard-edged harridan. Was he mimicking the sharp edges of the new photography? He was fully capable of matching the masters, so he must have chosen not to. Why not?

"The hypocrites!" hissed the duchess. "As if there were a man in this room who has not visited a prostitute nor a woman who has not gone to great lengths to copy the courtesan's fashions!"

Olympia all but shouted Parisian society's filthy secret: the city was in the midst of a plague. Tiburce had told me that of every five men we know, one had syphilis. He said that the walls of the *pissoirs* on the boulevards were covered with notices warning of the dangers of consorting with prostitutes. Yet such consorting was accepted. Prostitution was so common that women were sorted into types. Most of the gossip one heard when paying calls or enduring dress fittings was about which gentleman was seeing which *grisette*, courtesan, or denizen of the officially regulated brothels, *les maisons de tolerance*. For anyone who didn't understand the artist's message about sexual barter, a black cat, that symbol of promiscuity, arched her back in seduction at the right edge of the painting. Tiburce, a font of information about things he shouldn't know, had advised me that *cat* sounded like a crude term for a woman's most private part.

We maneuvered our way out past a corpulent woman who was crying, "What a horror!" When we were seated on a bench outside and able to breathe, exhausted after walking through only half the eight miles of the exhibition, I asked the duchess what she thought of Monsieur Manet's Salon entry.

"I don't know what to think. After last year's fiasco, I thought he would submit something more acceptable to the Salon."

The duchess was referring to the solo exhibition Manet had staged at his own expense after being rejected by the Exposition Universelle. According to the accounts of my friend Fantin, it was a massive showing of his work that went largely unnoticed. Fantin told me that Manet wrote a manifesto to accompany the show that concluded with a plea for the public's goodwill. But he continued to earn only enmity and ridicule.

"He is quite talented, to be sure," the duchess said. "And he so desperately wants to be accepted by the Academy."

I was puzzled. "But you wish your work to be recognized, also." Manet wanted to be accepted, but he demanded that it be on his terms. I understood that he was trying to teach us to respect the Masters, but also to claim our own time. Was it possible that I intuited better than the duchess what went on in the mind of Manet?

"My sculpture is in the classical style. But *Olympia*—that ludicrous creature? What a mockery!" She regarded me with concern. "I hope that you are not in danger of being influenced by Manet's outlandish style. Perhaps bringing you here was a mistake."

She thought I was a child. I responded to the insult with studied politeness. "Duchess, I am grateful that you have allowed me this opportunity." We stood to leave, but she laid her gloved hand on my sleeve.

"I suggest that you keep to your airy landscapes, unless you want to be spurned by all of society."

"Manet is unaccepted as an artist, yet he is still a part of society," I pointed out.

The duchess wore a grave expression unlike any I'd seen during our short acquaintance. "But if a woman were to produce a painting so shocking, she would jeopardize her social position," she said.

I wondered if the duchess herself had felt spurned following her debut at the Salon five years before. Her marble bust of a Renaissance noblewoman won an Honorable Mention that year, yet her success had been more social than professional, resulting in invitations from the Empress Eugénie to visit the Palais de Fontainebleu instead of prizes from the Academy. The duchess, who had no doubt hoped that exhibiting under the name "Marcello" would earn her more respect, had deceived no one. Word had quickly spread that it was a stunning, aristocratic woman who had sculpted the bust. It was a woman's old dilemma: her beauty had blinded them to her talent. Studying myself with the objective eye of an artist as I had matured into womanhood, I'd concluded that my refined features, combined with my exotic, dark eyes and hair, qualified me as beautiful. How could I avoid the duchess's fate?

"My landscapes will never earn the respect of the Academy, and I am unable to paint the history scenes or portraits of notable men that will," I said, my resentment boiling up and making me as bold as Manet.

I would need to find a way to navigate the art world in order to find a place for images of women as I saw them, neither Classical nudes nor courtesans painted the acidic colors of unripened fruit. I wished I could discuss this with Manet. Only he was painting Paris as it was this very minute, modern life shown in a modern way. Until now. I planned to do the same.

Chapter Nine

Paris~Boulogne-Sur-Mer~Passy
Summer 1868

The newest Madame Manet was rather plump. Of course, the former Suzanne Leenhoff's matronly figure was the result of being a married woman with a child. Her son, Léon, was seated next to Eugène Manet, brazenly displayed in front of all society. I examined Suzanne at length while she performed—beautifully, I had to admit—at one of the Manets' Thursday evenings soon after the Salon closed. I'd seen little of Édouard Manet during the past few years while I worked on my painting and waited out his marriage. But I couldn't resist getting a look at Suzanne Manet at one of the few social events she attended.

If Manet liked her blonde hair and white skin, then he would never notice me. I was dark as a gypsy. On the other hand, if he preferred someone with eyebrows and only one chin, he might take note of me after all.

When I peered over my fan just so, I could see that Manet, too, was watching his wife, the woman who had been his former piano teacher. He leaned against a wall with his arms crossed, careless of the First Empire, hand-painted mural behind him. It was impossible to distinguish whether he watched her with fond contentment or barely disguised ennui. I had been willing him to glance my way for the last quarter of an hour, a harmless game to pass the time, I told myself. So far my efforts had been unsuccessful.

"Berthe," whispered Edma. Then, an emphatic *"Berthe!"* when she saw me watching Manet. "You mustn't smile that way at a married man!" I forced my gaze back to Suzanne as she began yet another Chopin étude. Why not something livelier, like his *Minute Waltz*?

Soon, Fantin, sitting next to us, appeared to have tears in his eyes.

"Mon Dieu!" he whispered. How could he be so moved by someone so stolid and dull, a Dutch *hausfrau*? She had none of the traits admired in a French woman. And she had to be almost forty years old. I, on the other hand, considered myself the very vision of a chic parisienne. Tonight I wore my most sophisticated evening gown, a black, bustier dress with endless flounces that pulled back into a ruffled train, set off by the black velvet ribbon around my neck.

I was glancing out of the corner of my eye to see if anyone might be admiring my intricate chignon when I saw Manet looking at me. No, more than looking. The room grew stifling and the music melted away as his eyes paralyzed me. I couldn't breathe or turn away or even manage to raise my fan. I was saved by Edma's discrete but painful elbow squeeze. As if emerging from the summer heat trapped in this drawing room into a snowy night, I snapped back to my senses in time to applaud Suzanne as she finished her performance with a flourish.

When Fantin turned to speak with Edma, I was quick to move to the back of the room to visit with the Claus sisters before they took their turn playing for us. They performed professionally as the Saint Cecilia Quartet, and I admired them for so many reasons: their virtuosity, their pleasant demeanor, and the fact that they were as far away from Manet as one could be in this room.

"Won't you join us across the hall for some refreshments?" Fanny Claus asked me. We moved, if not at a rapid enough pace for my liking, into the dining room for champagne and pastries.

The dining table was heaped with silver trays stacked high with sweets—tartes of caramel, vanilla, or citron; almond and pistachio macarons; chocolate éclairs. Crystal decanters and iced champagne were lit by the flickering tapers of two enormous candelabras. The heat of too many bodies crowded into one room on this August evening, with their cloying perfumes and shrill voices, did nothing to calm me.

"What will you be playing this evening?" I asked Fanny, as we sipped our champagne in a corner. She was describing her violin solo—an energetic Wagner work, so unexpected from this shy young girl—when I felt someone staring at me. I peered to my left and almost dropped my éclair when I found myself looking up at Manet. He was close enough for me to feel the warmth of his body and to smell his light lilac cologne, a dizzying combination.

"You are the image of a woman from a Goya painting this evening," he said, without any prelude. Did he think I was too dark, like a Spaniard? Or did he find my looks appealing?

"I have been dreaming of a painting in the Spanish style. Figures on a balcony." His deep voice was so intimate that Fanny began to move away, but I shifted my position to trap her between us. "But it will only be as I imagine it if you will pose for me, Mademoiselle Morisot."

"Pose? I am not a model!" He was confusing me with the immoral woman he'd chosen to marry. It was completely unheard of for an unmarried woman of my class to pose for a painting.

"Mademoiselle Claus, I would like to include you in the painting, also," Manet continued. "Antoine Guillemet has already agreed to pose for it."

Guillemet was a respected artist who had served on the jury for the Salon. I didn't understand how people of fashion could think such an undertaking was proper. Manet's ability to blur the line between conformity and controversy left me perplexed and awed by the range of possibilities that he enjoyed.

Fanny whispered to me, "After all, Berthe, many artists are painting portraits of their friends these days. It's the latest thing."

My eyes darted around the room as I struggled for a response to Monsieur Manet. When I spied Maman approaching, I thought I had never been so happy to see her in my life.

Manet wasted no time before engaging her in conversation. He turned away from me to say, "Madame Morisot, good evening. My mother is at our country house in Gennevilliers, but she sends you her very best regards."

"I miss her company. Please tell her I expect a call as soon as she returns to Paris," Maman responded.

For a time all I could make out was the mesmerizing timbre of his voice behind me. The voices of the guests crowded into the dining room increased in volume with each glass of champagne so that I could only catch fragments of Manet's conversation with Maman. Then the sonorous melody again broke up into words. "...and it was not only in Spain that I became interested in the idea of the balcony. As a young man, I visited Rio de Janeiro; there, the only sight of a respectable woman is a glimpse of her at her balcony..." A burst of laughter from a group next to us drowned out the rest of Manet's sentence and the beginning to Maman's response.

"...Goya, you say?"

"But it was last summer in Boulogne...I was bored to death, of course, being away from Paris. As I was strolling, I happened to glance up and see vacationers—as bored as myself—watching those of us on the street below. I had an idea..."

More murmuring, indecipherable beneath the clinking of champagne glasses and high-pitched conversations, then Maman's clear voice: "I suppose, if she can choose her own dress and pose."

"And, naturally, you would be present to chaperone, Madame Morisot."

"I'm sure that's not necessary for a close family friend, but I would love to watch you work."

So, thanks to Maman's friendship with Manet Mére, my modeling for Manet was to come about. I would pose for the man I considered to be the greatest living artist. He had noticed me, chosen me. Peering at my mousy companion, the realization that I was to be the star of this show changed my opinion about the entire endeavor. "Fanny?" I asked, all innocence. "What will you wear?"

So there we were, enduring our fifth—or was it the sixth?—sitting for *People of Fashion at the Window*. Of course, we were not anywhere near an actual window, but in Manet's summer studio in Boulogne-Sur-Mer, a fishing port north of Paris that benefitted from the occasional ocean breeze. The day before, I had caught a glimpse of the painting as we were leaving. Suzanne's son, Léon, was in the dark background, portrayed as much younger than his actual age. Manet had made Fanny, with her plain face and a blank stare, somewhat resemble a mound of bread dough—dowdy for a girl of eighteen. As for me, I was scarcely blocked in yet, only a large white triangular shape in the foreground.

I hoped that I would be a more distinct character than the others were turning out to be. In fact, I meant to make certain to be. That day, Manet's endless legs were clothed in light-colored trousers, his torso encased in a frock coat with a nipped-in waist, and his neck circled by a cravat, complete with stick-pin. This was his painting ensemble? All that was missing was his silk top hat.

For this dandy, I had dressed with special care. When Fanny told me she would wear street clothes, as if she had just stopped by to pay a call, I was inspired. Let her wear her walking dress and stiff crinoline, her gloves, her hat with its silly white posy, and high-buttoned boots. I wore a floating, white silk organza peignoir, a dress such as I would wear when receiving my most intimate acquaintances at home. It was of Japanese style, with wide pagoda sleeves. My signature black velvet ribbon and locket hung around my neck. And my head was uncovered, again to indicate that I was at home, with my hair down, ringlets and curls cascading to my shoulders.

At last, today I was the object of Manet's regard. He stared, transfixed. Even with my focus off-center, I was aware of his intense gaze. I could have shielded myself with my fan, as coy as Lola de Valance performing a sultry Spanish dance for Manet, but closed it with a curt snap to signify that I was unafraid. I would let him read my message without resorting to the language of the fan.

All artists should be forced to model at least once. I gained an appreciation for every aching muscle that could not be stretched, every itchy nose that could not be scratched, the boredom that could not be relieved. I let my eyes slide over to Maman, who was immersed in her book. To her credit, she had said nothing about my costume.

Sometimes she was terribly modern.

Then I shifted my focus to her left, to Manet, whose eyes met mine. Mon Dieu! How could his pale blue eyes bore into me with such force? He stroked the canvas with his brush. He must have seduced many of his models that way, giving each woman hours in which to imagine his sensitive touch until she was helpless to resist when he put down his brush and approached her. I refused to let him see how he affected me. But it was all I could do to control my breathing, not to look away. I hoped my dark complexion hid the blush I felt surging through every millimeter of my body.

After the initial shock of his gaze, I was satisfied that I had controlled myself. Now a step beyond—to channel all of my churning emotions through my eyes, aimed back at Manet. I felt I could melt him with my molten glare. Ah! His eyes fluttered and moved away. Success calmed me.

What did it matter if Édouard Manet was married? It was me that he wanted. Knowing that gave me the confidence to devise a scheme to make him leave Suzanne. I had to find a way to model for him again. Alone.

As I resumed my pose, I saw that my clever Maman was no longer reading her book. She had seen everything—our charged visual exchange and my refusal to shield myself from it with my fan. She arched a brow, but I busied myself with my fan and pretended not to see her.

After fifteen grueling three-hour train trips and modeling sessions, Manet had to admit that the painting was finished when even the patient Fanny Claus cried out, "It is perfect—there is nothing more to be done over!" With September's arrival, summer visitors to Boulogne had disappeared, and all of us who had modeled were ready to return to Paris for the season.

The painting was accepted for exhibition at the Salon in May of 1869. Papa must have been working harder than usual, because he was too fatigued to attend, and Edma was attending a concert that evening with Adolphe Pontillion and his parents, which left Maman to accompany me to the opening gala. The instant we stepped down from our landau amid the crowd of carriages before la Palais de l'Industrie, we were surrounded by hundreds of fashionable gentlemen in colorful vests and ladies in gowns of springtime hues. Their voices created a growing thrum of excitement as we made our way across the piazza to the Renaissance-style palazzo. Its main entrance was a three-story triumphal arch topped by an allegorical sculpture of France crowning Industry and Art, flanked by wings of endless windows punctuated by pilasters. I felt like a Medici princess. Inside, a large painting by Puvis de Chavannes loomed at the top of the grand staircase in the exhibition hall. He was a reputable, if rather coldly conventional artist who had become a regular at Maman's Tuesday evenings, where his attentions had shown his interest in courting me, not the duchess, as I had suspected. The painting above us, *Marseilles, Gateway of the Orient*, was typical of his work, with muted colors and still, flat figures. What kind of husband would such a correct man make?

Upstairs, spectators crowded the hallways, some socializing, some studying their guidebooks, and some even taking in the paintings. There were statues, too, which seemed almost alive in the flickering gaslight. When we found Manet, he appeared dazed, but happy to see me.

"I must see the painting, monsieur. Tell me where it is," I said.

"Berthe, let us rest here a moment," Maman said. "I am afraid that I feel a headache coming on." *Oof!* We had just arrived to see Manet's completed painting, finally named *The Balcony*. Now I was expected to sit and wait? If only I could have come on my own. But societal mores didn't allow an unmarried woman, even one of my age, to go out in public alone.

Manet rescued me. "Madame Morisot, why don't you rest here," he suggested, "while we take Mademoiselle Berthe to see the painting?"

No woman could resist the man, so after Maman allowed him to show her to a sofa at the end of the hall, for a quarter hour Manet, in his top hat, showed his mother, Suzanne, and me around the exhibition, one minute laughing and saying "It will be a great success," and the next minute worrying that his painting was very bad.

Outside Salle M, Manet stopped. "Go and see it, Mademoiselle Berthe. I don't dare move a step," he said. The confident Édouard Manet suffering from nerves? Proof that he was a mere mortal! I found the contradictions in his temperament quite appealing. The Mesdames Manet and I went off, leaving him muttering to himself with a vague smile on his face.

Somehow, I became separated from the others and bumped headlong into Puvis de Chavannes. He was of impeccable background and wealth, but where others saw him as *distinguished*, I saw him as *old*, a full twenty years my senior.

"I am delighted to see you, Mademoiselle Morisot," he said. He had a way of holding his head back so that he squinted down on me as he spoke. "I was hoping to meet you here. May I accompany you for a few minutes?"

"Certainly, Monsieur de Chavannes."

"I beg of you, let us talk for a while first."

"But I want to see the paintings …"

"There is plenty of time for admiring the paintings."

Such is the life of the unmarried woman. I had neither the protection of a husband nor the independence of a man. He led me to seating in the corner of Salle A. "Did you receive my letter yesterday?" he asked.

"Oui, monsieur. It was kind of you to invite Maman and me to your studio. I apologize for neglecting to send a message in reply today." Where others might have noticed his red ribbon of the Legion of Honor, I focused on his prodigious nose and his Louis Napoleon-style moustache with curled waxed tips too whimsical for his courtly demeanor.

"Mademoiselle, the more withdrawn you become, the more I am

intrigued." I responded by lowering my eyes. It was aggravating that I was expected to keep myself chaste for such suitors, men that even Maman could not tolerate. The week before, she had come upstairs while I was preparing to meet yet another eligible gentleman, crying, "Hurry! I can't stand to spend another minute with that idiot!"

Another quarter-hour slipped away while I endured Monsieur de Chavanne's enthusiastic courting. When an aristocratic couple swept up and captured his attention. I used the opportunity to slip away in order to continue my search for Manet's work.

It took some effort to work my way through the crowds. On the way through Salle B, I saw that the tall Bazille had painted a young woman—his fiancée?—seated in the shade of a pine tree, with a glimpse of a village in the valley behind her. Sunlight struck the front of her white dress and the golden sandstone structures in the village. He had succeeded in showing what I had so often attempted of late—a figure in the outdoor light. In Salle D hung a pretty little portrait by Degas of a woman in black. Fantin had an insignificant sketch hung "at the skyline," near the ceiling in Salle F, a woman in fancy dress reminiscent of a Renaissance Venetian costume. Despite his admiration for Manet, Fantin had never broken away from the sober, classical style favored by the Academy any more than had most of the artists represented at the Salon.

Then, finally, Salle M. I pulled down the veil attached to my hat, held my program in front of my face, and positioned myself behind the group gathered in front of Manet's painting to see *The Balcony* for the first time in its finished form. It was nothing like any of the other paintings in the Salon exhibition. The title was perfect since it referred not only to the Goya painting Manet loved, but also to the modern sandstone apartment buildings lining the new boulevards of Paris, all of which featured balconies.

My figure seemed to be imprisoned, my tense fingers grasping the green wrought-iron railings. I had refused to communicate with Manet through the fan; closed, it created a red exclamation point in the composition. The way I leaned forward in my chair was my natural pose, I had to admit. But did I really twist so, as if struggling to break free? And my face! He had painted my eyes like large, black coals burning with desire.

All who saw *The Balcony* would presume that I was Manet's newest mistress. Censure swirled in the whispers around me.

"He does not even pretend to hide her passion for him!"

"What must the Morisot family think of their femme fatale?"

"And that dog! Who is being faithful to whom, one might ask."

In the painting, Manet's little Japanese dog, Tama, sat at my feet. Everyone knew that a dog signified fidelity. Trés bien. Let them say what they would. I didn't care whether my identity was protected or not. If Édouard Manet dared to paint me this way, it would mean that he shared my defiance and was willing to risk tarnishing his own reputation as well by compromising not a courtesan but a young woman of his own class.

All of us in the painting were awkward, spiraled away from one another, contained only by the pattern of greens. We were caged by the greenish-black balcony and framed by phthalo-green shutters. But wasn't this how life felt? The missed connections, the feeling of isolation even among family and friends? It did for me, at least. It occurred to me that the modern setting was appropriate for a depiction of this subject matter—it was all sterile new buildings and boulevards.

"Monsieur Manet," I reproached when I found him with his top hat tipped down over his eyes, pretending that no one could recognize him, "it was improper for you to leave me to walk around alone!"

"Mademoiselle Berthe," he replied, "You can count on all my devotion, but nevertheless, I will never be a child's nurse."

He was right to mock me. I was a woman, and if I wished to pursue our friendship, I would have to let go of the bourgeois perception of propriety. "I am not a child," I assured him.

"Good, because I intend to paint you again. Your mother has agreed that she needn't chaperone this time."

As I registered this surprising information, Suzanne returned and whined in my ear, "What a pity Édouard spent so much time working on *The Balcony*. What a lot of nice things he could have painted in that time." Philistine! She might have an ear for music, but she had no eye for art. Suzanne was a *hausfrau* who did not deserve her husband.

I was asleep that night when Edma tiptoed in and touched my shoulder. I awoke from a dream of falling through endless darkness, my nightmare since childhood. It was a relief to see my sister, but I could not shake off a sense of dread. "What is it?" I asked. "Is something wrong?"

"Nothing at all. I've just returned from the concert with Adolphe and his parents," she whispered. Her face glowed in the light of the candle she held.

I sat up and moved over to allow room for her to sit on my bed. "How is Lieutenant Pontillion?" I asked, tamping down my apprehension. "Did you enjoy the evening?"

She smiled in a way I hadn't seen before, a half-smile she seemed to try to hold inside. But her happiness could not be held in, and she burst out, "He has asked me to marry him!"

I shook my head. "Non!"

Edma reached for me. "Berthe, it's time. I'm thirty years old." I knew that it was past time for us to marry. Only one year older than I, she still felt the imperative to be the first. And it seemed that she was smitten. No wonder she'd been so agreeable during Maman's marriage talk.

"Bértât, you wouldn't understand," she said with a distracted half-smile. "Marriage is the most important step in a woman's life, and one must make a responsible decision about who can best provide for a family."

I began to tremble. My worst fear had come to pass. I grasped at the only deterent I could think of. "What about the Bonheur Society? We were going to devote our lives to art."

"We will still paint. We can write to each other about what we are accomplishing." Write to each other? *Naturellement*, she would leave Passy and follow Lieutenant Pontillion to wherever he was stationed. "But if you marry a naval officer, you will always have to live near the sea, far from Paris," I pointed out. Edma smiled and stroked my hair, as if I were a child and she, suddenly an adult. She seemed not to comprehend the enormity of her decision.

"We will visit often and paint together."

"You don't understand!"

Her eyes were soft and dreamy as she responded, "Understand what?"

"How this will change everything, all of our plans to conquer the art world."

"Berthe, maybe marriage is my fate, after all."

Her serenity was horrifying; I had already lost her. "Edma, don't leave me!" I begged in a quavering voice. "I can't do this alone."

So focused was she on her interior secret that I could not reach her. She leaned over to kiss me on the cheek before going to the door. "Be happy for me, little sister."

I reached for her, but she was gone.

When the door clicked shut, I slid down onto my pillow, feeling a bud of blackness begin to unfurl inside me. I remembered my childhood fear of the dark, when I'd felt the floor disappear beneath me and had fallen into an endless void. Then, I would fly into Edma's room and jump into her bed.

I still relied on her. How would I live without my sister to run to? Frantic, I cast about for a light. Some hope. Then I remembered that there was something to cling to as I struggled through my sadness. Manet still wanted me to model.

PART TWO

Les Coups Cassées

Broken Brushstrokes

Chapter Ten

Paris

Autumn 1868~Winter 1870

*E*dma married in the fall. After allowing the newlyweds a decent interval to settle in to their new home and hire their help, I visited them at Adolphe's post in Lorient. It was a delightful reunion, and I loved the painting of Edma by the harbor that I made. But once back in Paris for the winter, I was lost without my sister. Again and again, I found myself at Manet's Paris studio that winter.

Knowing that friends generally made their calls in the afternoons, I would arrive in the morning. I wondered why Maman said nothing about my visits, but hesitated to inquire. My theory was that my mother was shrewd enough to know that reining in her twenty-eight-year-old daughter would only lead to rebellion. She was continuing her search for a husband for me. In the meantime, she would allow these private visits to a close family friend. Then too, Maman understood how devastated I'd been by losing Edma. Manet provided the artistic camaraderie I craved. His company made my loss just bearable.

Like Manet, his studio was luxurious and refined, with high windows, oak paneling, and a large fireplace with a Chinese vase and a bust of the helmeted Minerva, the Roman goddess of war, on the mantel. There was a piano in one corner and a standing cheval mirror in another. An overstuffed crimson sofa sat beneath a small Japanese screen painting of a woman overtaken by a giant wave.

Because Maman no longer felt the need to accompany me on my visits to a member of our social circle, I experienced for the first time a magnificent freedom.

In the beginning, I would sit at the piano, playing subdued Beethoven sonatas in order not to disturb the artist. A man so absorbed in his work, so sensitive to the effects of color, and so delicate in his application of paint must possess immeasurable passion in his soul. I yearned to convey to him that I understood who he was, and that I, too, could hardly contain my vast emotions.

When Manet took a few minutes from his work, he showed me his current paintings. One was a portrait, a symbol of gratitude for the young naturalistic novelist Émile Zola's favorable review of his work. Zola, holding a book, sat in profile at his desk with Japanese prints on the wall behind him, the very picture of a progressive intellectual. The idea of having the freedom to keep company with such people, and to have the ability to paint them in such a crisp, fresh style left me dizzy with envy. I was baffled about my feelings for Manet. Was I falling in love with him, or did I wish I could *be* him?

It wasn't until one snowy day in December when I arrived wearing my mink jacket and muff that Manet asked to paint me again. "You are a vision in fur," he said. As his eyes raked me, they stopped at my face, not my furs. He took in my dark eyes and chilled pink cheeks, my sharp nose and chin, the curve of my lips. He reached to move a stray curl on my forehead, but caught himself. "A vision," he murmured to himself as he led me to the chair where I would sit for him.

As the afternoon wore on, my thoughts turned to my sister. "I miss Edma," I said, sounding more like a sulky child than I would have preferred.

"You can't be unhappy about your sister's marriage," he said without looking up from his canvas.

"We had never been separated, and now I have lost my confidante and my competitor. I wish you had never introduced Adolphe Pontillion to Edma."

"I introduced Fanny Claus to her fiancé, too, you know," Manet said in the sailor's drawl he sometimes affected, when his only sailing experience had been the training voyage he'd taken in his youth in preparation for an ill-fated Naval Academy entrance examination. "Oh, I can't fight my natural talent as a matchmaker." When he saw that his humor did not change my mood, he became serious. "I have known Pontillion since our days at sea. He's from a good family with an estate in Maurecourt. It's right that a woman her age be married." Oui, Edma had turned thirty. But was a mere number sufficient reason to betray the tenets of the Bonheur Society? "Twelve years ago, we agreed to devote our lives to art," I informed him.

"And so neither of you was to have a woman's life of marriage and children?"

"Isn't it possible to do both?"

"Tell me about one woman who has done so." Rosa Bonheur? Unmarried. The duchess? Widowed. I shrugged, but made a mental note to find one.

"Voila!" he exclaimed. *"Berthe Morisot with a Muff."* I was all pointed nose and chin, engulfed by my luxurious mink coat. The thought that Manet saw me as that beautiful and sensuous woman started my heart thudding beneath my furs.

My face was nearly covered in *Berthe Morisot in a Veil.* Manet again invoked his idol Goya when he painted me peeking through the black lace fan I held before my face like a mask, conveying the message "I love you."

He chose to talk over the language of the fan.

"I've been intrigued by the Spanish masters since my youth. My uncle, the only artistic member of the family, used to take me to visit the Spanish gallery in the Louvre." I found the image of Édouard Manet as a boy appealing. How I would have loved to have witnessed those hours when his burning urge to become an artist was first ignited.

"I paint Parisian characters with the simplicity of Velázquez," he told me. "No one understands that."

"They should. All of Paris has become interested in Spain since Empress Eugénie married Louis Napoleon."

"Can you say her whole name?" he asked.

"Eugénie…Non, Marie-Eugénie…"

"Marie-Eugénie Ignacia Augustina de Palafox-Portocarrero," Manet rattled off, causing us both to break into laughter.

In January, he painted me in profile, wearing my black hat with the white feather. He always depicted a different aspect of my personality, but he never painted me in disguise, as he did most of his models. He had once portrayed himself and Suzanne as Rubens with his wife, and he'd shown Victorine Meurent as a toreador, of all things. During the hours that I sat there in my feathered hat, I came up with two theories about Manet's penchant for costumes. First, he considered bourgeois society to be based on hypocrisy, so it made sense that he often depicted its members as characters other than themselves. Then too, he seemed to enjoy confounding the public, so perhaps he simply used masquerades to that end.

But I was always portrayed as myself, unless you considered my accessories to be the costume of a fashionable parisienne.

For another painting, I placed my hand over my throat with exaggerated modesty and settled in for a long session. To occupy me, I begged Manet to describe Café Guerbois, the daily meeting place of the most avant-garde artists in Paris, which placed that particular café at the center of the artistic universe.

"Oh, it's very elegant," he assured me. "The interior is white and gold, with gilded mirrors that reflect the gas lights and the marble table-tops."

"Oui, oui, I can see that much through the window!" He delighted in exasperating me. "But how is that so different from the tea salons or chocolate shops?" It was the difference between being relegated to chatter about fashion and hairstyles or being engaged in a discussion of Realism with fellow artists. I would have given anything to be able to be a part of the Guerbois circle.

When Manet saw the desperation in my eyes, he was frank with me. "Joining friends at the Guerbois is a relief, an escape after the day's work or when the light is gone by four o'clock in the winter." It was just that kind of companionship that I'd missed since Edma married. "At the Guerbois, I am King Arthur, surrounded by his knights of the Round Table!"

73

"That is not so far from the truth."

"Why not just say I am Jesus, surrounded by his disciples?" he scoffed. That was even closer to describing the devotion of his followers, from what I could see. But he disagreed. "I have no interest in being the leader of any group. Although I enjoy socializing at day's end, the true artist works alone."

It was impossible to imagine Édouard ever alone.

He fell quiet as his painting engrossed him. The hand I held at my throat grew cold, then numb. I wondered if Manet had ever considered that his models might study him as much as he did them. From my vantage point, the light pouring in from the window behind him brought out sparks of red in his wavy hair that hovered above the canvas. Below it, his long legs shuffled about in an artist's choreography. I felt I could never tire of watching him. At liberty to observe him as much as I liked, the hours glided past like a lissome skater on an icy pond.

Finally, Manet clucked his tongue in satisfaction. When he raised his head, seemingly surprised to be reminded of the world beyond his canvas, he sighed.

"What is it, Monsieur Manet?"

He paused. I waited until he was ready to confide in me. "The public wounds me constantly. Sometimes my springs are completely broken. *Mais oui!*" he insisted, seeing my expression of doubt. "There are those who avoid me in order not to have to talk about my paintings. I lose courage to ask anyone to model for me."

"So that is why I am chosen—because I am one of the few who can tolerate you?"

"Non, that is not the reason." He gave me that look, the one I was always waiting for. Only he made me feel truly seen. He painted my dark hair and my pretty gowns, but based on the varied ways he portrayed me, I believed that he saw beyond those into my soul.

"Mademoiselle Berthe," he said, stroking his forked beard, "May I call you simply Berthe? And please, call me Édouard."

I extended my foot from beneath my black dress to reveal a playful peek of a decorative rosebud on the toe of one of the pink slippers that I always wore, confident enough of his feelings by now to flirt with him. "As you wish, Édouard."

"I can tell a lot about a woman by how she holds her feet," he volunteered. "A woman who turns her foot out has a sensual nature." I contemplated my turned-out foot. Édouard tried not to smile, but I had no doubt that he was pleased to have discomfited me.

In an attempt to divert the conversation from my sensual nature, I said, "Tell me more about café life." My attentive expression encouraged him to continue.

"Sometimes we move on to the Café Riche for dinner."

"I've heard of *sauce à la riche*."

"Imagine a fish reduction with cream and lobster butter, and brandy and cayenne."

Even the idea of such a concoction made me almost gag. Either that or I so coveted the exciting life of the *flaneûr*, so far from the prescribed pattern of my days, that it was hearing about Édouard's rambles about the city that knotted my stomach.

"You may roam the boulevards and enjoy all that Paris has to offer, while I stay at home and receive calls or go for few excursions more exciting than dress fittings. Without your freedom, I'll never be a real artist."

How to explain my circumstances to a man who took his freedom for granted? Had he never realized that the only women he knew who enjoyed lives of freedom were those who occupied the demimonde? I pointed to one of Édouard's unsold paintings hanging on a wall, *A View of the 1867 Exposition*. "There, do you see how you've compressed space to show Paris closer to the viewer? The life of commerce and modernity is within reach."

"That was the point of the Exposition—to show the world that Paris is the future."

"If I were to paint the same scene, from a woman's point of view…"

I broke my pose to move closer to the painting.

Édouard came out from behind his easel and came to stand behind me. "I challenge you to do it."

"*Ça va,* when I paint the same scene, I will keep Paris in the distance. And these people—the gardener, the soldiers..." Édouard was standing so close that his sleeve brushed against my shoulder. My frustration at the obstacles I faced was compounded by the confusion his nearness brought about.

"Did you notice Léon, walking his dog?" His breath tickled my neck when he leaned in to point them out. I struggled to concentrate.

"Oui. And the hot air balloon available for hire, the amazon on horseback—they all inhabit the world. I will illustrate women from my smaller world, unable to associate with most of your people, haute-bourgeois wives and mothers restricted to their homes and gardens. *Mais oui,* I will depict the Trocadero as little more than the extension of a woman's garden." My voice cracked in helpless frustration.

When I had composed myself, I turned to face him and said, "I will tell the truth about the barriers that keep women isolated from the world. Only then will I consider myself a real artist."

"But you *are* a real artist, no matter how stifled you feel. You are all the more amazing for rising above your conventional circumstances." Perhaps he did understand the extent of my hindrances. Did he understand that he, too, was a source of frustration for me? I chose my next words carefully.

"I am not sure I am brave enough to defy the social order as you do. The consequences are more severe for a woman." Édouard's aggrieved grimace told me that he had intuited my meaning. I watched his eyes soften under my adoring gaze. Our conversation was taking a turn. Were we talking about the unconventional life of an artist, or something else, like flouting all that was respectable in order to be with the man I loved?

"Berthe, if I were free...That is to say, if I could make myself free..." His thumb stroked his beard with great energy.

Was Édouard suggesting what I thought he was? After six months of increasing intimacy, it seemed possible that he was ready to act on his feelings, to leave Suzanne for me. Our faces were inches apart. I held my breath and ventured a peek from under my eyebrows, awaiting his declaration of love for me.

But he quashed his emotions and rushed to return to the subject of our discussion.

"Just by being an upper-class woman who paints, you are being defiant."

I wonder how defiant you'd consider me if you knew how little I've painted over the year that I've been modeling for you, I thought. *Would you lose what respect you have for me as an artist?*

But I remembered that I was more to him than a fellow artist when he said, "You are the only person I know who is in a position to fully understand how confined I feel."

And then he pulled back from the verge of melancholia and became once again the light-hearted optimist. "And you have brought me luck! I've had an offer for *The Balcony.*" Given his history of poor sales, I hoped for his sake that this claim was factual, not just Édouard's attempt to impress me.

Back at his easel once again, his features taut, he became engrossed in his sweeping brushstrokes, and I didn't wish to interrupt him. There was no longer any need for the seductive gaze. Our attraction to one another was unspoken but understood. These were the parameters to our courtship. We could go no further without cataclysmic consequences.

One afternoon, inspired by the unseasonable warmth of a February day, I arrived at Édouard's studio wearing a filmy, white lawn dress set off by black ribbons at my neck and waist. When I sat down, my full skirt gave the impression that I had been dropped onto his red velvet sofa with one leg folded under me. Édouard handed me a fan, perhaps to complement the Japanese screen above the sofa. My other hand rested on the sofa cushion, with a lace handkerchief dropped next to it.

"*Mais oui*, your white dress provides a nice contrast," he muttered to himself. He leaned forward with one arm braced against the back of the sofa, trapping me where I sat. His fingers brushed against my face as he arranged my curls in front of my shoulders. I stopped breathing.

"But this is too casual a pose," I protested, aware that we were poised on a precipice. If Édouard painted me like this, anyone would think I had flung myself down before this man with abandon. But he did not stand up.

"I want to imagine you as free as you wish to be," he whispered into my ear. The touch of his breath set a shiver coursing through me.

I was afraid to imagine how free I might wish to be, afraid even to meet Édouard's gaze. He put a finger under my chin and lifted it. I forced myself to meet his eyes. Now that the moment I had anticipated so many times was here, I felt like the woman on the Japanese screen hanging on the wall behind me, overtaken by the giant sea-blue wave of Édouard's regard. If I allowed that wave to crash over me, who knew what frightening creatures I might find in the murky depths? When Édouard moved to kiss me, I turned away. "Édouard, my leg is asleep. I must move now."

He stood and backed away as if nothing had happened.

"Non! Your dress is arranged perfectly, and I am just finishing your ankle." So my ankle was showing? Later, I saw that he had painted the small portion of stocking that was revealed in a stark white, calling attention to a bit of exposed feminine anatomy. Ah, *tant pis*, I didn't care. My ankles were slim and neat, and if they caught Édouard's eye, so much the better.

I believed beyond doubt that this non-conformist, unconcerned with scandal, intended to leave his wife in order to marry me. Until then, I reveled in the attention of the man I loved.

Paris
7 May 1870

Degas,

I want to thank you for taking me to Longchamp last week. My first time at the racetrack was a revelation. Of course I enjoyed watching the fashionable spectators as they strolled the grounds and filled the grandstand. But, not one to enjoy the outdoors as a rule, I was surprised to be so seduced by the smells of the earth and animals. The bright silk costumes of the jockeys glowed as the sun burned through the diffused light of the early morning fog.

I watched you, Degas the Great Draftsman, with your flat-brimmed hat and blue-tinted spectacles to shade your bad eyes, sketching the horses and jockeys before the race. You are not a spontaneiste. I know you think works of art should be as carefully plotted out as the perfect crime, while I say the only way is to paint straight off what you see. If you catch it, all right. If not, then you try again. All the rest is nonsense.

Like me, you prefer to paint in your studio. But at the racetrack, you recorded the many poses you would later arrange into a composition using those funny little horse armatures you'd made. You were as skilled at showing the stallions ready to move as when they were in motion. You were a marvel at capturing the nervous energy, the barely suppressed tension of their magnificent bodies as they pawed at the ground and snorted, steam blowing from their nostrils.

Do you remember the conversation we had that day about marriage? After a few drinks in the beer garden behind the grand stand, you were holding forth—something about "It is really a good thing to be married, to have children..."

Easy for a bachelor to say. "Things always look better from the outside, mon ami," I assured you. Behind you, I noticed that giant clouds peeked over the line of trees at the edge of the racetrack.

"But to be free of the need to be gallant to every eligible young lady! Mon Dieu, it is really time one thought about marriage!"

"It's simpler to have a mistress," I maintained. "You have admirers enough to choose from—what about Mademoiselle Cassatt?"

I recall that you snorted in an equine fashion. "We became quite close during the months we worked together in my studio. I would marry her, but I could never make love to such a plain creature. She is one hell of a fine horsewoman, though!"

"What about the charming Mademoiselle Morisot, then?" I suggested. You gave me a quizzical smile, which I ignored. Did you suspect my feelings for Berthe?

You couldn't have known that, looking at those restless horses, I was thinking of the last time Berthe Morisot had modeled for me. After almost two years of painting her, I'd reached the pinnacle of my ardor. Over the last year, our intimacy had progressed to the point where she felt at ease reclining on my sofa, stretched out like a panther. How she captivated me! Her ardent attention pulled me in to the paintings she modeled for and made me a part of the composition. Her insolent gaze was more erotic than any nude I'd yet painted. Her deep-set eyes missed nothing. She was aware that I was painting her naked emotions, and she allowed it. Her whole being conveyed elegance and distinction, but her refinement and reserve barely concealed the passionate soul within.

I was driven to a frenzy, painting with brutal brushstrokes. Only in that way could I possess her. The more composed her lovely face, the more delicate the foamy lace at her neck, the more I loaded the brush and hurled myself at the canvas with a vengeance. When one brush broke, I threw it to the ground and took up another, building a thick impasto in an attempt to bury my feelings for Berthe. I felt like one of your horses, ready for his race. Are you surprised that I've been so consumed by a woman? I live for my hours with Berthe. Her sultry beauty, her acute intelligence, and her desire inflame me more than any other woman I've ever known.

You can see what a state I am in, mon ami.

What were you thinking, sipping your beer while I prattled on about Mademoiselle Morisot? "It's a pity she's not a man, but she could still do something in the cause of painting by marrying a member of the Academy and bringing discord into the camp of those old dodderers."

You hunched your rounded shoulders in your salt and pepper suit. "Would you sacrifice innocent virgins at the altar? Surely not!" Your indignant tone was muted by the banners surrounding the beer garden that flapped in the breeze as the distant clouds grew tall and marched in our direction.

"You will never marry, Degas. You lack spontaneity. You aren't capable of loving a woman, much less of doing anything about it." You nodded in begrudging agreement. "In that case, the brothels will suffice." I raised my glass in a toast: "To the maisons de tolerance!"

"Occasionally, but to be a serious artist today, one must be immersed in solitude," you retorted. "There is love and there is work, and we have only one heart!" As is your habit, you held out your hand for a congratulatory shake for this bon mot. I downed my glass of beer and slammed it to the table.

Shadows grew long, the last race ended, and people started to return to their parked carriages. I watched les belles holding their hats and skirts against the stiff wind brought by the menacing clouds now directly overhead as their escorts handed them up into their landaus, barouches, and four-in-hands. It was time to move on.

For reading my ramblings, and for holding my secret, merci.

Édouard

Chapter Eleven

Passy~ Paris
April 1870

My months of modeling for Manet had flown by like a dream, but on a gray day in April when *la grisaille's* low, leaden clouds bore down on me, I missed Edma more than ever. My gentle sister had left me, and we would never live together again. Who else would ever understand me as she did?

Leaning against the rain-streaked window of my bedroom, I re-read her latest letter:

> I am often with you in my thoughts. I follow you everywhere in your studio, and I wish that I could escape were it only for one quarter of an hour to breathe again that air in which we lived.

The tentacles of panic began to reach under the door of my boudoir. I had to be with a sympathetic soul. I flew down the stairs.

"Those damned Germans!" railed Papa in the dining room. "Now King Wilhelm is trying to put his son on the throne of Spain."

"Empress Eugénie must have something to say about that," Maman predicted, before calling out, "Berthe! *Le déjeuner!*"

Feeling trapped in my parents' house, apart from both of the people I loved most, brought on the usual result—the very thought of food was sickening. Maman found me weeping in the foyer, with my nose pressed against the wall.

I had sent for a horse and carriage, too desperate to take the long streetcar ride into Paris. When the driver pulled in front of our house, I grabbed my cape and a package, and went out. The ride to the Quartier Europe and the long blocks in the rain to the rue Gujot were a blur, but seeing that I was approaching Édouard's studio, anticipation replaced anxiety. I clutched my package, the painting of *Harbor at Lorient,* intended as a gift for Édouard, stepped down from the carriage before the driver could come to give me his hand, and rushed up the stairs to the studio.

Never had I been so gratified to see Édouard's excited greeting. So much so that it took me several minutes to realize that his charming chatter was not about me at all, but about a new "student" of his, Eva Gonzalès.

"She requires private lessons," he said, "because the prospect of copying in the Louvre makes her take to her bed." She was unable to go into society? How absurd!

"But you do not take pupils," I protested. Did he imagine that I had been his student?

Édouard did not even register my remark. "You could take Mademoiselle Gonzalès as an example, you know," he said. "She has perseverance, she knows how to carry something through." What was he saying? Was he referring to my portrait of Edma and Maman?

When Edma spent her first confinement with us, I'd decided to paint a double portrait of her with Maman, similar to something Fantin had done with his mother and his new fiancée. I liked how he'd used the edge of a picture frame in the background to structure his composition, but his painting was dark and gloomy.

In contrast, I had posed my subjects in the drawing room, with morning light pouring in the front windows, reflecting off the gilt-framed mirror behind the white sofa and falling on Edma's white peignoir. I painted her without gesture or expression. The book Maman was reading had been the focus of my sister's reverie.

She was no longer an artist and not yet a mother. What, then, was the essence of Edma? It seemed that an absence of detail would allow the viewer to search for what she withheld from the rest of the world. A silent, still woman was nevertheless a woman with a complex inner life. She was well-dressed, prosperous and proper, but what was deeply feminine about her—about all women—was separate from that. To me, this secret self, keeping something unknown, was what defined a woman.

I had been struggling with that painting, and it appeared to be getting the best of me. At one of Maman's Tuesday evenings, I had shown *Reading* to Puvis de Chavannes, who declared it "neither done nor doable." I undid. I redid. Tired and enervated, I went on a Saturday to Édouard's studio, and he promised to come the next day to tell me how I should repair the painting.

When Maman poked her head into my studio to say, "Bértât, Édouard has arrived." I tucked up my loose tendrils of hair and pulled off my painting smock as Maman led him in.

Édouard swaggered in, an indication that he was in one of his manic moods. "I came as soon as I sent off my own pictures."

"Thank you for answering my plea for help."

He examined my canvas. "It's incomplete," he announced, confirming Puvis' assessment.

I fumed with frustration but suppressed one of my dark looks. "If I have had difficulty finishing it in time, it is because I have spent so much time modeling for you!"

"I will tell you what needs to be done," he said, taking my paintbrush and palette.

"Perhaps you will still be able to submit your painting to the Salon," said Maman.

"That doesn't seem possible, since the carter is coming at five," I pointed out.

"It's very good," Édouard said, "but the lower part of the dress…"
Maman agreed. "*Mais oui*, exactly."

"Non!" I cried, as he took the brushes and put in a few accents.

"A touch here…and here." Once started, nothing could stop him.

"That is enough. Please stop!" I entreated Édouard as he moved from the hem of Maman's dress, to the bodice, then to her head, to my increasing distress.

"Édouard! You know perfectly well that the painting will be rejected if anyone learns I had help with it." He only laughed and handed my palette back to me. Half the painting was now taken up by Maman's black dress. I hadn't intended to cover my light-filled room with what looked like an ominous encroaching storm cloud. Anyone seeing it would presume that she was in mourning, not happily contemplating the birth of Edma's first child. Never again would I paint with black. "Her face, her hands…this could have been done by Goya himself. Everyone will know it is yours." Was that what he wished? Was he determined to present his image of Berthe Morisot not only in his paintings, but in mine, as well? Still laughing like a madman, he grabbed my palette again and continued painting.

After he left, and the carter arrived to transport the still-wet painting to the Salon, Maman responded to my fierce expression by agreeing that "the improvements he made were atrocious."

"What do you want to do?" she asked.

It was terrifying to think of the scandal that would ensue, should anyone discover Édouard's involvement with the painting. "I'd rather be at the bottom of the Seine than learn that the picture has been accepted," I managed to say.

Maman rushed to the studio door and called, "Boy, bring it back!" The carter toted the painting back through the courtyard and eased it into the studio.

Half of the double portrait no longer resembled my original vision. Yet the portrait of Edma remained mine. "I've changed my mind. Go ahead, take it," I almost moaned. The carter blinked in confusion, then carried the large canvas out the door again.

Maman shook her head in exasperation. "The smallest thing here takes on the proportions of a tragedy."

While I had been reliving the agony of my painting debacle, Édouard was still going on about his new pupil. "Oui, she is a very good example of perseverance," Édouard repeated. "Degas would do very well to marry Mademoiselle Gonzalès. There is a woman who is ravishing in every respect, and so intelligent, and such good manners!"

I was without words when he brought me around the easel to reveal that what he was working on was a portrait of this Mademoiselle Gonzalès.

"You have shown her as an artist." He had never done this for me, out of deference, I thought, for my social position. She somewhat resembled me, and judging by her dress, she was of our class.

The truth stunned me into silence. He had found a replacement for me. *Pourquoi?* Did he no longer find me attractive? Was I so old that he had come to desire someone who possessed more youthful freshness?

"I'm having trouble with the head...every evening I wash it out with black soap," he prattled, as I struggled to make sense of the situation. The woman's head appeared feeble, not pretty at all. She was painting only a still life, making ineffectual dabs at some flowers in a vase. And what woman in her right mind painted in a white muslin dress? Did she think she was Elisabeth Vigée-Lebrun, the coquettish court painter from a century ago?

"Your work!" exclaimed Édouard, spying the package I was still holding. "Let us see what you have brought me." He unwrapped my painting of Edma sitting on the sea wall in Lorient. She was all in white, with pink and violet in the folds of her skirt. Her face was in the shade of her parasol, her features just smudges.

"Decidedly, the best thing you have done!" he declared. "How did you reproduce the marine air of the Normandy coast so exactly, when it changes from moment to moment?"

"By mixing the light into the paint, I suppose. The light was wonderful in Lorient."

"Maybe I will try painting *en plein air*, after all."

"It is in the Japanese style, with Edma seated far to the right of the composition."

"Asymmetrical," Édouard murmured to himself. "*Très intéressant.*" He urged me to go on.

"The light on the, on the water…" My voice was choked. Édouard peered over my canvas to see me sobbing in silence.

"What is it, Berthe?"

His solicitous tone encouraged me to pour out my heart. All of my natural reserve vanished, and I listed all of my grievances to what I thought was a sympathetic ear.

Then, a knock on the door, and Eva Gonzalès was there in the flesh, swathed in a long burgundy pélerine over a matching gown. She was little more than a child with tiny, gloved hands that poked out from the slit sleeves of her mantle. Édouard, bright-eyed and grinning, was delighted to introduce us; he was bubbling over with good spirits. I had to face her, but the young woman's dark eyes and hair were so like mine that I had the disconcerting sensation of falling into a mirror. I understood that Édouard's attention had slipped away from me. While I was waiting for him to separate from Suzanne, he had formed a new attachment. How had I lost his affection?

"I am so happy to meet you, Mademoiselle Morisot. I have heard so much about you and your work."

Édouard turned my painting toward her. Non! I did not paint it for the amateur scrutiny of Eva Gonzalès, but as a gift for Édouard.

"I must go," I interrupted. "I only intended to stop in for a moment." There were more words as Édouard handed me my cape, but I didn't hear them. Darkness enveloped me like a shroud, so that by the time I reached the street, I had to pinch my hands to keep from revealing my desolation in public. I had been such a fool! Of course he had nothing to offer me, not as an artist nor as a woman.

In my rush to reach Édouard, I had neglected to tell my driver to return for me. Regardless of my desperate condition, I would have to take public transportation home.

On the omnibus, I forced myself to focus on a child sitting across from me until my dark glower made him turn toward his mother and hide his face. If I was so repulsive that I even frightened small children, how could I have ever imagined that I was attractive to Édouard Manet? I thought of Edma, who could always make me feel better when I was distraught. But she was gone.

I managed to stay conscious until I was back in my boudoir, where I let myself slide down and down into the oily blackness of despair.

❧

14 June 1870

My dear Degas,

You alone know my feelings for Mademoiselle Morisot, so I can write about them to only you. I have reached a crisis point.

The last time Berthe visited my studio, she was in the midst of describing a painting she made of her sister in Lorient when she broke down. It all came out—her longing for her sister, her questioning of her ability to paint, her lack of means to sell her work. I should have expected it. Love carries enormous responsibilities, which is why I've avoided it in the past.

Berthe's constant brooding is tedious, and having her every mood depend on me is impossible. I've listened to Baudelaire's incessant diatribes on the subject of his own depression, and I can't take any more. "Sacre nom de Dieu," I think I muttered, using one of his expressions.

I fully understand that melancholia is the lot of the artist. Baudelaire describes my swings from supreme confidence to desolation as "cyclothymic oscillation." I say it takes that level of confidence to break down borders in art, but it's difficult to maintain when neither critics nor customers support one's efforts. My feeling is that we can overcome our afflictions by pursuing an enjoyment of life. The society of congenial friends and the pleasures of Paris—these constitute the cure for melancholy. You know how I adore the perfumes and dazzling delights of evening parties.

Yet Berthe seldom experiences those highs, only the constant lassitude of neurasthenia, brought on by her domestic dilemmas and utter inability to change her circumstances. Over the course of the winter, her love for me has become yet another onus I must shoulder. Berthe is too beautiful, cultivated, and talented for me to let her become a burden.

Now it is spring. If I divert her attention back to her work she might lessen her dependence on me. I will try to find a gallery owner who will show her

paintings, or maybe a patron who will give her a commission.
Victoria Meurant has returned from her adventures in America—Olympia
herself. I think it is time to begin using her as my model again.
I have enough portraits of Mademoiselle Morisot, for now at least.
Confession is relief, but now I have burdened you in the same way I've been
complaining about being burdened myself. Forgive me, mon ami.

Édouard

Chapter Twelve

Passy

Autumn 1870

*T*he duchess gave up her enviable apartment on the Île St. Louis and moved to the south of France in June. She left behind legions of admirers, including the Emperor Louis-Napoleon himself. When she came to say goodbye, she explained that she was leaving because of a dream she'd had. In it, lightning had ripped a summer sky and a flame-colored moon had appeared from among the clouds, which to my wise friend signified trouble approaching. Napoleon proved the veracity of the duchess's dream when he declared war on Germany in July of 1870.

The war seemed to come out of nowhere. Even I, too miserable to paint after Édouard's rejection, had been aware of the pleasures of spring. The Salon was a tremendous success, with both *Reading* and a portrait of Edma by a window well received. A mare named Sornette won at Longchamp, so her jockey's pale turquoise livery inspired the color of the season. And Maman bought me the latest bonnet, the chapeau pomponette, topped with roses and tied in a large bow under the chin, to try to cheer me. I could only wish that Édouard could see me in it. No one had given a thought as to what was going on in the Emperor's palace.

Napoleon's wife was a member of the Spanish royal family, so when Germany's King Wilhelm proposed the idea of seating his son on the Spanish throne, her blood must have boiled. Empress Eugénie insisted that Napoleon exact retribution for Wilhelm's affront to her native country. So, Napoleon demanded a retraction of the Prussian proposal, as well as an apology and a promise never again to suggest such a thing, or else risk retaliation. In response, Wilhelm's Prime

Minister Otto von Bismarck made sure the threatening documents were printed in German newspapers, inciting the bellicose citizens of the Prussian states.

The people of France were first insulted by Bismarck's obvious ploy intended to goad them into war—right up to the hour that they decided that they *must* go to war. A matter of international importance, the attempted Prussian appropriation of the Spanish throne, was reduced to a volley of accusations: Napoleon's demands were too exacting! Bismarck's publishing of those demands was an incendiary act! The only reasonable man in government, former President Thiers, protested that the empire was ready to pour out buckets of blood over a mere matter of form. And so an absurd quarrel, less suited to statesman than to fish merchants fighting over a stall in Les Halles, led to war.

After the initial chauvinistic outbursts—throngs holding flags ran through the boulevards singing *La Marseillaise* and shouting "*Vive la guerre!*"—Paris, the sparkling jewel of Europe, returned to its origins as an ancient fortress. Bridges were blown up to prevent the German army's entry into the city, the pleasure boats on the Seine were fitted with guns, and search beams were installed atop every high point—the half-built new opéra house, l'Arc de Triomphe, and the windmills of Montmartre. The city of lights darkened as theaters and restaurants closed and fewer street lamps were lit each night. Department stores were converted to hospitals, and the flag of the Red Cross flew atop the Grand Hôtel. Even baguettes and café au lait disappeared, as wheat, coffee, and milk were shipped to the front lines.

It was difficult to imagine any need to prepare for war on a glorious day in the Bois de Boulogne, as Maman and I strolled under a canopy of jewel-colored leaves through warm September breezes. But I took note of changes. There should not have been thousands of sheep and cows grazing in the meadows. Farmers from the outskirts of the city thought to protect their livestock by bringing their herds within city limits. And there should not have been soldiers in their red and blue uniforms trotting their horses down the tree-shaded boulevards where fashionable people normally rode by in their carriages. What seemed impossible to believe must be true. War was approaching.

"Are you certain that we should not go to stay with Edma and Yves?" I asked Maman. Edma and her baby, Nini, had come to us when Adolphe was called up for service. We had sent them to the south of France to join Yves in the safety of Mirande the week before, after Napoleon, suffering from a bladder stone and piles, was captured.

"You know that the highest government officials will not leave Paris now that the Second Empire has collapsed—least of all your father!" Maman protested. "They are hard at work constructing the Third Republic."

I observed the boulevard, empty of other strollers. "The isolation is becoming difficult," I said. The duchess had been away from Paris for only a matter of months, yet it seemed years had passed since we'd shared one of our tête-à-têtes. Some of our friends had abandoned Passy, leaving their empty houses in the hands of their servants. The shuttered houses and overgrown gardens up the hill loomed ominously over our home.

"Monsieur de Chavannes has remained quite attentive," Maman pointed out, stepping around a pile of horse droppings.

Oof! His political views were as conservative as his art. "Puvis is a royalist. Would you have us return to monarchy?"

"You know I am a staunch republican. Why, President Thiers himself was a witness at your baptism, and he performed Edma's wedding."

"Then you must agree that Puvis' political views are very far from my own."

"As though you have any number of suitors and can afford to simply check another name off your list," Maman sniffed, as she adjusted her parasol.

"Should suitors be foremost on my mind, given the circumstances?"

"Circumstances? Nonsense! Our brave soldiers will repel the

Prussian invasion within days." She held her tongue about Puvis—until she could not. "I'll admit," she allowed, with a fond look, "his actions reveal that he does not understand the high-strung nature of the object of his affection." We continued in silence, enjoying the beautiful autumn afternoon, until we passed under the archway that led us out of the park, from heaven to hell.

The street was thronged with Parisians trying to escape the city and those from the provinces arriving to seek refuge in it. The privileged crowded into carriages, their furniture vans pulled by straining horses. The less fortunate struggled with carts piled high with mattresses, chairs, and cook pots, with children and birdcages balanced on top. A cacophony of clomping horses, church bells, and frantic shouting assailed us.

"It appears that everyone but us is leaving Paris," I said, forcing myself to sound calm amidst the mayhem. These people were running for their lives. Did they imagine Prussian soldiers invading Passy? Cannon balls shooting into the Bois?

"Cowards!" Maman choked out the word, her strongest censure. As we passed a gentleman hustling his family into a carriage, she raised her voice to say, "This is not my idea of how a man should behave." She was thinking, no doubt, of Tiburce.

Never able to settle upon an occupation, Tiburce had seen the war as an opportunity to embark upon a military career. He had been among the first to enlist and the first to be captured at the battle of Sedan, and he was now imprisoned in Mayénce.

"The German line is forming at Passy," the indignant man responded. "Shall I not protect my family?" It was plain to see that escape was the only protection he had to offer; his bald head and weak chin made him look as defenseless as a tortoise without its shell. He climbed up next to the carriage driver, shouting, "To the train station!"

I wished Papa would see fit to take us away from Paris. But he felt that we were protected by his government position and social status. *My* position and status as the only unmarried daughter in the family dictated that it was my duty to stay with my parents.

One of the peddlers working his way through the crowds, a young boy crying *"Papier!"* stepped in front of me. "Mademoiselle, paper and pencil to write your will?" Appalled, I could only shake my head before I hurried to catch up with Maman, who had sailed down the street with her head held high.

Édouard visited me in early September, after Napoleon had been disgraced and Léon Gambetta had taken over the provisional government. He arrived panting as if he had run across the city and up the stairs to our sitting room. "Suzanne and Léon are off to the Pyrénées. I've just come from the train station."

"It must put your mind at ease, knowing that they are evacuated to safety," I said, maintaining a measured tone.

My calm left Édouard was incredulous. "Do you understand the danger we face?"

"I know that Empress Eugénie has demanded that the French ambassador extract an official statement from Prussia, renouncing any claim to the Spanish throne forever."

"Don't you see that any demands from France only unify Germany? Our countries have been at war for centuries. The threat of attack always brings together the Prussian states."

A terrifying prospect, but perhaps Édouard was exaggerating, as he was inclined to do. "Prince Leopold declined the position, at any rate," I said, hoping to calm Édouard. But he saw that he had upset me, and he curbed his political passion in favor of less contentious topics.

"Have you thought of protecting your paintings?" he asked. Non, my paintings were far from safe. Which meant that we weren't, either. "Papa doesn't believe that the war will come to our very home, so I have made no such provisions," I admitted.

"I've stored my most important work in my friend Duret's basement. It should be safe there while I am off fighting. "

Fighting? Impossible to imagine this elegant man maneuvering a rifle rather than a paintbrush. I looked up at him, unable to hide my distress. His eyes mirrored my concern, if for a different reason.

"When will your family leave Paris?" he asked.

I was thoroughly frightened by that point but wanted Édouard to remember this visit fondly when he needed a respite from the horrors of battle. So I forced a light tone when I told him, "Oh, we'll stay on here. Papa thinks it's best."

His effort to temper our conversation forgotten, Édouard scoffed, "Does he? So much so that he's willing to risk his daughter's life?"

Maintaining social niceties was proving to be more than I could manage. I began to feel faint.

Édouard pressed on: "Who will marry you if you are wounded in the legs or disfigured?"

Who indeed would marry me? I wondered.

Belying our belief that France was invincible, Bismark proved that Paris was vulnerable when, on 13 October, 1870, the Prussians put the city under siege.

Along with our fellow residents of Passy, we congregated each day at the newspaper kiosks for the latest news and battle reports. Maman and I got as wet as water spaniels when we went in stormy weather to the telescopes above the Trocadero to watch the action below as though it were a theater spectacle. We were shaken when we came upon a corpse being taken away on a stretcher, one of the first casualties of the battle at the city's border. The light was gone from the poor boy's eyes, and the horror of his flat stare led to my first fainting spell.

Maman and I made one last foray to the Bois. In little more than a month, the forested park had been sacrificed for firewood; only a vast field of tree stumps, sharpened to deter invaders, remained. The sheep and cows had disappeared from the meadows, then the zoo animals—the camel and the antelope—were slaughtered at local butcher shops that were hard pressed to provide meat for the majority of the two million citizens of Paris who remained in the city. Word spread that when Castor and Pollux, the beloved elephants that I remembered swaying from side to side when patriotic songs drifted from the bandstand, were shot, their keeper collapsed, weeping, in their pen.

The hungry lion and tigers who remained dared anyone to approach them.

We returned to our home, no longer a sanctuary now that soldiers were billeted on the ground floor. I couldn't stand even a glimpse of our elegant drawing room, but rushed upstairs to our reduced living quarters and locked the door at the top of the staircase, as Maman had instructed me to do whenever I entered our house. The everlasting odors of unwashed men, gunpowder, and cheap wine that wafted from below, I would always associate with the war.

From the window in Maman's upstairs sitting room, I wrung my hands as I watched the militia in the courtyard below carry their furniture and supplies into my studio, now their quarters. The war had, indeed, come to our home. Too late, I remembered Édouard's warning about protecting my paintings. When I caught sight of soldiers piling my canvases out in the courtyard, en route to the wine cellar, I turned on Papa with a wrathful scowl.

"It seemed prudent to allow the officers to requisition your studio," said Papa, hiding behind his newspaper to avoid my ire. "Surely they would not choose a position likely to draw fire."

I expected Maman to speak up for me, but she focused on the needlepoint seat cover on which she was working, unwilling to displease her husband.

"Why are we still here?" I demanded. Maman gave me a warning look, and Papa stayed silent behind his newspaper. I more and more felt trapped, the longer we waited here for the Germans to arrive. But my parents were deaf to my objections. I blurted, "If I can't paint, what am I to do while we wait for our doom?" I stormed out of the room in a fury.

In November, we received news of the first of our acquaintances to die. Frédéric Bazille had gone north to fight with the Zouaves in the Army of the Loire. After his commanding officer fell, the tall Bazille led an assault in the Battle of Beaune-la-Rolande. He was shot twice. A week later, his heartbroken father travelled to the battlefield with a wheelbarrow to retrieve his son's body and return it to Montpelier. By then, I was ill. I had never had a healthy digestive system, and my inability to eat resulted in a constant battle with chlorosis— weak blood. That, combined with the depression induced by our dire circumstances, resulted in my hollowed cheeks, and I fainted on a few more occasions after that first time, when I'd seen the dead soldier. On top of everything, I developed an infection in my chest that Maman was sure was consumption. The infection spread to my eyes, and my vision began to fail. Our gas was cut off just as the first snows began to fall. War had come to Passy.

Chapter Thirteen

Passy

Winter 1871

J became hardened to the smells and the continuous cannon fire. But the feeling of an anvil on my chest and of my skin hurting all over—these were hard to bear. Since the war began, my life had become a leaden nightmare.

"You know you have become prone to melancholy, dear," Maman said, laying her hand against my forehead to check my temperature.

"This is the worst it's ever been, Maman." I pulled my shawl tighter and my duvet closer, but they were no match for the frigid winter, the coldest in memory. The ground was frozen to a depth of over one foot. With no heat, the windows were panes of ice, and our breath came out in puffs.

"It all comes of not eating! If you would only have some consommé, I'm sure your disposition would improve." Maman thought that she could argue me out of illness, when the very mention of food, or what passed for food that winter, made my stomach cramp again. We were on a diet of horseflesh; donkey was regarded as a feast fit for princes. Pasie did her best to make her roasts edible, but nothing could convince me to try even a bite. Nonetheless, Maman wrapped her own heavy shawl around herself and swept out of my room, resolved to find me something to eat.

I heard my father in the hallway. "How is she today, Cornélie?"

"Don't worry too much about her melancholy," whispered Maman. "It's become second nature to her since Edma married." I couldn't argue with that. My episodes of depression, brought on by my powerlessness to control my own life, had increased since I lost my sister, and even more after Édouard had turned to Eva Gonzalès. Almost frozen and going blind, could anyone blame me for suffering from melancholia?

"Will she eat?" asked Papa.

"I'm going now to search for something that might appeal to her. It disgusts her to swallow that rationed mess of beans and straw that Préfet Ferry calls bread. She hasn't eaten half a loaf this week. For all their professed fondness for our daughter, none of her former suitors has shown up at our door with firewood or food," Maman fretted on her way down the stairs. "I fear her health is permanently impaired."

"And you forced to play nursemaid. You are as thin as a rail, yourself. I pray you don't fall ill, my dear. If only she had gone to stay with Edma and Yves when she had the chance."

At this I gasped, which brought on a prolonged, hacking cough. How the story had changed in his mind! I'd stayed in Paris out of duty. We were in real danger in Passy, close to the German lines, yet Papa had never suggested that I leave. What I would have given for Edma's company now, to be safely away from the city, eating real food. The thought of food made my stomach start up again, but a resounding *boom!* diverted me. Ah, it was ten o'clock. For the last three weeks, the Prussians had bombarded the city every night. It wasn't enough that Paris starved. We were to be deprived of sleep—the only hours when we didn't think of our hunger—as well.

The house shook and my head rang. It would have made me feverish if I were not already in that state. And the odors! Following our family physician Dr. Rafinesque's instructions, I kept a cloth over my oozing eyes, and my lack of sight resulted in a keener sense of smell. Every breath was tainted by the stink of gunpowder, and I could not begin to describe the foul stench following the bombing of the chemical plant across the Seine, surely the cause of my eye infection. I peeled the cloth off my eyes and the explosions outside my window blossomed into many-colored flowers that, with my poor vision, resembled smeared paints.

After the Germans cut its underground wires, the telegraph company set up a balloon corps so those of us trapped in the city had a limited means of correspondence. That autumn, while I was still well enough to write, I'd been able to send occasional letters to Edma and the duchess. We paid a boy to carry our letters to the Place St. Pierre on Montmartre, the highest point in Paris. Launching in the dark of night, aeronauts carried hundreds of pounds of mail out of Paris in hot-air balloons.

The ingenious system that transported mail to Tours and points south also transported carrier pigeons for return mail, as the air currents that lifted the balloons generally flowed in only one direction. The duchess let me know that she was returning home to the safety of Switzerland, so I shouldn't expect to hear from her again until the war was over. Edma sent a note that described the antics of her daughter Nini and of Yves's children. Imagining them with the light shimmering on their blonde heads as they cavorted in the southern sun was like a vision of heaven. Best of all, we received word that Tiburce had escaped from his prisoner of war camp.

"Superb!" pronounced Maman, before collapsing into tears of relief. She had to admire the behavior of the artists of our acquaintance. Édouard and his brother Eugène were fighting in Paris with the artillery of the National Guard. So were Degas, Puvis de Chavannes, and Oudinet. I worried about my friends always, but my concern did nothing to alter the fact that all of my conversational companions were gone. I was stupefied by the silence.

We had observed the first day of 1871 in sadness and tears. The only bright moment that month had come when Édouard and Eugène were able to leave the front for a rare visit. Édouard strode in wearing his National Guard uniform with its grand artillery cloak and jaunty red stripes down the sides of his trousers, while Eugène had changed into civilian clothes. I met them in Maman's frosty upstairs sitting room, ignoring Dr. Rafinesque's warning that I must stay in bed to conserve body heat. I was willing to take the risk to see Édouard. When he caught sight of me, what I saw in his soft eyes relieved the pain in my poor lungs, and I breathed with ease for the first time in many weeks.

We sat by the empty fireplace in the winter chill, dressed as if we were outdoors, on the straight-backed chairs around our dining table, the only furniture remaining since Maman had stored away her precious mahogany First Empire pieces. Were the velvet chaise longue and the spindle-back chair any more valuable than the contents of my studio, I wondered? Because oil and even candles were scarce, we sat in the twilight of the winter afternoon, a lifetime away from last July when Napoleon had declared war on Germany, and the streets were filled with men crying, "*À Berlin!*"

"Mon Dieu, you look worse than I do, and I have been in battle." Those were Édouard's first words to me. If my circulation had been better, I would have blushed. I'd have preferred that Édouard not see me so gaunt and pale, but staying in bed and missing his first visit in months would have been unthinkable.

I sized up his dashing garb through blurry eyes and, summoning up an attempt at humor, countered, "And yet you appear to have spent the war changing uniforms."

"Hardly. I stand guard in the freezing wind with pads of drawing paper inside my cloak for insulation. To break up the monotony, I carry dispatches under fire."

Fear and admiration wrestled in my stomach as I thought of him returning to the front on the outskirts of the city.

Out of smiles, Édouard directed a serious question to me: "Do you have consumption?"

I shrugged. "I suppose it *is* 'siege fever,' but please, let's not speak of it."

"I begged you to leave Paris four months ago, before the siege."

I replied, "Maman thought you exaggerated the situation."

"I had no need to exaggerate. You are sheltered from scenes that are burned in my mind. The last painting I managed before evacuating my studio was of the daily pre-dawn queue at a butcher's shop across the street, hundreds of women waiting hours for whatever they could get—dog meat or horse hooves." His angry voice, expressing what he could not say to my parents, echoed around the bare room. "Thousands have died in the last week alone from starvation and hypothermia. I hope you will not join them."

Eugène, standing behind me, put a gentle, shaky hand on my shoulder to comfort me. Or was he trying to steady himself?

Édouard knew that I could not speak against my mother, so I did not reply. I felt Eugène's hands grip the back of my chair and turned to peer at him over my shoulder. His face was rigid but calm as he said, "I do not expect to come out of this alive. I should be proud to give my life for the glory of France—pardonnez-moi for my cowardice."

Men weren't supposed to confess to fear, but Édouard was accustomed to his weaker brother's sensitivity. He flung a protective arm around Eugène.

"Eugène," I said, pulling a small book from my pocket, "this volume is the last I bought before the bookshops were shuttered. It has helped me. Why don't you take it?"

"The Sonnet of the Vowels."

"It's a fascinating notion—Rimbaud sees each letter as a color."

The light came back into Eugène's eyes. "I've missed music and books. Merci, mademoiselle."

Édouard took a softer tone toward me. "Of all the privations the siege is inflicting on us, that of not seeing you often is certainly one of the hardest to tolerate."

I was feeling weak from sitting up for just this short time, and exhausted, too, from the emotions stirred up by Édouard's presence. I willed myself not to faint.

"I have a present for you," he said. What joy, to know that I was still in his thoughts despite everything and to receive a gift after months of scarcity! I tore the package open. It was a brush and three tubes of paint. When I tipped my head toward him with tears in my eyes, he searched my face, as avidly as if I were still beautiful.

"That's all I could find," Édouard said, "But it will help you keep in practice."

"Merci beaucoup," I whispered.

He squeezed my hand, and he was gone. I would have endured another month of illness for him to stay.

There was hope, then, if Édouard imagined we would one day be thinking of our art, and not of eating rat paté or the ostriches and llamas from the zoo in the Bois de Boulogne. We would again think of beauty, not of corpses in the streets.

Another *boom!* reverberated throughout Passy, shattering my memory of Édouard's visit. A new morning had dawned. It was 14 January 1871, my thirtieth birthday. *Incroyable!* There I was, suffering in my parents' house like an overgrown child. I had managed to fend off an undesirable marriage, but for what? Where was the career for which I had sacrificed marriage? When had I last touched a brush to canvas? My hands ached to paint.

Pasie tiptoed in with a plate of the crackers I had lived on for the last two weeks and set them on the table next to me.

When war was declared, I'd asked Maman, "Shouldn't we send Pasie home to Toulouse, to be with her family?"

"Pasie is better off here," was Maman's reply. "Her family can no longer provide for her. That's how she came to be in service for us in the first place."

Pasie must have learned that I had advocated for her return to her family, or perhaps she felt sorry for me in my pitiful state. Whatever the reason, she had become my devotee. It was selfish perhaps, but since our maid was to remain with us, I was happy for her company as our social circle dwindled.

It took all of my strength to lift my arm and reach for a cracker. If Jules Ferry's tedious discussions with Papa about the municipal debt at Maman's Tuesday evenings hadn't killed me, the bread rationing he authorized as the Préfet of Paris almost did. I labored to chew the cracker, but I could do no more than gag and return the cracker to the plate.

My skin ached where the cold air touched it, and each breath chilled me more. I dared not keep my eyes closed for too long, or I would begin that familiar swirling descent into desolation. But when I opened them, all of the forms and shapes in the room—the wardrobe, the bureau, the window frames—were dark smudges against the murky gray light that seeped in between the heavy drapes.

"Would you like to study your fan, mademoiselle?" Pasie asked.

"Oui, that would occupy me," I said. Pasie took the fan down from where it hung on the wall and brought it to me.

It was a gift from Degas, who had painted on it a scene of Spanish dancers and musicians done in watercolors and brown ink. I examined the figures as best I could through gummy, infected eyes. I was sure that Degas had discerned my feeling for Édouard and took pity when the man I loved deserted me for Eva Gonzalès. While Édouard was the light that illuminated all of Paris, Degas knew all too well how that light could be extinguished on a whim. The fan was the only beautiful thing I had to cling to for the time being, but it helped.

In that barren winter of war, I could not ignore stark realities. It was long past time for my parents to be looking after me. And I was not a dilettante, working to become someone's accomplished wife. It was not enough to work at developing my own artistic style. Someday, and soon, I must become an independent professional artist, supporting myself with my own earnings.

As I folded the fan, I began to feel something, like a warm ember in a cold stove. It was my pride in being an artist. If a small fan could give me hope, what could larger, lovely paintings bring to the world? A painting like the one of Edma in Lorient that I gave Édouard could perhaps sell, and earning my own living through my work was what I most cared about now.

I was angry with myself, too, for letting my obsession with Édouard distract me from my painting these last two years. I needed to recommit myself to being responsible for my own achievements, without help or support from any quarter—not father, not husband, not any man. I don't think there has ever been a man who treated a woman as an equal and that was all I asked, for I knew I was worth as much as any man.

If I regained my sight—*when* I regained it—I would make my living by painting scenes that would bring light and beauty into peoples' lives. I wanted to shout this vow to the world, but I held it in, a silent scream. If I could have used my eyes, I would have written a letter to Edma declaring my goal. Instead, I reached into the drawer of my bedside table, pulled out the paintbrush Édouard had brought me, and began brushing the air, painting a scene that only I could see.

When Papa came into my room, pushing past Pasie, who made a hurried exit, I was so bursting with resolve that I almost shared my dream with him. Then I remembered that this was a man who had turned away from his own artistic aspirations. He had studied architecture and had even published a magazine on the subject but did not have the fortitude to pursue his interest. He found it easier to collect Gavarni prints than to create his own. With his world crumbling around him, how could my father see my artistic goals as anything but frivolous? In addition, he would also have found my desire to support myself financially to be improper.

Non, I would not divulge my goal to my father.

"My dear," he said, sitting down in the chair next to my bed, "I've just received a brief from the provisional government. Paris cannot hold out much longer. We must surrender to the Prussians within a week. They will take Alsace and Lorraine, as well as five billion francs in reparations."

The war had changed my father. Shame over his inability to protect the Treasury had aged him ten years during the siege. He still had thick, white hair, but had grown stooped and slack. Papa was disgraced, while I dared hope that the four-month siege would soon be over, no matter what the terms. Would the new government be republican or lean to the right or—worst of all—return to monarchy? Whichever it was, it would only drive a deeper wedge between Papa and myself. He stood again, with difficulty. "I swear that I will have my door broken in rather than open it. I will sacrifice my life rather than yield!" He shook his fist. "Paris must die on her feet!"

I felt his same passion, if for a different reason. My purpose was now as luminous as the searchlight on the Arc de Triomphe, and no one would deter me. If I had indeed survived the war, then I must be strong enough to fulfill that purpose. I reached for another cracker.

Chapter Fourteen

Cherbourg

May 1871

The war had come to an abrupt end when the Germans left in January, seizing parts of France for themselves. But relief at having our house to ourselves again and real bread to eat was soon replaced by the realization that our troubles weren't over. The National Guard, frustrated by their defeat, still wanted blood. When the fighting had ended, the Guards had moved four hundred cannons into working-class neighborhoods around the city so that the workers could defend themselves, should the new government turn out to be a monarchy instead of a democracy. A horrific childhood memory of the revolution that had brought King Louis Phillipe's downfall flitted through my mind, but I pushed it away. Monarchs seemed doomed to fall, and they took their people down with them.

When citizens of France's new regime, the Third Republic, democratically elected Adolphe Thiers to serve again as president in February, his first task was to cut off pay to the Guards, enraging them further.

"The Guards still refuse to hand over their weapons," Papa told Maman and me at dinner. "Thiers will have no choice but to send army troops to confiscate the guns."

In March, President Thiers ordered a raid. Chaos followed. No doubt worried that anxiety might lead to a recurrence of my winter ailments, my parents left me out of their conversations for weeks after that. My eyes were healing, but my vision was still too poor to read the newspapers myself, so I was forced to eavesdrop from behind the dining room door. What I heard about the renegade guards was chilling.

"They've executed two generals," Papa told Maman in a hushed tone. "They've abolished the church," Maman read from *Le Monde* in a low voice. "There is talk of destroying Notre Dame." A sob, and then, "They've murdered more than fifty priests—Oh, mon Dieu, the Archbishop of Paris was executed and left in a ditch."

We were in more peril from March to May than we had been during the siege. French forces had kept Germans from attacking Paris, but the renegade Guards surrounded us within our own city. Our neighbors again left for safer locations, but Tiburce had joined a group of a few hundred patriots to constrain the rebels, and Maman refused to leave her son in the thick of fighting.

In early May, when Edma wrote asking for her painting materials, I saw my chance to escape Paris for a time, even if it meant bundling up in warm clothes and shading my weak eyes with a wide-brimmed hat to travel by train to her husband's latest naval post. By the time President Thiers and Préfet Ferry were forced to flee the city for Versailles, leaving the Guards to elect their own legislators, the Commune, Maman and Papa agreed that I had recovered enough to risk the two-hour journey to Edma's new home in Cherbourg.

I could not say which part of my visit to Cherbourg was more of a relief—the fresh sea air and open skies, or being with Edma again. The hardships of war had left me frail, but the sensations that engulfed me while walking out of doors with my dear sister made me begin to feel alive again. And I was elated about the return of my eyesight.

The very day of my arrival, we set up easels in the dining room, eager for an opportunity to paint together again. Within mere moments, Nini's nurse appeared to tell Edma that Nini would not take her nap unless her Maman came to kiss her. Edma, pregnant again, climbed the stairs with as much speed as her condition would allow. After she returned, the cook came in with a question about dinner. As soon as we had again set our attention upon the still-life arrangement of fruit and crystal on the dining table, Adolphe joined us, settling into a chair and regaling us, he thought, with tales of his travels.

"Let me show you something." When Adolph left the room to retrieve what he wanted us to see, Edma's eyes moved back to her painting. I saw how difficult it must be for her to focus on something all the way through. Then Adolph returned, wearing a silly straw hat that made her laugh, and she turned all of her attention to him.

Adolph plucked a rose from the vase on the dining table and burst into song. He thrust the rose like a sword, singing in an unfamiliar language, and finished by plucking petals off the rose and letting it fall to the ground.

Edma could hardly speak through her laughter, but managed to ask, "What did that mean?"

"It's a song about a war between a carnation and a rose. It's Portugese, *meu amor*," Adolphe exaggerated the rolled "r" as he bowed and left the room.

"He's learned how to say *my love* in the language of every country he's visited," Edma explained.

"He adores you, Edma. And you love him?"

"I do."

"And what about the more intimate marital love?"

Edma sensed my anxious curiosity. "It's all perfectly natural. You needn't worry about that." Baby Nini toddled in, having escaped her nurse's hold. Edma swept her up. "And you end up with this!" Nini smiled and babbled as she tugged at Edma's hair, earrings, and nose. Women like us, from good haute-bourgeois families, must marry. But I didn't think I would survive the life of a typical woman. At least not this particular arrangement, isolated from society in a house with relentless views of gray sky and sea. Edma's role as a wife demanded that she follow her husband wherever he was stationed, no matter how dreary it was.

Edma saw me taking in the drab view from the dining room window and said, "It is always the same: a remote naval outpost, the rain pouring down—without the lavender Yves sends me from the south, my linens would forever smell of mildew—and sitting by the hearth listening to Adolphe's incessant chatter. What I would give for some

109

witty conversation with Degas!"

I thought how thrilled Degas would be to be acknowledged as a master of the bon mot.

"I just finished reading a book Degas recommended, *Adolphe*. I'm afraid he was ridiculing me for my choice of husband. What do you think?" she asked.

Knowing Degas, I was sure that ridicule had been his intention. But I assuaged Edma's fear with flattery, "He always thought you the more talented sister."

"I don't know if that makes me feel better or worse. My passion for painting has not left me. I thought I would continue to paint after my marriage, but I only manage to produce a mess, which both annoys and tires me."

Before my visit, I'd written to Edma, "I wish you would tell me whether it is really possible to work in Cherbourg." It might be for me, but it never would be for her.

"Why didn't you marry an artist?"

"And condemn myself to a life of poverty?" Edma was surprised by my question. "But living away from Paris, and Adolphe's continuous need for entertainment…Non, I did not foresee that painting would be so impossible."

"Be careful that you do not turn into Madame Bovary," I teased. I had sent my sister Flaubert's newest novel when it came out before the war to help her pass the bleak winter days. I might also have intended it as a cautionary tale. She must not allow herself to become so dissatisfied that she find herself tempted to do something unwise. "I would never be so foolish," Edma assured me.

I understood what it was to want a purpose in life. Emma Bovary tried religion, then love. What I had learned is that some of us must have a creative occupation to make life worth living. Flaubert's description of a life "as cold as an attic studio facing north" would stay with me forever.

Edma sighed. "I am expecting a second child. My heart is filled with love, yet I still feel empty. You cannot end up like me, Berthe. No one knows better than I the turmoil you are experiencing. You need to use your utmost charm and skill to find someone who understands your need for both work and love."

After a few days of indulgence, I made my first tentative painting excursion in many months. I set up my easel and palette on a rocky point jutting into the English Channel. The easel's spindly legs teetered on the very northwest tip of France, in danger of being blown away by the wild wind off the water, blowing my dress and hair in all directions until I almost felt that I was in a boat at sea. The acrid smell of kelp was invigorating. Seagulls showed off their elaborate choreography, swooping low over the water, as the poet Mallarmé's wrote:

> The flesh grows weary. And books, I've read them all.
> Off, then, to where I glimpse through spray and squall
> Strange birds delighting in their unknown skies!

This strange bird observed the harbor scene to the east from above, just as in Japanese prints. Before beginning, I looked and looked again, the most valuable advice my teachers—from my first drawing teacher to Guichard, and then Corot—had ever given me. From behind me emanated a roar from the sea that had been building all the way from England. Great silvery humps overtook the waves in front of them, which seemed to throw up their white petticoats in surprise and whisper, "Hush!" Quietest of all were the hissing wavelets, like shiny silk scarves, overlapping and sliding away from each other on the rocky shore.

When I was ready to begin, I hurried to pencil in a ship cutting through the harbor below me, an armored frigate returned from the blockade of northern Germany. Then I marked over the pencil in crayon, sketching in masts that pitched and heaved in the background. Finally, I dabbed my brush into water and cakes of watercolors in blues and blacks. Corot had shown me how to use transparent colors to paint the air. My thought was that watercolors would be more translucent than oils, and as I brushed the colors over paper, I could see that I'd achieved the effect I desired. I don't know how long I was absorbed in that pursuit, but when I straightened up, the wind had grown so robust that it was all I could do to gather everything together.

I was not strong enough to stay out long. By the time I returned to Edma's house, cold air in my weak lungs had brought on the hacking cough left over from last winter. My sister seated me near the fire and proceded to stuff me with all of the foods I had missed. A cup of tea offered a sharp tang. Cream softened it. The yeasty taste of real bread contrasted with velvety, dark chocolates. Heaven! I could have spent the entire afternoon studying various combinations of flavors. "You are here to restore your health, not to catch pneumonia," Edma reminded me. She was right; I had no interest in infecting my eyes again. But I felt rejuvenated and ready to work. My objective was to turn my preliminary study of the harbor into an oil painting as incandescent as watercolors. I was filled with the smells of the sea, the wind in my lungs, and all of the ideas for paintings saved up over the last year.

I attempted small watercolor vignettes of Edma and Nini in the meadow at the edge of the forest behind their house. I painted Edma in a gray wash, sitting heavy and immobile on the grass. Here was my sister, expecting her second child, when I did not even have a serious suitor. She started in on her favorite subject—matrimony.

"You've mentioned Puvis de Chavannes several times. Is there anything that you want to tell me?"

"You mean, has he asked me to marry him."

"Well, has he?"

"Is marriage so wonderful?" I asked her in order to avoid the question. "Don't you remember what you wrote to me about facing the realities of life 'without a hint of bridal bliss?' And that was only weeks after your wedding."

"Which was two and a half years ago. I was still adjusting to provincial domesticity when I wrote that letter."

"Do you feel different about married life now?" I suspected that she did not. Men were willing to believe they filled our lives, but however much affection I might have for a husband, I couldn't imagine abandoning my vocation.

Edma proved that she agreed with me when she said, "Sentiment is all very well, provided you have something else to fill your days." She shifted her weight, trying to find a comfortable position.

"*S'il te plaît*, move your umbrella closer to your feet," I left my easel to prop a pillow behind my sister as I organized my thoughts.

Nini became distracted by a butterfly and toddled away. It was très difficile to portray a wandering child. I painted her from the back, with a blur of blonde hair and a quick scribble of blue to indicate her sash. For the first time, I considered how enchanting it would be to have my own toddling two-year-old. What would I be willing to sacrifice in exchange for such a gift?

"Occupation alone is not a *raison d'être*, either," I said. "Women have an immense need for affection. To try to make ourselves self-sufficient is to attempt the impossible."

"Then why not Puvis de Chavannes?" Edma asked. "It's obvious that he is devoted to you."

I shrugged. I had received a letter from Puvis, demanding:

> Take a good pen and a big sheet of paper, and write me sweetly everything that passes through your brain, which is set in such a strange and charming head…whether you are working, whether you are succeeding—in other words, everything. Boom!

Boom, indeed. Puvis assigned me duties, while the light-hearted letter I'd received from Édouard intimated that I was missing out on a return to light and liveliness:

> I hope, mademoiselle, that you will not stay a long time in

Cherbourg. Everybody is returning to Paris; it's impossible to live anywhere else.

He was entertaining "everybody," according to Maman's reports, which I read with a tinge of envy, with tales of his heroism during the war. I could overlook his boasting and falsehoods in light of his desire to please his public as a renowned raconteur.

Puvis was so domineering that I shrank back, afraid of being obliterated by the certainty of rightness that wealth and position had bred in him. He mistook my hesitation for reserve. "It is hard to find even a gleam of light," he wrote, "I strain my eyes trying to find you in the fog." Wasn't his aggressive pursuit rather vulgar?

"Even Maman and Papa don't care for him." I told Edma. "He is so old and pompous." And what of this Romanian Princess Contacuzene, whose name was often connected with his? Maman had let slip that Édouard advised against allowing a closer connection with Puvis, no doubt because of the Princess. I suspected that she was the real reason for my parents' disapproval of Puvis, while I hoped that Édouard's criticism of Monsieur de Chavannes was a sign of his continued affection for me.

"He is not so pompous that he doesn't appreciate Degas and Manet. And you," she pointed out. "Can't you try to think of him as distinguished, instead? He comes from a good family, he has money, and he would let you continue painting." That was something to consider.

The crowded buildings of Cherbourg and its harbor peeked above the trees at the border of the meadow, but I ignored them and surrounded my two subjects in a nest of green, stroke by stroke, so that I had time to ruminate. Edma was right. It was imperative that any potential husband support my work.

"I always enjoyed my conversations with Puvis," Edma said. "He could philosophize on any topic."

"That's part of the problem. He goes on and on until I am exhausted."

I remembered his most recent visit, after the surrender to Germany.

He'd planted himself in a chair and begun holding forth on his royalist views before I'd had a moment to settle myself.

"Louis Napoleon is gone. Now is the time for the Compte de Chambord to take his rightful place on the throne." I hadn't had nearly enough energy to present an argument against monarchy. *En plus*, I wouldn't have argued with Puvis de Chavannes. He had decided that I was a soft-spoken, delicate young woman, and somehow that is who I became when we were together.

Puvis continued, "Chambord is the direct descendent of Louis XV; he is our legitimate leader." Puvis went on to list generations of the Compte's family tree, but I couldn't follow the lineage. My head had been ringing and, with my bad vision, Puvis looked like a blurred watercolor. The war might have been over, but I had only begun to recover from my illness. The mighty Monsieur de Chavannes did not notice what his visit cost me.

Edma's voice broke into my thoughts. "If talking too much is his worst fault, you would do well to overlook it. I speak from experience."

"But his face is so red!" I couldn't help but burst out. We started to laugh, but my laughter turned into a choking cough.

"Stop laughing and fold your hands again," I commanded Edma when I had regained my voice. The vision of my skeletal self with that florid man was too much for her.

"Oh, you are impossible" she giggled. "Why don't you just admit that you don't want to marry?"

"A part of me does." Solitude was very sad. But who then to marry? Maman's list of available bachelors had significantly diminished. Jules Ferry, now the Préfet of Paris, I had found gauche and unrefined, and his failure to look out for my family during the siege was unforgiveable. As for Eugène Manet, he seemed to be a sweet and sensitive man, but he didn't hold a candle to Édouard, nor had he ever expressed a romantic interest in me.

"Then that part has no choice but to marry," Edma teased.

What even Edma did not know was with how much gravity I had considered Puvis. How I had written to him suggesting that he call on Maman and Papa to try to win them over. It was unfortunate that they were not at home when he went to visit, so this gentleman had been reduced to standing outside my studio, dreaming of me.

> Your Passy studio was open, but dark and sepulchral, the curtains three-quarters drawn. I searched for you in a white peignoir, but had to content myself with my own imagination.

During the last week of my visit, Edma and I took Nini on an outing to Honfleur, a nearby fishing village. On the harbor wall was a plaque commemorating William the Conqueror's departure for Hastings in 1066. I realized at that moment that I must conquer Puvis, or at least conquer my reluctance to marry him. There was no one else left to marry, and marry I must. This was as important as pursuing my artistic career. I could no longer be a burden to my parents, nor could I any longer abide being a child in their home. My months of solitary rumination had left me with clarity beyond what my improved vision provided. I would meet with Puvis as soon as I returned to Paris.

When I turned to tell Edma of my decision, she was staring at nothing. She looked so confused, either by the outcome of her compromise or by not knowing how to advise me. To set her mind at ease, I offered my own concession, whispering, "I promise to consider Puvis."

By the middle of May, the letters I received from Paris were no longer light-hearted. I read Maman's aloud to Edma. "President Thiers organized a new army and marched sixty thousand soldiers into the city."

"If Haussmann had designed the city's broad new boulevards especially for military invasion, they could not have better accommodated soldiers entering Paris on the avenue des Champs-Élysées," Edma pointed out.

The news in Maman's next letter was no less alarming.

> Paris is on fire! This is beyond any description. The desperate Guards set fire to the city—the Palais de Justice, the Hôtel de Ville, even Papa's Ministry of Finance. The Tuileries Gardens are reduced to ashes as the city burns.

"Limoges," Edma and I gasped in unison. The mention of fire brought back memories of the Revolution of 1848 that had brought down King Louis-Philippe, when the rabble had surrounded our home and demanded Papa's resignation as Préfet of Limoges. Awakened during the night, we'd peeked over the window ledge in the nursery to see angry workers from the porcelain factories of Limoges filling the street in front of our house, waving torches and shouting, "Burn his house!" Were there dozens? Hundreds? In my memory, their number seemed infinite. Edma had put her hands over my eyes.

Yves had shrieked, "Maman!" and had run to find her.

When the mob had broken into our house, Edma had pulled me to the floor and pushed me under my bed. She'd reached up to snatch my pillows and cover our heads with them. We were safely out of range of flying glass when a rock had shattered the window where we'd stood a moment before. Edma must have been as terrified as I was, only seven or eight years old, yet she'd always had the instinct to protect me.

Maman had found us huddled together, shivering in fear of the angry voices below us. Then Papa's calm voice had broken in, reasoning with the workers. Eventually, the shouting stopped and our house emptied. Still, we packed and moved the next day.

"Go on," Edma urged. "What else does she say?"

> Papa and I have been forced to take up residence with my cousins in Saint-Germain. We can hear the shelling of the Commune's battery on the Trocodero, just below our home in Passy. Paris is in a civil war!

117

I could almost hear Maman's shrill, panicked voice. Once again, I questioned my father's stubborn refusal to leave the city when his own wife's safety was at risk. Here I sat in my sister's comfortable drawing room overlooking the ocean. Our mother should have been with us.

Maman's next letter was the worst yet.

"Edma, listen. Maman says that General MacMahon's troops finally overran the Communards. They shot anyone who aroused the slightest suspicion of having been a Communard. Mon Dieu! They executed people by the thousands in the Bois de Boulogne."

A news clipping from *Le Monde* that Maman had enclosed confirmed that twenty thousand men, women, and children had been slaughtered during one bloody week, the *semaine sanglante*. It was too much to bear. I handed over the remaining pages of the letter to Edma. "'The rank smell of the mass graves reaches as far as our house,'" she read, unaware that she had placed a protective hand over her rounded belly. "'The Seine runs red with blood.'"

If I had not lived through the siege, I would have been unable to believe the descriptions of atrocities that filled the pages of Maman's letters. At the end of my month with Edma, and five months after Paris had surrendered to the Prussians in January, there was peace—even if it was the stillness of death.

It was time to go home.

Chapter Fifteen

Passy

June 1871

*E*dma returned to Paris with me to spend her second confinement with us. She was eager to see with her own eyes that Maman and Papa had survived the war. We found our father unwell and our mother not herself. Our furniture had been retrieved from Saint Germain, twenty kilometers west of the city, where obliging relatives had provided storage. So the upstairs sitting room was restored, and Maman sat in her favorite chair. But her eyes were downcast and there was no needlework in her hands, where in the past there had always been a pillow or seat-cover spread over her skirt.

She returned my hug and kiss, but when I asked, *"Comment ça va?"* she sat silent, unable to summon even a rote response. I sat on the footstool at her feet and took my mother's hand. "You wrote that the stench of blood was so strong, you could almost taste it. How did you brave it?"

Without taking her eyes off her lap, she finally spoke, but said only, "It's good that we sent you away." I'd never seen Maman without perfect posture, but now she drooped over her empty lap as if she might cave in on herself.

I owed it to my parents to make a good marriage. I wrote to Puvis de Chavannes right away.

The mood in the house during the last days of Edma's confinement was somber. It was difficult to remember that we were waiting for a happy event. Yet nature took its course, and a few nights before the date Dr. Rafinesque had determined the baby would arrive, Edma felt the stab of pain that announced the onset of labor. It was the first time I had witnessed the suffering of childbirth, and as she writhed

119

and moaned on sweat-soaked sheets, it appeared to me that we had made sure of Edma's safety during the war only to risk losing her now. But she gave birth to a healthy girl, whom she named Blanche, and within a short time, Edma was sitting up and introducing Nini to her baby sister.

Holding Blanche's small, warm body melted me. When I had to make a conscious effort not to nibble her toes, I understood that forces beyond my control were at work—I was overcome by maternal feeling.

Blanche was beautiful and perfect, but she never stopped crying. Edma and Pasie and I took turns walking her, trying to keep her quiet so that Maman could sleep. Finally, one evening our mother came into Edma's room and demanded, "Give her to me." Maman carried Blanche out into the hall, where we could hear her singing, "Here is the tale of the Lord of Framboisy, tra and tra and tra-la-la." Edma and I gaped at each other. Maman's lilting voice triggered our earliest memories. "Who married the most beautiful girl in the country, tra and tra and tra-la-la."

Edma fell asleep between one line and the next. And when Maman returned, Blanche was sleeping, too.

"There, she'll be fine now," pronounced Maman. Blanche had more fussy nights after that, but Maman was quite herself once more. Becoming a grand-mére again gave her a purpose and restored her belief that life would go on.

While we'd awaited Blanche's birth, Papa had been back at work writing a pamphlet supporting President Thier's appeal for a national loan to repay the Germans, convinced that an official publication issued by the Old Guard could influence current affairs. And Maman had resumed social calls to friends who had returned to Paris. But I'd been at loose ends until one afternoon when I'd found Edma in the drawing room leafing through the fashion plates in *La Moniteur de Mode*. She sat on the settee once again positioned beneath the tall front windows. If I hadn't looked too closely at the floor gouged by soldiers' boots, or at the cracked windowpanes in the doors to the garden, I could almost have believed that all was as it had been before the siege.

I'd managed to squeeze in next to my very pregnant sister on the settee and join her in perusing the out-of-date fashion plates. We'd come upon an engraving of a mother sitting by her baby's cradle. It was a universal image, almost a Madonna and child motif. But one could see only the mother's back as she looked out a window. This had irritated me—it wasn't right that she was turned away from her child.

So after Edma gave birth to Blanche, I painted her with her new baby to make my point. I kept certain elements of the offending fashion plate—the cradle, the mother in blue, the lawn curtain in the background. But I chose to show a woman's point of view of motherhood, depicting the profound bond that Edma felt with her baby. The painting was tender without being sentimental. I abhorred the popular paintings of mothers and clinging infants, even as I hoped that their popularity would create a market for this work, which would provide me with an income.

Edma was happy to coopérate. She sat in her already-familiar position next to Blanche's cradle in her everyday clothes, no fashion plate, while Blanche was covered in a cloud of gauze indicated in washes of gray and white, the edges of the diaphanous net canopy dotted in pink. Mother and child were enclosed by drapery made of the softest of fabrics, muted blue with glimpses of white where the sun touched the curtains' ruffled edges. Blanche stirred, but did not awaken. Her hand opened and closed like a sea anemone. Her bent arm rested on the pillow, almost—but not quite—touching Edma's elbow as she leaned over the edge of the cradle.

I rushed to catch the transient moment. I looked at my sister looking at her sleeping baby. Where most who might have viewed Edma at this moment would have seen maternal love, I perceived my sister's melancholy and included my own longing, each of us wanting what the other had.

When the painting was finished, I showed it to Edma and asked, "Does this seem more like your experience of motherhood?"

Edma examined the work as an artist and as a mother. She nodded. "I am so proud of your gift—your own style, new techniques. If only one of us was to become a notable artist, it is right that it be you."

"This painting *does* feels like a turning point," I said.

I heard Edma's voice tremble when she murmured, "One that I will never reach."

When I'd written to Puvis suggesting a meeting, he'd responded with immediate enthusiasm: *"This will be a very, very great pleasure for me...I shall be waiting."* Because I believed he intended to propose marriage, I'd suggested this particular location, slightly elevated above Lac Inferieur, from which one could see as far as the village of St. Cloud. I entered the Bois de Boulogne with trepidation after Maman's letters describing the carnage that had taken place only weeks before. Yet on this superb summer morning in June, there was little evidence of the unspeakable brutality that had transpired there. Below, in the lake filled with water lilies, an Oriental folly that had once decorated a small island had disappeared, sacrificed in the "wood riot" that had taken place the day after Christmas. But tender new grass filled the meadows, covering burial mounds and softening the jagged edges of felled trees. Birdsong filled the air. The rhododendrons were spent, but the lilac bushes and hydrangeas were beginning to bloom. Dahlias and irises, their bulbs safely hidden underground during the siege, now emerged, victorious. It was enough to make one believe in life after death. Magnifique!

My stomach swooped like the birds above me when I saw Puvis approaching, clutching his top hat to his head. His double-breasted frock coat left him far too buttoned-up for a balmy day. Every one of his forty-seven years showed, and even this small exertion emphasized his flushed complexion. A rush of impressions washed over me: Puvis' flat, emotionless paintings, his royalist politics, his princess, and all the privileges to which he felt entitled by his wealth. Puvis' face brightened with happiness when he saw me, yet as he called out, "Mademoiselle!" I realized that I could not possibly marry this man. His devotion would never outweigh his stolid nature. Married to Puvis, I could never expect life to hold another surprise. I would feel gratitude, but not passion. He would *allow* me to continue painting, rather than anticipate each new work with excitement. Spontaneity, encouragement, passion—I had already known these characteristics combined in one man. How could I be satisfied with less? I let myself imagine working side by side with a fellow artist who would both challenge and support me, attending effervescent social events with him each evening, falling into his arms at night. Monsieur de Chavannes was not that man.

Puvis approached, ready to take my hands in his, but I twisted them together to avoid his grasp. Scrutinizing his beak-like nose from below, all I could think of was Degas's biting description of Puvis as the condor in the zoo. I turned away, suppressing my nervous laughter.

"I was delighted to receive your note," he huffed. "How eagerly I have anticipated seeing you again."

"Bonjour, monsieur." Why had I chosen such a private setting? And why couldn't I have chosen to meet Puvis on a Sunday, when thousands thronged the Bois? Or at least they had before the war. Too late, I remembered hearing that people of fashion had resumed the afternoon promenade, *aux heures de la fashion*, on the Pont Neuf, not here in the Bois de Boulogne, where they might find themselves reminded of events they would rather not remember. Where were les amazones, riding side-saddle, or the bicyclists? It appeared that I was to negotiate this delicate situation on my own.

"Mademoiselle Berthe, my barouche and driver are waiting just outside the gate. I thought we could go to your house together so that I could speak to your father." This chain of events must be halted before it progressed one step further.

"Shall we sit for a moment first, monsieur?"

"*Mais oui, certainment.* What an enchanting setting." I chose a rock with room for one and angled away from him, not wanting to be seated next to my suitor when I explained my decision. After an awkward shuffle, Puvis sank to one knee on the ground next to me, putting him into a proposal position.

"Please, don't ruin your trousers!" I cried, as if the cause of my panic were sartorial.

He struggled to stand. "My trousers? What about my heart?" *Boom!* Another passionate declaration. Puvis was perplexed.

"*Je ne sais pas.*" A lone carriage traveled the curved rue de Boulogne below us. If only I were on it.

"Well, I think I know. I believe you have had a change of heart since you wrote to me."

Decency forced me to turn toward my suitor; still, I couldn't face him. "I'm sorry for everything, Puvis."

"But I am prepared to offer…"

Oh, *agonie!* I fixed my gaze on the ground, and when he again reached for my hand, I moved it away.

He apprehended my lack of interest. Ever the gentleman, Monsieur de Chavannes recovered in an instant. "Think nothing of it, my dear. I was privileged to have had your attentions for a time. Rest assured that I shall remain your lifelong friend."

"*Merci beaucoup.*" I could not think of one more word to say. In the silence that followed, I became aware of doves cooing their two-note song, with the accent on the second note.

But the eminent Puvis de Chavannes was never at a loss for words. "May I offer you a ride home, mademoiselle?" he asked, extending his arm.

"That won't be necessary. I think I will sit here for a while longer," I replied, keeping my eyes cast down.

"If you're certain, then I'll be off. *À bientôt,* Mademoiselle Berthe." He managed to disentangle my clutched hands in order to kiss one.

"Au revoir, Puvis."

I turned away so as not to watch him make his way down the hill. My "lifelong friend"—I hardly deserved that, given how my guilt and embarrassment dissipated in an instant, giving way to the bucolic pleasures of the Bois de Boulogne. I was quite happy to be back in this Parisian park, left alone with the flowers and the doves, whose song was now acutely clear: "Édouard! Édouard! Édouard!"

Chapter Sixteen

*I*t was stifling hot that late summer evening when I saw Édouard again. All of the women in Manet Mère's drawing room waved silk fans painted with Japanese scenes in an attempt to cool themselves. Degas, with his heavy-lidded, Bassett hound-face, was somnambulant. "Even the drinks are warm," he muttered. It was such a pleasure to return to my first of the Manets' Thursday evenings since the war and to be surrounded by people I cared about that I even enjoyed Degas's grumbling.

Across the room, I watched Édouard conversing with Eva Gonzalès and her parents. In one of her letters to Cherbourg, Maman had written, "Mademoiselle Gonzalès has grown ugly," and while I would have liked to be able to agree with her, the evidence was to the contrary. She was young and lovely, her rounded shoulders and bosom blooming from her deep green gown, one of the somber colors that all the ladies deemed appropriate after the war.

For the first time, I questioned my preference for the simplicity of wearing only black or white. But when I had told Pasie to make me trés belle, as I would be seeing someone special tonight, she'd insisted, "You must wear the short-sleeved, white silk dinner dress, Mademoiselle." A quick inspection of my white gown had assured me that her choice was the correct one, so I'd instructed Pasie to take in the dress to fit my thin, post-war figure. White set off my olive skin and contrasted with all the dreary dresses in the room. I was through with mourning for poor Paris.

I bided my time, waiting for Édouard to approach me. Maman had come to one of the Manet's first post-war evenings while I was still in Cherbourg, and she said that Édouard had asked about me, wondering whether I would stay in Normandy forever, surrounded by suitors. Even this facetious inquiry encouraged me. Since I had broken with Puvis, I'd had time to think. And with startling clarity, all my thoughts came back to Édouard. Three years after he had deserted me, after war, after illness, I found that none of it mattered—I still wanted only Édouard. Now that I was stronger, I would regain his affection the best way I knew how. I would offer to model for him again.

Meanwhile, I watched Tiburce, now Lieutenant Morisot, entertaining the middle-aged women of means who were the preferred targets of his amorous campaigns with the tale of his daring escape from the Prussian prisoner of war camp.

"It was nothing," Tiburce said, studying his boots with affected modesty. He was a feather-headed hero.

"The Morisot men are very brave." Papa stood beside my brother, his chest thrust out with pride for his son's heroic deed.

I wondered what I could ever do that would earn a comparable response from Papa.

"You poor boy!" gasped one rouged and bejeweled society matron, the type called an *ogresse*.

"Mon Dieu!" exclaimed another, fanning herself with a frenzy.

When the ladies had fussed over Tiburce enough for his liking, he moved on to a nearby group of men and began boasting about being invited to luncheon by General Vinoy.

"We formed a fraternal bond on our neighbor's terrace in Passy," he explained. "The Prussians began shelling directly at us. I'll tell you, surviving something like that brings men together."

"And did you know that General MacMahon and *all* of the Versailles chiefs of staff honored the Morisot family by attending a luncheon at our home?" Papa said.

Maman jumped in. "I had to retrieve the family linen and china from all over the city, at a moment's notice." Her complaint held a hint of satisfaction. "And put our wine cellar at their disposal."

I couldn't listen to any more of my parents' fawning. I turned to survey the room and saw that Madame and Monsieur Gonzalès had stepped away, leaving Édouard beaming at Eva like a lighthouse off the coast of Normandy. When she noticed me watching them, Eva waved her fan. I mustered most of a smile in response.

Maman turned to me, tipping her head toward Suzanne, who had somehow grown fatter during her stay in the countryside while the rest of us starved through the siege. "Manet must have experienced a great shock at the sight of her bucolic blooming," she said. "By the way, I have just received a note from Monsieur de Chavannes, inviting us to visit him tomorrow."

At that moment, Édouard ambled over to me with his sailor's swagger. Only the new web of lines around his eyes and his receding hairline that left only a single remaining tuft of hair above his forehead showed that he was in any way changed by the war. Bending close enough to remind me of the scent of his lilac cologne, he whispered in my ear, "Don't hold back. Tell him the worst things you can think of about his painting!" Then, loud enough for the others to hear, he boomed, "Bonsoir, Mademoiselle Berthe."

"Bonsoir." I fanned myself and waited for him to set the tone of the conversation. Would he offer me his scintillating but indifferent self? Or would he speak to me with the sincere intimacy that was his real charm? At first he tried the former.

"Tell me what you've been working on since your return to Passy." Très bien, I could do that.

"I lost a great many canvases and sketches. Everything in my studio was covered with stones and dust, and only three panes of glass survived the siege. Workmen are still making repairs, so I have not painted much."

"Nor have I." His shoulders slumped, and I noticed now how his jacket hung on his frame. "I seem to be feeling the belated effects of the war. During the Commune, while your brother entertained Thier's butchers, I roamed the streets, sketching the horrors. It broke me, Berthe." He gave me a quick sidelong glance, afraid that he had revealed too much.

I pretended to be concentrating on my fan, so he continued. "Out of it all, I produced only one lithograph of soldier shooting a Communard by a stone barricade. I caught his expression of surprise above the cloud of smoke from the gunshots that killed him. It was hardly more than a sketch—I couldn't bear to finish it. I don't know if I'll ever be able to paint what I saw during this terrible year." The lines around Édouard's eyes deepened as he described this atrocity. "Now all I do is wander the cafés. It's difficult to concentrate. I am beginning to believe what Baudelaire says about melancholia being the affliction of the modern artist."

"No one understands better than I what you mean when you talk about *le spleen*."

Neurasthenia, melancholia. The condition went by many names, but the strain of modern life combined with the anxiety of war ensured that everyone was familiar with the ennui and depression suffered by victims of this ailment.

Édouard appraised me in his old way. Anticipation of the evening had brought color to my cheeks, and Pasie had piled my hair on top of my head, leaving a few tresses trailing down over my ears. Curls over the forehead were the current style, but my little maid had advised me not to detract from my eyes, which looked even larger since I'd lost weight during the siege.

"It's as you say," Édouard murmured. "No one understands me better."

To turn his thoughts away from death and depression, I gave him a coquettish look from under my eyebrows. "Non?"

"Berthe, I think I could work if…would you let me paint you again?" Ah, c'est ça! I did not even need to offer my services.

"Moi?" I snapped my fan shut and tipped my head in Eva's direction with raised brows. "You do not find me too old and unattractive?" I glanced around the room, as if I were capable of noticing anyone but him.

His old sly grin appeared. He was laughing—not at all neurasthenic— when we were interrupted by my brother, who was tucking a cluster of ladies' *cartes de visite* into the inside pocket of his jacket as he announced, "Berthe, it's time to go."

"So soon?"

"Papa is exhausted."

"Come by my new studio as soon as you can!" Manet called after me as Tiburce took my arm and escorted me to the door.

I made Édouard wait, but no more than a week or two. After sending him a note the afternoon before, on a crisp morning in early September, I set off for Édouard's new studio in the rue de Petersbourg. As I worked my way through a maze of dusty paving stones signifying the reconstruction of Paris, I was cheered by the sound of cathedral bells, as much a part of the city's atmosphere as the yeasty scent of the boulangeries. It had been a year since the war began, a year during which I had stayed away from the City and hadn't smelled the stink of rotting vegetables in rubbish piles on the streets, the heady perfume of the flower markets, nor the odor of sewage dumping into the Seine. The cafés and restaurants were full once more, and the boulevards were backed up with all manner of carts, carriages, and horse-drawn omnibuses. Servants, heading home with market baskets filled high, wove their ways between the soldiers who were ever-present in any public venue since the Commune.

When I reached Édouard's studio, I thought I would go to the piano, as I had in the past. But, the moment I walked in, he abandoned what he was working on. "I must paint you exactly as you are," he murmured. I did not even have a chance to remove my beribboned black hat before he seated me in front of a plain backdrop, handed me a nosegay to pin to the lapel of my black wool walking suit, and set to work.

Édouard's new studio had the same oak paneling and exposed beams that the old studio had, with the same high windows. I recognized the same piano in the corner, piled with music and books—including his bible, Charles Blanc's "*Histoire des peintres de toutes les écoles*," the

Japanese screen decorated with the woman overtaken by a wave, the standing cheval mirror, the Chinese vase on the mantel of the large fireplace. Only the stuffed raven resting on the helmet of the bust of Minerva was new.

"I am illustrating Mallarmé's translation of Poe's works," Édouard explained.

Mixed emotions eddied within me as I sat there silent and still, the quiet only interrupted by rumblings from across the street when trains barreled through the Gare Saint-Lazare. How happy I was to see Édouard working! How familiar it felt to be covered by his gaze. And how agonizing it was to realize once again that he was the man I loved. But I avoided any appearance of the melancholy from which he always ran, fearing its contagion. Matching his breezy manner, I said, "If I were to paint you, the world would learn that your right ear sticks out *un peu*."

"I would turn my head so that no one could tell," he said without taking his eyes off his work.

"And that your hairline is creeping ever higher."

"That is what hats are for."

I sighed. "Of course, it would be improper for me to paint a portrait of any gentleman outside my immediate family."

He stroked his beard with his thumb as he exclaimed, "Thank heaven!"

An hour passed before he spoke again. "You are an intriguing creature," he told the canvas before him. "You are almost smiling, yet your eyes are tragic."

This was my moment to speak. We had not been alone for such a long time, and I could no longer withhold my feelings. "How could they be otherwise?" I blurted out. "I am a woman who cannot have what she most desires." He frowned—in concentration, or displeasure?—and said nothing.

A servant came with a tray of food from Manet's house around the corner; Édouard took the tray and waved her away. The sun had moved across the long windows when he began clucking his tongue, and I knew he was pleased with his results. He stepped back from his canvas. "Bon. Would you like to come and see yourself?"

I stood, stretched my painful, stiff legs, and came around to see his canvas. *C'est moi.* There was my fan, my long dark curls and olive skin, but those eyes! My hands flew to my mouth to keep myself from crying out at the naked desire revealed there. Had I been so obvious? I turned to the door.

"Berthe, please stay and talk for a while." My hand still covering my mouth, I let Édouard lead me, not to the sofa, where we could sit side by side, but to a café chair at a marble table. Instead of sitting, I spun around to face him. For the first time, I was in his arms. "Édouard!"

He lowered me to the chair as if I were an invalid, and I realized that I didn't want to hear what he had to say.

"Berthe, as an artist you are my equal, but as a woman…" he began. "Non!"

"No matter what you believe, I desire to be *un homme honnête*. I could never do anything that would destroy your reputation."

"Or your own—that is what you are afraid of, *n'est-ce pas*? It was your precious reputation that made you marry your pregnant piano teacher!" His features contorted in horror, disbelieving that I would break the great taboo by speaking of his family's secret.

"I did it partly for my father, who could not hope to maintain his magistrate's position with a scandal in the family."

He was lying. I could not conceive that he would waste himself on a loveless marriage just to preserve his father's good name, as there was hardly a gentleman in France who was without scandal. There must have been more to the story. If I composed myself, maybe he would tell it. I sat down and clasped my hands. "*S'il te plaît*, if you can explain your situation, I will try to accept it."

He lowered himself down to the chair on the other side of the cold marble table. "I don't know what my mother was thinking, suddenly deciding that her grown sons required music lessons," he began. He squirmed so that he appeared to be reassembling all his limbs. I had never before seen him this awkward, or anything but elegant.

"Eugène and I were at too an impressionable age to spend so much time with a woman scarcely older than ourselves. But it was Father, the virtuous, self-righteous judge who yielded to temptation." He stood and turned away from me, and then his words came out in a rush. "When Suzanne became pregnant...I was only nineteen, an art student; the scandal would be so much less for me than for him. And then, of course, I never wanted my mother to know who was responsible."

I struggled to understand. So Manet Père had fathered the child? That meant that Léon was Édouard's...brother? I clutched at my hands, not sure I could speak even if I dared to try.

"I hope you believe that I am a gentleman. I had to do the right thing for Léon. My father refused to acknowledge him or to provide for Suzanne. But after father died and I received my inheritance, I had the means to marry Suzanne in order to support her child, a Manet child. There was a certain satisfaction in defying my father's wishes, even after he was gone." His stare was as hard as the marble table.

Now I had to say something. "Why didn't you acknowledge Léon once you married?"

Édouard stiffened. "It was Suzanne. French law considers a child to be illegitimate if his father is married to someone other than his mother." He exhaled mightily. "But Suzanne refused to admit she had given birth to an illegitimate son, even if she later married the alleged father. And even if that 'father' adopted the boy. She stands by her story that Léon is her brother. She denies that he is a Manet, so I must, as well. It is my deep shame."

I was stunned. The situation was more hideous than I had thought. A memory came to me of Édouard's distraught expression while watching *Don Carlos*—the story of a father and son who share the same woman.

When he looked up at me, all of the passion had returned to his eyes. "Berthe, I have never met anyone as dazzling as you."

The painting on the easel, Édouard's vision of me as I wished I could be, showed an intelligent and seductive beauty.

"What about the day you painted me reclining on the sofa? Did you love me then?"

His eyes were tender as he remembered. "Your hair was up, with a few wisps coming loose on your forehead…that black lace decolleté against your skin…"

"You had your way with me on canvas. Why, you had to trim the final work in the name of decency!" He'd cut the canvas at my shoulders so that no one would see my wanton pose.

"My dear, if anything was of questionable decency, it was the way you gazed at me, with no hat, not even a fan between us. I treasured those most private moments together."

He seemed to be softening, so I allowed myself to speak in a gentler voice. "I always thought of the portraits as your love letters to me." I reached across the table to run my fingers up his forearm.

"They are letters which you must not answer." He stood, frowning as he struggled to control his emotions. But his nostrils flared and the tips of his ears reddened, revealing the havoc in his heart.

I stood, too, and threw myself at him. "But I am willing to give myself to you completely! I don't care about the consequences. There can be no one else for me!"

A miracle—he embraced me. "Berthe!" His husky voice was almost a growl. Then he had me at arm's length again, and his expression combined disappointment with desire.

"*Ma chère* Berthe…If we make love, this must be the only time." Sure that I could change his mind, I answered him with a kiss. His whiskers were silky. His mouth became my whole world.

Nights spent dreaming of this moment made me bold. His jacket and waistcoat emitted an odor of flowers when I pulled them off. He did not resist as I untied his cravat and removed his collar. Even his skin smelled of lilac cologne, mixed with something warmer.

I stepped back to begin the laborious process of unfastening my clothes as Édouard went to the door and locked it with a practiced gesture. I, who had seldom even seen my own nude body, was now frantic to free myself of whatever came between me and this man. I stepped out of my skirt, but it took forever for Édouard to unbutton my bodice and another eternity to loosen my corset. When I was almost naked, I grew conscious of how thin I was still from the months of near-starvation during the siege.

"What is the matter?" Édouard asked. I crossed my arms to cover the bones poking up from my shoulders. Smiling, he pulled open his shirt to show me his own protruding ribs. I smiled in turn, and Édouard drew me down to the sofa, sliding the straps of my lace chemise off my shoulders. He gazed at my breasts as though he were seeing God. I hid my face in his neck, but he lifted my chin with one finger, forcing me to meet his probing stare, to fall into those deep-set, cerulean eyes. I held his face in my hands and let myself fall.

Once I was persuaded that he wanted me, any remaining reserve evaporated. I averted my eyes during a mortifying moment when he worked a lambskin sheath onto his *vierge*. At last, he leaned over me. His shirt created a tent around us, and I was enveloped by his body. His white skin, which appeared as cool as the marble table next to us, almost burned me. I watched him through one eye with terror, and through the other with wonder until I was too blinded by sensation to see anything at all. Édouard grew desperate in his passion, groaning, "*Sacre nom de Dieu.*"

"*'Crenom!*" he cried out as he attained his satisfaction. Édouard had given himself to me. He was mine.

He lay back, stroking my hair and crooning, "My beautiful Berthe." His deep voice, resonating at my very core, caused me to wriggle closer to him. I thought our lovemaking was finished, but Édouard began touching me again, putting his hands on every part of my body, possessing me. When *le petite mort* overwhelmed me, I felt that it was a death from happiness.

Afterward, we lay entangled on the crimson sofa. Édouard gave me his fine, blue-trimmed handkerchief to tidy myself and covered me with his jacket. I was the picture of contentment, stroking Édouard's long, narrow nose and the one remaining curl that fell on his forehead. His expression was pained and tender as he searched my face, something he had done a thousand times while painting me.

It seemed the last barrier between us had fallen. Speaking more freely than ever before, I broke the silence with an idea that had been the subject of my most recent fantasies. "What if we went away together? We could start a new life, maybe in England." I spied the tray Édouard's servant had left on a table by the door and realized that I was ravenous.

"Our work would be more appreciated there," he admitted. I slipped my chemise over my head and retrieved the tray, watching Édouard smile as he considered the acclaim he would enjoy across the Channel. I couldn't consume enough bread and cheese.

Then the smile faded; which obstacle confounded him? Was he considering Suzanne and Léon? He could arrange to leave funds for them so that they could go on as usual. "But we wouldn't know anyone," he said, as if he were pointing out that there would be no oxygen in London.

"We would have each other," I said, cutting a pear and handing Édouard half of it. We were Adam and Eve in Paradise. "And we would certainly meet new people, other artists." The pear was the most delicious thing I had ever tasted.

"No one in polite society would receive us, under the circumstances. You know I am not happy unless, when I board the omnibus, someone asks me, 'Where are you going, Monsieur Manet?'"

It was an inarguable fact that Édouard enjoyed his social position more than anyone I had ever met. He knew everyone in Paris, took great pleasure in gossiping about them, and seldom spent an evening without companions from the highest echelons of society or the most shadowy corners of the demi-monde. I had presumed that because we had given ourselves to one another, our own society would take precedence over Édouard's love of the beau monde. Yet I saw that in the aftermath of our lovemaking, he, too, was speaking more openly than he had during even our most intimate conversations.

As I began to comprehend that the man I loved was not prepared to sacrifice anything to enable us to be together, I set the tray piled with bread crusts, cheese rinds, and pear cores on the floor and began to gather up my clothes. Not only had I thrown myself at Édouard, I had suggested something too audacious for him even to consider.

He watched me, his bewildered expression suggesting that he was seeing who I was for the first time. And I was stupefied to realize that he wanted no part of my truest self, the self that was willing to sacrifice everything to be with him.

He spoke in a choked voice. "There is a way in which we could be forever connected." I turned to him, hoping. "The bonds of family are the strongest there are," he said.

Again he was talking about something beyond my ability to understand. It took me a moment to realize what he might be suggesting, something so monstrous that I looked up at him in amazement, searching his face in desperation. "Family?" My voice was tremulous. "You mean...?"

I fastened my clothes with frantic, shaking hands.

"Just listen," he pleaded. "If you married Eugène, we could continue to meet, to discuss our work without fear of gossip. We could use the informal *tu* in front of others. And would greet each other with a kiss, *comme ça*." His face serene, he stood and gave me a tender kiss on each cheek. He was pleased with himself for having come up with a solution to our dilemma.

I turned on him with the fierce expression I'd been careful never to let him see, tears of humiliation coursing down my face. "You can't be serious! Is that what I am to settle for?" I hurled the fan and nosegay at him and ran out of the studio.

That same evening, the Morisots were expected for dinner at Manet Mère's apartment. I had to attend so that Maman would not suspect anything was amiss. When I arrived home from Édouard's studio, Pasie had laid out my clothes for that evening. But I needed a few moments to myself, so after she had fastened my corset and buttoned my bodice, I dismissed her. At the sight of my stricken expression, she crossed herself and rustled out of the room. I performed my toilette and dressed myself as if I were blind, too numb for tears. Yet in the carriage I heard myself speaking in a sprightly tone.

Careful not to look at Édouard during dinner, I thought I was carrying off my charade quite well, until my frozen numbness wore off. I felt as though whatever held me together had been loosed, so that my limbs were in danger of dropping off one by one, like melting icicles. As the men were engaged in a political discussion at one end of the table, something about Gambetta and the emerging Third Republic, I focused all of my concentration on keeping my body in one piece. I couldn't remember in what order to arrange my features, which seemed at risk of sliding off my face. And that was only the outside. Within, organs were cracking and collapsing like dissolving glaciers. The roaring in my head sounded like a multitude of clashing instruments, an orchestra tuning up before an overture. That cacophony broke down into recognizable music—*La Danse de la Reine*, the dance of the queen who was loved by both Don Carlos and his father. Small wonder that Édouard had looked so miserable at the opéra that night.

From where she sat gossiping with Manet Mère across the table, Maman managed a sharp glance at my untouched plate. She scrutinized me, surprised, as I had been eating well during the past weeks.

When I managed the elaborate manipulations required to turn my uncoopérative body away from her, my eyes met Eugène's. He seemed to ascertain my distress, if not its cause, and he responded with a kind smile.

My situation was impossible in every way. Yet even in my desolation, I did not doubt Édouard's love for me, whether or not he was brave enough to act on it. I was sure of it, even if he was capable of suppressing his feelings. It was his willingness to give me up that was most baffling. Then I remembered that he had abandoned me before.

I needed to put Édouard out of my mind, and the only way to do that was to leave Paris.

The next morning, Maman came into my room, and, observing my breakfast tray, asked, "So, you're back to starving yourself?"

"Maman, I want to go to England. It seems Fantin made a fortune in London with floral paintings—he was able to retire to Normandy with his new wife. And you remember my fellow model from *The Balcony*, little Fanny Claus? She was delighted with her trip."

"But there is no one to chaperone you. I can't leave your father." Papa's constant exhaustion had turned out to be a sign of heart disease, so Maman was confined to caring for an invalid at home. "And your sisters have their own families to attend to. Yves's family is planning a trip to Spain."

I seized upon the notion that my older sister might be able to help me escape Paris. "Spain, then. I will see the paintings of Goya and Velázquez for myself."

Pasie knocked and brought a package into my room. "This just arrived from Monsieur Manet, mademoiselle."

Afraid of what my mother might see, I snapped, "Give it to me." When I ripped open the wrapping paper, a folded note fell to the bed.

Pasie saw it. The clever girl twirled around to say, "Madame, see how beautiful it is," holding up the small canvas in order to divert Maman's attention while I slid the note under my duvet.

"Merci," I mouthed.

It was a painting of the nosegay I had thrown at Édouard when I rushed away from him, inscribed with my name just above his, so that it read:

To Mlle. Berthe

E. Manet

"Violets?" noted my savvy Maman. "The symbol of love?" She shook her head. "Oui, I think you *should* go to Spain, and stay there for a very long visit."

I touched the still-wet canvas; my fingers came away daubed with violet paint.

Chapter Seventeen

Spain

Summer 1872

With no possibility of a trip to England, I had to settle for traveling to Mirande, near Toulouse in southwest France, where I joined Yves and her family for their annual excursion to the coast of Spain. It was yet another compromise that did little to fulfill my dreams of travel and independence. And I was forced to wait for even that small reprieve through an interminable winter and spring until Yves's husband could take time for a holiday. Still, from the moment my train pulled out of the Gare Saint Lazarre, I breathed more easily than I had in months. After cloistering myself to avoid encountering Édouard in public, each mile separating us brought increasing relief. Yves, Théodore, and their two children took me to a resort in Saint-Jean-de-Luz on the Basque coast, a place I found arid and ugly. It was tiresome in every way. The resort was full of Spaniards, whose language we did not speak. The sea was dark and dull. And it was impossible to fight the fleas.

Yves was kept busy caring for her children and anticipating every moment when her husband, who had lost his arm in the Mexican war, would need her help. But for me, there was nothing to do and nothing worth painting, since the constant sun created a light that made everything look as flat as I felt. I saw why Édouard did away with shading in his paintings. He was copying his idol, Goya, who had shown the effects of the scorching Spanish sun with faithful accuracy. Parasols were no protection against that crushing heat.

Our only relief from the torpor came in the evenings, when it was cool enough to sit out in the square, or by the sea. Yves brought needlework, just as Maman always did. But Cornélie Morisot embroidered so that she could socialize while her hands were busy, whereas Yves worked in silence. How had Edma endured the long winter of the siege that she spent with Yves's family in Mirande? "Don't you tire of all of that fussy detail?" I asked Yves.

"This is my art, painting with a needle," she replied. I remembered that she had attended those first drawing classes with Edma and me, but when we went on to study painting with Monsieur Guichard, Yves had bowed out. Thinking back, this was when a distance began to grow between Yves and we two younger sisters.

As she worked, I noted that my sister had retained her fine features and light hair. I thought of her as middle-aged, but at thirty-five, she was only four years older than I. Because she had married and left the family when I was fifteen, I considered her to be almost a generation beyond my own. At the time, I could not understand why anyone would have accepted a disfigured man who seldom spoke. Maybe Yves had found it romantic that Théodore Gobillard was a wounded veteran of Maximillian's war in Mexico. Now he served in provincial Mirande as a tax administrator. One could hardly imagine a marriage more confining and compromising.

I had to ask, "How did you decide to marry Théodore?"

"There was no decision. He asked me to marry him, and I did. I was the eldest daughter of three whom Papa and Maman needed to marry off."

As I observed Yves's tranquil expression, an idea for a painting came to me, colors and shapes springing up around her. She would sit just as she did now, with the same ambiguous aspect, alone in a drawing room. The viewer would wonder why she sat there, idle—was she expecting a visitor? Ah, to add to the uncertainty, I would include other figures who had nothing to do with her. I could see them, standing in the sunlight on a balcony beyond the drawing room, while Yves remained indoors, lost in her private reverie. As the picture painted itself in my mind, the title came to me: *Interior*, referring both to the room and to Yves's secret thoughts.

"I'll tell you why I married." She startled me out of my vision. "For one thing, I was an obedient girl, and I did my duty." There was no question that she was dutiful. I thought of her watching after Papa during the summers when Maman took Edma and me on painting excursions. "And for another, I was lonely," Yves said. "I've never felt that way since marrying Théodore."

"Lonely? But why?"

"You and Edma were so close. I remember when you took that trek through the Pyrénées. Papa said that we would never hear all of the incidents of your holiday, and he was right. When you returned, you whispered and laughed in the secrecy of your rooms. I was never included in those tête-à-têtes."

Why had we never bothered to describe for our older sister the cliff-clinging ruins of a Cathar castle or an eagle swooping over the Mediterranean, when it was only because she agreed to stay home with Papa that we had had the opportunity to enjoy those sights? I promised myself that I would make Yves very beautiful in the painting I imagined.

There we sat, my sister, content with her life, and I, fighting to avoid her fate. I, too, wanted to be a dutiful daughter. During the siege, I had accepted that I must marry. Indeed, I would rather be married and have my own family than be dragged along on holiday with my sister's family, another duty for Yves. Still, I hoped for a life that included holidays more stimulating than the one we were enduring in Saint Jean-de-Luz.

My frustration became so evident that Théodore offered to take the children home while Yves and I continued on to Madrid by ourselves, a bustling city sure to be a more exhilerating site than dismal Saint-Jean-de-Luz. It was a generous gesture that earned him Yves's spontaneous embrace. "Your husband is quite accommodating," I said, hardly able to keep from hugging him myself.

"We try to make each other happy. That is what marriage should be." Pleased to learn that she had married a man devoted to her happiness, I made the slightest revision in my opinion of Yves's life.

We left for Madrid on a stormy day. The air was heavy, and although we dressed as lightly as possible, the ride to the train station left us drenched in perspiration. The temperate climate of Paris seemed as far away as the frozen Arctic. Still, if heat was the price to be paid for distance, it was worth every degree centigrade I had to bear.

Maman must have mentioned my trip to Édouard, because a letter from him was waiting for us at the hotel. My heart jolted when I saw his familiar pointed handwriting on the envelope, but the letter merely explained that his friend, Zacharie Astruc, would be our guide in Madrid. What Édouard no doubt intended as a kindness was an unwelcome intrusion. So much for the benefits of distance.

In my youth, I would have thought Astruc, a dark-eyed, handsome Frenchman living in a foreign land, to be a great adventurer. Since knowing Édouard, however, I suspected that most men had something to hide, and I imagined that Astruc had fled a woman, debt, or worse.

Monsieur Astruc put himself at our disposal. Without him, Yves and I would have been confined to one of the hotels favored by foreign visitors where we would have spent our days having teas and dinners with English or French tourists.

On our way to dinner that first evening, he escorted us to the Plaza de la Constitución, the main square in the heart of the city, enclosed by ochre buildings atop arcades, like the rue de Rivoli.

"Sometimes there are bullfights here. People watch from their balconies." I must have looked stricken, because Astruc went on, "Then I suppose you wouldn't have been interested in watching heretics burned here during the Inquisition."

Astruc showed us in to one of the cafés. He spoke fluent Spanish, so Yves and I were grateful to have him order dinner that first night. We were happy to find that foods with unpronounceable names turned out to be nothing more than soup, steaks, and peas. Édouard had told me that Madrid had no character, but I found that I enjoyed the mild evening breezes, and the melancholy guitar music wafting into the blue-tiled restaurant almost allowed me to overlook the stray dogs and dust in the Plaza. We pounced on our meals with voracious appetites.

"How is my friend, Manet?" Astruc asked me, when he paused for a sip of wine.

I had expected Édouard's friend to ask after him, but the query still came as a blow to my stomach. It was bad enough that he continued to work his way into my thoughts. Astruc's mention brought him to this very table.

I answered with caution, "He was well when we last met."

"I haven't seen him in several years," said Astruc. "He visited Madrid right after he painted *Olympia*. What year was that? '62? '63?"

I became aware of the tough steak sitting in a pool of rancid oil in my stomach.

"What a masterpiece!" Astruc continued. "Did Manet ever tell you that I wrote a poem about it:

> When, tired of dreaming, Olympia awakes,
> Springtime enters on the arms of the sweet black messenger..."

Yves's mouth dropped open. Even in the provinces, she'd heard enough to be aghast at the mention of an infamous courtesan in polite company.

I turned to the soup, a watery concoction of mysterious origin. I remembered Édouard describing his trip to Spain: "When you sit down to the table, you want to vomit rather than eat." The voice of the man I had left in Paris still rang in my head, proving once again that distance would provide no relief from his presence, after all.

Indeed, I began to feel that I might vomit. This time, my loss of appetite did not result from melancholy. In that foreign place, far from home, I recognized that it never had. Any dark depressions or digestive troubles came not from sadness, but from a feeling I could not identify yet was so intense that every muscle and organ within me contracted when I tried to contain it.

"Berthe," whispered Yves.

"Oui?"

"Why have you stopped eating?"

We talked of a day trip to Tolédo, or attending a bullfight if we were stouthearted enough. But I had no intention of exerting myself in the stifling afternoon heat for anything but the paintings I had come to see, so the gorgeous Astruc obliged me by arranging a visit to the museum the next day.

The Prado was magnificent, with marble floors of varying hues and tall fan windows—both of which made the place cooler than the rest of the city—as well as a glass-domed roof similar to the one in the Louvre. I was there to see the Goya paintings, and that gentleman himself greeted us in front of the museum. His statue frowned down at us. With one heavy boot striding forward, and a long overcoat swirling around him, it appeared as though the last of the Old Masters could not be bothered to stop for us. I would not have expected anything else from this intrepid artist as he stepped into his new role as the first modern painter.

Inside the museum, the paintings of Goya were a revelation. Small wonder that he was Édouard's idol. His depiction of the Spanish resistance to Napoleon I, *The Third of May*, was a ground-breaking work, the first faithful depiction of war. Here was no illusion of nobility or heroism, only the all-too-realistic slaughter of human beings shot at close range. Yves turned away from the brutal image of the battle, no doubt thinking of what her Théodore had endured in Mexico.

But I was absorbed by the scene, set at night, with a wedge of light that emanated from a lantern at the feet of the French executioners illuminating the defenders of Madrid, who were lined up against a boulder. The central figure, a Spaniard whose white shirt almost glowed in the light, stood with arms outstretched, reminiscent of Christ on the cross. As he glared at the rifles pointed toward him, awaiting his fate, I could almost hear his defiant shout. In the darkened background stood a church or some other grand edifice, a sign of civilization so removed from the butchery at the forefront of the painting that it might have been on a planet distant from our own.

This was the work that inspired Édouard's *Execution of Emperor Maximillian*, one of the paintings I'd seen in his studio that had never been shown in France. He had copied the composition almost exactly, but had turned the tables, substituting Mexican resistance fighters for Goya's French executioners, and the French Emperor Maximillian for Goya's white-shirted victim. And he had used the same composition again for his only depiction of the terrible *semaine sanglante*, the lithograph of a French soldier shooting a Communard that he'd described to me on that first evening I'd seen him after the war. Édouard was not a Realist painter, but by all of the accounts I'd heard, the ruthless brutality in his images of war was accurate. I admired his determination to record the events in modern history that many wished forgotten. As Édouard crept back in my thoughts, I found myself missing my idealistic friend.

"Shall we move on to the next gallery?" I asked my companions. Yves dabbed at her eyes and stuffed her handkerchief in her sleeve. "Oui, mademoiselle." Monsieur Astruc took me by the elbow, signaling an unwanted interest in me. It hadn't crossed my mind that I would need to fend off advances in this foreign place. I hadn't sensed any particular regard from Astruc, but I presumed that he saw me as an unattached woman conveniently placed in his path. With his dark beard and long hair, brushed back from a wide forehead, Astruc resembled any other French gentleman to me. He was nothing like the tall, light-haired man who lived in my head. When I shrugged my shoulder, Astruc released my arm and put his offending hand safely inside his jacket in the first Napoleon's famous gesture before guiding us into another room full of Goya's work.

I stopped in my tracks when I saw the artist's *Portrait of the Duchess of Alba*. She was swathed in black lace, with pale pink slippers showing beneath the hem of her gown, just as I had appeared in *Berthe Morisot with a Pink Shoe.* I knew that Édouard had been influenced by Goya, but now I saw that more of his paintings were almost exact copies of the Spanish master's works. In *Majas on a Balcony*, two Spanish beauties leaned forward on the railing with shadowy male figures in the background, unquestionably the source for *The Balcony*. The memory of Édouard's eyes upon me as I modeled for that painting stabbed me with desire and at the same time suffused me with grief, remembering that he had chosen not to fulfill my desire ever again.

But it was *The Naked Maja* that stunned me into silence. That alluring beauty spread across a divan, with dark eyes and black curls, even breasts similar to mine, displayed her charms as boldly as *Olympia*. I could well imagine what effect the Maja's brazen, seductive pout would have had on Édouard as a boy touring the Louvre's Spanish gallery with his uncle. And I could almost believe that he had always been waiting to meet me, a woman who happened to be the living version of his youthful fantasy. Yet he *had* met me. How could he have let me go?

If I had kept Édouard from using a *préservatif* when we made love, he might have had reason to feel as responsible for me as he did for Suzanne. I was torn between the wild wish that I carried Édouard's child and the fantasy that I had slashed every one of his precious paintings that day in his studio.

There was no doubt that he was the most gifted painter the world had seen in the half century since Goya's death. And there was a good chance that he would be remembered as the one artist who told the truth about his time. But I could not love him for his painting or his potential alone, and now I knew that he offered little more than those. His charm and dashing figure were no more substantial than clouds, and I did not choose to live in the shade they cast. Non, Édouard and I would never be together.

In a sudden epiphany, I knew that it was not despair or disappointment that caused my hands to shake. It was fury.

As my sorrow turned to anger, the weight in my stomach began to lift. When Astruc touched my elbow to guide me out of the gallery,

I turned on him with a volcanic glare. I strode out of the museum on my own.

What if I failed to be as obedient a daughter as Yves? What if I never found a suitable husband and became a *vieille fille* painting instructor, as Maman had threatened? Bien, I would live my life alone. I cut our trip short—did I sense relief on Yves's part?—and returned to Paris, with plans to visit Edma at the Pontillion estate in Maurecourt before going home to face my parents.

When I stepped down from the train in the Gare St. Lazarre, the sun glinted off the tall windows of Édouard's studio across the rue de Petersbourg. For all I knew, he was watching me at that very moment. I would have to channel all of my anger toward him, my family, and society into achieving my ambitions.

I hurried on to catch the train to Maurecourt.

Chapter Eighteen

*T*he darkness of late-summer thunderstorms had closed in on Passy by the time I returned home, and the political climate was no less dreary during the year that followed. In the aftermath of the siege and the Commune, the public's reaction was to cling to patriotism and religion. What was worse, all art became suspect. In hindsight, the people of France had decided that cultural decadence had been the reason for the demise of the Second Empire, villainizing prostitutes, homosexuals, and artists, and holding them responsible for our hardships. If a conservative milieu leading to a distrust of artists weren't enough, there was also an economic crisis, so that buyers for paintings became scarce. There was nothing for me to do but wait—for the economy to improve, for paintings to sell, for my life as an artist to begin again.

I missed the duchess. After the war ended, she had remained in Nice, reluctant, it seemed, to return to Paris. She was said to be associating with minor European royalty, the Count de Kergolay and Prince Louis Windisgraatz.

"France is well on its way to monarchy again," Papa announced from behind his newspaper barricade. President Thiers—to whom I remembered Édouard referring as "that little twit"—had been forced to resign.

Papa was beside himself. "I must schedule meetings with representatives from the other ministries." I knew how much he would have liked to meet with his politically powerful friends behind the scenes, but his heart trouble that had worsened since the war prohibited any such pursuits and had forced him to give up his position with the Treasury.

I was inactive, as well. In truth, years of modeling, and of war and its aftermath, had prevented much painting on my part, a welcome relief from the panic and self-doubt that overwhelmed me whenever I worked. One day, I returned to my sanctuary, the Bois, to draw the swans, but I ended up crumpling the paper and throwing it into the lake. After that, I sequestered myself in my studio. I was frozen by my desire for perfection; all the confidence I had acquired from completing *The Cradle* had dissipated. I wandered my studio, in a constant spin. Unfinished canvases accused me.

I found myself thinking about how Édouard, as a man, was capable of setting the terms for his career.

He was not recognized by the Salon? It was his choice to submit his most controversial paintings to that outmoded organization. He did not sell paintings? By cultivating the members of the Academy, among them the jury for the Salon, he could have reassured buyers that his officially recognized works were good investments. "The public wounds me constantly," he had complained. What nonsense! In the end, Édouard's career was determined by Édouard.

I had no such choice. Where was my endless circle of social acquaintances from which to cull buyers for my work? Where were my models?

What I felt was neither grief nor envy. The roiling in my stomach, the heat that flooded my body, the blood that engorged my very eyeballs so that I was blinded by a scrim of red—these were incited by rage. That spoiled man! That self-pitying child! He indulged himself at every turn, when he had every opportunity—time, money, the fact of being a man—to achieve his desires.

I tried to subdue my seething frustration to a simmer when I was with my parents, but one day when Maman came into my studio and settled on the pouf to needlepoint a pillow cover, she discovered me scowling before a pastel portrait of an aristocrat's children. Édouard had recommended me to the family, which was both the least and the most that he could do for me.

"Such a fierce expression!" remarked Maman.

I shrugged. "I won't know if it's any good until Edma tells me."

"Edma is far from here. Are you incapable of accomplishing anything serious on your own?"

I turned on her like a lioness. "Why don't you take the brush yourself, then?"

At that, she softened her tone. "Bértât, I can't bear seeing your poor little face so bewildered and dissatisfied over a fate about which you can do nothing." We had never spoken of my feelings for Édouard, but I sensed that she was coming close to doing so. What did she suspect as she glanced at Édouard's painting of violets out of the corner of her eye?

"Never have you chosen what was within your reach. Your work was refused by the Salon this year; doesn't that mean something?" Bon, we were pretending to speak only of painting.

"It means that I am getting farther and farther from what that jury of petrified painters still deems worthy, and closer to a style that is truly mine."

"Is the life of an artist worth all this misery?"

I often wondered. Lately, I'd begun to doubt whether it would be possible to fulfill my goal of supporting myself through my work. That morning, I'd written to Edma: "I'm so sad. Everyone is abandoning me. I feel lonely, disillusioned, and old." Who could say which of us was more miserable? I had no answer for Maman's question but forced myself to respond, "I am well aware that you would prefer me married."

"At your age, I was a *préfet's* wife with three children."

At that, I threw down my brush and resumed my aimless pacing, clutching at my hands. I stopped in front of the cheval mirror. "Maman, do you think I'm fat?"

Her eyebrows shot up. "How is that possible when you don't eat?"

It was puzzling. Most food did not agree with me, yet when at times to me it looked as if my reflection swelled—like today—I made an effort to eat even less. At least this one part of my life I could attempt to control.

Maman came and stood before me. I would not meet her eyes, but I knew she saw with her usual acuity that the source of my despondency was not painting or plumpness.

"You act like a woman with a broken heart. You can't still be thinking about Édouard Manet, surely?"

There it was. I felt more relief than shame. "You've known all along and never said a word about it."

"As a gentleman and a friend of the family, it didn't occur to me at first that there was any danger. As time went on, it was apparent that you had developed a *béguin* for the man. So I was happy when he married. I was certain that no daughter of mine would become involved with a married man."

"It's not a true marriage, you know."

"It's true enough.

"Why did you let it go on?"

"Bértât, how was I to stop you? Pack you off to a convent? I thought it wisest to let it pass. And it seemed only natural that another man would eventually draw your attention. I was even willing to let you marry Puvis de Chavannes, although it was difficult to believe that you wanted him."

"But it's more than a *béguin*, and it hasn't passed. I don't think it will ever pass. I feel condemned to love only him." In truth, my feelings for Édouard were consistent only in that they consistently changed. On a Tuesday, I might yearn to see him, while on a Wednesday, I might remember his maddening ways and feel determined to avoid him. But today was a Tuesday.

Maman sighed. "I can see what bonds hold you to him. You are both sensitive artists. But he has chosen his life, and you must go on with yours." She gathered her needlepointing, but before she left me alone, Maman had to have the last word, declaring, "You are no longer in his thoughts."

As if I had received a blow to my chest, all the air left my lungs. I dropped to the pouf in misery, clutching at the frame of the cheval mirror. Was it possible that she was correct, that Édouard had simply put me out of his head, when he existed always at the edges of my mind?

I stared again at my reflection in the mirror. My sharp angles and frown began to soften then disappear into a white void where I did not exist. The shapeless, colorless vision reminded me of the childhood day when, watching the clouds from my prone position on the bench in our garden, I saw for the first time that they were not white at all.

From my hiding place under the big, round, dining table, I'd watched Papa's legs as he walked to and fro, carrying my new baby brother, Tiburce. I couldn't make out his words, but he'd spoken in a tone I had never heard from him. I was the third daughter, which was a disappointment. Now he had his son.

When Papa was at the far end of the room, I'd scooted from under the table, run around the corner to the front hall, and raced upstairs to Maman's boudoir. She was in bed with her eyes closed.

"Maman?" I whispered. There was no answer, so I was forced to try again, a little louder: "Maman!" She started and searched the room until she saw me in the doorway.

"What is it, my little fawn?" She was such a pretty invalid, with her pink cheeks and her eyebrows like perfect half-circles. My governess, Louisa, said that I was a lucky girl to have such a young and beautiful mother. Louisa had brown hair pulled tight over her ears, and she always wore a plain dark gown. She must have wished she made as pleasing a picture as Maman, with her soft, wavy hair and her delicate lace nightgown.

"Um, were you missing me?"

"Come here, Bértât, and give me a hug. Gently now," she said as I threw myself into her arms. I'd lain very still. If I were quiet, maybe she would forget I was here. But after a moment, Maman had said, "Why don't you go and play with Edma and Yves?"

"They are busy with their studies." It wasn't fair that I was not

154

included. I was five years old, only one year younger than Edma. I was sure that I, too, could learn to read.

"They will be finished soon. You must let me rest now." Then Papa had come in with the baby, and they hadn't noticed when I'd left.

Back downstairs, I'd stomped down the hall to the back door and into the garden, where I wouldn't get in everyone's way as I did in the house. I scuffed my shoes along the pebbled pathway, even though I knew this would earn me a scolding from Louisa. Sometimes I stopped and squatted to count snails. There was a sharp smell in the mossy, green shade of the hydrangea bushes. I continued along, scuffing and squatting, until I reached the garden bench. I climbed up to lie back on the cold, iron bench, gazing at the sky and tracing the clouds with my finger, detecting animals and faces in their ragged shapes. It was surprising to realize that the clouds were not really white, but contained many colors. What fun it would be to float among the clouds, slowly changing colors. When I got up, the back of my dress was damp from the bench. I would no doubt be scolded for this, too. I scuffed my way along the pathway back to the house. After a very long time, Louisa and my sisters joined me for supper, some kind of soft fish with a thick white cream over it—*oof!* Louisa frowned as I nibbled on a piece of bread. I never ate enough to make Louisa happy.

Yves tried to explain why Louisa was so determined to feed me more than I needed. "It is because you were delicate when you were a baby. Maman and Papa want you to be strong."

After supper, we had our baths, and then it was time for bed. Louisa took us to Maman's boudoir to say good night.

"Berthe has refused to eat, again, madame," said Louisa.

"Did she eat nothing?" asked Maman.

"Very little, madame. She is headstrong."

Maman studied me with an expression both proud and worried. She circled my wrist with her thumb and finger as she told Louisa, "She is a very little girl, so I'm sure that whatever she consumed was quite enough."

We three girls took turns kissing Maman. I thought she held me a little longer than she did my sisters. As we filed out of her boudoir, I heard her tell Louisa, "Have cook make a tarte tatin for Berthe, tomorrow. She will eat that."

Yves and Edma went to the bedroom they shared, but I still slept in the nursery. What would happen when the new baby grew old enough to stay in the nursery? Where would there be a place for me then?

Louisa listened to my prayers. "Don't forget to pray for your brother Tiburce," she reminded me. I supposed I must.

"Louisa, will you read to me tonight?" I asked as I climbed up into bed. She had been reading bits of Shakespeare's plays to me. He was English, like her.

"Not tonight, Berthe."

"Will you tell me about your English garden?" Louisa had taught me the names of the flowers in the garden of her childhood home. There were foxgloves with blossoms you could wear on your fingers, roses that climbed, and other flowers with funny names like Grannie Bonnets.

"It is late, Berthe. No, don't flash those black eyes at me; it will do no good to make your sulky face." She tucked me in and left the room. I was so sad. Did everyone forget that I was the baby of the family? From her small room adjoining the nursery, Louisa said, "I hear you crying. You must learn to build a strong character, Berthe."

When she closed her door, everything turned black. I felt the floor disappear from under my bed, and I was falling, falling into the darkness. I was still little, and I was all alone. There was no one to save me! Nothing to hold on to! I was swimming or running or flying with all my might. I was not delicate—I did have strong character!

I found myself in my sisters' bedroom. Edma threw back her duvet, as she always did, and I crawled into bed with her. Once I was safe and snug, I whispered, "Edma, did you feel this way when I was a baby?"

"What way?"

"Like you didn't matter anymore?"

She took so long to answer that I thought she'd fallen asleep. But then she whispered, "A little bit."

"I'm sorry."

"Go to sleep, Berthe."

I did, dreaming that I was a cloud equal to all other clouds, changing colors as I drifted through the sky.

For an instant I remembered the wonder of that child, myself at five years old. What a marvel it had seemed then that colors put next to one another could create shapes, pictures of whatever one imagined. It felt marvelous still.

When the contours of my face became visible in the mirror once again, I pulled myself to my feet and went to my worktable, where I squeezed paints that comprised the colors of clouds onto my palette.

The horse-chestnut trees lining the boulevards were just beginning to bud into froths of chartreuse, which meant that another year had passed since the war had ended. I marched through the city streets with Pasie following behind, carrying the wrapped painting she had toted all the way from Passy. As in my old copying days with Edma, Pasie and I had taken the tram to the Place de la Concorde. Our destination was only a few blocks beyond. We had an unobstructed view of the Louvre from the rue Royale, because the Palace had burned down during the Commune. The smell of ashes was still noticeable when a breeze blew our way. At the Place de la Madeleine, we turned right onto the rue de Capucines. The dusty rubble and blocks of stone still stacked outside shop windows displaying the latest styles were as incongruous as the people of fashion mingling with the workers in their blue smocks, a sight seldom seen before the war. A *joli garçon* in tight trousers and a bowler hat, straggling home from a night of dissipation, claimed the sidewalk ahead of us, forcing a family returning from their night's work at a textile mill to step into the street.

We crossed the boulevard at rue Lafitte, dodging between carriages. I stopped on the corner to unfold the note in my pocket. For the hundredth time, I checked the address on the back of the note that had fallen from the painting of the violet nosegay that Édouard had sent me. The pictures propped in the windows flanking the door in front of us left no doubt that this was the gallery belonging to Paul Durand-Ruel, one of the new, private art dealers competing with the Salon.

I'd vowed to become a professional artist as the siege came to an end, but it took time to rebuild Paris—yet another thing for which I'd had to wait—and somehow I'd thought I could win buyers for my paintings on my own. Now, more than two years later, I admitted that I needed help to bring attention to my work.

"I'll go in first," I told Pasie as I steeled myself to open the door.

"Oui, mademoiselle," she said, acknowledging my instruction, and adding, "*Bon chance!*"

A bell jingled in accord with my nerves when I entered the small anteroom. A short, dapper, clean-shaven gentleman emerged from behind a velvet curtain, adjusting his lapels as he greeted me. "Good afternoon, mademoiselle. How may I help you?"

"I am here at the suggestion of Monsieur Édouard Manet."

"Yes, I have some work by Manet that I can show you." He turned to step behind the curtain again.

"Non, non! Monsieur Manet told me that Paul Durand-Ruel is representing new artists…" The gallery owner was known to be conservative, a proponent of Catholics and kings, but progressive in his patronage of avant-garde artists.

"I am Paul Durand-Ruel. Which new artist is it that you are interested in?"

"Myself. I am Berthe Morisot." I signaled through the window for Pasie to come in. She was quick to carry in the wrapped painting and set it on a display easel as I told Monsieur Durand-Ruel, "I've brought a painting, hoping that you'll agree to represent me."

He unwrapped *The Cradle* and considered it for too long a time for my taste. After what seemed like hours, he spoke. "It's very pretty, Mademoiselle Morisot, but I have never represented a woman before."

It was far more than pretty. Couldn't he see that I had shown a complex woman lost in reverie? "I've been accepted by the Salon for ten years," I told him. "I am ready to be a professional artist."

"Still, in these dire economic times I have been unable to support many of my long-time artists. I am not certain that my customers would pay much for work by a woman."

I reached for the painting. "Thank you for your time, monsieur."

"Please, wait." Once more, he inspected the portrait of my sister and her baby. He must have noticed that, instead of depicting the typical Madonna and child, this mother's expression held weariness and worry, and *un peu de tristesse*. I was certain that Monsieur Durand-Ruel had never seen anything like it. Manet's matadors and Degas's racehorses did not delve into a woman's interior life.

Without looking away from the painting, he said, "This reminds me of my wife. I often saw her sitting like this with our five children. I lost her during the war." I held my breath. After a long moment, he nodded to himself and said, "I opened a gallery in London during the war. Would you be willing to send this painting abroad?"

"*Bien sûr*, I've heard that the English have more progressive ideas about women artists."

"Let us wait to see how this is received in London. Then I'll decide what is to be done here."

Once again I was waiting, a skill I'd so finely honed that I should have been considered an expert. But I wouldn't wait much longer.

Chapter Nineteen

Paris

October 1873

Édouard was socializing with visitors when I arrived at his studio on an autumn afternoon for a private showing of his painting that had been rejected by the Salon of 1873. Curiosity had overcome my qualms about seeing Édouard, and because I didn't want to explain my need to see his work to Maman, I'd slipped out of the house by myself. Now I stood alone before the mantel, trying to keep my eyes off the red velvet sofa that had been the scene of my life's only indiscretion. I focused instead on Alfred Stevens, the Belgian painter with the English name, and his wife, Marie, sitting at the marble café table, and on Eugène Manet near the easel that held Édouard's rejected painting, chatting with a young man I didn't know.

I was still at my position by the fireplace, studying the painting across the room, a depiction of a mother and child in front of an iron fence that separated them from a blast of steam heralding a train arriving at Gare Saint-Lazare, when Degas greeted me. "You are recognizable even from behind by your erect carriage and distinguished attire." He noticed that I was just pulling off my gloves and added, "You must have arrived just before I did."

"I haven't seen you since that evening at the Manet's, right after the war."

"I've just returned from Nouvelle Orléans, where I went to stay my brother while Paris recovered."

He saw that I was alone, deduced that I required a chaperon, and discreetly assumed the role, all in an instant. I was aware that he was examining me as we conversed. He may have noticed, perhaps for the first time, that I was almost his age. My cheeks were still hollowed, long after the end of the siege. I returned his pleasantries in a rush, eager to get to the real object of my interest.

"I haven't seen this latest work. Have you seen the painting, monsieur?"

"Not finished, non." We moved over to where *The Railway* was displayed. The regular rumbling of the floor and the smoke billowing from the train station across the street almost brought it to life.

"This model, she is Victorine Meurent, *n'est-ce pas?*"

"Oui, mademoiselle," Degas replied. "She is a bit plumper than in Manet's earlier paintings."

"Oh, but I recognize her red hair and pale eyelashes. The little girl peeping through the bars was my influence, you know. Édouard saw my painting of Edma and her daughter on our balcony. Little Nini's hair is just this color, and she wore a white pinafore and grasped the bars in just this way."

He regarded me with new respect. "I have always thought it a challenge to depict modern life just by painting someone's back."

"Are they lovers?" I asked, looking at Degas out of the corner of my eye.

It took him an instant to realize that I was asking about Victorine and Manet, before he answered, a discrete "I wouldn't know." Then he relented, nodded toward the red velvet couch, and murmured, "I believe she is Alfred Stevens's mistress."

This confidence might have satisfied me, if it hadn't been for the incident that followed. A penetrating voice behind us exclaimed, "But this is wonderful!" and we turned to the doorway to see a gleaming woman, her beauty as hard as the gems draped from her neck and arms.

Manet, charmed, turned to her from across the room like a flower to the sun. "Who are you, madame, to find good what everyone else finds bad?"

"May I introduce Madame Méry Laurent?" asked her escort, an older American man who seemed accustomed to being ignored in her presence. When I heard her name, I recognized her as the so-called stage actress popular for appearing close to nude at the Théâtre

Châtelet. So that must be Dr. Evans with her, the man responsible for making her the highest-paid courtesan in Paris. I could forgive him his foibles, remembering that during the war he had established a large field hospital for French soldiers with his own funds. But I could not be in the same room as a courtesan. Nor any other woman who attracted Édouard's interest. I was finished with Édouard, but it was unbearable to watch him with another woman.

Hearing my slight intake of breath, Degas asked, "Mademoiselle, would you care for some fresh air?" My posture and expression had not altered, but he must have seen my face go as pale as that of a betrayed wife.

"*Oui, s'il vous plaît*," I whispered. "If you will escort me to the omnibus stop, I will go home now." He offered his arm, and he gave our perfunctory farewells as I gathered my skirt with my free hand and swept out of the room, passing close enough to the bejeweled courtesan for me to admire her cold glamour. I maintained my aloof demeanor as Degas led me out of the studio.

On the street, I kept my composure, hoping that my politesse masked my vast sadness. But Degas saw through the mask. He'd seen how my eyes had never left Édouard and how my jaw had tightened when Édouard spoke to Méry Laurent.

I struggled to maintain my poise as the omnibus approached. Degas filled the silence. "I would like to talk with you about joining a group of like-minded artists. We all enjoy the challenges of painting modern life."

I nodded, unable to speak. Degas pressed on. "With your permission, I will call on you next week."

The omnibus arrived, and he handed me up the steps. After the driver called, "*Allez!*" to the enormous clomping horses drawing the vehicle and it pulled away, I turned to the window and saw that Degas still stood on the sidewalk, his attention on my sharp profile.

162

That is how Degas came to dine at the Morisot home the following week. We sat at the round table in the dining room, just our one special guest, my parents, and myself. As in the drawing room, the décor was simple: glossy parquet floors, simple striped wallpaper, a small faïence fireplace, and a buffet against one wall. My mother was known for social events that were all light and gaiety, but this was a business meeting.

Wasting no time, Papa began his offensive before the first course. "I have heard of other groups who tried to break away from the art establishment, to no avail."

"I know some of them, Monsieur Morisot. Rousseau and his fellow landscape painters. Realist artists, with their naturalistic style."

"Neither group earned the acceptance of the Academy."

"But if you trust my opinion, you must believe that our group is of a much higher caliber than ever assembled before."

Without Papa's approval, there was no need even to imagine joining Degas's new group. Since the war, Papa's main concern was that I would be taken care of after he was gone. Whether that was to be through marriage or professional success remained to be seen. My only hope was to appeal to the man Papa had been before the war, an art lover who was pleased that his daughters loved art as well. I leaned in from across the table to make my case. "Monsieur Degas is the finest of draftsmen. No artist today draws better."

"I've just made my first sale to a museum, which will help my reputation considerably," Degas added.

"*The Cotton Exchange*," Maman said. "I read a favorable review of it in *Le Monde*."

Papa did not even look up at her as he plunged his spoon into the leek and potato soup Pasie had set before him, pronouncing, "There is more to success than mere talent. Who is to manage the business affairs? No doubt the artists involved are near-paupers who expect me to fund this opération."

"We would be a *société anonyme*, an incorporated group, democratically sharing expenses to mount an exhibition independent of the Salon system," Degas said.

I again tried to catch my father's attention. "Claude Monet is a master of light-saturated landscapes. The effects of light are precisely what I am interested in. Papa?"

Papa was having none of that. He swiveled back and forth between us in exasperation. "Has any one of the members of this group attended l'École des Beaux-Arts? Or earned a medal at the Salon?" His face was growing red, and I noticed Maman eying him with concern.

"Non, Papa, and neither have I," I pointed out, firm, despite my soft voice. "It is a great honor for me to be invited to join les Independents. I cannot think of a more propitious circumstance."

Maman added, "It must be a respectable enterprise. Monsieur Degas is the essence of polite decorum." Her voice seemed to calm Papa. We turned to our soup, a simple dish that our bachelor guest no doubt enjoyed more than the others at the table, Degas being at the mercy of an Italian housekeeper who, he complained, prepared the same meal every night—boiled veal and macaroni, with preserves made from no fruit he had ever identified.

I could see Degas trying to think of something else to convince my father to allow me to exhibit my paintings with his group. "Mademoiselle Morisot's name would not be printed on the exhibition posters," Degas assured him, slurping a last leek from his spoon before Pasie removed the soup bowls.

"Certainly not," Papa snapped.

"And I assure you that she would not be expected to attend the organizational meetings with the other group founders."

"Out of the question. I will not have my daughter thought as unconventional as Adèle d'Affrey has become." Indeed, public opinion of late seemed to have turned on the duchess. The art critic Edmond Duranty had turned his hand to novel writing, and the character of Lucie Hambert in his latest work bore a striking, unflattering resemblance to the duchess.

"But she is a duchess, after all," said Maman.

"She is a 'New Woman,'" Papa pronounced with contempt. "Would you have our daughter putting herself forward in conversation? Or shaking hands with men?" I stared at my sole with velouté sauce, our second course, stirring a bit of fish in the sauce before setting down my fork. Degas tried to catch my eye, no doubt to encourage me to continue argue our cause, which was starting to feel hopeless. I turned my gaze away from the table to focus on the leaves falling outside, where I would have preferred to be at that moment.

"Is it not it shameful enough that Manet's portrait of Berthe has been the subject of caricatures in the newspapers?" Papa had to stop to catch his breath. Maman put a hand on his arm as an unhealthy flush rose from his neck and congested his features.

"Calm yourself. Think of your heart."

Papa was right. Édouard's portrait of me on his sofa, which he called *Repose*, hidden in a basement along with *The Balcony* for the duration of the siege, had been finally exhibited at the Salon to tremendous public ridicule. One could hardly open a newspaper without seeing a cartoon of the disheveled Mademoiselle Morisot, sprawled on a couch. One such caricature was labeled, *Seasickness*. The critic Armand Silvestre described me as "wilted, wretched, and ill-humored." When even the gossipy *Le Petit Journal* deemed the painting "an abhorrence," I knew that I was at risk of becoming almost as much of a laughing stock as any New Woman.

To change the subject, Degas turned to Maman. "Madame Morisot, perhaps Madame Pontillion would like to remember that she was a painter like her sister and could be again." Oui, that was inspired. Edma and I had been allowed to exhibit at the Salon together; perhaps it would put my parents at ease if both of us joined les Independents.

I spoke up. "I wish she would remember that." Perhaps now that her children were past their infancy, her life might be more her own.

"Oh, I don't think Edma could join your group," Maman demurred. "She is busy with her family now."

"Then Mademoiselle Berthe must represent the Morisots," Degas insisted. "We find that her name and talent are too important for us to manage without." Papa was frailer than he'd been before the war, but he still wasn't ready to capitulate.

"I haven't yet decided what's best," he announced. For the first time, I noticed the resemblance between my father and me—identical fiery eyes beneath dark brows.

Degas was distracted by Pasie, who carried a dessert that smelled like lemon soufflé. Still, I'm sure he saw Maman give me a reassuring nod.

Chapter Twenty

Paris

February 1874

S'il te plaît, think of your reputation! Do you suppose your tenuous social position as a woman painter can withstand such an act?" Édouard lectured me, ignoring the fact that I sat before him draped in a voluminous black cape with a thick black mourning veil cascading over one shoulder. Although his offer to paint the customary mourning portrait had been kind, my ashen and emaciated appearance elicited no mercy from him.

"But I've been considered a non-conformist from the first time I modeled for you," I said.

"Your father would never have allowed such behavior," Édouard grumbled, careful to keep his eyes on his canvas. Perhaps he was trying to reign in his attack.

"Ah, oui, but Papa is gone." My father had died from a sudden heart attack, reminding me that he did have a heart, after all. We had buried him the last week in January. Since then, I had experienced the profound grief that is inevitable when too much has been left unsaid. I remembered the days when Maman had been unable to escort Edma and me to our copying sessions, so Papa would walk his daughters to the Louvre on his way to his office in the Ministry of Finance. During our trek down the rue de Rivoli, Papa liked to point out that the lines of streetlights on either side converged in the distance at the Hôtel de Ville—a perfect lesson in perspective. What had happened since those days? I suppose it was that Papa could never accept that I had become my own person, with different desires and political views than he had planned for me. We had never resolved our differences and now we never would.

I smoothed my skirt and asked, "I wonder what he would think of you berating me while painting my mourning portrait?"

"If he knew that you were contributing his money to this undertaking—mon Dieu!"

"I'm only happy that the inheritance he left has enabled me to do so."

Here was a side of Édouard I had seldom seen. Of late, he had adopted an avuncular attitude with me, if one's uncle were both a cad and a curmudgeon. He was enraged at the idea that I would consider participating in an exhibition outside the Salon. He made a series of slashing strokes.

In the past, our conversations while I modeled had been stimulating, but never rancorous. Was he alone allowed to be unconventional? Few might purchase his paintings, but his dissolute habits were accepted within the confines of our caste. I knew all too well, however, that there were limits to his bohemian behavior.

"And you agree with the principles for which these independent artists stand. You yourself were the first to do away with the layers of glazes to let the brushstrokes themselves show through." My tone remained mild only because I did not have the energy to exhort him.

"Oui, oui, I eliminated the 'brown gravy,' but..."

I cut off his protest. "Why don't you join us, then?"

"I will never exhibit in the shack next door to the Salon." Édouard held his paintbrush in the air, forgotten, as he recited his credo. "I will enter through the main door and fight alongside all the others." Then, for an instant, his bravado failed him. His shoulders slumped, and he turned to me, pleading, "Why don't you remain with me? You can see very well I am on the right track." He picked up a smaller brush, then seemed to decide against adding fine detail to my portrait and tossed it aside.

"It was your friend Baudelaire who called upon artists to depict everyday life. You know as well as I do that I will never be able to paint the huge, operatic opuses that the Salon values. This group *wants* me to paint small, domestic scenes." I was determined to make Édouard admit for once that my choice was the right one, but it was an exhausting venture. "And they don't even seem to have noticed that I am a woman. As for propriety, who could be more proper than the artist who invited me to join the group—Monsieur Degas?"

"Degas be damned!" Édouard's palette clattered to the floor as he marched around the studio, ranting. "He is using you to get me to join the group. How dare he compromise you by connecting you in any way with Renoir, the son of a grocer, or Monet, the son of a baker, or, or, or," he stammered—"Pissarro, who is both a Creole and a Jew!"

I had always valued Édouard's opinion above all others', but I would not listen to him condemn Degas. He seemed to believe that he held the moral high ground. Did Édouard think that rejecting me, which he no doubt thought of as his refusal to risk compromising me, was a noble act? Edgar Degas could be a difficult man, but he had earned a place in my heart when he'd included Edma in his invitation to join this new group. Édouard was not in a position to tell me what to do, much as he enjoyed trying. In fact, now that Papa was gone, I was released; I did not need to obey any man's orders.

"Monsieur," I said, with every bit of dignity I could muster, "I do not intend to socialize with these men, but I will not pass up this opportunity." I was making a regal exit, sweeping cape and veil past my sputtering critic, when I spotted my painting, *Harbour at Lorient,* leaning against the wall. When I'd given it to him as a gift, Édouard had said that it was my best work yet.

"I will borrow this for the exhibition," I announced.

"You are disloyal to me, Mademoiselle." I gasped, setting off one of the coughing fits that I'd suffered from every winter since the war.

"*I* am disloyal?" Incredulous that he could resent my joining a group that might help my career, I spun around and saw that the desperation in Édouard's eyes belied his words. It was a look I had seen when he doubted that he would sell another painting. He had lost me as a lover, and now he was afraid of losing me as a colleague. I'd worked at hardening myself toward Édouard, but he could still make me weak, if only by revealing his pain. My heart stuttered.

But when he sensed my hesitation, the glint of victory returned to his eyes. His manipulation of me was as dexterous as the wielding of his brush. How revolting to think that I had loved this louche rascal. That gloating in Édouard's blue eyes was all I needed to see to come to my senses.

As I resumed my exit, now somewhat more encumbered by my painting, he called after me, "At least I still have Eva on my side!" I refused to respond to that taunt. If he could not find it within himself to show me mercy even while I was in mourning, let him lecture Eva Gonzalès from now on.

The last thing I heard from the bottom of the stairs was Édouard railing, "Radicals and madmen!"

12 February 1874

Ma chère Berthe,

You were possibly more beautiful in mourning than I had ever seen you, or simply more yourself, the very essence of both intelligence and femininity. Wanting to capture that essence in your mourning portrait, I painted heavy black, slashing strokes circling in to frame one slender arm and isolate your white face with those haunted eyes that grieve for more than the death of your father. Do you also grieve for what might have been between us, as I do? Your pain is almost too excruciating to witness, but those dark eyes do not spare me. No heroic nor erotic image will ever measure up to the image of pain. That is the core of humanity, its poem.

I could never have compromised you. But I did disappoint you. My emotions remain hidden, as they must. I let you go, but I've kept your portraits close, more than I've painted of anyone else—seven of them have never left my studio. After you stormed out today, I allowed myself to take the other portraits out of the armoire where they are stored, line them up against the wall, then sit before them until my eyes were full.

From the first portrait, in which your intensity seemed hardly contained by the balcony that bound you, to the coy flirtation in the paintings where you revealed a pink slipper or peeked over a Spanish fan, to the beautiful mature woman in full possession of her power in Berthe Morisot with Violets and Reclining, up to the spectral apparition of today's mourning portrait, I've depicted a different aspect of a complex woman each time you've posed for me. I have to content myself with these testaments to the many ways you looked, and the ways you looked at me.

Next to these, I set another painting from the back of the armoire. Now I will confess something that you might find shameful, but which will reveal the depth of my desolation in the knowledge that I will never possess you. One night I spotted a barmaid who bore you a superficial resemblance, and I hired her to model for a nude portrait. I gave her a black velvet ribbon to tie around her neck. She had dark curls, and her round breasts were quite like yours, even if her features were coarse and her eyes blank. I trusted that these differences would keep anyone from ever suspecting that this was my way of keeping you for myself.

Édouard

PART THREE

Les Belles Taches

Beautiful Touches

Chapter Twenty-One
Paris~Fécamp~Paris
April-July 1874

The Anonymous Co-opérative Society of Artists, Painters, Sculptors, Engravers, Etc. opened its exhibition on 15 April 1874, two weeks before the opening of the annual Salon. We held the show in the upstairs rooms of a bright red building on the corner of the boulevard des Capucines, an area of Paris in the midst of change, a location as modern as our art. Just down the avenue de l'Opéra, the new Opéra National was close to being finished. It was a hub from which radiated the boulevard des Italiens, anchored by the Café Tortoni, and the rue de Paix with its fashionable shops.

We hung the paintings in two rows only, so that one could see all of them, rather than in the cluttered floor-to-ceiling manner of the Salon. Renoir's brother painted the walls of the small rooms a deep russet, so that the effect was that of paintings hung in one's drawing room, as they were intended to be. Windows filled the rooms with outdoor light, while also providing views of the modern world we sought to portray. The feeling was intimate, which was quite a change from the Salon.

A few days after our opening, I brought Maman to the exhibition and let her tour the rooms while I stood in front of my paintings. I felt calm, so sure was I that this was the right place for my work. In addition to *Harbour at Lorient*, I had submitted *The Cradle*. It hung close to Cézanne's *Modern Olympia*, his reworking of Manet's reworking of Titian's *Olympia*, this time as a scribbled sketch. I amused myself at the opening by watching Maman's discomfort as she stood between the two paintings.

"I would have preferred that a portrait of my daughter and granddaughter not hang next to a portrait of a courtesan," she said, averting her eyes from Cézanne's work. *Modern Olympia* was mocking and playful, but her profession was made perfectly clear by the presence of a gentleman in a top hat at the right side of the painting. More than one mother hurried her daughter past. Cézanne's painting, with its thick impasto and outlines and bold juxtapositions of color, made as jarring a statement as the workman's clothes he wore to the exhibition opening.

I had hoped people would pay more attention to the other Independents to whom Degas had introduced me, the founders of this society. Camille Pissarro, a reserved man, was the oldest in the group. Monet, a visionary with wild, dark hair swept back from his wide face, was the center of the circle. His friend Renoir was a stylish young man with a goatee. Sisley had been Monet's first mentor.

Monet had been selling pretty paintings of women in gardens as fast as he could produce them. But the soft-edged images of London that he was showing here, images seen through an atmosphere imbued with coal-dust, were unlike anything I had seen. Many newspaper critics scoffed at what was, to their eyes, an unfinished style, accusing us of merely sketching our subjects. One of Monet's paintings in particular, *Impression: Sunrise*, inspired a critic to dub us all *Impressionists*. The representatives from *Le Globe, Le Monde, Le Gazette des Beaux Arts*, and dozens of other newspapers—some of which had come into being just to be able to review this exhibition— had the authority to influence the taste of our potential customers. Newsvendors were stationed at street corners all the way down the boulevard des Italiens. The newspaper critics had power, but I could also sense their excitement at having new subject matter to write about.

"Maman, isn't it wonderful that almost this entire wall is filled with my work?" I was able to show landscapes and portraits, new and old, oils and pastels—nine paintings in all. Relieved to be torn away from her examination of Cézanne's objectionable subject matter, she turned to study a painting of Edma and Nini playing hide and seek. I was also showing *Reading,* the double portrait of my mother and sister, so Edma was in the exhibition after all. And there was a pastel portrait of my little cousin, Madeleine Thomas. Armand Silvestre described it as "vigorous and charming"; the critic redeemed himself in my eyes after having described me in his scathing review of *Repose* as "an exhausted slattern."

I attracted quite a bit of attention simply because of my gender—having a woman in the group made us all the more radical—but the critics also had a lot to say about my work itself. Most of the reviews commended my use of color. The respected Phillipe Burty mentioned the freshness of my palette. And the review in *Le Siècle* included this flattering mention:

> Berthe Morisot has wit to the tips of her fingers...You cannot find images handled more delicately than *The Cradle* and *Hide and Seek*.

On the other hand, Alfred Wolff, the dreadful German whose name suited his personality, wrote a review that might have been the end of my reputation:

> There is also a woman in the group, as is the case with all famous gangs. Her name is Berthe Morisot. She is interesting to behold. With her, feminine grace manages to preserve itself in the midst of the ravings of a frenzied mind.

I hadn't expected such viciousness from the vain little man who wore rouge and a corset to the exhibition opening. Pasie was contrite when she spilled ink over Wolff's review in *Le Figaro*, but I assured her, "It got what it deserved."

Among my detractors were some of my former teachers. Papa Corot did not condemn me publicly, but personally, he advocated "escaping from that gang."

When I saw my old painting master, Monsieur Guichard, approach Maman, I ducked behind a corner. A newspaper critic set upon me there, leading with a compliment: "I am enjoying your paintings,

Mademoiselle Morisot. You convey emotions without showing them."

"Thank you very much, monsieur," I replied, but my attention was elsewhere. Because the rooms were uncrowded, I could hear everything Guichard had to say.

("When I entered, I became anguished upon seeing your daughter's works in such pernicious surroundings."

Maman glanced around at the surroundings in question. "Surely, monsieur, this is no worse than any other exhibition.")

I turned to the critic. "But no one is selling a thing. You are one of a very few critics who have something kind to say about the Independents."

"That may be because I am a poet, and your works are visual poems."

("*Au contraire!*" Guichard said to Maman. "To associate with these artists will destroy all your daughter's efforts, all the aspirations of past dreams."

"Do you think so?")

There was much more at stake now than when Guichard had made alarming statements while Edma and I copied at the Louvre. Maman revealed her distress by pulling her head back and furrowing her brow, an expression she tried to avoid because it could lead to a wrinkled forehead.

"Ah, a critic *and* a poet." The critic could see that I was only half listening.

("…not only madness, but a sacrilege! She must go to the Louvre twice a week, stand before Correggio for three hours, and ask for forgiveness for having attempted to say in oil what can only be said in watercolor.")

Guichard thought of watercolors as an inferior medium and saw the Impressionists as lesser artists. I rather liked his description of my sin—trying to make oil paintings look as spontaneous and light-soaked as watercolors. As he doled out my penance, once again I thought myself fortunate that I no longer had to listen to the advice of others.

The critic was still standing at my side. "Your use of color is of the highest caliber. Is this the influence of Manet?"

"Him? I am far ahead of him." How annoying to still be associated with Édouard. I waved my hand at the paintings. "Just look at my brighter colors. Édouard Manet does not work *en plein air*, and these hues cannot be achieved in a studio, no matter how renowned the artist."

"I will consider that the next time I am in Manet's studio."

Now I focused on the critic and remembered seeing him conversing with Eugène Manet the day Édouard showed *The Railway* in his studio. I saw that even though he was scribbling in a little notebook with the stub of a pencil, he had something of Édouard's elegance himself.

"He is one of my closest friends, and I call on him almost every day." He gave a small bow. "Stéphane Mallarmé, at your service."

"Oh, you are *that* poet. It's a pleasure to meet you." Not only had I enjoyed reading his work in Papa's literary magazines, but I remembered that this was the man whose translations of Edgar Allen Poe's work Édouard had illustrated. Édouard had raved about this new poet, but as Mallarmé was still struggling as a schoolteacher and a sometime newspaper critic, I'd never had occasion to be introduced to him.

As evidence of his uncanny ability to be in the most socially advantageous place at any given time, Édouard chose that moment to come up the stairs to the gallery, with his brother Eugène one step behind. Édouard had time only to greet Mallarmé before both were surrounded by critics.

"The King of the Impressionists has arrived," announced one, referring to a caricature of Édouard wearing a crown and holding a paintbrush as his scepter that had appeared in *Le Siècle*. They insisted on including Édouard with us, and Degas and Monet had more than once asked him to join our movement, but he remained adamant in his determination to be accepted by the Academy.

"I am not an Impressionist, gentleman," Édouard said, looming above the cluster of newspaper writers. "I have only come to lend support to my friends."

"Don't you mean your disciples, Monsieur Manet?" asked an eager young reporter.

As the circle of men broke into laughter, Eugène turned to me. While we were close to the same height, he would not meet my eye. "What a pleasure to see you, Mademoiselle Berthe. How lovely your paintings are, as if they were painted with light."

"You are too kind, monsieur."

With a diffident smile, he asked, "Will you walk with me as I take in the others' paintings?"

"I think I will wait here for Édouard's opinion of the show," I said, meaning his approval of my paintings, so much more important to me than any newspaper review.

Eugène pointed to Édouard, towering over the gaggle of newspapermen. "That could be quite a long wait," he suggested.

It was thoughtful of him not to leave me stranded, with Édouard turning the critics' attention away from the artists they were here to write about. Still, I said, "I don't mind. You go on and visit my colleagues."

"You are sure that you want to wait here?" he asked.

I nodded.

"Then I believe I'll wait here with you, if you don't mind." Eugène stayed by my side for the rest of the afternoon.

In all, 3,500 visitors climbed the stairs to our exhibition that month and paid one franc each for a ticket. It was a respectable number, but we finished in debt.

I did not sell a single painting. No matter. I was known now, even notorious, which was another change.

"'Mademoiselle Morisot is not interested in reproducing trifling details. When she has a hand to paint, she makes exactly as many brush strokes as there are fingers, and the business is done.'"

Maman persisted in reading aloud the reviews of our exhibition, in spite of the fact that seeing the name of her unmarried daughter in the newspaper during the entire month of the Independent exhibition had been a disgrace for her. My remorse over causing my mother shame had me in a vulnerable state when she suggested that we spend July enjoying the cool ocean air at Fécamp, a popular summer destination on the Normandy coast. With Maman still bereft over Papa's death, I wished more than ever to please her. So I packed up my paints while Pasie packed my clothes and Maman's, and we loaded our trunks into a carriage bound for the Gare du Nord.

The shouting conductors, shrieking whistles, and clanging bells at the train station were deafening. Eruptions of black smoke intermingled with an inordinate number of young women bound for summer resorts where the slight relaxation of social rules increased their chances of forming connections with potential *fiancés*. It was humiliating to be among their number. But once on the "marriage train," in our summer travelling costumes and surrounded by other pleasure-seekers fleeing the heat in Paris, I began to look forward to the trip. It was still an adventure to race along the new train lines connecting the city to the Normandy coast.

"'Stupid people who are finicky about the drawing of a hand don't understand a thing about Impressionism,'" continued Maman, reading another review.

I dismissed this sarcastic statement with a shrug. I no longer felt compunction when breaking Papa's rules, or Édouard's. Letting go of limitations was becoming easier for me. Now, realizing that the opinions of the critics had nothing to do with what I wanted to create, I shed yet another layer of constraint.

"This is written by Louis Leroy, the most respected critic in Paris."

"Respected? By whom?"

"Well, then surely you respect your former teacher. Bértât, Monsieur Guichard is an experienced artist. If he doubts your abilities, who are you to believe in them?"

"It's Impressionism he doubts, not my abilities. He is nothing more than a second-rate copiest." I turned to the window. I believed that my painting career was more than a dream, yet I also knew that Maman's single-minded goal was to find me a husband this summer, and that she was right to be so determined. I could not continue to be a burden for her, now that Papa was gone, and I had learned the hard way that waiting for love was a foolish fantasy.

When Manet Mére and her son Eugène joined us in Fécamp, I resolved to be amiable. Or was it that I was simply too weary to be embarrassed any longer about us being thrown together by virtue of being the only still-unmarried man and woman in our social milieu? Edma and her family were also with us, and together we made many excursions.

Edma made a point of making the shy Eugène comfortable, drawing him out in conversation and gaily laughing when he said anything close to humorous. She was particularly proud of arranging an afternoon at the shore, so that Eugène could admire me in my bathing costume. Edma and I stood shivering in shallow water, the overskirts of our woolen bathing costumes floating on the waves, scrutinized by Maman and Madame Manet, who had the advantage of being fully clothed—complete with bonnets and parasols—on the bluff above us.

"I feel like a prize cow at a country fair," I said.

We watched Adolphe and Eugène, in their street clothes, enter the back door of the men's bathing machine. Two brawny attendants wheeled the contraption into the sea where, having changed into their striped bathing suits, the gentlemen could jump into the water from a door on the far side of the machine, for modesty's sake, so that we would be unable to see them. Adolphe dove in with a mighty splash and swam away, thrashing and shouting for Eugène to follow him.

"Eugène is far too cultivated to let you feel that he is appraising you," Edma assured me. She was all smiles, relishing her finest hour in doing what she felt was best for me. "Don't you think he looks like

Édouard?"

As Eugène and Adolphe swam back and forth. I did think I glimpsed Édouard's blonde beard out of the corner of my eye, but as I pointed out to Edma, "He's not as tall," Eugène waved a white arm and dove under a wave. "Nor as vain."

Eugène Manet was an amateur painter, and we spent many days painting at various spots around Fécamp. One such day we set up on a rocky point over a little harbor where boats were being repaired in a dockyard.

From the beginning, Eugène had supported the Impressionists. He agreed that Édouard had broken open the wall of tradition, but he admired even more those of us who chose to walk through. "I am not the painter my brother is, but I know enough about art to appreciate your talent," he said.

"You are very kind to say so." I was concentrating on getting onto canvas a complex arrangement of logs in the foreground and ships in their cradles beyond. A sliver of water bisected the composition, with the village of Fécamp and low green hills on the far side of the harbor. A full third of the painting was given over to pale blue sky with thin clouds blowing in from the right.

"And I appreciate the Impressionists for what you are giving us—nothing less than a new beginning for France."

"You know it was decadent atheists like us who brought about our defeat to Germany," I teased him. Many artists and writers lived lives of dissipation—Baudelaire's was the most recent death from syphilis, and our neighbor Gioachino Rossini had succumbed to the disease a few years before—but no more than did the general population.

"Good citizens of the new Republic should only desire paintings honoring our glorious fallen soldiers," I continued, to provoke a response.

"I am sick of death. And I'm not alone in also being sick of the dead, stale paintings of the Salon!" The quiet Eugène was catching fire.

His voice rose. "We lost the war, but we have rebuilt Paris, and we have already paid our debt to the Germans." He took a step forward and almost stumbled so that I feared he was having a seizure

Eugène regained his footing, but his voice rose still more. "We must remind the world that Paris has been its artistic capital for one hundred years and will be for hundreds more to come."

Talk of the war brought back his old feelings. Eugène rubbed his temples and dabbed at his damp forehead with a handkerchief. I remembered how he had responded to the fighting, anticipating death. He was a sensitive man, yet this reaction bordered on alarming. To calm him, I turned his attention to my painting. "What do you think? A bit more yellow in the clouds?"

He gathered himself together to focus on my work. "No, I think there is quite enough. You don't want a jaundiced sky, do you?" Aside from Édouard, Eugène may have been the only man I knew who gave me an honest opinion. In their desire to behave as gentlemen, most were too complimentary.

We worked in companionable silence for a time. I added dashes of blue to the boat-workers' coats as I contemplated whether it might be possible for a high-strung man and a headstrong woman to create a life together, a choice that seemed ever more inevitable. If there had been no Édouard, Eugène might have seemed perfect for me.

"I wouldn't mind at all if you were to compliment me a bit on my painting," Eugène ventured with a small smile. His seascape was made of muted colors, with careful brushstrokes. I searched for something to say.

"Your composition is good. Oui, you have caught the moment."

"You are humoring me. Edma would have had the grace to come up with less general comments."

While I craved honest estimations of my work, Eugène required compliments. "Edma is the diplomat," I agreed. "I am more troublesome." It was only fair to warn him.

"I was quite neglected as a child," he said, "disregarded precisely because I *didn't* get into as much trouble as Édouard."

183

"But attending to a troublesome child is not the same as accepting her," I assured him. "I was far from neglected, but seldom have I felt accepted. In all of my paintings of Edma and Nini, the child is partly me, separate from her mother, isolated and sad."

Every unmarried woman knows that she must never mention marriage or children to an unmarried man, lest she appear desperate. But, as I approached middle age, there was no use in pretending to be someone I was not. And I was someone whose desire for a child grew as my chances to have one diminished. I couldn't help but add, "If I am ever fortunate enough to have a child, I will never turn my back on him."

I returned to my painting, but I could feel Eugène's focus still trained on me. It was not like when Édouard pierced me with his lightning-bolt stare. It was more like when you knew your faithful dog was watching to intuit what your next command might be. His attentive regard turned out to be quite pleasant.

Eugène, with his eyes on the ground, finally spoke. "I think you are a woman of incomparable worth." I realized that he was declaring himself. I thought of Edma explaining to me that *one must make a responsible decision about who can best provide for a family*. Yves had said of her decision to marry, *I did my duty*. If I accepted Eugène, I would be choosing a good provider and doing my duty. But it was remembering Yves's other reason for marrying, her loneliness, that convinced me I must marry Eugène Manet. No lightning emanated from him, only a kind understanding. We would try to make each other happy.

I stood before him and waited until he lifted his chin and looked me straight in the eye. "Berthe…would you?" he whispered. "What I mean is, if I were to ask you…?" He looked as though he might faint before he finished his sentence, so I came to his aid.

"Oui, Eugène. I accept."

This inevitable moment was not at all as I thought it would be. I had been afraid that I would feel trapped, and more, that I was being forced to settle for second-best. Instead, Eugène's gentle admiration enveloping me felt like sliding down into my first warm bath after aching with cold throughout the siege.

In response, I handed Eugène the painting I was working on. "I would like for you to have this as a souvenir of our day," I said. We packed up our paints and strolled through the fields. When his tentative hand reached for mine, I felt the dual consolations of the promise of companionship and of fulfilling my duty to Maman.

When I returned to Paris, Édouard insisted on a last painting of me. I agreed, because I wanted an engagement portrait. I arrived at his studio as a respectable betrothed woman, wearing a dark dress and velvet neck ribbon, as usual. Also as usual, I held a fan, this time fanning myself quickly, indicating that I was engaged. I held the fan with my left hand, to show my ring. When Édouard tried to catch my eye, instead of returning his gaze I turned away and looked in another direction. But nothing could erase the image of us, naked and entwined on the crimson sofa in the corner, the farthest thing from respectable.

He worked in silence at first. After a while, he clucked his tongue and sat back in his chair as if about to speak. "Berthe," he began.

"What is it, Édouard?" I asked, maintaining my pose with my eyes focused somewhere over his shoulder.

After a long pause, in a strangled voice, he said, "Oh, it is nothing, *rien de tout.*" Perhaps he had thought to talk me out of my plans, but he seemed to think better of it. He was correct in concluding that there was nothing more to say. He had suggested that I marry his brother, and I would soon do so. He knew all there was to know about me, and now he would never have any of it.

Eugène was eager to marry in the autumn, but I wanted to complete a year of mourning for Papa. We compromised by marrying three days before Christmas. A deep snow and heavy fog muffled Paris, enveloping us in bridal white. From above, our party must have resembled the black marks on a Japanese print.

PAULA BUTTERFIELD

We were a small group. After the war, Tiburce had gone off to make his fortune in America, and Yves could not travel because she was again expecting. So only our mothers, along with Edma and Adolphe to act as witnesses, accompanied Eugène and me to the civil ceremony at the office of the *maire* in the Sixteenth Arrondissement. I felt Papa's absence on this one occasion when he might have felt proud of me. I imagined him taking my arm, as pleased to escort me as he had been when he walked me to copying sessions at the Louvre. Instead, Adolphe escorted me into the office, wrapping me in a burly embrace and wiping a tear from his eye before handing me to Eugène.

I went through the ceremony without the least pomp, without any guests, as was fitting for a thirty-three-year-old woman—no dewy young bride. My new husband, over forty himself, signed the church register: *Eugène Manet, a man of property*. I wrote: *Berthe Marie Pauline Morisot, no profession*, as I owned no property, nor did I make my living by my work. As I set down the pen, my new husband touched my cheek and whispered, "I vow to make you the most adored woman on earth."

Eugène was an honest and excellent man. He did not fill me with passion, nor would he break my heart. Maman's marital advice was to fight against that part of myself which disposed me to excessive sensibility and melancholy. She needn't have worried. Eugène was intelligent, kind, and accepting of me. With his support, I finished four paintings, country scenes of farmers and laundresses, at the Manet estate in Gennevilliers that spring.

For the first time in my life, I was content. And that was the biggest change of all.

Chapter Twenty-Two

Paris

Spring 1875

*W*hat could be more delightful than sitting in a chocolate shop with the duchess, surrounded by packages proving a successful shopping trip? At long last, my friend had returned to Paris for a visit. We had everything to say to each other.

"I will have the bonbons with mint ganache," said the duchess. The waiter seemed mesmerized by my friend's fine features and blonde hair. "Did you hear me, garçon?"

Her imperious tone spurred the graceless young man into action. His voice broke as he replied, "Oui, oui, madame!" He took her menu, dropped it and picked it up, and scrambled to rush her order to the kitchen.

"Une momente!" she called after him. "You have neglected to take madame's order."

Even six months after our wedding, I was almost as flustered as *le garçon* to hear myself referred to as a married woman. "I'll have *chocolat à l'Africain*," I stammered.

After the waiter stumbled off, the duchess turned her attention to me. "And what will you do to keep painting, now that you are married, dear girl? Join one of the women's art organizations, *peut-être?*"

"And make watercolors of fashionable ladies doing needlepoint in their drawing rooms, to keep in an album?" I scoffed.

"More than that, I should hope," she said, touching her dangling earring.

"My paintings are limited to the domestic sphere—what choice do I have? But that is the only thing I have in common with amateur painters." Conscious that I was wearing my fierce expression, I unlocked my eyebrows and continued. "Non, *les arts d'agrement* were

187

enough for my mother's generation, but if I want to be accepted as a professional, I cannot be associated with that sort of group."

"I could get you mentioned in *La Gazette des Femmes*," my friend offered.

"But being on the board of directors for that newspaper hasn't kept you from being rejected by the Salon for the last two years." Irritation slipped into my voice. "Connections with women never help."

The duchess was not willing to relinquish her representations of social status. "Being introduced to Empress Eugénie allowed me to paint the most illustrious members of society."

That, and your astonishing beauty, along with your unencumbered but still respectable marital state as a widowed aristocrat, I thought. "More parties than patrons," I murmured.

The duchess knew when to pretend not to have heard. "The hat from Le Printemps will suit you well, my dear. I do think we should go back and buy you that cunning fur muff."

"But I already have one quite like it. Manet painted me with it one day. Maybe you noticed that portrait when you visited his studio?"

"Oui, that is where I got the idea of painting you myself. Manet's portraits of you are so severe with you always in black. I pictured you as a mature, happy woman in a delicate pink decolleté evening gown."

Mature, *sans doubt*. My shoulders and breasts were full and rounded in the duchess's sketches. Was that from happiness, or my encroaching middle age?

"Did I tell you that Manet asked if I would model for him?" Her mention of this was so casual that I struggled to match her tone.

"Non, I don't believe you did."

"Naturally, I declined. I told him that I already had so many artistic enemies that I didn't want to add his to mine. He seemed dumbfounded." She raised her eyebrows as she leaned in over the table so that the ladies sitting near us would not hear. "It is one thing to visit his studio, especially since it's so close to mine, but quite another to be associated with him further."

This uncharitable remark was too much. What did she think of *my* artistic association with Édouard? I felt compelled to defend him—and myself. "But he is a great artist! Possibly the greatest in Paris."

"But he is an artist, most of whom are uncouth, and he in particular has known nothing but scandal. My commissions may have declined since the fall of the Empire, but they could disappear completely if my name were linked to his."

It occurred to me, not for the first time, that the duchess might be the one who had things all wrong. What had her social circle done for her art? I found that my career was progressing at a slow but steady rate. *My* circle of colleagues—Monet, Renoir, and Sisley—had organized an auction at the Hôtel Druout following the Impressionist exhibition, where a dozen of my paintings had sold. Ernest Hoschède, the department store magnate, paid four hundred-eighty francs, the highest price of the day, for *Interior*, the painting of Yves I'd imagined in Spain. I would have liked to witness this victory, but it didn't seem suitable for me to attend such a commercial enterprise.

And now I had a husband, which the duchess did not. For a shocking instant I wondered if this remarkable woman would end up ruined like the sculptor in Alphonse Daudet's current popular novel, *Le Nabob*, that parodied her life even more cruelly than had Duranty's book—a drug addict, a "monster," condemned to live and die like a man." Non, impossible!

Noticing that I did not respond, my sophisticated friend broke our silence by rustling through her packages. "It is impossible to find gloves of this quality in Switzerland. And of course, Paris is where one finds the most talented milliners. Mother will adore this hat."

When the waiter arrived to set the porcelain chocolatière and tiny cups on the table, I was unable to drink it. Mention of Édouard still had the power to unbalance my life, that composition I had created with such care.

"My dear, is there something that is making you unhappy?" the duchess asked with genuine concern. "You know that I am not easily shocked."

I could confide everything in her. Except perhaps, the subject she had brought up. I had never spoken to anyone about my feelings for Édouard, loathe to be mistaken for yet another in his long line of conquests. I twirled the *moussoir* sticking out of the chocolate pot, pretending to concentrate on stirring the chocolate. "Duchess, I am perfectly happy, I assure you. I am devoted to my husband and to my work." As she knew that Eugène and I were to take our honeymoon trip later in the summer—she had offered to provide letters of introduction to her acquaintants in England—I was surprised to hear her question my happiness.

"Ah, then it is regret that haunts you."

I started. How did she know? The moussoir rattled on the marble table when I dropped it, and the dark paneled walls of the shop began to close in on me. What a relief it would be to speak of it. "There was someone…"

"Of course there was."

"He could be so spirited, so optimistic and full of life."

"But…"

"But I could not endure his changes of heart! He would share with me the greatest intimacy I have ever know, then turn me off like a gaslight."

"You have made the better choice, ma chère. A man who is capable of such a volte-face is not to be trusted. But tell me, did he write you marvelous letters?"

The duchess did understand. I should have known she would. I let my guard down and confided, "The most endearing I have ever received."

"Burn them," she said. "And make sure that he does the same." She was quite right. I would do it as soon as possible.

"How efficient you are in these matters." Only a fluttering of her eyelashes revealed that the duchess was aware that this might not be a compliment.

"It is starting to rain," she said. "We will have to use our new umbrellas."

Her features remained smooth as she pronounced, "Try to remember that the dream of perfect happiness is a chimera. At the same time, you must do what you must; respectability is no substitute for...well, anything else. And work is the most important of all." She touched her napkin to her lips and laid it, neat and folded, on the table. "Come, my fascinating friend. We have enough time before dinner for me to continue working on your portrait, my gift for the new bride."

"*Mais oui!* I would love for you to finish it before you return to Nice." I said this knowing the painting would never be finished, as we were never in the same place long enough for all the necessary sittings. We began gathering our things.

"Mon amie," she asked, absent-minded as she picked up her packages, "will you take care of the bill? I never carry money." It was understood that there was a price to pay for the pleasure of her aristocratic presence.

҈

Paris
30 July 1875

My dear Monsieur and Madame Manet,
I trust that you both are enjoying your carefree gallivanting through England while some of us remain in Paris, toiling away. Yesterday, the summer sun streaming through the windows of my studio as I painted through the afternoon left me lightly sautéed by evening. Happily, I remembered that it was Wednesday, when I, without fail, make the two-minute walk from the rue de Petersbourg around the corner to the Café Guerbois.
The glass door grated against the sanded wood floor of the café when I entered, a welcome, familiar sound. Célèstin, my favorite waiter, gave me a quick nod and a "Bonsoir, Monsieur Manet," and barked my order back to the kitchen, knowing without asking what to bring me. The bright lights and din of clattering dishes, clacking billiard balls, and chattering patrons were a tonic to me after the long hours alone in my studio. I cut through clouds of cigar smoke toward the laughter and shouting from my friends at

our regular table by the front window, hung my cane on the coat rack next to it, and sat down beside Monet. Across the table, Renoir's little seamstress, Camille, draped herself on his shoulder.

Even Degas made one of his rare appearances. You might be interested to hear that the Impressionist exhibition is still a primary topic of discussion, over a year after it closed. Degas decried the critics' negative responses. "What else could we expect from the critics? They are lackeys of the Academy. Their accolades would be meaningless!"

He lives to argue, and I was happy to oblige him. "All that contempt, my boy, is nonsense," I said. "Reward is a weapon, and in this dog's life of ours, one is never too well armed."

"Then you yourself are unarmed!"

"I haven't been decorated? That is not my fault, and I assure you that I shall be if I can, and that I shall do everything necessary to that end."

"Naturellement," Degas said. "I've always known how much of a bourgeois you are. Leave it to us to move art into the future."

"The Academy and its Salon must accept us, on our terms," I insisted.

Célèstin slipped my glass of aged red wine before me. What a comfort it was to have a white-aproned, black-vested waiter stationed like an attentive penguin behind me.

"You are as famous as Garibaldi—what more do you want?" Degas continued. As usual, he thrust out his hand for me to shake in congratulations for what he thinks of as his great wit.

"If only I could unify artists as Garibaldi unified Italy." I turned to Monet and Renoir. "Why don't you stay at the Salon with me? Degas, even you might earn an honorable mention."

Although Monet was more interested in giving Célèstine his dinner order than in listening to our repartée, and Renoir was wholly occupied with Camille, Degas went on. "Manet seems to be obstinate in his decision to remain apart. He may very well regret it," he prophesied.

"Your independent exhibition was hardly a resounding success!" I fired back.

And so it went. You see that things are unchanged here, and that all will be

familiar when you return from your travels abroad.
Until then, fond regards from your brother, and brother-in-law,

Édouard

❧

30 July 1875

My dear Degas,
You were at the Guérbois last night, as I'd hoped you would be.
The rude remarks and the affectionate insults were as usual. No one goes there for flattery, but rather to enjoy a few hours of stimulating conversation about art, philosophy, the world. When I am in the midst of a painting taking weeks or months to complete, even your sarcasm can provide the enthusiasm I need to go on until the idea takes its final shape. Last night, you were holding forth once again on the Impressionist exhibition. By now, we all know where you stand, having heard your opinions on the subject for over a year. The critics don't understand, art will die unless the Academy embraces change, et cetera. But the conversation took an alarming turn when Monet spoke up.
"Still, the world knows us now. Some paintings sold. Berthe Morisot sold more at the auction afterward than any of the rest of us."
Edgar, did you imagine the emotions that welled up within me upon hearing this news? Mention of Berthe left me silent. Pride, envy of her growing success, and most of all, fear that my feelings for Berthe might be discerned roiled inside me and threatened to reveal themselves. By force of habit, I concentrated on not allowing my face to reflect those sentiments.
"I'm glad of it," Renoir said. "We couldn't have staged the exhibition without her financial backing."
Regaining my composure, I took advantage of an opportunity to dispel any idea of a romantic connection between Berthe and me when I said, "Mademoiselle Morisot has talent, to be sure, but she has learned most of what she knows from me."
Under your breath, you muttered to Renoir, "I definitely believe him to be

much more vain than intelligent." If that was, as I suspect, your attempt to steer the conversation away from Berthe, I am indebted to you. I forced myself to roar with laughter at your remark. The others joined in, then we all clinked our glasses together and finished off another of the many drinks that we imbibed last evening. What could have been a crisis for me was averted.

While the conversation continued, I sat there thinking of Berthe spending the summer on her honeymoon trip with my brother. I would never be certain whether I had given her to him, or he had won her. All that mattered was that, at this very moment, it was Eugène, not me, who was enjoying Berthe's conversation and seeing England through her artistic eye. I could not bring myself to think of what else he might be relishing about his new bride. I know only too well what delights Berthe can offer a man. But what would she enjoy in return? Eugène has never been accused of being a sensualist, any more than you have!

Monet married his mistress, and it looks like Renoir might do the same, but had Berthe become my mistress, I would still have been unable to marry her. Even if I had been unencumbered, I would not have inflicted myself upon her.

While my new sister-in-law has been enjoying her holiday in England, I've been laboring over a painting of a young woman with a book. Each day, a beautiful brunette model lies back against overstuffed couch cushions in my studio with her volume abandoned on her lap. She is reminiscent of Berthe, but Berthe she is not. Still, if Berthe will never be mine, then I must find pleasure where I can.

When I tried to catch the eye of the pretty young woman who hovered by our table, her downcast glance made her seem almost demure. If she was a seamstress like Renoir's Camille, or a milliner or glove-maker, even if she stooped to consorting with men to make a few extra francs, I had to respect a young woman who earned her own living. "Célèstin," I called out. "Bring a glass of pastis for the mademoiselle."

Did you judge me, Edgar, when I reached out for the shy grisette with the fine eyes and pulled her down to my lap? You needn't bother.

I am a miserable dog.

La Luministe

Édouard

Chapter Twenty-Three

England~Paris

Summer 1875~Spring 1876

*P*uvis used to tease me about having British blood; although I was Parisienne to the core, he thought my love of watercolors was explained by my "English eyes." C'est vrai, I felt at home on my honeymoon trip. Perhaps it was the influence of my English governess, Louisa, but I found England enchanting.

London was a painting heaven. On the shore of the Thames, I rushed to daub a forest of yellow masts and the dome of St. Paul's Cathedral shimmering in a golden haze.

Eugène and I spent hours in the National Gallery. Eugène was fascinated by the just-opened Barry Rooms, arranged in a cross under a central dome, although I felt that the monumental architecture overpowered the paintings there. I was struck by how British artists painting one hundred years before me had been as fascinated with the light as I was. Tumultuous clouds churned above Turner's seascapes and served as backdrops in portraits of aristocrats and their dogs. The portraits of women still depicted them in the midst of their many children, though. Or sewing.

The atmospheric paintings of clouds and light excited us so that we chattered over one another. "Berthe, do you see? Constable was interested in the effects of daylight."

"Even the light on the wind-blown trees varies from leaf to leaf."

"His reflection of sun on water resembles Monet's, don't you think?"

At the Tate Museum we came upon the work of the Pre-Raphaelites, a group of English artists who had broken away from the British Academy twenty years before, just as the Impressionists were doing now.

"Rossetti's colors are as bright as Renoir's, and he paints over a white

background, too," I mused, in front of *The Girlhood of Mary Virgin*.
Eugène was examining the painting so closely that a museum guard positioned himself next to us, but Eugène was too absorbed to notice. "But his paintings are all precision and detail, unlike the quickness of the Impressionist style," he said of Rossetti. "He is concerned with conveying a moral message while the Impressionists want only to express the fleeting moment."

"Where we are anticipating the future," I observed, "they are looking back."

But what was this? A painting of a group of women clustered on a bluff drew my eye. While not understanding the effects of outdoor light, the artist had attempted a plein air scene, painted in a stippled technique that stood out against the polished style of the other paintings in the room. A standing auburn-haired woman, in particular, was absorbed in her thoughts. The label read: *Sir Patrick Spens,* Elizabeth Eleanor Siddal, 1856. So there had been a woman among the Pre-Raphaelites, one who was interested in the same aspects of painting that captivated me—outdoor scenes and women in reverie—over twenty years ago. I found it encouraging to think of myself as part of an unbroken line of women working to present our artistic visions to the world.

We were pulled from one painting to another, as happy as children playing. Eugène had become almost as close a companion as Edma. It was a bit bewildering. Was I confusing him with Édouard, or were my feelings for Édouard receding? Was it possible that what I had perceived as love for Édouard was no more than a series of scenes I had painted in my imagination? The feeling persisted that I was betraying my great love, but I told myself that there couldn't be anything wrong with enjoying my husband's company.

The duchess's letters of introduction came to nothing, as in August all of fashionable society left for the country, shooting birds or riding to hounds, or doing whatever the British did during that month. The duchess wrote that I gave her "the impression of being always on the way to some other spot on the globe where I won't be able to see you." Who was she to complain, when one never knew whether *she* were in France, Switzerland, or Italy!

The art dealers were gone, too, which was disappointing. I would have liked to see Durand-Ruel's London gallery, or to find English dealers who would pay me three hundred thousand francs for each painting, as we heard they had done for James Tissot. After the war, Tissot had moved to London, where he found great success in painting society ladies in a style that, to me, resembled the polished work of Alfred Stevens.

I left London hopeful about my new marriage, with my head full of Hogarth's scenes of daily life and Gainsborough's informal portraits set against natural backgrounds.

The beach on the Isle of Wight was the prettiest place for painting, like an English garden next to the sea. The little river full of boats created a charming scene. I would have considered moving to England for my career, but the man I'd married would not hear of it. He was not as coopérative a model as my sister. Not until we were forced by cold weather to stay indoors one day did I convince him to sit for me. He straddled a chair and sulked as he scanned the world outside the window, a restless gentleman awaiting his escape.

I laid in Eugène's figure on the far left, with flower pots on the window sill in the center of the canvas, and fragmented marks for the dazzling, pellucid light pouring in through sheer curtains on the right. To cheer myself, I made a sunny outdoor scene with ships' masts in the distance and a mother and child passing our garden fence in the middle ground. Eugène had soon had enough.

"C'est fini?" he asked again and again. You would think he had never modeled before, though he had been a central figure in Édouard's *Afternoon in the Tuileries*, and that Degas had painted him as well, for our wedding gift. Finally, I finished *Eugène Manet on the Isle of Wight*. It was a portrait, a still life, and a seascape all in one painting. Bien. The notion of having a child like the one outside our garden fence to walk along the harbor with me was so much more appealing than accommodating a husband made bad-tempered by poor weather that I wrote to Edma, "Couldn't you see your way to sending little Nini and her nurse over for a visit? I could paint lovely pictures with them on the balcony."

Eugène and I rented a boat and attempted to paint harbor scenes as we bobbed back and forth in it. The light changed every instant, so that I was painting not even an impression, but only a glance. Dashes and wobbly lines like Japanese writing, scratches and scumbles of vibrant color conveyed the movement of water, boats, wind, and light. The spontaneity was as thrilling as riding a speeding train.

Eugene complained about "the infernal lapping of the water."

I had secured my hat against the brisk sea breeze with a black lace scarf. Yet somehow a gust of wind managed to loosen the lace bow and blow the hat into the sky. The sailors stacking cargo on the dock, struggling to keep their own flat hats on their heads while their wide, white trousers flapped in the breeze, burst into raucous laughter.

Eugène was upset to see me disheveled, with my hair in my eyes. "Is that what you want? To call attention to yourself in front of English sailors?" he demanded as he gave me a brusque yank to the other side of the boat. His rough behavior shocked me. I was surprised to see him let such a small thing cast a pall over our perfect day, but I was to learn that abrupt changes in mood were common for him.

Eugène no longer pretended to join me when I painted. The last time we'd painted together, he had developed one of his terrible headaches.

"Is it eyestrain?" I asked. The crystalline sunlight could become a painful glare at times.

"No, it is another kind of strain," he grumbled. "I've come to the conclusion that two painting Manets are enough," he said. Did his frustration spring from feeling that he was in competition with my artistic talent? Or with Édouard's? "I have an idea for a novel," he said, "and I must think it through."

Back in Paris that autumn, we settled into our apartment at 9 avenue d'Eylau, between Passy and the new neighborhood near the l'Arc de Triomphe. Maman was a widow and I was her only child in Paris, so it was only right that she sell my childhood home and come to live with us. Eugène agreed that it was our filial duty to look after our mothers. Maman brought her maid with her, and when I saw Pasie, now a slender young woman of twenty-four with chestnut hair, standing in the doorway to the dining room, an idea for a painting sprang to mind. I would show her just there, with the light from the kitchen beyond. I was happy to have a new model, and an old friend, in our home.

Édouard brought Manet Mére, Suzanne, and Léon—who escaped to the kitchen with Pasie—to our first family dinner. Just the sight of him brought all of my feelings thundering back. While caring for Eugène and Maman at the same time that I was settling into a new house kept me busy, my most difficult challenge would be socializing with Édouard. We had found a way to be around one another before I married. Édouard would act cross, while I drew upon the technique developed during my hours of modeling of looking past him. But now I was ill at ease during those times when he witnessed me in my role as Eugène's wife. And Édouard's general irritability seemed to have solidified into disdain for his brother, which made me wonder how he could have allowed himself to lose me to Eugène.

After we dined, I led everyone into the drawing room. The men lit up their pipes near the windows opening on to the balcony while I served the women their tea by the fireplace.

Édouard broke the silence in a sonorous voice, which initiated a vibration within me in places my husband's hesitant explorations had yet to discover. "Eugène, have I told you that I painted the Monets in their garden?"

"More sugar, please." Manet Mère, seated by the fire, passed her cup to Suzanne. Édouard's mother had the same long, narrow nose and thin lips as he did, but her pursed mouth and heavy-lidded eyes made it difficult to guess her thoughts.

"Here you are," said Suzanne. I strained to hear Édouard over their voices.

"I have finally discovered the color of the atmosphere—it is violet," Édouard went on from his position by the window. I could feel him watching me and was tempted to communicate with my eyes. But I didn't dare risk revealing my feelings, so I focused on stirring my tea. "C'est vrai, one must really paint outdoors to realize true colors," he pronounced. It was obvious that Édouard was speaking to me, responding to my years of pleas that he paint *en plein air*, but I clutched my hands and forced myself not to react.

Suzanne broke into my thoughts. "Berthe, now that you are settled in Paris, we can visit every day."

"I would love to see you," I paused to sip my tea before I continued, "when I'm not working." This was a polite exaggeration. Nothing about her plain, round face or thin hair pulled into a tight bun encouraged any desire to rest my eyes on her more than was necessary. Still, her eager expression told the story of the solitary life Suzanne lived. What must fill her days, other than cooking and keeping house? These family dinners were the only social occasions she shared with Édouard.

"Surely a lady needs a daily social hour."

"Just as an artist needs her working hours." I heard a low chuckle behind me. If Édouard was listening, I would respond to him. Referring to his announcement about painting Monet's family in their garden, I suggested, "Perhaps I could paint you in your garden, instead?"

"Perhaps," was her curt retort to my rebuff. When I could not deny my need to look at Édouard for another instant, I glanced in his direction while leaning forward to set my cup and saucer on a table— just in time to see him turning back to face Eugène.

After our guests left, Eugène and I sat before the dying fire in my sitting room.

"I came back from England feeling strong and eager to work, but I have yet to find time to paint at all. Suzanne expects now to be my best friend."

"It wouldn't hurt for you to be friendly with your sister-in-law." He rubbed his temples; the evening had brought on one of his migraines, or I might have brought it upon him myself because I was in poor spirits.

"No one would expect Édouard to spend his afternoons paying calls and writing notes."

"But one must be congenial."

"It is so time consuming. I have my work to consider!" My husband's affronted air alerted me that he interpreted this comment to be critical of the fact that he had received no offers of employment as yet. The income we received from the Manet property in Gennevilliers that Eugène oversaw and from his family's other investments was substantial, and a gentleman as retiring as Eugène was not inclined to pursue an occupation. He was doing so at my urging.

"You know I am considering that tax collector position in Grenoble through your mother's connections." He spoke in the almost inaudible tone that he used when struggling to remain calm. I could understand how he might not think that his duty to Maman extended to allowing her manage his career.

But I was too irritable to suppress my feelings in order to accommodate Eugène's. I went on, "Maman has seen for herself that holding a civil servant post is a good idea when the stock market is so volatile." Stocks and bonds had lost almost half their value during the war, so our family had been grateful that Papa had had a position to return to when it was over. "And I agree with her that every self-respecting man should earn an income, no matter how impressive his inheritance." The idea of an indolent husband repelled me. I wanted a man whose ambition matched my own.

"I've applied for interesting positions from Istanbul to Africa, as you well know, but nothing has come of any of them."

"All the more reason for me to sell paintings."

This comment cut him to the quick. "Are you implying that I cannot support my wife?"

"That's not what I meant." We examined one other, as we each revealed another layer of ourselves to the person whom we had married.

"I'm not an artist, but I have much to recommend me." My husband's voice was still quiet, but filled with repressed fury. I supposed this sprang from his frustration at not being able to live up to my expectations.

"Eugène…"

"Nor am I the most exciting man in Paris." Now his words were an icy hiss. "Still, I believe I am worthy of your respect."

"Please. Stop."

"When you modeled for my brother, he no doubt regaled you with tales of his nightlife." I couldn't deny that; I'd listened to Édouard's stories with rapt attention. "Wouldn't it be better if he spent some time with his son? Instead, I am the one who takes Léon on outings."

"I hadn't realized—Eugène, that is so good of you."

"Perhaps you find me too good. Shall I spend my evenings with the demi-monde and take mistresses? Would you prefer a philanderer?"

"How dare you think such a thing!"

"I must know: did Édouard seduce you as he did his other models?"

"Do you think of me as a common model, willing to do whatever an artist requests in order to earn a few more francs?"

"I can see that he still fascinates you."

"We have artistic interests in common that few can understand." I regretted my words even as I said them. Now I had made Eugène feel excluded as an artist as well as a husband.

"You have the shell of a heart," he said as he stalked out, leaving me alone in the room.

❧

How comforting to have the duchess to tea! She was impeccable in the latest style, a fringed skirt and a short, fitted jacket, with a cunning arrangement of ribbons and feathers at the back of her tiny bonnet. She gave the impression of being smaller than the last time we'd met. And, in the year since our last visit, her face had splintered into a thousand fine lines, her delicate beauty shattered like one of the porcelain cups I'd unpacked after the siege. I wondered how she had aged so quickly. Still, it was wonderful to see her.

"Let me look at you, fresh from your honeymoon trip. You'll be sure to tell me if there's to be any addition to the family, won't you?"

I busied myself with the teapot as I thought of my marital relations with Eugène. When he came to my room at night, he never undressed, only lifted his nightshirt. He was gentle, too timid. I had been truly taken only once in my life, and my husband's faltering manner promised that I never would be again. Even Édouard had seemed taken aback by my wanton behavior, so I was careful that Eugène not witness any passion on my part.

"I've been waiting on events, and till now fortune hasn't favored us."

I held out a plate of profiteroles, but the duchess shook her head and waved them away.

"No, thank you. I have no appetite. But please, enjoy one without me."

I set down the plate and moved a large pastry to one side so that it balanced the two smaller ones on the other side. "Are you ill?" I asked. She did appear pale.

"Only poor health could keep me from Paris," she admitted. When she coughed into her handkerchief and left a tell-tale stipple of blood on it, I realized with a fright that she was battling consumption.

"Have you contracted the artist's disease?"

"No, I'm only sick at heart."

"Ah oui, the gossip." There was no point in dissembling about her downfall. Her face was drawn. She appeared too exhausted to evince either indignity or shame. But I felt indignant on her behalf. The public ignored her refinement and talent in favor of malicious rumors.

People were still talking about Alphone Daudet's vile novel that featured a character based on the Duchess of Colonna. The author referred to her "virile" sculpting ability and implied that this masculine trait led to promiscuous behavior:

> She has, because of her name as a society lady and an artist, that court of admirers a free woman can allow herself, that seductiveness accorded by liberty and independence.

Daudet was rumored to be yet another Parisian syphilitic, so I did not see him as being in a position to judge my friend.

The duchess had remained unmarried for too long. Behavior which society might excuse in a young widow became shameful in a woman of a certain age, fodder for *Le Petite Journal.*

"What hurts more than the disgrace is feeling too weak to work. I've decided to go to Italy."

"Have you considered a stay at a sanatorium in Germany?" The best health facilities were said to be there.

"I want to be home, in Italy."

"Who will accompany you there?"

"I am on my own these days."

"I hate to think of you all alone!" I also meant that I hated to think of myself without any opportunities to see my old friend.

My uncharacteristic outburst had startled her. She had too much pride to be seen as a lonely invalid, so I reigned in my emotions and poured us each more tea. "I will miss you," I said, managing an even tone to avoid upsetting my fragile friend.

The duchess was trying, in turn, not to upset me. She called up all of her charm to continue the conversation. "I hope you will soon be working, producing those paintings which seem to be windows open to nature."

To match her faultless façade, I mustered an enthusiastic response. "England was like a brisk breeze coursing through my soul. I can't wait to get started on new paintings."

"Do get started, mon amie," she said, before coughing again.
"I wouldn't dream of doing otherwise," I promised her.

Chapter Twenty-Four

Paris

Winter~Spring 1876

But there were obstacles. My mother-in-law expected the same fawning attention from me that she got from Suzanne, which I was unprepared to give to her. And Suzanne stopped by uninvited and chattered without pause as I unpacked my paintings from England and set up a work area in my small sitting room, where my work wouldn't interfere with our family life. Eugène and I had been eager to move into one of the modern apartment buildings on avenue d'Eylau, but while there were many rooms in our apartment, only the drawing and dining rooms were spacious. With the two overstuffed chintz chairs from our home in Passy before the fireplace, there was little space in the sitting room for an easel and stool, let alone walls where I could to hang canvases to dry or a worktable at which to mix paints.

Later that day as we had our tea, Maman sat in the same chair that had accommodated Suzanne an hour before and listened to my grievances about my sister-in-law. I had accepted that I would never have Édouard, but to have to count his wife as one of my sisters was too much to ask.

"Really, you are so superior to her," assured Maman, "that you shouldn't pay her any more heed than if her plump person were not of this world." Perhaps it was because I was becoming acquainted with Monet and Renoir, as courteous as any gentlemen I knew, but I was starting to see that Maman was a bit of a snob. And I was, too, or at least I had been. Surviving the siege and submitting to marriage had humbled me.

Maman leaned back in the chair with a sigh. Since our return to Paris, both Eugène and I had observed how enervated Maman often seemed to be.

"You must paint. When I took your painting of the Boursier sisters to Durand-Ruel's gallery while you were in England, I was impressed to learn how much he's been charging for your work."

While she paused to catch her breath, I considered how widowhood and war had made Maman even more modern. No longer needing to please Papa, she was free to engage with society in ways she'd never have considered when she was a proper wife. And after the privations of war, she saw the sense in my creating paintings that would sell—the higher the price, the better.

"And when Monsieur Hoschède stopped in and purchased the painting right out of my hands," Maman went on, "I was staggered by the sum he offered—eight hundred francs!"

The Sisters had finally sold! It had hung in my studio for years. Buoyed by my satisfaction with *Harbor at Lorient,* I'd pushed the settee in our drawing room up next to the double glass doors, and had finally managed to capture the light for an indoor painting. I'd been happy with the way that double portrait turned out. What at first glance appeared to be no more than the usual pleasant depiction of two well-dressed, attractive sisters—one could almost take them for Edma and me—was unmistakably mine. On closer examination, the careful viewer would notice that the sisters' hands almost, but did not quite, touch, and that they stared, unseeing, into the distance, their focus inward. The women's lack of sentimentality and their reverie marked the painting as a Morisot.

The owner of Printemps and La Samaritaine, the new department stores in the city, had already bought some of my other paintings. He'd called my work spontaneous and delightful.

"I remember how much I adored the strong will you displayed as a child," Maman mused. "I've seen how fearless you are in pursuing your career. What I saw at Durand-Ruel's gallery convinced me that you are on the right path. I made a vow to myself that day, to help you in whatever way I could."

"Merci, Maman. But you are not well. Let me…" I reached to adjust a needlepoint pillow behind her, but Maman waved me away.

"You go on now, ma chére. Use this time to paint, not to pamper your old mother." She leaned back in her chair, exhausted.

"I am happy to care for the woman who nursed me through the siege." Her criticism of me had slowed after she saw me married. And it had ceased entirely since she'd witnessed Durand-Ruel and Hoschède, two men of the world, enthusiastic about my work.

"Bértât," she said, taking my hand, "all the ordeals we have endured together have considerably strengthened the bonds that link mother and daughter." She gave me a fond smile. "But you must paint, whether I am well or not."

Through the sitting room doorway, I took in her boudoir. It wasn't England, but if I could not leave the house to be in nature, I could use these familiar surroundings as my studio. The dressing table, the cheval mirror, and the settee would have to serve as backdrops for my models. "Then I will paint right here!" I announced.

Through the winter months of 1876, I produced a series of women at their toilette. The first was of a young woman with a hand mirror, powdering her face. Maman watched with interest from her chaise longue as I employed the sketchy, fragmented style I had developed while attempting to capture the bobbing ships in England. I painted another model washing her feet in a basin. We'd had a ceramic sink and toilet installed in our home in Passy after Papa read about the ones on display at the Great Exhibition at the Crystal Palace in London. But the water pressure in Paris was so minimal that we still used washbasins and pitchers in our boudoirs. I mixed white lead paint into ultramarine blue for water, then added still more white. For a touch of violet accent on the washbasin, I mixed vermillion with cobalt blue.

For the third boudoir painting, I posed a woman arranging her blonde hair before Maman's First Empire cheval mirror. I had become enamored with white, painting long, overlapping strokes just tinted with blue or pink. Maman paused in her needlework to pluck a creamy camellia from the flower arrangement on the table next to her. "Place it on the dressing table, there, between the powder puff and the crystal decanter," she said. The painting became a symphony in white. I loaned the model one of my black velvet ribbons to draw the viewer's eye to the nape of her neck. That should show my fellow artists that other parts of a woman's body could be as alluring as a bare breast.

I used short sittings to preserve the freshness of the moment and finished the paintings using the memories of my sisters and mother and myself in the privacy of our boudoirs—washing, arranging our coiffures, fastening our gowns.

These were not the bold, provocative women of Manet's paintings, but real women, lost in their daydreams. I looked at them looking at themselves, not as a man who would eat them with his eyes, but as a woman familiar with the preparations required for such masculine appraisal. A woman performing her toilette for male delectation is a work of art of her own making. Until she has placed the last hairpin, tied the last ribbon, and turned to make a final assessment of her reflection in the mirror, she is unfinished, just as Impressionist paintings were described as being unfinished.

It was refreshing to re-enter this feminine world after spending every day of our marriage with my husband.

By the following spring, a second Impressionist exhibition was planned. Both Édouard and Eugène were invited to participate, but both had declined, one out of pride and the other out of humility. So I was the only woman and the only Manet whose work was on display at the opening in April 1876, held in Durand-Ruel's gallery. Drawings, watercolors, and pastels were in the first room and paintings in the second. I showed several works from our trip to England, along with the oil paintings of women at their toilette.

Édouard and Degas strolled together to where I stood in front of my paintings. "You've pushed you-know-who down to fifth position,"

Édouard murmured in my ear. I didn't know who, but I liked hearing that.

"All infused by your feminine vision," was Degas's verdict.

"*Merci beaucoup, monsieur.*"

"The critics are praising your palette," Degas said, snapping open the afternoon edition of *Le Temps.* "*She finds the utmost delicacy in the grays and the most refined pale tones among the pinks…*"

Édouard leaned down to tell me, "Zola described your boudoir paintings as veritable pearls."

I was thrilled by Zola's words and, in spite of myself, by Édouard's deep voice.

Degas shuffled through *La Tribune* and said, "Théodore Duret writes that one has the idea that you scattered flower petals over the canvas." I found that to be an appealing image. He bent over to examine the bottom corner of a painting. "I see you still sign your maiden name."

"I don't want to be confused with that other Manet," I said with a sideways glance at Édouard. He responded to my taunt with smiling eyes, the small way in which we still connected with one another.

At that moment, we heard a commotion near the gallery entrance. Eugène rushed toward us, flushed and overexcited, almost maniacal. "He called you a *gourgandine!*" he burst out, pointing to a sour-looking little man. "I challenged him to a duel!" Eugène shouted, before running to the front room of the gallery where Pissarro was holding back the foul-mouthed man.

"Monsieur Degas! Please!" I begged.

"I'll stop him!" Caught up in the excitement, my short, round-shouldered colleague dove into the fracas and clutched Eugène's arm.

"It may be brazen of me to show my work in public," I said to Édouard, who stood outside the skirmish with Renoir, both of them too debonair to become embroiled in a brawl. "But a *gourgandine?* I am not a street walker!"

"You are saved by your delicacy of character and innate inability to be vulgar," Édouard assured me before calling out advice to his brother, *"Courage, mon frère!"*

Mon Dieu, the man was impossible.

I turned toward the mêlée just in time to see the retiring, white-bearded Pissarro punching one of our paying customers in the face. The sour little man who had maligned my virtue sank to the floor.

Degas extracted my hectic husband from the fray. He came out with his fists swinging as Durand-Ruel called to a gendarme in the street. Monet came to the aid of his friend, pulling Pissarro back with brawny arms.

Sans doubt, some of my colleagues were rough around the edges. But what a shock to witness such explosive behavior from my self-effacing husband, who had most recently been busying himself with framing and placing my work. After little more than a year of marriage, I was starting to get used to his changes in mood, his anxieties and anger. But observing Eugène with his jacket unbuttoned, his hair disheveled, and a sheen of perspiration on his livid face, I feared I had married a madman.

Chapter Twenty-Five
Maurecourt
February 1877

My productive streak was halted that winter when Edma, who was pregnant for the third time at the advanced age of thirty-seven, came to stay with us for her confinement while Adolphe was at sea. My sister's fertility seemed to mock me.

When Edma caught me eying her rounded figure, she said, "Don't envy me, little sister. Your time will come."

"I can't deny that I would like a child of my own," I said, an understatement that did not hint at my tearful nights spent yearning for a living creation, one that would fill my arms. "But for now, I am happy that you provide a reprieve from my domestic life."

"Your work serves that purpose, doesn't it?"

"When I can fit it in. I don't fulfill my duties to my family's satisfaction or work enough to satisfy myself."

"I wish that I had the chance to experience your dilemma," Edma sighed.

"But you have your precious Nini and Blanche, and another baby on the way. You may one day take up painting again, but I cannot conjure a child from the air."

Edma considered that. "Why don't you go to Maurecourt to paint for a few days?" she suggested. As always, she knew just what I needed and was ready to provide it. She must have intuited my unspoken concern about our mother's failing health, because she added, "I can care for Maman."

"Your house in the country? Alone? That would be heaven!"

❧

I escaped to the Pontillion estate in Maurecourt, an ivy-swathed, stone château topped by a mansard roof and surrounded by brown winter fields. There, I lost myself under the restless, shifting clouds of late winter in the Île de France. Since my marriage and our move into a small apartment, there had been no vantagepoint from which to paint landscapes, and my domestic duties precluded painting excursions. Now I remembered the healing effects of creating transient little dream worlds that only I could control. Life was chaos, but my small, gentle scenes were organized just as I wanted them to be. When I was lost in the darkness of melancholy, I could paint not just light colors, but the light itself. Only my nervous, broken brushstrokes revealed my inner turmoil.

Best of all was the separation from Eugène. His headaches and delicate health I could understand, but "high-strung" did not begin to describe my husband. Nor did his health explain his physical reaction to the mere memory of the war or his enraged response to the sailors who witnessed my hat flying off. I, too, suffered from the anxiety and fatigue of neurasthenia, but not to such a debilitating degree. In fact, it was only work that pulled me out of that dark hole. And, unlike my husband's behavior at the last Impressionist exhibtion, I would never resort to violence under any circumstances. Apart from the lowing of the golden jersey cows in a meadow across the river and the chatter of passing geese, I luxuriated in quiet solitude that first day while I painted two small watercolors. My group portrait of cows consisted of green scrawls to indicate grass in the foreground, and jots of brown for the bovines. This painted portion of the paper created an oval shape, so that the white edges framed the scene.

After a simple dinner, I pulled a chair near the fire and basked in the quiet of a country evening. My thoughts turned to Eugène. How had we come so far from the comfortable companionship we'd enjoyed during our honeymoon only a year-and-a-half ago? Perhaps I should not press him to find employment. After all, I was almost as reserved as my husband; I would abhor spending every day in a public setting. Or maybe having Maman living with us diverted too much of my attention away from my husband. The crackling fire lulled me, and I drowsed, dreaming of the kind of marriage I wanted.

The postal delivery the next day brought a small package from Édouard. Inside was a note that read, "My dear Berthe, do not be surprised to receive this latest style easel, very handy for pastels." He was staying nearby in Bellevue, he wrote, undergoing therapy for recently-diagnosed neuralgia in his leg.

The following day brought an even bigger surprise. I heard crunching gravel and poked my head out my boudoir window to see a closed-top brougham carriage pull up to the front door. As I glanced in the mirror to make myself presentable for company, Edma's new maid, Marie-Louise, stuck her head in the door to say, "Madame Manet, the gentleman says to tell you that Monsieur Manet has arrived."

Disappointment that my solo adventure had been interrupted mixed with hope. Perhaps my husband sensed that we needed some time alone, away from family demands and career concerns. But both of those sensations coalesced into a feeling like an electrical shock when I saw a familiar long leg and silver-tipped cane emerge from the carriage below. Édouard and I saw one another at family gatherings, and we corresponded about our work, but it was beyond the pale for a man—even my brother-in-law—to visit me alone. Thinking fast, I said, "Marie-Louise, tell the cook that my husband will be joining me for lunch," as I pinched my cheeks and smoothed my hair.

"Oui, madame." She turned to go down the stairs, but I passed her, flying, with no need for feet to touch wood. Édouard and I arrived at the entry hall at the same time. I held on to the heavy oak newel post and he tapped his cane against the slate floor as we waited for the maid to retreat to the kitchen.

"I hope you don't mind my intruding unannounced," he said with a wry smile. "Suzanne returned to Paris, so I am all alone."

With a sidelong glance at Édouard, I replied, "Welcome to Maurecourt, *Eugène*," loud enough for the help to hear.

Over soup and bread, I asked Édouard about the treatments he was having at Bellevue. He made light of them, saying, "I highly recommend ice-water massages—if you are a polar bear or an arctic seal."

"The pain from your damaged nerves must be excruciating."

"Enduring an enforced rest with Suzanne as my only company is far more trying than any medical procedure," he said with a wink. He'd always assiduously avoided any derogatory remarks about his wife, which I might once have enjoyed. But I did not respond to his comment, unable to play the woman scorned, or the gracious *belle-soeur*, or anything but a happy hostess.

It was a perfect day. After lunch, we bundled up against the chilly breeze and walked for a while, leaning into one another and laughing after a group of geese turned and chased us. Every woman imagines the man she loves when he was a child. I could conjure an image of Édouard as a tousled and flushed boy at the Manet country home in Gennevilliers, tormenting the geese, running through fields, and leaping into the river. I wished I could have a little boy like that for myself.

When Édouard began limping, leaning on the cane that had in the past been no more than a fashionable accessory, I realized that he was experiencing discomfort in his leg. We turned back to the house. "Shall we sit on the terrace?" I suggested, when we arrived. Édouard bundled up in blankets, and I set out my new easel in the wan February sun to paint another small watercolor of the river.

"I was thinking of you recently, while I was working," Édouard began, as I took up my brush.

"Oh?"

"I was so taken by your painting of the woman before the cheval glass, that I, too, was moved to paint a woman at her mirror."

"Did you paint her from behind, as I did?"

"Oui, madame, I followed your example exactly." He tapped his cane on the stone terrace to emphasize his point.

"It's not the first time you have emulated me."

"Non, but this was my most successful attempt. The light palette—

not a drop of black—the feathery strokes, *les belles taches*, all were my homage to the artist Berthe Morisot." His expressive face held my attention a second too long. I let out a long breath. When he noticed, I looked away.

Had I really been holding my breath during the two years of my marriage? Being in the presence of the suave intelligence of the artist I most admired again made me feel like I was gulping fresh air. The afternoon disappeared while we talked. As the sun lowered and the late-winter light struck him full-face, Édouard's blue eyes almost glowed. Was that silver in his beard? To myself I tallied that it had been almost twenty years since we first met in the Louvre.

We shivered as a chill February wind came up off the river. "It's getting late," I said. "Will you stay for dinner, Édouard?"

"If I may."

"I'll go speak to the cook." I went to the kitchen where the cook had already foreseen the change in plans and had a terrine in the oven. "I won't require your services after dinner is served. Please tell Marie-Louise that she is also free to go," I told her. I advised her about which wine to bring up from the cellar, then went upstairs to change for dinner.

Alone in my boudoir, I had to admit to myself that this visit was more than a call between artistic colleagues. It was yet another of Édouard's highly irregular impulses. I considered sending him away. He could be in Bellevue by dark. The alternative was an evening of lively conversation, nourishment for my very soul. My mirror revealed a face that was brightened and lifted, the decades since I'd met Édouard erased from my countenance. I dressed with the utmost care for dinner.

The dining room at Maurecourt, with its wood-paneled walls and crackling fire in the small, red-veined marble fireplace, felt intimate despite its high ceilings and tall windows. We had finished our dinner, and a bottle of wine had made Édouard garrulous. Alone, our defenses fell away and we reverted to our former intimacy. Édouard was able to speak, unguarded, and I was unafraid to meet his eye.

"You of all people know that I am like Paris, a well-dressed exterior covering the darkest of secrets," he insisted. I focused on my wine glass, not wanting to acknowledge what I knew, how Édouard had taken on the onus of his father's sins. "But if you want to truly know me, you can study *Ball at the Opéra*."

"I have seen your painting, of course."

"Have you noticed Polichinelle the clown, on the left? That is me, a man in disguise."

"As I recall, *all* the men in that painting are masked—black masks with their black evening clothes." I didn't mention the women he'd depicted, the ones who attended those Saturday night balls in their short pants and fancy costumes. It was beyond the limits of my imagination to conjure up the lights, the music and noise of the crowd, the frank sexuality of such a gathering.

"*Oui, les foules noire*, like a crowd of undertakers!" He glowered over the half-melted candles between us.

"Mallarmé raved about your 'dark harmonies' and the nuances in the blacks…"

"Yet that did not keep the Salon from rejecting me once again. But did you notice that only the clown is in full costume, just as I am the most complete hypocrite in a city full of them?"

"Édouard, you are too hard on yourself. It is not your fault that you have been forced to hide your father's actions."

"Ma chère Berthe, I'm not talking about that particular hypocrisy, although I can understand that the litany becomes confusing." A long sigh escaped him. "Non, I am referring to my entire career, the way I grovel for acceptance from men I despise. The way I've turned my back on politics—my head is full of scenes of the war that I have never painted." He pushed himself away from the table. "And the way I walked away from love, pretending that I was doing the honorable thing."

Speechless, I held up another bottle of wine, and Édouard nodded. "Instead, I've embraced a life of sad pleasure, like a tired café singer seducing the barmaid at the end of the night."

"Stop it, please." I pulled the cork and poured another full glass for each of us, although I had already imbibed far more than I was used to. "You are the most admired artist among artists and one of the most beloved men in Paris."

"If that is so, why does abuse rain down on me like hail?" He drained his glass.

I had no answer. *Certainment*, civil servants and merchants with money preferred paintings they could understand, but it was a mystery to me that a larger portion of the public hadn't yet recognized Édouard's brilliance. Society loved the charismatic *roué*, but not his paintings. To supplement his family income, he was forced to paint portraits of his society friends.

"The fools. They've never stopped calling me inconsistent." With a raised eyebrow, he said, "They couldn't have said anything more flattering."

My feelings for Édouard made me a match for his inconsistency, but I didn't find the word flattering.

He gave me his old debonair smile. His air was studied nonchalance, but I was familiar with his look of desperation.

He asked, "Are you happy, Berthe?"

Was I to complain about how his brother treated me? Or the fact that I still had no baby? Even if Eugène gave me a child, it would be Eugène's, not the child of the man I loved.

But would a baby have to be my husband's? Who would ever know the difference between one Manet child and another? I was so desperate for a baby and, at thirty-five, I had so little time left to have one. A plan sprang, fully-formed, into my head.

It seemed safer to return his smile than to answer his question, though I couldn't help but add, "I am at this moment."

"You are still exquisitely beautiful," he said. Then he came to me, offering his arm. On his face was a question; on mine, an answer. I stood. He bent toward me and whispered only, "Berthe." As if I had been waiting for him to speak our secret language, I leaned to blow out all of the candles except for one, which I carried as we climbed the stairs.

Once in my boudoir, I set the candle on the bureau and went straight to the bed. This most practiced of lovers seemed frozen by the bureau, but now I was committed to my objective, so I reached out and drew him down next to me. I traced his fine profile with the tip of my finger, from his high forehead down his long, narrow nose to his flared nostrils. He closed his eyes and lay back against the pillows, like a battle-weary warrior.

"Don't you dare fall asleep," I warned him, tapping the ear that jutted out a bit more than the other. I couldn't help but think how Eugène might have been irritated if I had bothered him when he was tired. But Édouard laughed and opened his eyes to watch me undress. I took my time, luxuriating in the fact that, this once, we had the whole night together.

"You look just like a girl I once met at the Louvre," Édouard said, when I unpinned my hair and it fell down my back. But after I unhooked my skirt and let it drop, untied the bows on the front of my bodice, and let my chemise fall to the floor, he said, "I must be mistaken. You're a woman, not a girl."

Our bodies were still familiar to one another, after all those years. His crooked ear, the mole on my left thigh. When I slid next to him on the bed and lay my leg atop his, Édouard winced. I saw that it was pain that exhausted him, so I was careful with his ailing limb after that. We laughed as I fumbled with the lambskin sheath he provided. We made love with more tenderness than passion. Hearing his heartbeat against mine and feeling our breath mingle replenished the élan vital that I'd been lacking. Afterward, I kept the candle lit and watched Édouard fall asleep in my arms.

"I will never stop loving you," I whispered.

He mumbled, "Berthe" in his sleep and pulled me closer to him.

Tears rolled down my face and onto his shoulder as I mourned what might have been.

The next morning I stood again at the window of my boudoir, watching Édouard's carriage disappear under turbulent clouds down the tree-lined allée. There was no way to tell if I would ever again spend a night with the man I loved. But it was a comfort to think that I had another precious memory of him to keep with me always. When I turned away from the window, feeling beloved and desirable, and caught sight of myself in a mirror, I was smiling.

The night I returned from Maurecourt, Eugène came to my room, emboldened by his joy at my homecoming. His tap at my door was so light that I was uncertain whether I had heard anything. But then, a soft "Berthe?"

I had been looking forward to snuggling up in bed and reliving my night with Édouard in my imagination, but Eugène was my husband, after all, so I came to the door.

"Are you exhausted from your journey, my dear?" he asked. Far from weary, I felt more alive than I had since we'd returned from England. I did not rebuff Eugène after my rendezvous with Édouard in Maurecourt. *Vraiment*, in the dark, the scent of his skin helped me to pretend that it was Édouard in my bed.

"I must take you on holiday more often," my husband murmured as I moved and sighed beneath him.

Chapter Twenty-Six

Paris

March 1877~Spring 1879

Cornélie Morisot, who had once epitomized all that was feminine, attractive, and captivating, was debased by cancer. It seemed that during those few days I had spent in Maurecourt, she had become skeletal. Edma met me at the door in tears upon my return to deliver the news that our lovely mother did not have long to live.

I tried to have a final conversation with her. "Maman, I've caused you so much trouble in the past. I want to find a way to thank you for allowing me my art."

She would have none of it. "Don't be morbid," she snapped. "I'm not going to die tomorrow." It was not our family's way to discuss emotions, the less pleasant ones such as fear or sorrow in particular. That night I dreamed of Maman at her most vivacious, when she was a préfet's wife, off to host a ball in honor of the President—and future emperor—Louis Napoleon. My sisters and I could hardly breathe when she drifted down the stairs in a cloud of rose-scented perfume, wearing a pink satin gown with layers of tulle embellishing a full skirt and train. She was the picture of youth and happiness. In the morning I woke up knowing what Maman needed. Edma and I came into her room with champagne flutes and chocolates, calling out, "Madame Morisot is invited to a soirée!" She couldn't drink or eat, but she sat up in bed and smiled as her daughters toasted her. A ghastly vestige of the charming Cornélie responded by reflex to laughter and gaiety.

When she died, our small, black-garbed group—my sisters, Tiburce, Eugène, and I—once again made its way through a late-winter snow to huddle by a fresh grave, just as we had after Papa's death. Maman's last weeks had been hideous, but it was even more awful to think of the weeks, months, and years ahead, with a hole where she had been. After dividing Maman's belongings with Edma and Yves—Tiburce had collected what he wanted after Papa died—Edma returned home to await her baby's birth. I cast about for something to do. Lacking any desire to engage with society, I found myself following Pasie around the kitchen, compiling market lists for foods that grief had left me too nauseated to eat. I ordered mourning gowns, but when the fittings were finished, I declined all invitations to events where I might have worn them. I thought writing down my thoughts would bring relief, but found my words dull.

I fell back into my painted world. I'd always worked to prove to Maman that I could succeed, but as I grasped that she was gone and not coming back, I now painted—for the first time—only for me. To cheer myself, I engaged a model and returned to a favorite motif, a young woman in a gilt chair next to a window, surrounded by flowers, immersed in light. I was less concerned with a depiction of modernity than with developing my own personal style, for my own satisfaction. Using bold jabs of white, I tried to duplicate the dazzling play of sunlight on a summer's day that made the woman's features melt into the vibrations of the atmosphere.

When Édouard spied my finished work, *Summer,* while at our house for a Manet family dinner, he'd proclaimed his ambition also to produce a similar work in which figure and background were indistinguishable. Thinking back, I remembered that I had been the one to convince Édouard to paint *en plein air.* And he'd told me that night at Maurecourt that he'd painted a woman at her mirror in light colors and feathery strokes in homage to my style. The great Édouard Manet wanted to emulate *me.* I had become an artist in my own right.

Gustave Caillebotte was a gentleman painter from Argenteuil, recruited to join our group by Monet and Renoir when they met him there on one of their painting excursions. An engineer with an ordered mind, he took it upon himself to organize a third Impressionist exhibition. He wrote to me after he'd held a meeting with the other members of our group. I had never attended such meetings, as it was improper for me to be involved in the business end of our artistic endeavors. Yet it would have been nice to receive notification of the meeting before it had taken place, so I might have sent Eugène as an emissary to express my opinions about such details as dates and locations.

I had to rush to prepare for the April 1877 exhibition, only a month after Maman's death, but focusing on the paintings gave me strength and purpose. I assembled five oils in all, with a few watercolors and pastels. I was most proud of the painting where I had perched my model on the edge of her chair in a white dress with a sash of flowers and her hair drawn up, wearing opéra gloves and a diamond necklace, waiting to go to her first ball. She looked off to the side, seemingly calm, but the frenzied green and white background conveyed her nervous excitement.

Young Woman in a Ball Gown was hung in the same room as Renoir's huge *Ball at the Moulin de la Galette*, a painting that showed members of the working class enjoying their day off with dancing and drinking in a beer garden. My *Woman* would seem to be going to an altogether different ball. I thought of what Maman would have said about positioning an exquisite young debutante next to lower-class revelers. Still, it would have pleased her to see how many people visited our show, five hundred each day, drawn in by the banners announcing the Third Impressionist Exhibition that hung all over the city.

Monsieur Caillebotte turned out to be a master of organization. He rented a large apartment for us, across from Durand-Ruel's gallery. Visitors entering the first room were assailed by depictions of modernity, surrounded by Monet's huge paintings of the puffing trains under the high glass ceiling of the Gare St. Lazarre and Caillebotte's life-sized scenes of the new Parisian boulevards. The large room in the center held Renoir's high-spirited *Ball at the Moulin de la Galette*, without question the centerpiece of the show, along with his *Girl on a Swing*. The disconcerting perspective, alarming style, and bold colors of Cézanne's works set off the soft-edged figures and subtler hues of my paintings and Renoir's.

Degas had a small room at the back all for himself, to which I returned again and again. His portrayals of ballet dancers were like my toilette paintings; both revealed the work required to create the illusion of effortless beauty. I saw the influence of Japanese prints in Degas's diagonal lines, as well as the way he often painted from slightly above and cropped scenes close. Harsh stage lighting created stark contrast with the soft pastel costumes of the dancers.

I was thrilled to see Edma and Adolphe in the crowd. They had traveled to Paris for the express purpose of attending the exhibition. Edma broke away from her husband to join me, and I took her arm and walked her to my wall of paintings, asking about Edme, her new baby boy, whom she'd named after Papa and herself. Edma seemed exhausted by her train travel, responding to my questions with one-word answers.

"Edma, what do you think of my boudoir paintings?" I asked when we reached my work. "Not as energetic as my English paintings, but don't they have something of Utamaro's prints, the intimate gesture?"

Edma seemed distracted, but still she was drawn to the paintings. "I like the strokes of light on the figures," she said with her eyes fixed on *Woman at her Toilette*. I noticed the camellia tucked into the composition and remembered that had been Maman's suggestion.

"Oui, oui, I think it brings them to life." She didn't respond, lost, I thought, in her examination of my work. "Thank you for coming, dear sister." I stepped forward to kiss her cheek.

She pulled away and turned on me, balling up her gloves and blurting, "I know what you did."

"What do you mean?" I asked, knowing in an instant to what she was referring.

How could I have thought she would not find out? Her maid must have remarked that my "husband" had visited me in Maurecourt. I'd chosen to believe that Edma's servants would think that Édouard was *my* Monsieur Manet, but any mention of Eugène would have struck Edma as false, since she saw him every evening while she stayed in our house to care for Maman. If only I could have taken Pasie with me. She would not have seen nor said anything—the perfect accomplice. "Edma," I pleaded, ashamed that I'd deceived my sister. "Nothing happened."

"Do you think you can have everything?" Her face twisted, but she struggled to compose herself. I knew she would sooner die than shed tears in public. "A husband, and another man," she waved toward the wall of paintings—"and this, as well?"

It was "this" that bothered her the most, I suspected. "You could have this, too," I pointed out.

She wheeled around. "I'm not speaking out of envy, but out of common decency!"

I tried to stop her, but she spun away. I called out, "Edma!" but she did not turn back. We had attracted unwanted attention—side glances and eyes peeking over programs. I was dazed and felt on the verge of fainting. I sat down on a small gilt chair, unsure if it was strong enough to hold the weight of my heavy heart. I had just lost Maman; was I now to lose Edma, as well?

Eugène emerged from the throng, exulting, "Who could have predicted that only four years after the disaster of our first exhibition, our third show would be a notable Parisian event?" I couldn't muster a response, but in the over-excited state the exhibitions always incited in him, he didn't notice. "What you have worked to attain for almost twenty years is finally coming to pass."

"It appears to be." My flat voice caught his attention.

He looked puzzled. "You are being taken seriously as a professional artist," he pointed out.

I forced myself to use a brighter tone when I added, "And yet, I don't care as much as I might have in the past."

"Don't care?" His brow furrowed in puzzlement.

I even managed a smile when I said, "Non. You see, Eugène…"

I turned to my husband, with one hand at the waist of my black mourning gown. His eyes widened in astonishment, and he took my hands. I was already nodding when he whispered, "You are with child?"

I stopped everything, even painting. Pregnant for the first time at thirty-six years of age, I needed to be careful. After the weeks of nausea ended, I felt the same as before. Was I carrying a child? It seemed unreal. And if I couldn't feel anything, was my baby healthy? Soon enough, though, I felt tiny fingers tickling my ribs from inside, and later, vigorou kicking after meals.

"I'm certain that it's a girl," Eugène told me over and over again, with unwavering conviction. "Our child will want for nothing."

The thought of becoming a father brought out the sweet tenderness that had first drawn me to Eugène. My husband prepared for his new role by furnishing the nursery, having the room papered with a light floral print and fitting it with a cradle and rocking chair. When I came upon him hanging white-ruffled curtains at the windows, he turned to me with a radiant smile and said, "I've fallen in love with her."

I waited endless months, eating more but sleeping less, until I was ready for my pregnancy to be finished. I grew ever more terrified at the thought of giving birth but was willing to go through it because I wanted so much to meet my child. I finally did on 14 November, 1878. I endured the pain of labor, blunted by chloroform. Dr. Rafinesque observed the latest medical practice of washing his hands before approaching me. He preserved my modesty by maintaining eye contact with me throughout the proceedings and working by touch alone. Then I had my precious baby girl. We named her Julie, but called her Bibi.

I regretted that she was not a boy to perpetuate the Manet name, and for the simple reason that each of us, man or woman, is in love with the male sex. But Julie was sweet as an angel, with fat cheeks and a rosy complexion.

And yet, for the first time in a long while, the black days came again. Being confined to bed for the weeks of my recovery reminded me of those months of illness during the siege. Then too, that winter was the coldest since the siege, with icy winds that crept in through the keyholes. I kept to my bed with the curtains drawn, in a dark depression.

One morning while reading *Le Monde*, I came upon a notice of the death of my friend, Adèle d'Affry, the Duchess of Colonna, at the age of forty-two. I dropped the newspaper and fell back against my pillows. My poor, dear duchess was the only one in whom I had dared to confide. I had lived too long. Too many I had known and loved had disappeared. Papa, of course. And I was still mourning Maman. Fanny Claus had died young due to the deprivations of the war, and Monet's wife Camille had succumbed to cancer. The void was great. My grief was made worse by the bronchitis I suffered during the cold months.

It didn't help to hear that Degas, who was always including outsiders in our exhibitions, had invited an American woman to join our uniquely French movement and to take part in the next Impressionist show in April. I had painted only fanciful fans during my confinement. And while Degas planned to dedicate a whole room to the decorated fans in vogue at the time, including his own and Pissarro's, I did not want those to be my sole contribution when the critics were sure to compare me to this American, Mary Cassatt. Adding insult to injury, Durand-Ruel was snapping up her paintings when he still took only one or two of mine at a time, and he had never offered me a solo show as he did the other artists in our group.

Degas presumed that I would participate in the upcoming Impressionist exhibition, but I had already decided that I would not. All would think that I had missed the exhibition in order to care for my infant, and I would let them believe that was my sole reason.

One day, weeks after Julie's birth, I was in bed with her when Pasie came in with a tray.

"Just what you need," announced Eugène. "Something to eat." He took Julie and walked her around the room, speaking to her in a tender tone.

"You know I have no appetite, Eugène. I am so tired; I only want to sleep."

"Yet you don't sleep. And you are as emaciated as if the siege had just ended. How do you expect to keep up your strength?"

He had hit upon my deepest fear, that I wouldn't be strong enough to care for my baby, or that I might become another name on the tally of the dead. "What if I die of consumption like the duchess?" I cried. "What would become of Bibi?"

I felt that I was a failure as a mother. Unable to do much to care for Julie, I obsessed about her health. The tiniest of mewing sounds emanating from the pile of crocheted blankets in the new father's arms sent me into a hand-wringing panic. "Is anything wrong with her?"

"Calm yourself," Eugène insisted. He called out the door to our wet nurse. "Angèle!" Our *second-mére*, the heartiest nurse my husband could find, came in and took Julie. "Try to get some rest," he said, taking the tray and slipping out the door.

I tossed against my pillows, missing my mother, who always knew what to do. "Maman," I moaned.

"Your maman was a great lady," said Pasie, who had remained in the room, tidying up in her unobtrusive manner. "But I am sure that she didn't know any more about how to care for her first child than you do now. You will learn."

"I wish I could be sure."

"I am here to help you, madame." Nearing thirty, an age when ladies' maids often returned to their villages to marry and have children of their own, Pasie was devoted to me, and now to Julie as well. Was it fair for me to keep her from moving on with her life? After a trip home to visit her family, Pasie told me that a gentleman had courted her, a widowed clock-maker with grown children.

"I know that you have someone waiting for you in Toulouse."

"I will stay as long as you need me, madame."

I breathed a sigh of relief. I did need her. Pasie was a treasure.

Eugène deserved credit for taking matters into his own hands. He brought Julie into my boudoir and left her with me, with instructions for Angèle to feed her there. And he brought in the baby's bassinette so that she could sleep near me. "From now on, your baby will never leave your side. Falling in love with her will erase your fears," he proclaimed.

I spent long hours in bed holding my Bibi, singing to her as she gurgled and waved her arms. Eugène was right; it was Julie who cured me. She was like a kitten, always happy, with shining eyes and a wide grin. With her blue eyes and blonde wisps, she was a Manet to her fingertips. I found myself pretending that she was Édouard's child.

I looked down at my daughter. "You are already like your uncle, not a bit like me," I whispered. But I realized that it didn't matter whether Julie was Eugène's or Édouard's. What was important was that she was mine.

As soon as I felt myself again, I began to make paintings of my baby, relying on watercolors in order to work quickly, before her next need arose. The first fine day of spring, I set up Julie and Angèle in the back garden. As always, I wanted to show my subjects surrounded by space and light. Perspective and modeling seemed beside the point. Angèle became a cloud of white in a whirling sea of green. Only her umbrella thrown to one side and her straw hat on the other anchored her to the earth.

From then on, Julie was my primary model. When she grew to be a toddler, I painted her holding her doll or floating her toy boat in the lake in the Bois. She became an angelic, round-faced child, if a sometimes-impatient model. A painting intended to be of Julie on the veranda revealed a tea table with abandoned cups and plates, and a doll thrown, forgotten, on a chair. She had run off before I could finish.

I imagined my grown daughter sitting perched on the edge of her chair in a diamond necklace and opéra gloves, as in my *Young Woman in a Ball Gown*. A vision of myself in my ruched, black-bodiced gown sprang to mind. I remembered Maman taking me to the dress designer to be fitted for that first grown-up evening gown and how much she enjoyed dressing my sisters and me.

It occurred to me that by doing for Julie what Maman had done for me, by embodying her best characteristics, Julie would know the grand-mère she had never met. She would become an attractive, fashionable woman with the *joie de vivre* that Maman would have wanted her to have. In turn, those feminine traits visible in my daughter would keep my mother fresh and alive in my memory. I determined to live long enough to see that.

Chapter Twenty-Seven

Paris

Spring 1882

My *grand-mère* had had what was considered a superior education for a woman of her time. She knew a smattering of ancient history and had an elementary knowledge of science. Maman had been an enthusiastic reader, and she wrote with great facility and charm. I, too, was an educated woman, even if my knowledge was limited to a bit about literature and foreign languages. But no one told me how much I would learn by being a mother. And Julie was only four years old.

One afternoon we took a walk in the city. We stopped at a map dealer's stall by the Seine, where an artist's rendering of the solar system led to a discussion of the sun and the planets. "Here is Earth, where we live," I told Julie.

"I want to live on Saturn," my daughter declared. "It has a halo!"

When we passed a photographer's shop with reproductions of Botticelli's *Primavera* in the window, Julie asked, in a ringing voice for all to hear, "Why is the pretty lady naked?"

"She is just born, like a new baby," I explained.

Along the way, we had to stop to speak with almost everyone on the street. The child taught the mother to be more sociable than she had ever imagined possible. Julie had noticed that some ladies wore slippers, while others wore boots, so she asked each one we passed, *"Chaussures ou bottes?"* When a young mademoiselle humored her by stopping and lifting her skirt to reveal dainty slippers, Julie declared, *"Chaussures!"* and laughed in delight.

I was pleased that the distractions of footwear and the bustle of people and traffic kept my daughter from noticing the men who exited the sidewalk *pissoirs* while still buttoning their trousers. Who knows what high-pitched observations she might have shared about them?

When we arrived in the Jardins de Tuileries, I sank down on an empty bench to catch my breath, put up my parasol to shield my eyes from the sunlight glinting off the water spilling in the Great Basin, and let my thoughts drift like the red boat my daughter dipped into the fountain. I was soon lost in happiness. I'd thought I wanted a son to carry on the Manet name. But a son would have had to go away to school, while Julie would always be with me. She made up for losing Maman, the duchess, and even Edma. Now, as Julie marched on the sandy, interlaced walkways around me, I vowed to myself once again to raise her with the utmost care, as *grand-mère* and Maman had raised their daughters, and to make of her a very chic woman. She could decide for herself whether or not to become an artist.

Julie climbed onto the bench with me, panting and smelling like an overheated puppy. I couldn't resist putting my face in her hair, but when she squirmed, I moved away and said, "Bibi, I have been sitting here contemplating the shadows on the sand. What colors do you see there?"

She considered with care. "I see violet."

"And what colors are in the light on the roof of the Louvre?"

She fidgeted, already finished with the game. "Pink!" she decided.

I decided against asking her to identify the marble statue of Mercury riding Pegasus by the West gate. "*Bien!* Off we go then." The allée de Diane would lead us through the formal flowerbeds and out of the gardens.

"Not so fast, I beg you," came a familiar, deep voice from behind the bench. I tilted my parasol down to hide my flushed and disheveled appearance. I should have remembered that Édouard always walked here at this time of day. Or had I? He and his friend Mallarmé seemed not to notice my state. But it felt strange to run into him in public, unprotected by our roles as relatives or fellow artists. The intimate liaison we had shared, now five years in the past, we had tamped down and never again referred to after we returned to our prescribed roles within the family.

"*Bon après-midi, Madame et Mademoiselle Manet.*"

"*Bonjour, Oncle Édouard!*" cried Julie as she flew into his arms. I confess that I felt a twinge still at her uninhibited embrace, something I could not share with him.

"We've just dined at the Café Tortoni," Mallarmé announced. I was quite familiar with Édouard's favorite luncheon location at number 22 on the fashionable boulevard des Italiens. "The white asparagus was superb."

Édouard sat down, and Julie perched on his knee. The two blue-eyed blondes exchanged wide smiles. He looked from Julie to me, and back again, asking me a question with his eyes. I could feel him calculating the time between our rendezvous in Maurecourt and Julie's birth, something he was only considering now that Julie was growing to resemble him.

I tipped my parasol further down over my eyes, in case Édouard might be inclined to read my expression. Instead, he, adept at letting go of troubling thoughts, turned back to Julie. "Did you know that I used to come here when I was your age?" he asked.

"*Vraiment?*" she asked in wonder. I could see that she could not imagine that her oncle Édouard had ever been so young.

"I lived very close by." He assumed that she would be fascinated by this information, but I knew that my little girl was getting restless sitting on that bony knee. When she hopped down, Édouard rubbed his leg with a grimace. Julie was not heavy. His arthritis must have been worsening.

"Bibi, shall we be off? We don't want to keep the gentlemen from their sketching."

Édouard rustled his drawing pad to indicate its importance, and Mallarmé gave his courtly "au revoir" before they continued on with their promenade. As we stood to leave the Tuileries for the rue de Rivoli, I turned back for a last look at Édouard and noticed that he appeared to be limping in pain.

"Are you ready for a sweet, Bibi?" I asked as I took her hand.

She turned her round face up to me. "May I have a macaron?"

"To the Patisserie Ladurée!" We stepped off the curb, and Julie skipped into the crush of carts and carriages as I held tight her small, slippery hand.

"Bonjour!" she called to a one-legged man wearing a tattered, gray National Guard military jacket, making his way across the street on crutches. His weary face broke into a smile. "*Bottes*," she informed me.

The child was like a ray of summery light streaming into the dark and dusty garret of my mind. With Julie, I didn't mind the first white hairs and wrinkles of age. She was all that was left to me of youth and beauty. And it was she I loved most of all.

Chapter Twenty-Eight

Nice

February~March 1883

Julie was like a rose in bloom. Her cheerful little face as she trotted through the streets of Nice was a pleasure to see, and a relief after her illness.

Northern Italy in the winter had been as cold as Moscow. While our family toured Genoa, Pisa, and Florence, Julie had come down with a sore throat that had turned into bronchitis before we reached Venice. We rushed to change our plans and made for the south of France, which seemed the best place for her to recuperate. The villa we rented in February came with a cook who planted a pot of steaming water in every room and insisted on adding a crushed bay leaf from the tree by the front door to Julie's honey and lemon tea.

Once Eugène had established us in these comfortable accommodations, he returned to Paris where he'd finally taken a position with the Ministry of Finance, where Papa had spent so many years.

I tended to our daughter. When she was feeling better, I supervised Julie's studies in the mornings. Once, I attempted to give her a history lesson while we strolled around the ruins of the Roman amphitheater. But she was more interested in climbing the stairs to view the stage from different vantage points than in hearing about the reach of the empire. Sometimes we painted side by side. And she practiced her violin, mandolin, or flute, according to her whim. But more often, Julie would loll in the grass under the orange trees with her parakeet on her shoulder, bringing to mind a peasant girl.

In the afternoons, we walked. One day we followed the goat paths into the hills, where the ground was cut by little streams. I managed to leap over one of the larger rivulets and called back, "Jump, Bibi!"

"I can't jump that far!" she wailed. Going back to help her cross, I lost my balance and almost pulled her into the water with me.

"Maman!" she shrieked.

We managed to regain our footing but made such a commotion that some women washing clothes downstream heard and came to help us across. When we were safely back in the courtyard of our villa, we laughed about the episode until we were in tears and promised each other we would never try to emulate goats again.

Another day we went to Grasse to view the Fragonard paintings in the museum there. Maman had spoken sometimes about the possibility that an ancestor of hers had married into Fragonard's family, so I was curious to see more of his work.

His eighteenth-century sentimentality was not to my taste, yet I had to admit that there were some similarities between his style and mine. Fragonard knew how to seize a moment. Only a true *spontaneiste* would think of depicting a lady falling off a wall. All I ever wanted to do was capture something that passes, a touch of the ephemeral—Julie's smile, the branch of a tree, a flower, a fruit. Just one of these would suffice.

I caught my breath when I noticed the falling lady's dainty, white-stockinged ankle exposed beneath her gown. Did Édouard have this image in mind when he painted my uncovered ankle in *Repose*?

Meanwhile, in Paris, my generous husband, my faithful friend and best supporter, was hard at work in his new post. He wrote: "I came back in the nick of time…my chief had written to Florence, insisting that I return." It was just as well that he had left us, as he'd been experiencing one of his moody intervals while he was here; whether it had been caused by our truncated travel plans or by work concerns, I could not say.

Eugène was also overseeing the building of our new house on the rue de Villejuste. "What is to be done in the courtyard?" he wrote. "Where shall the fountain be placed?" On top of all this, Eugène wanted all of my paintings in white frames for the seventh Impressionist exhibition, so he was running back and forth to the framer's shop, hurrying to have them made by the opening on 1 March.

I replied:

It seems to me you are working yourself to death, and all on my account. This touches me deeply and vexes me at the same time. I had thought of showing the small picture of Bibi and Pasie, the only one that Édouard likes; he wrote me that again yesterday. However, I leave it entirely up to you, and whatever you do, I won't complain. This is a solemn promise.

Even though I had been relieved to have Eugène depart with his moodiness in tow, I was a contradictory creature, and missed him once he had gone. I was always happier when a letter from him arrived.

❧

25 February
Paris

My dear wife,
How I wish you and Julie were here! I shall paint you a picture in words, and hope that you don't mind the outpouring of confession and detail.
Today was marked by cold, wet, and wind. Juggling an umbrella and unwieldy framed canvases while running over wet paving stones under a driving rain was quite exerting. I felt a headache coming on and knew that breathing in the cold, damp February air was doing nothing good for my lungs. I had climbed a mountain of paperwork at the Ministry in the morning, and in the afternoon, approved the architect's modifications for the Villejuste house. But I managed to reach the Salle des Panoramas in the rue Saint-Honoré while it was still open.
Berthe, imagine me, soaked and panting, as I struggled to close the umbrella while passing my precious packages through the doorway without nicking any corners. A somber, patriotic mural in the Academic style by an unknown artist, a work commemorating the French defeat at the Battle of Reichenshoffen in the Prussian war, will greet visitors to our avant-garde exhibition. I hope they will appreciate the irony; the Impressionists are the descendants of the artists who were deemed to be the cause of the France's

downfall during that war.

Everyone in the exhibition rooms was in good spirits, delighted to see me, if only because my purpose for coming was to exhibit my wife's works.

"My good man!" boomed Monet in welcome. You will remember that he has grown a beard, and he wore the floppy hat he seems never to remove since he settled in the country. Thirty of his shimmering landscapes filled the walls behind him. And Renoir! His hair glistening with macassar and his mustache trimmed to precise points, Renoir looked ready to enter his Luncheon at Bougival, the painting sure to be the showpiece of the exhibition. Sisley and Pissarro, in the far room, were varnishing their paintings of canals and countrysides.

"How good to see so many of our original group come together again," I responded, happy for the reunion of artists who had gone out on their own and missed the last two exhibitions.

Only Degas and Mary Cassatt were missing. Showing his work is as much a matter of financial urgency for Degas as it is for most other members of the group, so I was puzzled by his absence. As you know, he has been struggling to pay off the debts his father left, and not long ago his brother Achilles incurred legal fees as well. At first Degas claimed that his eyes were troubling him too much to provide paintings for the exhibition, but I suspect his absence comes because the other Impressionists have tired of the many and varied protégés that he allowed to exhibit alongside them, and Degas has tired of arguing about it. I think he took a stand, choosing not to participate if we would not let him have his way. Mademoiselle Cassatt followed his lead.

All of a sudden, as I was musing about Degas, it seemed that everyone was rushing toward me. I braced myself for the inevitable back-slapping and hand-pumping to come. But then I heard a familiar deep-voiced, "Bonsoir, mes amis!" behind me and realized that the excitement was, of course, for Édouard, who managed, even as he leaned on a cane, to swagger into the hall with Mallarmé. The painter and the poet wore elegant English overcoats, the latest fashion for French gentlemen, somehow untouched by rain.

"What's this we hear about the Legion of Honor, Manet?" Pissarro called out as he made his way toward us from the far room.

"You may call me Chevalier, gentlemen." Édouard was glowing. He wore his heart on his sleeve and his red ribbon on his lapel.

"His friend Proust put in a good word for him," Mallarmé explained.

"Oui, Antonin made the most of his two months as Minister of Fine Arts," I said, failing to suppress a sardonic tone. How convenient that he was in a position to bestow favors upon childhood friends.

"There is still room for your work here, Édouard," Monet reminded him.

"Toujours!" Renoir chimed in.

"I've already asked him," Pissarro told them with a resigned air, stroking his long white beard.

"Non, I must remain loyal to the state," Manet declared, "now that it has decided to recognize me!"

"France gives a man a ribbon and gains a patriot," quipped Monet.

"An aphorism worthy of Degas!" Édouard laughed.

I had to break off here to attend to Julie, who insisted that I take her for a walk to her friend's house.

Julie was very popular in Nice. She adored a little Russian girl, whom she ordered around like a puppy while at the same time threatening to overwhelm her with hugs. And when she made friends with the daughter of a ship's captain, we were invited to a reception on board the USS *Lancaster*, docked in the harbor. From every door we passed on our walks, one heard "Bonjour, Mademoiselle Julie!" When she was asked her name, her well-mannered answer was, "Bibi Manet." This made two *cocottes* walking along the sea wall laugh until they cried. They no doubt thought she was a daughter of the famous Édouard Manet (whose reputation cut a swath across the entire country) sent to be raised in this village far from Paris, as illegitimate children sometimes were.

Nice was filled with international tourists who made their promenade on the avenue des Anglais. When the duchess used to spend time here, she must have been in her element, with no end of social events to choose from. But after suffering indigestion (from mayonnaise and sauerkraut—*oof!*), I chose to forgo my neighbors' hospitality and insipid chatter in favor of having something wholesome for lunch with Julie every day. Bibi and I went to the market together to buy fresh fish. She ate the honey they sold there and was thriving on it.

My Bibi was delightful, but one can feel isolated when a five-year-old child is one's only companion. I hadn't heard from Edma in a long while. She had not forgiven my indiscretion, and I suppose I had never forgiven her, either. How could she have given up painting altogether? After all, no one had forced her to make the choices she'd made. I could never have imagined this distance between us. In her infrequent correspondence, she had complained of *ancient wounds* and a *wall of ice* between us. My own sister saw me as *cold and aloof.* I blamed my English governess Louisa for teaching me to suppress my feelings at a young age, under the guise of developing a strong character.

Before I had been able to finish my husband's first missive, another sweet note arrived from Eugène:

I feel very lonely without you; I miss your lovely chatter and your pretty plumage a great deal. I have wandered through every street in Paris today, but nowhere did I catch a glimpse of the little shoe with a bow that I know so well.

I replied:

Speaking of plumage, I have begun my lady with a parrot. I don't think I have posed her very well; I thought all the time how Édouard would do it.

After sending off my note, I returned to Eugene's first letter.

I broke away from this scene of hero worship to maneuver my way to the back room, where space had been reserved for you, my dear wife, and leaned your paintings against the wall as the searing pain of a migraine headache settled just behind my eyes. Your intimate family pictures from last summer in Bougival were to hang together, so I placed the painting of hollyhocks next to the one of Julie sitting at Pasie's knee.

"This one of the maid reading to your daughter is my favorite," said Mallarmé, who had followed me back. He tossed his gloves from hand to hand as he studied the work. "It must be called Fable."

"So it will be," I assured him. "Your words are gold."

I returned to my task. I needed to save room for the paintings of aloes and orange trees that you sent from Nice as they are still being framed, and I have no choice but to bring them next week.

"You have them all wrong, mon frère." Édouard had torn himself away from bantering with his adoring followers for the pleasure of irritating me. As you know, I never have been as brilliant or gregarious as my brother. Édouard hadn't wanted to study law. Neither had I, but somehow, before we were twenty, I was the son who found myself toiling over law books while he sailed off to Brazil on his training cruise for the Naval Academy. Now I am a civil servant when I, too, possess the soul of an artist. This conflict is one source of my migraines, without a doubt. A spike of pain drove deeper into my head.

Here I stopped reading again to think about the generous spirit of the man whom I had married. Eugène never competed with me. He was willing to put himself in my shadow, even after all the years he had lived in Édouard's. There was companionship, not passion, between us, and the former was what I needed in order to work. But the fact that my husband never complained about my limited ardor for him did not prove that he was deceived about my feelings for his brother.

I continued reading Eugène's letter:

The day began to catch up with me. "Édouard, I'm sure you have some excellent suggestions for me," I replied in an even tone. It annoyed me to no end that I had to look up at my younger brother.

"For one thing, The Washerwoman should be near the corner, so that it is close to Renoir's Laundress," Édouard said. Ça va. I moved the painting to the corner. A high-pitched whine seeped into my skull.

"And his Luncheon at Bougival belongs with Berthe's Bougival paintings. Surely even you can see that!"

"Édouard," interjected the quiet Mallarmé.

I am quite familiar with your work. I had watched as you painted most of it. I tried to hold in my mind a mental image of you standing before your easel, with your intense focus on your subject and your brush poised in the air.

"But I can't expect you to understand, par example, that the pastels don't necessarily belong in a grouping. Rather, each should be placed next to a painting of corresponding theme or colors." Édouard began to arrange the paintings himself. "I know Berthe would want me to make these decisions for her," he said, rearranging still more framed pieces.

With each painting that he touched, it was as if he were putting his hands on you. You will mock my jealousy, I suppose, but I can never think of my wife modeling for my brother without such scenes coming to mind. My vision started to blur—I had hoped that my headache wouldn't get so bad this time. I rubbed my temples where the pain was the worst and staggered when the dizziness overtook me. As everything went black — forgive me, my dear — I lashed out, driving my fist into my brother's face.

Rough hands pulled me so that I stumbled backward, and Mallarmé's low voice said, "Steady, steady."

The first thing I saw when my vision cleared was Monet, helping me up with a worried expression. Then I spotted Édouard, holding a blood-stained linen handkerchief to his nose. I had struck my brother, when I know how much pain he endures and what it had cost him to come here. As Mallarmé picked up his bowler hat from the floor and pulled him toward the door, Édouard leaned on his cane and turned back to hiss, "Imbécile!"

Berthe, you must see that he had driven me to it.

The Seventh Impressionist exhibition would mark the return of Monet, Renoir, Sisley, and Pissarro, which pleased me, although I would not be there to witness their reunion. But it was not their approval I sought. I wrote to Eugène: "You do not tell me what Édouard thinks of the exhibition as a whole. I think I can read between the lines that he was only moderately satisfied with it. Am

I mistaken?"

Eugène reported that, on the contrary, Édouard declared that with my double portrait of Eugène and Julie at Bougival, I had now far surpassed Eva Gonzalès. As if I hadn't known that.

While Parisians attended the Impressionist exhibition in March, I was delighted to stay on in Nice. But our happiness was halted one day in mid-month.

Julie and I were enjoying our déjeuner à deux, sliced potatoes with artichokes baked in olive oil with garlic and fresh thyme, in the courtyard of the villa when Pasie brought me a telegram. I tore it open, scanned it, and threw it down in an instant. "Wait!" I called out as Pasie went back inside. "Get the trunks and begin packing our things, quickly!"

I had known that Édouard continued to suffer from pain in his leg, diagnosed at various times as rheumatism, neuralgia, and lately, arthritis. He had spent last summer in Versailles, where he'd received daily hydrotherapy and massage. Even there he'd painted a scene of his ugly little overgrown garden with an ominous empty bench and discarded bonnet, just for something to do. We had received many letters illustrated with watercolors of flowers and fruit. Last Christmas he'd written, "This year is not ending very well for me as regards my health." But later he'd said that he was better and had discarded his cane. Édouard wrote of his illness that the doctor "seems to believe in an origin that might allow for some hope." That sounded more threatening than arthritis. It was possible that he was telling me, with as much delicacy as possible, that he suffered from gonorrhea, as did so many men who frequented the brothels of Paris. It was painful, but curable.

"What's wrong, Maman?" asked Julie. Her sun-kissed face was the picture of health, her bout with bronchitis forgotten.

"It's oncle Édouard," I told her. "He's very ill."

Chapter Twenty-Nine

*W*hen Édouard first became ill, he tried to carry on as usual. He remained in his latest lover's apartment in the rue de Rome as long as he was able. Méry Laurent, the woman in his life, whom I had met years before in Édouard's studio when she was just starting out as a cabaret dancer, had climbed the social ladder, man over man, until she now presided over the most celebrated salon in Paris.

Later, when Édouard could no longer live without the comforts of home, he left Méry and moved café society right into his studio, around the corner from his house. Friends and acquaintances from the boulevard drank beer or liqueures, delivered on trays from the nearby Café Nouvelle Athénès. After years of being little more than a glorified housekeeper, Suzanne was delighted to have her husband close by and to play the hostess, passing through the room with apéritifs of sardines with onions and celery with remoulade sauce. Sitting at his easel, Édouard was surrounded by the conversation and laughter that were his life's blood. He still dressed in jacket and cravat to paint. His only concession to illness was that he sat down during his bravura performances.

Many society *ogresses* came to sit for him, panting in the steel corsets that contained their middle-aged plumpness and raised their bosoms almost to the point of releasing them altogether. Wealthy foreigners and financiers escorted these ladies, the Englishmen in their bowler hats and the Austrians in fur-trimmed felt jackets. It was a festive atmosphere.

By the time I returned home from Nice, Édouard's crisis was over. But since my family was staying in an apartment close to Édouard's while our new house was being built, it was easy for me to come help with household duties and care for Édouard. Eugène gave Julie her lessons in the mornings before he turned her over to Pasie and left for work. I spent almost every waking hour with Édouard.

The lines between his eyes had deepened with pain, I observed, as had the hollows under his cheekbones. I couldn't imagine how he worked while suffering from the sharp pain and paralysis of nervous ataxia, his newest diagnosis, but he managed to maintain his arm muscle coordination well enough. I understood, of course, that his painting was what kept him going.

He finished *Bar at the Follies Bérgère* for the Salon of 1883 by having a marble-topped counter moved into the studio for his model to stand behind. He alternated between working and resting on a couch to chat with friends, although his animated conversational style had to have been more exhausting than restorative. Méry was in the background of the painting, in light colors, leaning on the balcony. My favorite part of the composition was in the top left corner, where tiny feet stood on a trapeze, shod in green boots the color of the crème de menthe bottle on the counter. This painting was as close as I would ever get to the dazzling Folies Bérgère and its operettas, dance troupes, acrobats, and circuses. No respectable lady could attend this most risqué of music halls. *Tant pis*. If Édouard had taught me anything, it was that glittering surfaces often cover what is fetid and rotten.

For those few weeks in March, his condition improved, but then there was an abrupt volte-face. Within days, the urbane Édouard Manet turned into a gaunt old man bent over his cane. His vanity was crushed.

No longer able to endure the long sittings with models, he closed up his studio and returned home. To her credit, Méry visited often, bringing sweets and tangerines. Édouard made small, elegant still lifes, using the spring flowers friends sent him, set in simple vases of water. The peonies Méry sent daily with her maid were his special favorites.

"A painter can express all that he wants with fruit or flowers," he said.

"I would like to paint them all." The little paintings were beautiful, but they had something of the sadness of the vanitas about them, the warning of impending loss.

As Édouard's health deteriorated, a new doctor tried more desperate measures. Dr. Hureau de Villeneuve prescribed ergot, derived from the fungus on rye bread. This had the effect of smoothing the muscle tissue in his leg, which gave Édouard some relief from pain. But there were less desirable effects, as well. Too much ergot constricted the blood vessels, leading to an almost unbearable burning sensation. Eugène, who stopped in after work each day, took me aside to whisper, "This charlatan has very nearly dispatched my brother into the next world!"

One afternoon I carried a tray of food out to where Édouard was painting in his small garden. "I've brought you something to eat," I said.

"Put it anywhere," he said without taking his eyes off his canvas. I set the tray on a wrought-iron table and turned to go inside. "Berthe," he added, as I was closing the door.

I opened the door again. "Oui, Édouard?"

"Aren't you happy that I'm painting in the open air?" He looked at me over his shoulder and smiled. "I've hidden myself away back here like a sick cat."

That made me smile, too, and something unclenched within me as I moved back out into the garden. At last, we were alone. Perhaps now we could talk about plein air painting, or discuss the new artists, Vuillard and Seurat and the rest. I sat down on a little chair by the table.

He said, "I long to paint women in the middle of greenery and among flowers where everything is enveloped in light, because, believe me, I'm not done for yet!"

"That is precisely what I love to paint." But I could never hope to have at my disposal the array of potential models that Manet had accumulated in the years after he discarded me, when his affairs multiplied at an impressive rate. I felt distant from all of that. Suzanne,

Méry, none of them bothered me any longer. Since Julie's birth, I had put away any passion I felt for Édouard, while the intellectual and artistic connection we had was so much a part of me that no one could touch it.

Édouard stood to join me at the table, then cried out from a sharp pain that caused him to stagger and fall. Suzanne and the maid appeared in an instant. It took all three of us to help him into the house. Only after the moment for us to be alone had passed did I realize how long I had been waiting for a chance to have Édouard to myself. I wanted to store up more of our lifelong conversation, all I would have left of him one day.

One morning, Mary Cassatt showed up at the door with her wealthy American friend, Louisine Havemeyer. I could see that she was shocked, but perhaps not surprised, to see me answer the door rather than the other Madame Manet. I had neither the energy nor the inclination to explain my presence. Helping a sick relative was the least of my scandals.

"He is ill," I told them. "He can see no one." It was a pity. Mary Cassatt had brought her friend in order to purchase paintings, and I would have liked to see some Manets in an American collection.

Their expressions reflected the strain in my voice. They hadn't known just how ill the man was.

Then, through the open door to the dining room, now transformed into Édouard's sick room: "Take them to the studio, Berthe." Of course. No one wanted Édouard's work in important collections more than Édouard. I did as he asked, grabbing my cape and his key, and walking the women to his studio around the corner. Fragrant absinthe wafted from the open door of the Café Nouvelle-Athènes when we passed. As he was everywhere, Édouard had been the center of the group of artists who met there. I resented the fact that his models could be a part of that gathering and I could not, when I was sure that a street urchin such as Victorine Meurent had been

248

when Édouard found her could not have been a conversationalist of my caliber.

I imagined Édouard stepping out of the twilight darkness of the café doorway to join me. "Conversation was not what men were seeking from her," he'd say in his familiar, husky voice. I pictured him tipping his hat to me, then leaning back to feel the sun on his face before replacing his chapeau at just the right angle. "*Allons-y!*" he would say, offering me his arm.

We would promenade down the boulevard, one of his favorite activities, mingling among the blue-smocked workmen with their berets and the gentlemen of the world in their top hats. There wouldn't be a hint of a limp in his jaunty stride. He would inhale the scent of the blossoming chestnut trees lining the sidewalk and comment on the row of new electric streetlights lining the boulevard. The contents of each shop window he would find fascinating, the fashionable women even more so. He would gaze at me, seeing me as I was in my youth, the most beautiful woman in the world to him. "Ah, Berthe, ma chère, isn't life wonderful?" he would ask.

With him, I remembered that it was. Was it my fate to meet him in order to learn the lesson of life's possibilities? Then his face began to fade, and I became aware of the brightness of the day and the rattling of carriage wheels on quarry-stone streets.

"This is the building, *n'est-ce pas?*" Mary Cassatt asked. I nodded, and led Mesdemoiselles Cassat and Havemeyer inside and upstairs.

I slid the key into the lock and pushed open the door to the cold, empty studio. This dark, dead place had once seemed to me the location of the very center of life. There was the Chinese vase on the mantel, there the piano I played for Édouard while he worked, and there, the crimson sofa where we had made love. I should never forget the days of my intimacy with Édouard, when his charm and his mind kept me alert during those long hours when I sat for him. Again, I was overwhelmed by the urgency to find a moment alone with Édouard.

I went around the dusty studio from window to window, opening the shutters to let in some light as the women stood before *Luncheon on the Grass* and *Olympia*, both of which still hung there, still unsold. I pointed out the superior attributes of Manet's masterpieces to Mademoiselle Havemeyer. But these controversial works must have been too much for the American. When I guided her to Édouard's more conventional painting of Monet's family in their garden, she seemed quite taken with it. "Here you see all of the characteristics of an Impressionist work," I told her. "It is a scene of everyday life that shows the effects of outdoor light." I remembered something Durand-Ruel once told me. "Americans don't laugh. They buy." Nothing would make Édouard happier. While my efforts didn't result in a sale that day, I parted ways with the women at the corner confident that Mary Cassatt would close the deal.

"Louisine, this is your opportunity to build the foundation of a great collection," was the last thing I heard her say as they walked away.

I rushed back to Édouard's house, eager to find an opportunity to speak with him in private. But Suzanne was so enjoying feeding him Dutch pastries, dusty with cinnamon and powered sugar, and playing Chopin nocturnes on the piano, that I couldn't think how I would find a moment alone with him. I would have liked to watch him savor a juicy fruit tart while I played some light-hearted Debussy,

By mid-April, Édouard was in bed with chills and fever. In desperation, he had ingested too much ergot. Chronic constriction of his blood vessels had led to the gangrene that now blackened his left leg. "Well then, if there is nothing else to do, take off the leg and let's be done with it," he said. Suzanne cried out in horror, but I stifled my cry. When Dr. de Villeneuve gave him chloroform, all of the pain left Édouard's face until he seemed as young as he had been when I'd first met him. I fled the room. Eugène, weeping but determined to be with his brother during the amputation, remained. Soon, that long, elegant limb was no more.

Sitting on the stairs with my hands over my ears to block out

Édouard's shrieks, I thought of the warning he had given me before the war, when he urged me to leave the city. "What if something should happen to your leg?" I remembered. Oh, I remembered.

When I stayed late one evening in order to organize a shopping list for the cook to take to the market the next morning, I found Suzanne asleep in the chair next to Édouard's bed. She was clearly exhausted. The amputation had resulted in infection, so that Édouard needed to be watched around the clock for signs that his fever was increasing. I wakened Suzanne and offered to take a turn watching over him. She shambled upstairs to bed.

I took my place in the chair near Édouard, examining his profile in the candlelight, aware of how few of these intimate situations we had experienced together. His ruined, sunken face, as white as the pillowcase on which he lay, was covered in perspiration. I wrung out the cloth in the washbasin next to his bed and patted his face with cool water. Afterward, I pulled my perfumed handkerchief from the pocket where I'd kept it in the days since the amputation, protection from the stench of his putrefying stump that filled the room.

After a time, Édouard's own groaning awakened him. He turned toward me, and when the cloud of sleep left his eyes, he gave me a wan smile. I saw that his teeth had turned gray as death began its decay.

"*Ma chère* Berthe …"

"Oui, I am here."

"You are all that stands between me and despair."

"I am familiar with that feeling." I was about to offer to play the piano to ease him back into sleep when he spoke through clenched teeth.

"My leg—I can't bear the pain." He raised his bedcovers, then lowered the fine linen sheet over his rotting stump without a word when he saw that his leg was gone. Watching him in this appalling agony reminded me of Maman's death—the fever, the convulsive shivering. It was too much.

"It's no good. I will die like Baudelaire, paralyzed and insane." Like Baudelaire! Then it was la verole—syphilis, not gonorrhea—that had destroyed his spinal cord. My sympathy for him transformed into utter rage that he would let his taste for women lead to the destruction of his genius.

"So which *demi-mondaine* gave you this gift, Édouard? Was it one of your models—Marguerite or Amélie-Jeanne?" I sputtered, "Or that diva Louise Valtesse?"

He clucked his tongue in satisfaction. "Don't forget the actresses, *ma chère* Berthe."

My anger, which in his enormous conceit he interpreted as jealousy, made him attempt a smile.

"I've been incapable of doing what you accuse me of for some time. It's possible that this is yet another problem I inherited from my father. Has Eugène never told you that Father died paralyzed by syphilis? He shouldn't have brought children into the world if they were going to turn out like this!" He caught his breath. "Things might have been different between us if I hadn't feared infecting you."

So he must have had the first symptoms of the illness when I began modeling for him. Everyone knew that the early stages of syphilis were the most contagious. Was that why he had resisted me? I was not prepared to contemplate just how different my life might have been, had Édouard not been afraid of passing on his disease, yet questions tumbled over one another in my mind. If he'd not had syphilis, might he have left Suzanne? He would not have bestowed me to his brother for whom he had no great respect, would he? To avoid thinking of the life I might have lived, I clung to anger and snapped, "Yet you had no qualms about the many women who followed me."

"You must know that they turned out to be no substitute for you." How did a legless syphilitic have the strength to try to charm me? I struggled to subdue the emotions that surged in response to his flattery.

"That remark is not appropriate, coming from my brother-in-law."

"Berthe, I don't have time for niceties. Just listen now. I want you to have the portraits—you alone should have them. They say everything I have been unable to say aloud. You said yourself once that they were my love letters."

Tears sprang to my eyes and seeped from their edges. He was digging up long-buried feelings too painful to be borne. I didn't know how to respond, so I pushed up my sleeves, again wrung out the cloth in the washbasin, and wiped his fevered forehead with a gentle touch as he gazed up at me. "You have been the model of strength for me," he said. Strength! I shrugged and put my fingers to his lips to silence such nonsense.

But he had more that he was determined to tell me. He grabbed my wrist. "I have loved life, and it has passed so quickly."

"Oui, no one has loved life more than you."

"I have ideas for paintings…there is so much more work to be done." I imagined the paintings the world would miss because of this artist's life cut short. "If one wins one's eternity by virtue of one's work, you will be remembered," I assured him as I fought to hide my tears. "I will make certain of it."

"Oh, I know all about justice being done one day," he said, choking on his bitter words. "It means one begins to live only after one is dead. I know all about that sort of justice."

His grip relaxed, and he let his hand trail down my bare arm.

"Say something kind to me," he whispered.

I stroked his unkempt beard into two points, the way he had always worn it, as I wondered how to set his mind at ease. What could I say that would convey what he had meant to me? A line from Song of Solomon came to mind, and I whispered to Édouard, "Many waters cannot quench love, for love is as strong as death." He held my hand to his lips as my heart broke yet again for this man.

કે

Manet died of blood poisoning on a beautiful spring evening, 30 April, 1883. He was fifty-one years old. He went before paralysis, blindness, and insanity could take him, but his last days were atrocious nonetheless. Once again, I witnessed death at close range in one of its most dreadful guises. This most fastidious of men, with the acute aesthetic of a great artist, was reduced to convulsions and delirium. It was a relief when he left us, as a fresh breeze blew flurries of cherry blossoms past the window like snow.

We held the funeral at the black-draped Église Saint-Louis d'Antin. While the choirs sang and the priest performed the offices of the dead, I tried not to think of Édouard's poor body, skeletal and mutilated, lying in the coffin beneath heaps of flowers.

Eugène and I picked out the burial plot near a pathway under a grove of linden trees in the Passy Cemetery. It was still peaceful there, just beneath the Trocodero, but it was only a short walk across the boulevard to a panoramic view of the city that was expanding westward. As Passy was absorbed by Paris, so Édouard would be engulfed by the modern world that had so fascinated him.

Under a pale gray sky, Suzanne, Eugène and I led five hundred black-clad mourners—artists, the cream of the Parisian haute-bourgiosie, and those who knew only of Manet's celebrity—all following the wreath-laden hearse in the procession from the church to the cemetery. The mood might have been judged by others to be somber, but I hoped that it was guilt that overcame many of the mourners for not having supported this great man while he lived. Some of them may have been among the crowds attending the Salon the evening Édouard died. I heard later that when someone arrived to announce Manet's death, silence fell over the galleries as, one by one, the men removed their hats.

Méry Laurent covered the gravesite with the first white lilies of the season. Claude Monet and Fantin-Latour came from Normandy; they, along with Émile Zola, were among the pallbearers, as were Phillipe Burty and Théodore Duret—the critics finally supported him. Antonin Proust gave an elegy praising Édouard's generosity and inspiration to other artists. Degas said, "He was greater than we thought."

I had always known his greatness. But I said nothing, showed nothing. People no doubt interpreted my behavior as cold hauteur. I hid behind my frozen façade, afraid to reveal the extent of my grief, which would have been seen as unsuitable for a sister-in-law. But I was even more afraid to acknowledge it to myself.

There was just enough room in the small plot before us for Eugène and me to join Édouard one day. I would spend eternity between my husband and my great love. With that thought to console me, I drew my black veil down tight over my face and clung to Eugène.

Two days later, we received word that Eva Gonzalès was dead. Hearing of Édouard's death, she had risen from her childbirth bed to make a wreath for him and suffered an embolism. My old nemesis was gone, and now I saw that there had been no reason ever to be jealous of her.

That same week, we moved into our new home. I did what I had to do during those days. I lined the walls of the salon with Édouard's paintings. The Chinese basin he gave me I put on the mantel.

But I did not cry, nor I did not eat at all that week.

With the burial and the move completed, I locked myself into my boudoir one evening, sat at my writing table in the dim light, and reached out in a letter to Edma.

Dear Edma,

I feel my entire past collapsing. Édouard was associated with all the memories of my youth. His was such a powerful personality, his mind was so young and alert, that it seemed that more than others he was beyond the power of death. How many silent dead behind us. I am aware that life is moving on and that it is time to reveal what is in one's heart. Can we not melt this wall of ice between us?

I am shattered.

Berthe

ॐ

I dropped my pen to the table and my head to my hands. I would have liked to relive my life, but that was a useless fancy. How could it have been different? Would I have run off with Édouard? Spent my life as his mistress? I sinned, I suffered, I atoned. We all die with our secrets.

My lifelong conversation with Édouard had been interrupted in mid-sentence. I was left with unanswered questions. If I was unable to fathom how I would survive that loss, then what means did I possess to reassure my husband that all would be well? If there was a hell, would I burn for marrying a man because the scent of his skin reminded me of my lover?

Still, no tears came. But a wail I could no longer suppress seeped out of me and grew until it filled the room. I fought to catch my breath as memories from the past twenty-five years suffocated me. Images of the most elegant and audacious of men swarmed around me: my awe at meeting the great pioneering painter at the Louvre. The titillation of reading the gossip about him and his paramours with Edma. Our tender liaison at Maurecourt. I pushed a fist into my mouth to muffle the moan that spilled out as I remembered falling in love with the fragile man who revealed his inner doubts when I modeled for him. The room spun around me as I relived the searing heartbreak of his rejection.

I was not strong, as Édouard had thought. I lacked his ability to carry on. I needed him to be in the world, even if I could not have him.

Eugène knocked at the door. "Berthe, may I come in? Berthe?"

I did not need to search for my reflection in the mirror to know that I was disappearing, not into a light-filled atmosphere, but into endless darkness. My dress crumpled around me as I slid to the floor.

Chapter Thirty

Paris
May 1883

Birdsong awakened me, which meant that the sun was out after days of drizzle. Their chirping evoked the fresh yellow-greens of the leafy Bois de Boulogne. The prospect of a pleasant day filled me with dread. People would expect me to be happy, when I wasn't sure that I wanted to be alive.

Julie tiptoed in and opened the curtains, flooding the room with light. I saw a luminous white cloud reflected in the mirror across the room before realizing that I was seeing my hair, gone completely white in the weeks since Édouard's death.

"The rain has finally stopped," Julie whispered. "Let's go to the Bois before the crowds arrive."

"I don't know if I feel well enough".

"I'll get the paints," Julie said.

"Really, I don't think so…"

"Here is your hat," said Julie, before scurrying off for her clothes and watercolors.

It was difficult to dress with limbs that felt weighted. But after Pasie had buttoned my clothes and pinned my hair, I was surprised to see that I looked presentable enough to pass as a human, not the subterranean creature I'd become following Édouard's death. In the deep black hole into which I'd fallen, I'd felt as weak and naked as a newborn mole. I was unable to eat and could not breath without a struggle. But I was Julie's mother, and she'd had enough of my month of mourning.

The short walk to the Bois de Boulogne entrance was almost more than I could manage. Yet as soon as we entered the Passy gates, I found it easier to breathe. Mallarmé had teased me about my love for what he termed the Bois' "moderate groves and mediocre shades—nature's parsimony." Ah, but the early morning light shimmering through the chestnut and elm trees did not seem tame to me. If he considered that most of my plein air work was done in my private garden or some other contained space, then he might have seen that, for me, the Bois was a wild Eden which provided me with all the landscapes I needed.

"Maman, the tulips have bloomed!" cried Julie. We were surrounded by banks of flowers in warm colors, complemented by a background of stately, deep-green fir trees. I remembered another spring when the floral abundance of the Bois had shown me that life continues after the horror of death. If flowers could emerge from blood-soaked ground to blanket it in scented blossoms, then a woman might be able to cloak her grief, although with what, I couldn't yet imagine.

"It's May. Is it time for the Fête des Fleurs?" Julie had transformed into the wood sprite that she always became in her natural habitat.

"At the end of the month. Another week or so," I replied. A short walk brought us to a grove of trees on the shore of Lac Inferieur, the site of my near-proposal from Puvis de Chavannes, now one of my favorite places to paint in privacy. I attempted to give Julie a short lesson in landscape painting, but she was more interested in kneeling at my feet to make fairy houses out of leaves and twigs.

Soon I was lost in making watercolor sketches of trees, a passing carriage, the swans gliding on the lake. Only the palest washes could convey the dappled light and the slight movement of air. My brush flew over the paper. More than simply capturing the moment—photography could do that—I wanted to seize a glance, a glimpse out of the corner of one's eye, the image one noticed before fully registering it in one's brain.

As I painted, I considered my work in a new way. It was a privilege and an imperative to create as much as possible. My days of sequestered grieving must now give way to productive employment. Édouard's death had reminded me that we all must die, but that we might gain immortality through our art. Édouard would be remembered by many, while I would be happy to have my paintings appreciated by family and a few close friends.

Entranced by my mission, I was aware on some level of experiencing an ephemeral instant of happiness.

"Maman, I'm hungry!" Julie called up to me from the edge of the lake. She was feeding the swans, whose gobbling must have reminded her that she'd had no lunch. What kind of mother could forget the presence of her child? An artist-mother, I suppose. But to neglect to feed one's child—that was an unforgivable sin. My penance was to stop mid-painting, pack up, and make for the Chalet on the island in Lac Inferieur.

One thing led to another. A poster in the Chalet restaurant announced a concert that very afternoon by Julie's "most favorite composer." So we were off to the outdoor Théâtre de Verdure, with stops en route for the marionette show and to feed the animals in le Jardin d'Acclimation.

We found seats near the stage, stowed our painting equipment below our chairs, and sat back to enjoy captivating young Cécile Chaminade's music. Julie watched me with bright, questioning eyes—Édouard's eyes. "Maman, do you feel better now?" she asked. The child had watched me mourning those past weeks. "I can take care of you," offered my daughter, slipping her arm through mine and leaning into me. I took in her apricot cheeks, the periwinkle blue of her day dress—the color of her eyes—and her waist-long blonde hair.

"Merci, Bibi. I am perfectly well now," I assured her.

Julie gave me her wide smile. "Isn't today wonderful?" she asked. My daughter embodied all of Édouard's lightness and joy, whether she was his child or not, so he wasn't altogether gone after all. I saw that being brave enough to love, even knowing that the loved one could be lost, was the real strength of character.

The concert began. Chaminade's Ronde de Crepuscule was the story of the fairy queen Mab, which reminded me of learning to read

Shakespeare, sitting next to my governess, Louisa. A snippet flitted through my mind:

> And in this state she gallops night by night,
> Through lovers' brains, and then they dream of love.

I couldn't help also remembering the words of Mallarmé, as I so often did, about how music is like a woman with an enormous head of wavy hair. Mademoiselle Chaminade's composition was curling and melodic and utterly Parisienne. It could not have been better suited to a spring afternoon.

Then, another of those fleeting instants of perfect happiness. I realized that it could not be captured, only experienced.

I decided to live.

PART FOUR

La Grande Dame de Peinture

The Great Lady of Painting

Chapter Thirty-One

Giverny

14 July 1890

For Bastille Day 1890, Eugène, Julie, and I took a horse-drawn cart from our summer home in Mézy to the train station in Mantes. There we joined Mallarmé with his wife and daughter in boarding a locomotive, bound for a reunion with Monet. From Giverny, we took a narrow-gauge train that passed along the foot of Monet's garden. Our motives for this pilgrimage were more than social. Mallarmé hoped to come away with a painting for himself, and I wanted to fulfill my promise to Édouard that his work would be remembered.

The Impressionists had scattered in the seven years since Édouard's death. Monet had moved to Giverny. Sisley, still penniless, had escaped back into the country and Cézanne to the south of France. Renoir was newly married and had returned to classical painting techniques with his latest successes—a series of indoor scenes of girls reading, in rich hues of Venetian red and juniper green.

As for Eugène and me, we had settled in to enjoy our home on the rue de Villejust. I'd made the garden the site of several paintings, including one portrait of a ghost-like woman whose pale face reflected my emotions in those first months after losing Édouard. I painted Pasie in the dining room and Julie with her English teacher, Miss Reynolds, in the Bois de Boulogne. During the years after establishing our home, we spent holidays chasing the light to Nice, where it reflected on the aloes and olive trees, to Reuben's gold-lit paintings in Holland, to our new country house, le Mesnil, in Mézy, where the atmosphere was suffused with an opalescent glow.

After Édouard's death, we held an exhibition of two hundred of his works at l'École des Beaux-Arts. While it was a financial fiasco, his work earned positive reviews, a revenge for so many rebuffs, but a revenge that the poor man obtained only in his grave. We had come a long way from the kind of dim-witted jokes that used to be made about his pictures. I experienced intense pride, along with disappointment that Edma would not attend, still estranged from me after all these years.

Because Édouard had stipulated that all of his work should be sold to benefit his wife and "god son,"—I'd wondered how he'd ever thought she would allow me to have the portraits he'd promised me—Eugène and some of Édouard's friends arranged an auction and raised 116,637 francs. Suzanne had hoped for at least two hundred thousand francs. She must have been desperate. How could she live on what she earned as a piano teacher? Suzanne's brother bought *Luncheon on the Grass* and the composer Emmanuel Chabrier purchased *Bar at the Folies Bérgère*. I obtained eight large canvases, including one he'd said I should have—his last portrait of me, wearing my engagement ring.

But my goal was to place Édouard's work in a permanent home. Monet had come up with the same idea while visiting a display of Édouard's work at last year's Exposition Universelle. It was difficult to fathom that over twenty years had elapsed since Édouard's unsettling Realism had broken through the stilted style of the Academy. Now we wanted to place *Olympia* in the Louvre, where her presence would mark the beginning of modern art. Today I would discuss our efforts to that end with Monet.

Claude Monet's house was a coral pink, with viridian green shutters and ivy climbing up to the second story. Monet led us through the rustic, blue-tiled kitchen, with trim painted aqua blue and a line of copper pots overhead, to the light-filled dining room with sunny yellow furniture, a red-and-white tile floor, and one whole wall of Japanese prints. The profusion of flowers in the garden outside the window resembled nothing so much as the brushstrokes of a glowing Impressionist painting. Monet had brought the outdoors inside by placing blue hydrangeas on the kitchen table and sunflowers in the dining room.

I took it all in with amazement. "*Vraiment*, you are a man who has entered his own painting!"

"*Mais oui*," he said. "Isn't it wonderful?" Monet's full beard had grown white, and he had the round belly of a rich man.

Next, he took us to his studio and showed us his new paintings, a series of the Rouen Cathedral. Mallarmé was in ecstasy, exclaiming, "It makes me happy to be living in the same age as Monet!"

"Choose one of these for yourself," Monet insisted, pointing to another wall of paintings. I encouraged Mallarmé to choose a large scene of the banks of the Seine with the Jeufosse church spire in the background and a plume of smoke from a passing train cutting a diagonal line across the foreground, and he took my advice.

We dined outdoors under an arbor heavy with purple wisteria, whose scent combined with that of a nearby lavender patch for an intoxicating effect. The heat of the day muffled the cries of Julie, of Mallarmé's daughter, Geneviève, and of Monet's son, Michel, as they ran around the garden paths, crunching gravel and clattering over the wooden bridge.

Monet presided over the table. "Have some more bread. It is fresh from the market this morning," he boomed. "And salad—I grew the lettuce myself."

"You are a happy man," Eugène observed.

"I am a pig in clover here in my little haven." Monet reached around the table to refill everyone's glasses. "I well remember the days when I had to borrow from Manet. Now all of my paintings sell. Haystacks paid for this house!"

I saw my opening. "And you have the influence to get *Olympia* into the Louvre. You alone, with your name and your authority, can break down the doors if they can be broken."

"And who is to pay for the painting?" Monet asked.

Eugène jumped in. "We have in mind to raise funds by public subscription, in order to purchase *Olympia* from Suzanne."

It wasn't unusual to raise money in this way. Artists sometimes used subscriptions to purchase expensive materials for large projects. And *Olympia* must be saved. Suzanne had proven beyond doubt that she was incapable of appreciating Édouard's work. We'd been horrified to learn that she had allowed Léon to cut up the stunning *Execution of Maximillian* to sell in separate pieces, reasoning that she could see more profit from several Manet paintings than from one. The work was only saved when Degas purchased and painstakingly reassembled the fragments.

"It is my great desire to present my brother's groundbreaking work to the state." Eugene said.

"You'd better hurry," said Mallarmé. "I've heard that Suzanne is about to sell *Olympia* to an American."

"Very well. She should be as happy to sell the painting to us as to anyone else," I pointed out, "since it is worth only money to her."

"We cannot let my brother's chef d'oeuvre leave France!" Eugène cried to the others gathered at the table.

"Don't say that in front of Mademoiselle Cassatt," I warned. "She won't be happy until all of our work is in America. And Claude, you must be gentle when approaching Monsieur Kaempfen." The director of the Louvre was not well liked, so he might be reluctant to involve himself in a controversial acquisition that could further reduce his popularity and jeopardize his position. For my part, if necessary, I would throw myself at the mercy of Jules Ferry, now the Minister of Fine Arts.

"Berthe and I can't thank you enough," Eugène said, "for helping to get my brother the recognition he deserves."

"He deserves more. I only wish he had joined with the Impressionists," Monet declared. He clapped my husband on his back. "Have some more of the local cider," he urged.

We leaned back in our chairs, encircled by protective pine trees. All was quiet for a moment, except for the buzzing bees hovering around the wisteria vines. I scanned the table, each person in turn. Monet, the son of a grocer, was a happy, productive man. In the past I would have scorned Alice Hoschède, who lived, unmarried, with Monet. But she had left her husband, the department store owner who had purchased several of my paintings, to help Monet when his wife Camille was dying. They had fallen in love and created a life together, including this home. And Stéphane Mallarmé's deft poems, seemingly written in feathery brushstrokes, mirrored my own work—that was our connection. These artists, with our shared history, were as much my family now as any blood relative.

"Édouard said that the artist must work alone," I said. "But that's not entirely so, is it?"

"Why, Berthe, I believe you have finally become one of us!" Monet insisted on pouring yet more cider for us all, and I raised my glass.

"To us!"

"To France!" Eugène chimed in.

"To Édouard Manet, the greatest draftsman since Ingres!" roared Monet.

We, the truly faithful, thought he was far greater.

Monet insisted on sharing his bounty with us, pressing bags of vegetables and jars of honey into our arms when it was time to go. Our trip back to the station was slowed by military bands and torch-lit Bastille Day celebrants blocking our small train. Eugène juggled jugs of cider while also trying to keep hold of Julie's hand. Mallarmé was concerned with protecting his painting. All I wanted was to protect was Édouard's legacy.

It fell to me, as Suzanne's sister-in-law, to negotiate the sale of *Olympia*. I called on her the following week. She was living with Léon, a lost soul who had settled upon an odd occupation: distributing a catalogue dedicated to the business of breeding and selling rabbits and chickens.

Suzanne insisted that dealers were clamoring for Édouard's works, which was difficult to believe, given the disappointing sales at his auction. Without Édouard to support her any longer, need drove her to authenticate paintings of questionable provenance. The couple of canvases I saw propped on the mantel might have originally been unfinished works by Édouard, but I could see that they had been repainted by artists of lesser talent.

"You don't consider these to be Édouard's, do you?" I asked.

"I can't say they weren't painted by my husband," she stated with stolid calm.

"You do understand that putting his name on a painting of this caliber will taint his reputation," I protested.

"You are meddling in what doesn't concern you." There was a challenge in her eyes. I saw that she had envied what I had shared with Édouard, our haute-bourgeois class and our shared profession. Did she suspect more? She had been powerless over her husband's life, but now displayed dogged determination to control what was left of him after his death.

I had a memory of Maman's frightening vision of my life had I remained unmarried, had my paintings not sold well, had my family money disappeared. For the first time it struck me: financial desperation might have kept Suzanne from fighting off Manet Père's advances for fear of losing her position. For all I knew, he had forced himself on her.

Her obstinance was frustrating, but I thought of what Maman would have done to disarm her and turned the conversation to lighter topics. "Have you heard the latest Saint-Saëns opéra? He dedicated it to Pauline Viardot, whom I remember singing at one of the Rossinis' musical evenings."

Suzanne was starved for gossip. Since Édouard's death, society had forgotten her. She mentioned that Victorine Meurant had written to her. Penniless and no longer able to model, Victorine, who had posed for some of Édouard's most famous paintings, reminded Suzanne of Édouard's promise to help her find a position as a theater attendant.

As there was nothing in this transaction to benefit her, Suzanne had never answered the letter.

It took every ounce of patience I possessed to deal with Suzanne, but now that I recognized her as another member of the sisterhood of women whom Édouard had disappointed, I felt sympathy for her. And now that I understood that money was her sole concern, I broached the subject of purchasing *Olympia* by offering a higher amount than our group had planned to pay. After some bartering, we agreed on the price of 20,000 francs. But I came away having secured her promise to sell me one of the modern world's greatest masterpieces.

Chapter Thirty-Two

Paris

Autumn, 1891

All of life is like a painting, isn't it? That gray November evening, the rain softened the edges of the ochre haloes around the streetlights outside the dining room, turning the window into a frame for an Impressionist painting. I offset the lack of color outside by turning up the gaslights and stoking the fire.

"Pasie," I called out, "More candles in the dining room!"

She rushed in with a candlestick in each hand. "But, madame, too much light will be painful for Monsieur Degas's poor eyes." Pasie knew my guests almost as well as I did.

"We will turn out the gaslights entirely when he sits down," I assured her. His other rules were easier to follow: no pets, and dinner precisely at seven-thirty. The aging bachelor had become quite set in his ways. Degas would be pleased that I had found orange—almost vermillion—chrysanthemums at the florist for the table arrangement. As he had said at last week's dinner, Orange gives color. And what else? I think it was, Green neutralizes, and violet is for shade. I would remove the flowers before we dined, though, as Degas refused to endure floral scents or perfumes.

That night Degas was to bring Mademoiselle Cassatt to dinner. I hoped that Mary Cassatt's intelligent conversation would entertain Eugène, who had not been himself since he'd contracted a respiratory ailment last winter. I'd fallen ill at about the same time, with a frightening bout of rheumatic fever. Mine was the more serious illness, yet I'd recovered, while Eugène's malady lingered.

Monet would also be making an appearance, rare since his move to Giverny. And Stéphane Mallarmé, literary Impressionist and honorary member of our circle, would also join us. Was I not like l'Arc de Triomphe, with all of Haussmann's boulevards coming together under me?

In addition to bringing my family of Impressionists together in our home, my aim was to entertain my husband. I peeked into the drawing room and saw that Eugène had not moved from the blue chaise longue on which he had settled that afternoon. He continued to lose weight, he was cross, and his horrible cough lingered, competing with the hacking of the bronchial old lady I had become. He was in his middle fifties, but could have passed for ten years older. It was a heavy burden to live with a person whose suffering was as much mental as it was physical. He almost never left his room. I often asked myself if I had fulfilled all of my duties to him as a wife; in any case, I couldn't manage to distract him from his ailments.

"Eugène, shall I bring some more tea with lemon for your throat?"

"How much tea can one man be expected to drink?" he grumbled.

I had always made an effort to follow Maman's instructions, to dress well for my husband, and to please others in order to please him more. "I'm wearing the gown you like," I said, stepping into the room. "How do I look?"

He paid no attention to me, lost in his own misery. "All the tea in the world wouldn't help me now," he muttered.

As autumn had closed in, I'd been surprised, after a long absence, to feel the contagion of Eugene's darkness in my own soul. For a time, none of my work struck me as any good. After more than thirty years of painting, I felt I had not done anything I had set out to do and was still a mere beginner. On several occasions, I found myself sitting paralyzed in my boudoir, listening to the hiss of the gaslights. But one night, when the familiar weight had come down on my chest and my stomach had begun to churn, when my arms had started to tingle and I'd felt myself beginning to disappear, something had halted the episodes. I'd remembered that to keep from falling into blackness, I needed to move toward the light. I focused on a photograph of Eugène, Bibi, and myself on a bench at le Mesnil. The love of my small family held me up until I could regain my footing.

Julie's presence reminded me that my life had not been in vain. She was worth everything. I was devoted to Eugène, but decided that if he chose to drown in despair, he would have to do it alone. I had no more incidents after that.

I turned back to the dining room. The Harcourt-style, flat-cut, Baccarat crystal, Maman's silver, and the Sèvres porcelain all caught the flickering light. The smooth surfaces of the table settings contrasted with the textured, geometric pattern woven into the white damask tablecloth. I pulled the velvet drapes over the rain-streaked windows. What else? I fetched my small still life of a glass pitcher and a cut green apple from Julie's room and hung it on the wall to complete the dining theme. Now all was as it should be. Bon.

We would dine *en famille*, at the round table Maman had left me. What would she have thought of that? She who gave a grand reception for Prince Louis Napoleon, a banquet for five hundred at the Hôtel de Ville in Calvados, when Papa was préfet there. But as I still could not meet my colleagues at the cafés, I was obliged to invite them into my home if I wished to discuss art. Besides, being the most financially comfortable of the artists in our group, I felt noblesse oblige to do what I could for those still just scraping by.

Auguste Renoir was almost starving. I didn't know how he managed to support his mysterious wife and child, neither of whom he'd ever allowed me to meet. I suppose he thought I'd look down upon the young dressmaker he'd married last year, unaware of how little I cared about such things anymore. After all these years, social distinctions between the Impressionists had been erased by years of shared critical contempt, the resolution of internal disputes, and mutual respect.

Strange that I had become so close to Renoir. But after all, we were only weeks apart in age, and unbeknownst to us at the time, we'd grown up within walking distance from one another in Limoges. We both enjoyed the opéra and, before Eugène became unwell, Renoir had accompanied us to matinée performances, regaling us all the way home with arias sung in a fine tenor.

My friendships with other Impressionists had deepened, as well. Once I had managed to persuade Monet to come stay with us at le Mesnil. I'd showed him my paintings of haystacks in the surrounding countryside, which inspired him to paint his own haystacks—the ones that he claimed paid for his house in Giverney.

To the kitchen then, to see how dinner was coming along. For Monet, we were serving scallops from his beloved Normandy, as well as oysters with vinegar, all arrived fresh at the marchand de poisson on the morning train. But had Pasie also remembered to stop at the traiteur?

"Pasie, did you pick up a *casserole à la boulanger*?"

"Oui, madame," she said with a smile. "I know men love their potatoes."

When the doorbell chimed, I went to greet my guests, trusting that Pasie would have everything in order when she called us to the table.

Another of Maman's instructions on entertaining: Each guest must feel especially attended to. During the fish course, I could see that Monet was pleased with the soupier de Saint-Jacques. When he pierced the pastry crust and was surrounded by steam, he cried, "La mer!" This reminder of the sea was my gift to him.

Degas was equally enamored of the seafood.

"You must allow me to take you to Goumard Prunier restaurant, mon ami," boomed Monet, leaning back to accommodate his increased girth. "There you can try raw oysters."

"It would be my pleasure to accompany you, Claude," replied Degas, my finicky friend. "However, I cannot promise to eat them raw."

I enjoyed every dish. My appetite had increased of late, and I was in danger of becoming plump, but with the satisfaction of my family and control over my career, I found that no longer concerned me. Eugène, seated nearest to the faïence stove, did not touch his plate, I noticed, understanding now how Maman had agonized over my eating habits.

As Pasie took away the soup bowls, conversation filled the room. "The study of nature is trivial!" pronounced Degas, waving his arms in his baggy salt and pepper tweed jacket. "Painting is an art of convention."

"*Certainment!* Art is falsehood!" Mallarmé agreed with enthusiasm. I concurred, but didn't say so. To me, the word Realist had no meaning; any painter hoping to render nature could call himself a Realist and none deserved the name in the absolute sense. They had all called Manet a Realist, when his artifice was obvious. His goal in referring to earlier painters, without using their conventions of volume or proper scale, had been to shock the viewer into an awareness of a painting as a painting. Yet another of Maman's litany of lessons about one's role as hostess dictated that I keep my guests conversing, but, for my husband's sake, I preferred to keep my conversation about Édouard to a minimum.

Eugène, almost too frail to join us at the table, came to life when Mallarmé asked, "How is that novel of yours coming along?" *Victims!* was a romantic tale with a hero who sacrificed himself for the good of the Republic.

"Slowly, but I have the essence of the heroine," Eugène said. "I based her independent mind and dark eyes on my wife." Me, as the heroine of a novel—*oof!* Still, writing his long-planned novel filled those months when he was too weak to go out.

His occupation allowed me the time to contribute paintings requested for exhibitions from England to New York. Julie and I took the train to Brussels to see my paintings in the exhibition of Les XX. I reminded myself daily that I was now an artist of international renown. The secret was to keep going; if one had talent, eventually it would be noticed. Prices for my paintings increased as my reputation spread, until I was earning more than any of my male colleagues except for Monet. Perhaps I should have shown my haystack paintings before he had showed his! Still, I felt that my best work was ahead of me, so maybe I would catch up with him yet.

For Degas, who would have loved to have been a poet, Stéphane

Mallarmé was the gift. Poor Degas was on his fourth sonnet. It was to be the literary event of the autumn, dedicated to Mademoiselle Cassatt in honor of her latest Belgian Griffon, Coco. I was curious to know whether the sonnets were poetic or instead, literary variations of his current unbecoming artistic theme of women climbing out of their bath tubs. But again, I kept silent.

"I am full of ideas, I have too many," Degas complained.

Mallarmé pointed out, "But Degas, you can't make a poem with ideas. You make it with words."

For Mademoiselle Cassatt, I called Julie downstairs to say good night after the main course of saffron rice and chicken with figs was cleared. Mary Cassatt had no children of her own and had lost her cherished sister Lydia not long ago. Julie illuminated the room when she entered, and it was not just the flash of her white dress in the candlelight.

"Miss Julie!" I saw Mademoiselle Cassatt appraising my thirteen-year-old child. She too had been painting mothers with children during the same years that I'd had the pleasure of painting my Bibi.

"Ah, the sweet and lovable Julie," from Monet, who insisted that Julie call him oncle Claude. "My lovely little future competitor."

"Mademoiselle Bibi!" Mallarmé used her pet name.

After circling the table for hugs and kisses, Julie floated off, a miniature Marie Taglioni performing *La Sylphide*.

There was a moment of quiet while we basked in the glow Julie left trailing behind. Did my guests notice that all of the objects in the room were now brushed in a lighter hue? Then Pasie entered with a tray of brandied plums and a cheese platter.

"Julie is a vision," murmured Renoir. "I would love to paint her."

"By all means," I said.

"Don't you think that in literature as well as in painting, talent is shown by the treatment of the feminine figure?" asked Renoir. "Think of Natasha, in *War and Peace*."

And the conversation began again.

At last, my gift to myself—the hour we spent sitting by the fire in the drawing room. As cigar smoke filled the room, I noticed that Mary Cassatt had succeeded in engaging my husband in a tête-à-tête. Her conversational skill—which I could appreciate now that she had become more confident speaking French—and her perfect posture evinced her good breeding.

Relieved, I looked down to see my hands lying still in my lap, not twisted together as they so often had been in the past. I allowed myself to fall into a contented reverie. The room pleased me. I kept it simple, tall and white, with parquet floors. The furnishings included the Japanese screen, the First Empire chaise longue, and the Louis XIV mirror over the mantel, all from Maman, and the black, spindle-backed chair and cabriolet-legged table from grand-père Morisot.

The drawing room also served as a museum of my life in paintings. Monet had painted *Villas at Bordighera* especially for the room. Images of Julie hung on every wall: sitting under an orange tree with her parakeet, perched at the garden gate, playing the flute. I could have filled the room with portraits of Julie.

Except, of course, that I had to leave room for Édouard's paintings. Along with the pieces I'd obtained at the auction, I had managed to acquire eight more paintings, including Édouard's portrait of me holding a bunch of violets, when Théodore Duret, the critic who had sheltered Édouard's paintings during the siege, fell on hard times and was forced to sell his collection.

While I would never forget the heartbreak of that day we made love, when I declared myself and offered to run away with him, the memory no longer stung as it had when I stood in the Prado and understood the full breadth of his genius and the depth of his weakness. I did not regret loving Édouard. Regardless, one cannot change the past. And, after many years, *Repose* was mine. As I relaxed into the calm of old age, that title suited me better than it ever had. I was not the woman in the portraits anymore. And I was. Aren't we

all of our ages at once? My memories of dancing at the balls of my girlhood were still vivid, especially the one where Edma and I had dressed in classical Greek attire. I wished I could remember what I thought at twenty. I recalled that I'd had a wild desire to taste life. Although, following the duchess's advice, I'd burned Édouard's letters and my journals from those years, each portrait I possessed— *With Violets, Mourning, Reclining*—transported me back to his studio. Those hours were etched in my memory.

Unimaginable now that I should have had even a fleeting thought of marrying Puvis de Chavannes. However, he had remained my loyal friend ever since, even if he came to my Thursday dinners less often after he had moved in with that young model, Suzanne Valadon. And now I was forty-eight years old, approaching the age that Maman had been when she died. How much longer did I have? I wore a crown of pure white hair and had earned every strand. But every year, I still felt the same joy and the same hope. *Isn't life wonderful?* Édouard would have said.

My contentment would have been complete had Edma and I been back on friendly terms. A hopeful thought sprang to mind. If I wrote to Edma, inviting Nini to visit, she might reciprocate the conciliatory gesture and send her. It would be an opening, at least.

My musings were interrupted by the aroma of coffee that Pasie poured as she moved among the guests. No one knew that this room served as my studio, but I liked to think of it. Had anyone noticed the armoire behind the Japanese screen that hid my painting equipment? I remembered the Impressionists' endless talk of "modern life," and the time when Édouard asked me years ago what woman had combined work and family.

I had. This was my modern life.

Mallarmé sat as he did in Édouard's portrait of him, slouched to the side, with one hand in his pocket and the other holding a cigar. He released a huge exhalation and leaned back, quoting from one of his poems: "This drawing room, rarefied by friendship and beauty; this luxurious exclusion of everything outside!"

His natural élan reminded me of Édouard. He had even taken up with his old friend's mistress, Méry Laurent. I appreciated the life he'd brought into this house during the past few years, inviting James Whistler and Oscar Wilde and other fascinating people to dine with us.

Mallarmé was reciting more of his work: "Oh end of century, winter! It disguises everything except emotions."

We were transprted, Degas by the poetry and I by the wintery images that Mallarmé loved to use—snow, ice, and cold distant stars that concealed burning passion. Renoir dozed.

"I have an idea for a new undertaking," Mallarmé announced. He described his proposed poetry project, to be called *The Lacquered Drawer*. "So, will you help me?" he asked.

"*Pardonez-moi,* Stéphane. What did you say?" I asked, brought back to the room from the white, frozen world to which Mallarmés words had carried me.

"He is inviting all of us to make etchings to illustrate his poetry," Degas told me.

"Mademoiselle Cassatt can help you with that. She's become obsessed with Japanese prints and has mastered the use of Eastern techniques."

First, I was thrilled at the prospect of working with Mallarmé. Then I was irritated with Degas, who was a master of printmaking but had never offered to teach me the medium himself, no matter how much interest I showed in his work. I suppressed my annoyance in front of my guests, but Mary Cassatt seemed to sense it. She'd had her own exasperations with Degas, no doubt.

"Please, I have been experimenting with dry point and aquatint," she said, "and it would be a pleasure to share what I have learned with you." Her generous offer vanquished the feeling that Degas had handed me off to his assistant.

"Your assignment will be *The White Water Lily,*" Mallarmé told me.

That caught my interest. I wondered whether I could create something as subtle as his words. I visualized the lightest of lines, the picture suggested by mere hints of color. Tomorrow I would begin sketches of the water lilies in the lakes in the Bois. Some quick drawings should be easy enough to translate into etchings. My new colored pencils would give just the right delicate effect. I'd go at first light.

The evening ended with a toast. First Renoir stood, unsteady from the wine, and pronounced, "A surprise for our hostess!" Then all of my other guests rose from their chairs.

"What is this?" I asked. My first thought was that they had brought a gift for Julie, whose birthday was approaching.

"Thank Mallarmé," boomed Monet. "He has convinced the Minister of Fine Arts to purchase the first Impressionist painting for the state." Mallarmé took a bow. So Jules Ferry, in his latest political incarnation, had redeemed himself. But which painting had been so honored?

"For four thousand, five hundred francs!" slurred Degas. I was amazed. Who had earned so much for his painting? That was ten times what my early work had sold for.

"What a curious thing is destiny!" Monet thundered. "For Berthe Morisot, a painter of such pronounced temperament, to be born into the most severely middle-class surroundings that have ever existed, when to have a child, never mind a girl, who wanted to be an artist was a dishonor to the family..."

Mallarmé cut off Monet's rambling toast and lifted his glass to me. "To your *Young Woman in a Ball Gown*, who now resides in la Musée du Luxembourg."

My painting—the nervous young woman in her first diamond necklace—was to be the first Impressionist painting in a museum! The magnitude of this honor was staggering, as was its rich irony. The Luxembourg housed works by living artists. Only after his—or her—death could an artist's creations move to the Louvre. Édouard, as always, had been an exception. The French government had obtained *Olympia* after we'd placed articles calling for subscriptions in two newspapers. We'd raised 19,415 francs in that manner, with a few private donations bringing us to the amount I'd promised Suzanne. But at the same time, no one was prepared to take responsibility for allowing that courtesan to inhabit a former palace. So *Olympia* had been consigned to the Luxembourg, where she and my *Young Woman* would live together through generations to come.

"And congratulations to *la grand dame de peinture*, whose vaporous painting conceals the surest draftsmanship," added Degas, praising me for the first time since I had known him.

Life is full of surprises. I felt cocooned in the warmth of the blazing fire and the affectionate respect of my colleagues. Then Renoir surprised us by bursting into song:

> They walk at night
> When there's no more light
> On the sidewalks…

Degas joined in on the chorus, leading me to believe that this must be a ditty from the café-concerts.

> Streetwalkers,
> Sidewalk stompers!

Bien sûr, this had to be one of popular café singer Aristide Bruant's favorites about the Parisian lower-class. Even Eugène had to smile.

> Hair frizzé,
> Breasts blasé,
> Feet worn away…

It wasn't Offenbach's *Barcarolle*, but I couldn't resist singing along when the chorus came around again:

> Streetwalkers,
> Sidewalk stompers!

I was still breathless from laughter when we saw our guests out into the rainy night, singing with great enthusiasm and stomping through puddles as they made their way down the sidewalk.

کے

After they'd gone, Eugène and I went upstairs to check on Julie. I loved this difficult and gentle man for creating a family with me. I loved the way he gazed at our angel. Édouard would have been incapable of caring for Julie and seeing to her education. How grateful I had turned out to be that, despite my insistence that he find a profession, Eugène had chosen to look after our child during her early years. How little painting I would have done without him! The careful attention my husband had put into planting a luxurious garden in the courtyard of our home was telling. He wanted a place which would serve both as a background for my paintings and a playground for Julie.

I had tried to represent the kind of father Eugène was to his daughter in the painting I made one summer of the two of them by the pond at le Mesnil. Eugène, in his summer hat, was reading to little Julie as she sat watching her red toy boat drift around in the water. The boat— the center of the composition—was for my enjoyment, reminding me of the boats of Lorient, Cherbourg, the Isle of Wight, Nice. My little family was the calm in a whirling composition, wreathed in green and yellow leaves dappled with white light.

I laid my hand on Eugene's cheek and turned his face to me. He leaned down to kiss my forehead. After we tiptoed out of Julie's room, I took my husband's arm and helped him up the stairs.

Chapter Thirty-Three

Paris~Valvins
Spring 1892-Winter 1893

$\mathcal{E}$ugène insisted on using the last of his strength to prepare a solo show of my work for the Boussod and Valadon Gallery. He assembled forty paintings to be hung in two rooms. As he had for each of the Impressionist exhibitions, he signed contracts and wrote letters arranging for the delivery of my paintings, this time hunched over his desk, coughing. He worked on my behalf until he could not work any longer.

I would have wished for Eugène to slip away, as my father had, but instead, he suffered, like Maman, like Édouard. "Please live," I prayed as I sat at my husband's bedside. When I heard a rustling skirt, signaling that Julie hovered just outside the door, I realized that I had spoken aloud.

"Come in, Bibi," I said, but she was afraid to see her father like this— suffering, emaciated, drained of all light. She was only fourteen, still a child. She shook her head and stayed in the hallway, twisting her hair and biting her lip, yearning for her papa.

I had long hours during those nights to consider our life together, weighing the gifts and the trials. I wondered, had being my husband been too much like being Édouard's brother? The artist's single-minded devotion, accepted as a sign of genius in men, was seen as selfishness in a wife who should properly have focused on her husband. Had my self-centered determination to succeed triggered Eugène's difficult behavior? Had I over-reacted to his high-strung episodes, exacerbating those situations?

Then, too, I feared that I had allowed guilt over my terrible secret, my love for his brother, to create a barrier between us. Once, when he woke, asking for water, I asked him, "Have I been a selfish wife?

Have I told you how I've appreciated your devotion?"

Eugène looked up at me with adoration in his eyes. "I've worshipped you," he said.

Each day brought my husband closer to his demise, but he fought death. Finally, that fight diminished to the point where his struggle was for each breath. At the end, every agonized wheeze seemed to tear at his lungs. I found myself breathing along with him, until his grotesque writhing froze in mid-gasp.

His soul had gone, I hoped, to drift among the ever-changing clouds.

After Eugène died in April, I overcame my reluctance to have my paintings shown and allowed my solo exhibition to proceed, although of course, as I was in mourning, I did not attend. I respected my husband's last efforts to secure a legacy for me as we had done for his brother. An icy veneer of guilt crusted over my scalding grief long enough for me to perform the duties required of me. I arranged the burial, deposited the checks brought in at my exhibition, paid Boussod and Valadon their commission, and acknowledged the flowers and gifts that friends had sent us.

As soon as all was in order, I allowed myself to descend to the depths of suffering. My face went as white as my hair and my skin sagged, but I attempted to spare a girl of Julie's tender years the sight of my grief. The poor thing was so broken that she had not cried nor even spoken her father's name since his death.

I arrived unprepared at another of life's stages. As a new widow, I had somehow to learn to make sense of my feelings and survive for my child's sake. If not for her, I would have wished I had not outlived my husband, whom I saw now had been the best friend of my life. Once again, I had lost my closest companion. I calculated that, with Eugene's support, we'd brought three hundred paintings to life during our years together.

My mourning was complicated by the burden of blame, as it always had been for me, When Édouard was alive, I had fantasized about what would happen if Eugène were somehow out of the picture. Those memories were excruciating now. And what if Édouard were still alive, now that I was alone? Grief on both our parts would have precluded any romantic feeling.

All I could remember now were Eugène's caring qualities. Édouard had told me once about his uncle who had taken him as a child to the Spanish galleries in the Louvre, a life-long influence on his work. But it was Eugène who had taken young Léon on regular outings, Eugène who had invited Maman to live with us, Eugène who had patiently taught Julie her lessons. His kindness outweighed his high-strung temperament.

I let Pasie go.

One day as she was helping me with the difficult task of sorting through Eugene's clothes, I asked, "Is your clockmaker still waiting for you?"

Pasie understood my meaning and burst into tears, saying. "But, madame, how can I leave you now?"

Tears sprang to my eyes, too, and I had to pause to restrain my emotions before I answered, "I've had my husband; it is your turn to be happy."

It pleased me to think of Pasie standing behind the counter of an *horlogerie*, surrounded by chiming clocks and glittering pocket watches, a much more pleasant position than working from dawn to dusk as the wife of a baker or grocer. I sent her off with a trousseau of my dresses and hats that I deemed too frivolous to wear as a widow. Pasie would return to Toulouse, where she would marry and work next to her husband, the prettiest and best-dressed shopkeeper's wife in town.

Now it was just Julie and I. After renting out our country home in Mézy and our family home in the rue de Villejust, where Julie had grown up and I had grown old, in the winter of 1892 we moved into a spacious apartment on the rue Weber, more appropriate for the two of us. As pleasant as the homes I'd lived in with Eugène had been, each of their rooms had been designed for a specific purpose, and none had offered the space and light required for an artist's studio. In the new apartment, I installed our cook and maid in rooms behind the kitchen, and combined three maids' rooms in the attic to create a studio, my first since the one Papa had provided for Edma and me. I'd told Édouard on his deathbed that he had won his eternity by virtue of his work. Now I needed to take those words to heart myself. Encouraged by the success of my show at Boussod and Valadon, I painted for my life through the hot days of summer when it would have been easier to retire to the blue chaise longue in the drawing room with a book and a cool drink. While Julie worked on her new endeavor—writing her memoirs—I produced a pastel self-portrait that, while not flattering was, in my view, a tour de force. I was struck by the desperate searching in my sunken eyes, the nervous slashes of color that conveyed my restless striving, the white chalk marks vibrating around my head. That was me, riven by guilt, but alive. I wasn't ready to reveal that much of myself to the world, so when my portrait was finished, I rolled it up and stuck it in the back of the armoire that held my painting materials.

In August, Julie and I accepted Mallarmé's invitation to visit his family in Valvins, in the Forest of Fontainbleau. My old friend gave Julie a greyhound named Laërtes, a badly behaved beast whom she loved at first sight and kept by her side as a constant companion.

We dined in Mallarmè's small, rose-covered house by the Seine with some of the younger artists who lived in the area. Crowded around the table in the one room on the first floor, we were enclosed by Mallarmé's bookcase full of English books, including his translations of Edgar Allan Poe; his Japanese cabinet displaying fans and lacquer boxes; and, on another wall, a rack holding his pipe collection.

Art had moved on since the Impressionists' day. In the 1880s, artists had become more interested in symbolism and structure than in light and color. These "post-Impressionists" used garish hues and unintelligible subject matter, yet at least one Symbolist seemed to find my light tints and focus on the interior life interesting. Odilon Redon had told me as much when he participated in the last Impressionist exhibition. He no doubt saw me as akin to an aging sailor who had been among the first to voyage beyond the edge of the known world. Another guest, Henri de Toulouse-Lautrec, seemed to me to embody the heritage of the Impressionists. He had the dark hair and whiskers as well as the haberdashery of the typical Parisian gentleman, but he was set apart by his wire-rimmed spectacles, by his bulbous nose, and, most of all, by his diminutive stature. When Lautrec took his seat next to me, he seemed to be of normal height, since his stunted growth had only affected his legs. After all, how much taller was Edgar Degas? He reminded me of Degas, in that both were damaged aristocrats, Degas in his bank account and Lautrec in his legs. Lautrec was descended from counts on both sides of his family, yet his disfigurement had diminished his social prospects to the point that he was said to live in a brothel in Montmartre.

"I understand that your family comes from Toulouse," he said. "I grew up in Albi, not one hundred kilometers from there."

We talked about life in the Pyrénées before I was bold enough to broach the subject of Lautrec's audacious prints. "I am too old-fashioned to think of your posters for the Moulin Rouge as works of art, but it pleases me to see that you have been influenced by Japanese prints."

He smiled down at the table, unsurprised that an old lady such as myself might not be taken by his blotches of black and red that represented café-concert singers and can-can dancers.

"The Impressionists were my other great influence," he offered, his generosity of spirit proving that he had been brought up to be a gentleman.

"Indeed, when I saw your work at the Les XX exhibitions in Brussels, I thought I was standing in front of Degas's prints of racehorses," I told him. But while Lautrec's horses and dancers were derived from

285

Degas, his bold contours and long brush strokes could have come only from Édouard Manet. Whenever my eye followed a line down the length of one of Édouard's paintings, it still made me shiver, as though his hand were running down my back from neck to waist.

Where would any of these artists be if the Impressionists hadn't broken the stranglehold of the Academy? My guess was that they would still be negotiating that Byzantine system, like rats living in the filthy, winding streets of ancient Paris before Haussmann opened the avenues up to the light. I would have appreciated some gratitude from the artists who followed the Impressionists, but meeting Édouard's artistic descendent was satisfaction enough.

The elegant and aristocratic Laërtes interrupted dinner with paws on the table, searching for remnants of our meal.

Edma did allow Nini to visit when Adolphe died, and throughout the years we continued to be estranged. The infant who had toddled through my paintings of her with her mother in Cherbourg had turned into a willowy young woman, an unwitting emissary for a chilly armistice. Yves's daughters, Paule and Jeannie, also came into my care when Yves died of cancer. Our home was filled with youth and beauty.

An idea was taking shape in my mind's eye. What had felt untethered within me after my husband's death began instead to feel expansive in my large studio. I was new to this stage of my life, and I felt the child-like sense of possibility that the young possess. This sensation of starting again made me eager to attempt a painting both larger and in bolder colors than I had ever tried before.

In the midst of all the activity during that year following Eugène's death, I'd finished fifty-six paintings and made endless studies of the work that I was determined would be my magnum opus. *The Cherry Pickers* was almost-life-sized. Julie modeled, holding a basket, and Nini stood on a ladder above her, reaching up to a fruit tree to fill it. Their white dresses formed a serpentine shape through swirling green branches, ascending to a patch of blue heaven above. The figures' weight and volume, both more graceful and more monumental than those in my earlier paintings, steadied the vibration of the vivid blues, yellows, and acid greens surrounding them. And the triangular composition I'd chosen revealed the influence of Renoir's return to Renaissance practices.

Eugène would have been ecstatic to see the work that I believed would establish my legacy, a combination of Impressionist light and Renaissance technique.

If never as happy as we had been when Eugène was alive, Julie and I had surmounted the major hurdle of grief. We were content, and I kept busy forging ahead with my new work.

Our full lives became even more so when, at long last, Edma returned to Paris.

Chapter Thirty-Four

Paris
Spring 1893

Julie, who had stationed herself on the balcony to keep watch on the narrow street below, waved her arms. She ran downstairs and across the courtyard, pulling the gate open with a metallic screech. "Tante Edma!" she squealed, thrilled that our familial feud had ended. I reached the door in time to hear my sister whisper, "Bibi."

It took a second look for Edma to recognize me, a plump, white-haired matron crossing the courtyard. "Welcome, sister," I said.

Edma clung to her daughter, and I was glad that Nini and Julie were there to cushion our reunion. Still, I felt that we weren't yet ready to sit and face each other across a tea table. "Won't you come see my studio?" I asked, and we all trooped upstairs, glad for something to do. The room was almost as cluttered as the studio Edma and I had shared in our youth, with easels crowded in the center and paintings covering the walls. My special lyre-shaped easel and low, wooden chair were positioned in a bright nimbus of light by the windows.

Edma inhaled deeply and seemed close to tears. "The odor of turpentine is still intoxicating, after all these years," she managed to say. "As familiar to me as the smell of my child's hair."

Nini pulled Edma around the studio from one portrait of Julie to another. "Look, Maman. Tante Berthe has painted me, too!" Nini stood before my portrait of a lithe young woman in Renaissance hues. With her sleeve fallen back, exposing her bare arm, and her dark head resting against her hand, Nini's casual pose belied the exhilaration that illuminated her like one of the new electric lights.

"Is this graceful girl draped on Maman's blue velvet chaise-longue really my little Nini?"

I nodded. Nini managed an indulgent smile.

"I see you've included a photograph of yourself with Eugène and Julie at le Mesnil on the wall behind her," Edma said. "You always insisted on combining your private life and work in just that way."

"That was my modern life."

Nini turned to me. "What was so modern about that?"

Edma and I shared our first smile. I shrugged and said, "Our girls are able to take so much for granted."

Edma continued her tour of my paintings. There was Julie sitting with Laërtes, in a dress made of long strokes of cobalt blue, and there again, playing the violin in the same dress, this time set off by the white mantel and a bold picture frame surrounding Édouard's portrait of me reclining, in the background.

"I'm happy to live in the age of the New Woman," Nini said.

"So that you can smoke cigarettes and ride a bicycle?" I asked.

"So that I can attend art school and study the nude. And be a *bachelière*."

Edma's face was a study in amazement.

"Our century is nearly over," I declared.

When Edma and I visited the Louvre, I couldn't help but feel that we should have been laden with palettes and maulsticks. "It seems no time at all since we copied here," Edma agreed.

"You will have to come and paint with me." I watched fear cross Edma's face as she considered my invitation. "What are you afraid of?"

"That I've fallen too far behind. That I won't remember what to do." I would have to think of a way to entice her to return to what was once a great joy for her.

We also visited Édouard, or his paintings at least, at the Musée du Luxembourg. More of his paintings had joined *Olympia*. When we reached *The Balcony*, Edma gasped. She hadn't seen it since it was first shown at the Salon, twenty-five years ago. "This was one of his works that ushered in modernity. I can't believe now that his Realism was seen then as vulgar. But——" I knew what was coming. "——only a scoundrel would have announced to the world how this young, unmarried woman aroused him. How on earth could Maman have let you model for the man who painted *Olympia?*"

"Maman thought it perfectly suitable to entrust me to a close family friend of impeccable pedigree."

"But Maman didn't truly know Édouard, did she? She knew his mother and thought that was enough."

I heard the harsh judgment in her voice, but she caught herself before falling into old ways that were as out of date as bustles. I understood that my sister was referring not to this particular painting of me on a balcony, but to the fact that I had gambled my reputation and my prospects for a cad.

"You no doubt think of me as boring and conventional. Still, I can understand a dalliance in one's youth—but not with the most dissolute man in Paris. And not in my house."

"That was thoughtless. But was that indiscretion worthy of a silence lasting more than ten years?"

"You stepped to the very brink of the abyss into which the duchess tumbled," Edma's voice shook with fear, "and I was not there to save you."

So it wasn't me she could not forgive, but herself, for not fulfilling her role as my protector.

She walked on ahead of me. I gave her time to calm down before catching up. "Edma?" My familiar inflection may have reminded her of the constant questions that had distracted her during our copying sessions at the Louvre. When I saw that I had her attention, my tone turned serious. I needed my sister's protection one more time. "I want to talk to you about something. A few winters back, I fell ill. So ill that I felt the embrace of death."

Her eyes grew wide. She had seen me during bouts of bronchitis and knew that I was not exaggerating.

"I was terrified at what could happen to Julie after I am gone. You must know that you are the only person in the world whom I would trust with my Bibi."

I could see that Edma couldn't grasp losing me after just finding me again. But she managed to murmur, "*Mais oui*, of course, if anything should happen."

Satisfied, I took her arm and, without a word, led her across the hallway to another gallery. We rounded a corner to be greeted by a vision in green, my *Young Woman in a Ball Gown*.

"Mon Dieu, Bértât!" she gasped. I scanned my painting for any detail that might have scandalized her. But it was enthusiasm that took her breath away. "You've captured the excitement of preparing for one's first ball."

"I wanted to show our lives, women's lives, as worthy of the freeing brushstrokes of an avant-garde artist."

"There is no question that your work deserves to be here." Edma took a breath before saying the words I'd waited too long to hear. "Berthe, I need to accept whatever path led you to this point."

I was already working in my studio when the maid brought Edma upstairs one morning, unannounced. "I'm sorry to interrupt you," Edma began. "This morning after Nini and Blanche rushed off, I realized that what I want to do today, more than anything else, was to take you up on your offer to paint."

I smiled and shrugged as I arranged a chair and easel next to mine.

"I don't know if I remember anything, or if it's buried under years of domestic duties and caring for others. Being half of myself. But Adolphe is gone and my children are grown. Isn't it time to think of the other half a little?" She gravitated to the painting of Nini on the blue chaise longue in jewel-like Renaissance colors.

"Renoir has led me back to the Old Masters," I explained. "The Impressionists are history now."

"This one must find its way to my apartment." Edma examined the painting. "You've given the mantel a greenish hue, to complement her deep orange dress. Hmm...maybe I haven't forgotten everything."

I handed her a paintbrush, issuing an invitation to her old life. She flicked the paintbrush against her palm as I nudged her toward the easel. "You were better than I," I said with a smile. "All these years, I have just been catching up to you."

"I suppose if there's no jury to judge me. But only if…" She turned her easel toward me as I set to work. My hair might be snowy white, but my gaze still penetrated the canvas as I leaned forward and applied a flurry of brushstrokes, as avid as though this were my first painting. Before I knew it, Edma was laying in the lines for a portrait of me.

And the Morisot sisters were again active members of the Bonheur Society, painting together, side by side.

Epilogue: Julie

Paris
1962

*W*hen Renoir wrote, inviting us to join him in Provence the following February, Maman was forced to decline because she feared that I was coming down with typhoid fever. It turned out to be only a bout of influenza, but what followed was far worse.

Maman contracted her final illness while nursing me through my ailment. As soon as I was feeling well again, I realized that Maman was not. Her lungs had been weak since the Franco-Prussion war, more than twenty years before. But this was worse than her usual winter bronchitis.

She took to her bed.

The next day, tante Edma came to our house with Dr. Rafinesque, both of them disappearing into Maman's boudoir as I waited in the adjoining sitting room with Nini, watching the snow fall and praying, "Dear God, please save my mother." After an endless afternoon, tante Edma emerged. "Julie, you'd better come in now," she said, her haggard face revealing how urgent the situation had become.

I sat on Maman's bed. "Please, don't cry," she managed to say in a faint voice. "I want to tell you something."

I curled up beside her. "Maman, don't go yet," I whispered.

"I would have liked to see you married." This remark evoked the future as an unimaginable void. We had always been together, Maman and I. She had raised me and cared for me with the utmost tenderness. The choking sobs I had held back for days came tumbling out.

"Work and be good as you have always been…You have beauty and wealth; use them wisely. My little Bibi, don't cry…I love you even more than I can say." Her head fell back against her pillows.

"Come, Julie," Tante Edma said. "Your mother is tired. You can visit her again in the morning."

"What did you want to tell me, Maman?"

"We'll talk again later," whispered Maman. "I want to see you one more time."

But that was the last time I was allowed in my mother's room. I hoped she would be cured; instead she died the next day. Tante Edma told me her last word was "Julie."

The suddenness with which my mother departed this world in the winter of 1894 left at first only a cold nothingness. I was an orphan at sixteen. Edma and Nini stayed with me, but I was unaware of them. The house felt vacant without Maman. Laërtes sat with me during hours of mourning, silent except for an occasional shivering sigh.

Yet within a year, les oncles—Renoir, Monet, Degas, Mallarmé—and I had put together a retrospective exhibition at the Durand-Ruel Gallery. There were more than six hundred works in various media, including Maman's only self-portrait, holding palette and brush, which I found rolled up in an armoire in her studio. Renoir pronounced her portfolio of watercolors delightful, and explained to me how to have them framed. Mallarmé wrote the introduction for the catalog. For the frontispiece, we chose oncle Édouard's portrait of Maman that he called *Reclining*. Of all the portraits by all the artists who had painted her, that one best conveyed her straight-forward intelligence, her alert beauty.

On 5 March, the morning of the exhibition, I went to the Passy Cemetery to visit Maman. Tante Edma waited in the carriage while I first stopped at the florist kiosk near the entrance, then lifted my skirt and trudged through the wet snow to the Manet plot. It was so small that Maman's casket was stacked between Papa's and oncle Édouard's. Yet a bust of Édouard Manet was the only monument for the three of them, aside from a plain marker listing all their names. I brushed away the late-winter snow, soaking my thin kid glove, and laid a white rose on the grave. Maman was buried between two Manets, Édouard and Eugène, but her name on the marker was Berthe Morisot.

So many unanswered questions. I wondered why Maman had stipulated that she lie between Papa and oncle Édouard, just as I wondered why her death certificate read, as her will had specified, "A woman of no profession."

I may be over eighty years old now, but my stylish kitten-heeled boots and the scalloped petticoat peeking out beneath my skirt are evidence that I haven't forgotten my mother's advice about remaining chic, even today. The American president's French wife, Jacqueline Kennedy, is an example of what good sense it is to make an effort to be attractive and fashionable at all times.

I sit on the blue chaise longue in the drawing room of our house on the rue de Villejust, to which I returned after I married to raise my family here. In our "Manet Museum," as Maman used to call it, I enjoy the clutter of Maman's paintings around me—memories of my happy childhood—arranged just as they were when she was alive. I was happy to have her paintings after she was gone.

Whenever I look at *Reclining*, Oncle Édouard's painting of Maman lying on a crimson sofa, my eyes slide back and forth between her scorching gaze and his signature in the lower right corner, *Édouard Manet*.

I'd found some of Maman's journals, rolled up in the self-portrait she'd pushed to the back of her painting armoire. I didn't read them for a long time. Seeing my mother's handwriting was as painful as having her words scratched on my skin with the sharp nib of a pen. And years after Maman's death, Degas had given me a packet of letters oncle Édouard had sent him. At about the same time, when I went to have another of oncle Édouard's portrait's of Maman reframed, *Berthe Morisot with Violets*, I'd discovered a note tucked behind the backing of the canvas. On one side of the paper, worn soft from many folding and unfoldings, was Monsieur Durand-Ruel's name and address. The other side read simply, *"Toujours le vôtre, Édouard." Yours always.*

Those words were the impetus for me to finally read all of the journals and letters. I learned about my mother's life, more complicated than I'd known. Rather than condemn her, I admired the strength required for her to emerge from dark places in her life to become *la luministe*, the woman who painted the light.

"Everyone dies with their secrets," she used to say. She would have told me her secrets herself, I think, but she ran out of time. She didn't marry until she was over thirty. Who else had held her heart before then? So many men had worshipped her. *Tant pis*, no matter whom she loved, nothing can change how much she loved me.

During my childhood, I used to imagine entering one of Maman's paintings and feeling as if I were enveloped in whipped cream, or swimming in sunlight. One day soon, I will leave here to join everyone I have loved. When I do, I imagine that I will become less line than color, less form than light. I shall be released from this angular, sharp-edged body and become an ethereal creature imagined by Berthe Morisot.

Glossary

A

à Berlin—to Berlin
à bientôt—until later
allez—come on
allons-y—let's go
après-midi—afternoon
arts d'agrement—the leisure arts
aux heures de la fashion—during the fashionable hours
maison de rendezvous—house of rendezvous, a brothel

B

bachelière—female bachelor
barouche—a style of carriage
béguin—crush
belle-soeur—sister-in-law
belles taches, les—beautiful blotches
bon, bon après-midi, bon chance—good, good afternoon, good luck
bottes—boots
boutonnière—a flower for one's buttonhole

C

café concert—informal concerts where chanteuses sang risqué songs for crowds that mixed high society with the working class.
cartes de visite—calling cards
chapeau pomponnette—style of hat (chapeau) decorated with pom-poms.
chassures—shoes
cocotte—a fashionable prostitute
cyclothymic oscillation—swinging back and forth in a circular arc (English)

F

flâneur—one who walks aimlessly, observing street life
foules noire, les—the black crowd

297

foyer de danse—dancers' rehearsal hall

G
gourgandine—a type of prostitute
grand dame de peinture—great lady or first lady of painting
grisaille, la—in painting, work in monochromatic gray, used colloquially to refer to leaden-gray, cloudy weather
grisette—a young, working class Frenchwoman, often so poor that she allowed herself to be "kept" by a student or other man

H
hausfrau—housewife (German)
Histoire des peintres de toutes les écoles—History of paintings of all schools
homme honnête—honest man
horlogerie—clock shop

I
incroyable—incredible

J
joli garcon—pretty boy

M
maisons de tolerance, les—house of tolerance, a brothel
moiré—a kind of fabric
morés—established customs
moussoir—frother, used in making hot chocolate

N
n'est-ce pas?—isn't it?
neurasthenia—medical condition marked by lassitude, headache, and irritability (English)
New Woman—a late-nineteenth-century term describing a woman who pushed against societal limits (English)

O

ogresse—female monster, colloquially used to describe a wealthy woman of a certain age with a taste for art and handsome men

P

pastis—a French liqueur
pèlerine—a style of cape
petite mort—a little death, colloquial expression for an orgasm
peut-être—maybe
pissoirs—public urinals
prix de Rome—a French scholarship for artists that paid for three to five years of study in Rome.

R

raison d'être—reason for being
retroussé—turned up, as with a turned-up nose
roué—a debauched man

S

Sacre nom de dieu—holy name of God (contraction:'crenom)
seconde-mére—wet nurse
semaine sanglante—bloody week, referring to the round up of the Communards
s'il te plait—if you please (familiar)
société anonyme—a type of corporation
spleen—usually refers to bad temper, but colloquially used to refer to depression or melancholy
spontaneiste—one who is spontaneous

T

tant pis—too bad
tante—aunt
toujours—always
traiteur—caterer

U

un peu—a little, un peu de tristesse—a little sadness

V

velouté—velvety, creamy
verge—penis
verole, la—syphilis
vieille fille—old maid
viérge—virgin
vive la guerre—long live the war
volte-face—about-face, a change of heart
vraiment—really

Author's Note

Berthe Morisot was notoriously private and discreet, a "sphinx," according to her friend, Stéphane Mallarmé. We can't know all of the exact conversations or inner thoughts of even the most dedicated journal-keeper, and Berthe complicated the issue by burning her journals from the years that she modeled for Édouard Manet.

So I've taken liberties with Berthe Morisot's story. Lives don't always follow a perfect narrative arc, but any adjustments or fabrications I've made are based on research. I adhere to Hillary Mantel's words to those of us who write historical fiction: "You have the authority of the imagination, you have legitimacy."

Some minor details that I altered: Édouard Manet had another brother who had nothing to do with this story, so I left him out. Berthe had too many suitors to mention without expanding her story into an epic novel. I had Berthe meet Édouard at a younger age than is commonly agreed upon, my reasoning being that contemporary readers tend to transpose today's morality upon characters from the past, making it difficult to believe how exceedingly sheltered Berthe was when she met Manet at age twenty-four. I decided that Berthe would be seventeen when she met Édouard.

Of the many mysteries about Morisot, the one that draws the greatest interest is the love affair between Berthe and Édouard. Did it really happen? Those burned journals and letters raise suspicions. Some biographers contend that the two artists restricted themselves to an emotional affair. Others suggest that there was an affair, but with no concrete evidence, they're hesitant to take a definitive stance. I say, look at Édouard's portraits of Berthe and then tell me that he wasn't passionately ensnared by her beauty and intellect.

Was Édouard Julie's father? Probably not. Was he Léon's father? Almost certainly not. Was he Berthe's lover? I believe that he was.

My task has been to amplify and illustrate Berthe's life, to infer her passions and frustrations in her time, place, and specific circumstances. For details that shaped my decisions, I've relied on the definitive biography by Margaret Shennan, *Berthe Morisot: The First Lady of Impressionism*. Anne Higonnet-More's *Berthe Morisot* was also a valuable, albeit more circumspect source. For readers interested in more about Berthe Morisot, Édouard Manet, and Impressionism, a select bibliography is available on my website: paula-butterfield.com. Images of Berthe's paintings and scenes that illustrate her life can be found at http://www.pinterest.com/luministe/.

Acknowledgements

Thanks go to so many. Early readers Margaret Butterfield, Sylvia Dakessian, Lori Latham, and Judy Zehr all contributed helpful comments. Andie Newton and Pamela Fedderson generously read several drafts of the book. Editor Jessica Morrell and members of my critique group—Linda Gallante, Rachael Spavins, and Loey Werking-Wells—provided structure, suggestions, and patient support. Jaynie Royal provided the opportunity to bring this book into the world, and Ruth Feiertag was its gentle, sure mid-wife.

The library at the National Museum of Women in the Arts accommodated me by bestowing a table piled high with all of their Berthe Morisot archives—news clippings, magazine articles, photographs, and letters—for me to gleefully wallow through. The First Place Award for Historical Fiction from the Chanticleer Book Reviews Writing Contest supplied much needed encouragement.

Thanks to my husband, Alan Dakessian, and our daughter, Drew, for the light you've brought into my life.